Sun-dr...
fiery-
and beauti...

Let these power...
seduce you in

At the
Sheikh's
COMMAND

Three spell-bindingly passionate
stories by three favourite,
bestselling authors:

Alexandra Sellers
Michelle Reid
Carol Grace

At the
Sheikh's
COMMAND

Alexandra Sellers
Michelle Reid
Carol Grace

M&B™ and M&B™ with the Rose Device
are trademarks of the publisher.
Harlequin Mills & Boon Limited, Eton House,
18-24 Paradise Road, Richmond, Surrey TW9 1SR

AT THE SHEIKH'S COMMAND
© by Harlequin Books S.A. 2008

Sleeping with the Sultan © Alexandra Sellers 2001
The Sheikh's Chosen Wife © Michelle Reid 2002
Taming the Sheikh © Carol Culver 2001

Sleeping with the Sultan, The Sheikh's Chosen Wife and Taming the
Sheikh were first published in Great Britain by Harlequin Mills &
Boon Limited in separate, single volumes.

ISBN: 978 0 263 86584 4

009-0308

Printed and bound in Spain
by Litografía Rosés S.A., Barcelona

SLEEPING WITH THE SULTAN

Alexandra Sellers

Alexandra Sellers is the author of over twenty-five novels and a feline language text published in 1997 and still selling. Born and raised in Canada, Alexandra first came to London as a drama student. Now she lives near Hampstead Heath with her husband, Nick. They share housekeeping with Monsieur, who jumped through the window one day and announced, as cats do, that he was moving in. What she would miss most on a desert island is shared laughter. Readers can write to Alexandra at PO Box 9449, London NW3 2WH.

For
Leslie Wainger and Isabel Swift,
who thought I should write about sheikhs.

One

"**L**ook, it's Reena!"

"She looks so different in real life!"

"What a dress!"

"Wow, she's practically *naked!*"

Dana Morningstar paused at the top of the short flight of steps leading down into the bar as the whispers ran in a little ripple around the rapidly filling room.

"Isn't she wearing *anything* under it?"

"She's *so* beautiful!"

"My dear, you are a ravishingly wanton nun tonight," said a gravelly, perfectly produced voice at her elbow, and she turned with a smile to greet one of the great theatrical "Sirs" of the old school who had entered just behind her.

"Hello, Sir Henry, how nice to see you."

"And how lovely to see you, Dana. Who, if I may ask, designed that very dashing frock for you?"

The very dashing frock consisted of a double layer of shimmery, sheer white fabric with a high, straight neckline, wrist-length sleeves, and a long skirt. By a trick of the light playing on the two layers of fabric, it looked opaque, and very demure, but at moments, with certain movements, it became almost fully transparent. Her warm mocha skin glowed through the fabric, and underneath she was wearing only a skin-coloured thong.

Dana smiled and put her hand on the arm Sir Henry offered, stepping down into the bar at his side as people gazed entranced. "Kamila," she told him in an undervoice. "A new designer launching here in the autumn. She says this dress is going to make her name."

Dana's black hair, long and thick, fell like a cloak around her shoulders and down her back. Her makeup was expertly applied to enhance her dark, heavy-lashed eyes and high, strong cheekbones. She wore delicate tan-coloured sandals and carried a tiny bag.

"On anyone but yourself it would be a dismal failure, but she is perfectly right. Every woman in this room will be knocking on her door tomorrow, foolishly hoping to be made to look like you."

Dana was five foot eleven with a perfect figure, curved and long, with high breasts, athletic legs, and a firm musculature. Her smoky skin usually meant that as an actress she was cast in "ethnic" roles—whether First Nation rebel, exotic outworlder, or Arab princess. Or her current soap role—Reena, the bitchy, repressed, high-flying South Asian lawyer.

"Would you like some bubbly, Dana?" Sir Henry asked, neatly whisking a glass of champagne from a waiter's tray and offering it to her. "Not for me, dear boy, my heart, you know," he added, waving one pale hand with studied elegance. "Do you think you could find me a scotch?—double, no water."

"Oh, yes, Sir John! Of course!" said the waiter, enthusiastically if inaccurately, and headed for the long bar, behind which men and women in black and white bustled to provide for the guests of the charity function.

"They are so young these days," Sir Henry complained mildly. "They don't show my Lear in the schools anymore, of course."

"I don't think they teach *King Lear* at all," Dana sympathized. "Not accessible enough, Shakespeare."

A man was staring at her from across the room. The whole room was manoeuvring, overtly or covertly, to get a look at the dress; she had been prepared for that. But this man was different. He looked disapproving. Dana flicked a careless eyebrow at him and turned her attention back to "the best Lear the world has seen this century."

"Ah, the new barbarians," he was saying. "And why are you here tonight, my dear, giving a view of your body to the masses? A particular interest in Bagestani Drought Relief, or merely part of the general celebrity sweep? I understand they've pulled out all the stops for this one." He glanced around the crowd with studied disdain. His mouth worked thoughtfully. "Too far, perhaps."

She laughed, as she was meant to. "A little of both. They did scoop the cast of *Brick Lane,* but I would probably have been targeted anyway—I'm half Bagestani, Sir Henry."

She glanced at the disapproving man again: he had a dark intensity that made him magnetic. She was annoyed by the compulsion, but couldn't resist it. For a moment their eyes met. Then, dismissing her, he dropped his gaze to someone who was speaking to him.

Who the hell did he think he was? Dana looked him over. He was wearing a dark red, matte silk, Eastern-cut jacket over ivory silk *shalwar* trousers, and some pretty impressive jewellery, as well as what looked like war medals. He also seemed to have a chain of office. Although by his looks he might be a Bagestani, no representative of the Ghasib regime would be at this function.

"Really?" Sir Henry replied, his eyebrows raised. "I was under the impression that you were Ojibwa—was that just studio publicity?"

Dana had played the small part of a First Nation woman brought to England from Canada during the early nineteenth century in a film in which Sir Henry had had the starring role.

"My mother's Ojibwa, my father Bagestani," she said shortly. She glanced around the room. People were still nudging each other and talking about her dress, but the dark man was now apparently unaware of her existence. "Usually they play up whatever side suits the publicity machine."

"Yes, of course," he said, eyeing her up and down. "Astonishing how beautifully some races mix. Makes one wonder why the great prejudice grew up against interracial marriage. I am sure we—"

"Sir Henry," Dana said abruptly, "that tall man over there was looking at you. Do you know him?"

He turned his head absently. "If a man was looking this way, my dear, and I am sure they all are, he—oh, good evening, Dickie," he interrupted himself as an actor of his generation accosted him. "Still kicking, then. Do you know Dana Morningstar?"

On Dana's other side a woman took advantage of the interruption to approach her and claim her attention.

"I have to confess that I watch *Brick Lane* regularly! And I think the show is going to be absolutely *destroyed* without Reena. I love you in that—you are so cool and bitchy, you never let Jonathan get away with it!" she enthused. "Everyone I know was *so* upset to hear you were being written out!"

Dana smiled with the charm that always made people comment on how different she was from bitchy Reena, and murmured politely.

"No, it's absolutely true! You make that show!" the woman overrode her, much more interested in her own voice than her idol's. "Do you know yet how it's going to happen to Reena? Is it going to be murder or anything like that?"

Dana had done her final day of filming last week, but—"I'm sworn to secrecy, I'm afraid," she apologized with a smile.

She heard much more in the same vein as the next hour progressed. For an hour the celebrities, major and minor, were rubbing shoulders in the bar with the paying guests, who had parted with substantial sums of money for the privilege, and would be parted from more during the course of the evening.

A magazine photographer's assistant was working his way through the crowd asking the celebrities, two at a time, to go and pose for shots under the special lighting that had been set up in one corner. A photographer from a newspaper was walking around the room taking candid shots.

Sometimes she thought she felt the man's gaze brushing her again, but when she glanced over she never caught him looking her way. Maybe she was imagining it. She irritably rejected the idea as soon as she thought of it—he was the last man in the world she would obsess over. She knew what he was like without exchanging one word with him.

She was sure that if she asked anyone about him he would notice, and she was determined not to give him the satisfaction. He was certainly on the "celebrity" side: women were drooling over him with the special fixity reserved for men who are rich, handsome, young *and* famous all together.

Not that he was all that handsome, Dana told herself critically, watching as he dutifully took his turn posing for the photographer. His face was composed of angles too strong and stern for handsomeness. There was too much strength in the set of his jaw, the discipline of the wide mouth. He had square, thick black eyebrows over black eyes that seemed to set icy fire to whatever they touched. He was slim and spare, his shoulders square under his jacket. There seemed to be a weight of responsibility on him, and she could only guess his age at between twenty-five and forty.

She didn't like him. She didn't like him at all.

But it occurred to her that she always knew exactly where he was in the room. Of course it was only because she was the tallest woman in the room and he was at least six-two, but still…

"Ladies and gentlemen, in a moment we'll be moving into the ballroom," one of the organizers announced, and she surfaced and realized that she had spent the past five minutes in a daze, with no idea what she had said or what had been said to her. "If you don't yet know your table, please check the charts by the entrance."

"Have you found yours yet, Dana?"

Jenny, the actress who played her roommate, Desirée, on the show, was at her elbow.

"Clueless," Dana replied cheerfully, as they kissed cheeks.

"I'm sure you'll be at Table G with the rest of us." The two women linked arms and moved towards the crowd around the chart beside the wide entrance to the ballroom.

"That dress is going to cause a riot, Dana," Jenny murmured, completely without envy. She was Dana's opposite in nearly every physical feature—she was a curly-headed blond, with a round, cheerful, motherly face and a short dumpy shape. But she was fun, loyal and a good friend, as well as an excellent actress, and she never seemed to envy anyone anything.

Dana laughed. "Is it shocking?"

"You have no idea, my pet! You turn your head or lift an arm and suddenly you're naked! I've seen more than one spilled drink!"

"Well, that's the idea," Dana observed. "It's supposed to get me noticed."

"And who is that broody alpha male you're carefully not exchanging glances with?"

Dana's cheeks got warm. "Who do you mean?"

Jenny laughed and squeezed her arm. "You know very well who I mean. First he looks at you, then you look at him, and you're both careful never to be caught at it. Darling, have you had a complicated affair with a handsome sheikh and managed to keep it secret?"

Dana jerked upright. "I don't even know his name, and I certainly don't want to learn it! Where did you get the idea I knew him?"

"Oh…just a certain sizzle in the air," Jenny said,

mock dreamily. "The air between you is distorted, sort of like when heat is rising over the desert sands...."

A man with a clipboard stopped them before Dana could argue.

"It's quite all right, I can check for you, Miss Morningstar!" he said, so obviously smitten that Jenny laughed. He riffled through his pages. "Table D," he announced. "That's about five o'clock on the inner circle if you take the dais as twelve."

This cryptic comment made sense a few moments later when they moved into the ballroom. Against the centre of the back wall was a raised octagonal dais where a Middle Eastern ensemble, including the traditional *tar, setar, nay* and *santur,* as well as zither and violin, was tuning up. Around the dais was a polished octagonal dance floor, and around that were arranged tiers of round tables, each seating eight people.

The band began playing as the guests entered and spread out to find their tables—a haunting melody that Dana recognized. It was a traditional Bagestani song called *Aina al Warda?*—"Where is the Rose?"—which had taken on a special resonance for the expatriate Bagestanis, all so bitterly opposed to Ghasib's terrible regime. Her father had played it to Dana and her sister throughout her childhood.

"I wonder why you're not at Table G with the rest of us?" Jenny moaned after accompanying her to Table D and discovering, contrary to both inclination and expectation, that the man with the clipboard was right.

"It's a bore," Dana agreed, but there wasn't going to be a seating change now.

"Who are you with, then?" Jenny bent to the cards on either side of Dana's own. The band was giving *Aina al Warda?* all it had, and as people around the room sank into their seats, Dana saw another stern dark man looking her way. He was dressed in the Western style, black tie, and looked as though he was wondering whether to cross over to her.

Her father.

Where is the Rose?
When will I see her?
The nightingale asks after his beloved....

She stared at him. Well, this put a whole new complexion on the fund-raising evening. This was no mere Drought Relief Campaign. Her father would not have come to any ordinary charity fund-raiser for Bagestan. He was convinced that, in spite of everyone's best efforts, most of the money raised in good faith in the West went straight into President Ghasib's own coffers and the poor scarcely saw a penny.

Dana took a fresh look around at the other guests. They were top bracket; the tickets to this affair had been very pricey. Only about half of them were the usual run of charity supporters and celebrity hunters, though.

The other half were wealthy, educated Bagestani expats—mostly those of a certain age who had been rich enough to get out of the country in sixty-nine, but sprinkled with a few who had come as refugees in the years since and made good. The next generation, the foreign-born sons and daughters like herself, were also well represented.

The women were mostly in traditional Bagestani dress of beautifully decorated *shalwar kamees* and trailing gold-embroidered scarf, and a number of the older men were in immaculate white djellabas. More than one of them, hearing that music, now had eyes that were brighter for tears.

Her father was still looking at her. She wondered if he had seen her dress. She hoped so. She was suddenly filled with a dry, dead fury, as if her father had somehow manipulated her presence here. Logic told her that was impossible.

"Hellooo," Jenny carolled.

Dana surfaced, nodded a cool acknowledgement to her father and turned away. "Sorry, what did you say?"

"Sir John Cross," Jenny repeated, pointing to the card at the place setting to one side of Dana's. "Who's he?"

"A diplomat, I think. Or, he was." She had a vague memory of her father's voice. "Wasn't he the British Ambassador to Bagestan at the time of the coup?"

"Search me!" Jenny shrugged. "Poor Dana! And Sheikh Ashraf Durran," she read from the card on her other side. "One of those boring old farts in white skirts, I bet. My poor darling, it's going to be a long night for you."

"It is going to be a very successful fund-raising night," Dana told her with dry sarcasm, unable to hold down her irritation.

"Is it? How do you know?" Jenny asked with a smile. She wasn't big on world affairs, Dana reminded herself. And her interest in such things as mind manipulation techniques began and ended with using her disarming, housewifely smile in fabric softener commercials.

"Because it may say Drought Relief on the banners, but the real story behind this little event is Line Our Pockets with Gold and One Day We'll Restore the Monarchy in Bagestan!" she told Jenny through her teeth. "God, these people make me sick!"

Jenny blinked. "What do—"

"Listen to that music! They're deliberately playing on everyone's insane hopes for Ghasib to be overthrown and a new sultan to come riding in on his white horse and turn back the clock to the Golden Age! It's not going to happen, but they will get a fortune from the deluded tonight! It's unspeakable!"

Jenny was looking at her in surprise. Dana wasn't often like this, except when she was on the set playing the overexcitable Reena.

"But, Dana, wouldn't you rather see Ghasib kicked out? Wouldn't it be a good thing if one of the al Whatsit princes could be found and restored to the throne?"

"You've been reading the Sunday papers, Jenny. It's nothing but ink and hot air. There *are* no al Jawadi princes! Ghasib had them all assassinated years ago. If anybody kicks Ghasib out, it is going to be the Islamic militants, and that's just going to be a case of out of the frying pan, isn't it?"

"But what about that one in *Hello!* magazine a couple of weeks back, who had amnesia? He was *so* gorgeous, too. He's a grandson of the old sultan, and it said—"

"Najib al Makhtoum is not a viable candidate for the throne, even if he is who they say he is, which I doubt. They are all completely deluded, these people, and somebody is making sure they stay deluded." She belatedly noticed the alarm in Jenny's eyes, heaved a sigh and smiled.

"Sorry, Jen, but I got this stuff all my life from my father, and I hate it. You're right, they are a bunch of boring old farts who want their palaces and oil rigs back and can't accept that it isn't going to happen. God, I wish I hadn't come! It might be tolerable if I were sitting with you and the others. This way—" she gestured at the label that read *Sheikh Ashraf Durran* "—in addition

to everything else, I'll have to listen to a whole lot of
demented ravings about how we've got Ghasib on the
ropes at last.''

''Never mind,'' Jenny murmured mock-placatingly,
''you can always marry him. He's probably got lots of
money, and that's what really matters.''

''Not if he were the last sheikh on the planet!'' Dana
vowed.

Jenny laughed, leaned to kiss Dana's cheek again and
moved off. Dana turned her head—and found herself
looking at the harsh-faced stranger from a distance of a
few feet. By the look on his face, not only was he an al
Jawadi supporter, he had overheard every word of their
conversation.

Two

For a moment she thought he was going to pass on by, but he stopped and faced her. His eyes bored into hers, but against a little shiver of feeling she couldn't define, she managed to hold her gaze steady.

"Are you an optimist, Miss Golbahn, or a pessimist?" he asked in conversational tones.

Typical of a man like him to call her by her father's, not her professional name. She was quite sure it was deliberately calculated.

"Don't you mean, am I a dreamer or a realist?"

"No, I don't mean that," he replied, in a careful tone that infuriated her. His eyebrows moved expressively. "I mean, when you say that the restoration of the monarchy is impossible, do you speak from your wishes, or your fears?"

He had absolutely no right to challenge her about a

conversation he had eavesdropped on in the first place. His arrogance made her grit her teeth—and tell a lie.

"I have no wishes one way or the other. I am simply calling it as I see it."

"You have no wish to see a vicious dictator who destroys his country and his people swept from power," he repeated, his face hardening.

She was damned if she would retract now.

"What good would my hopes do anyone?"

His burning gaze flicked down over her body, then back up to her face again. She suddenly felt what a disadvantage it was not to know whether she was naked or not. Had he just looked at her breasts?

"Do you feel you owe nothing to your father, Miss Golbahn?" he asked.

She stared at him in open-mouthed, indignant astonishment. Typical of a man like him to imagine a twenty-six-year-old woman should govern her actions according to her father's pride!

"Who *do* you think you're talking to?" she demanded, dimly realizing that heads were now turning in their direction.

"I—"

"My name is Morningstar," she overrode him in her coldest voice. "And how accounts stand between me and my father is absolutely none of your business."

His eyes narrowed at her, but if he expected her to be cowed, he could think again. She tilted her chin and gave him stare for stare. Her tone was no more insulting than his own had been, and she would be quite happy to point that out to him. But the man bowed his head a fraction.

"I apologize. I was given to understand that you were Colonel Golbahn's daughter."

"My father is Khaldun Golbahn. He is no longer a

colonel, and the regiment he was colonel of hasn't existed for over thirty years,'' she returned through her
teeth.

Before he could respond to this, a waiter appeared to
pull out her chair, and Dana gratefully turned away and
sank down to accept a napkin on her lap. Only a few
people were still milling around, tying up their conversations before heading to separate tables. People were
watching her more or less covertly, and she realized that
her argument with the stranger had given them another
reason to stare and whisper.

She could sense that he was still hovering behind her.
She hoped he wasn't intending to get in the last word.
Dana picked up the printed menu card propped in front
of her wineglass and wished he would disappear.

''Sheikh Durran!'' a crusty old voice exclaimed with
satisfaction.

''Sir John,'' his voice replied, and she almost fainted
with horror. Her eyes flew to the place card at the setting
next to her. *Sheikh Ashraf Durran.*

Ya Allah, she would be sitting beside him for the next
two hours!

The two men were shaking hands behind her, and she
heard the clap of hand against shoulder. ''I was hoping
to see you.'' The old man dropped his voice. ''How did
your brother manage? Can I assume your presence tonight means I am to congratulate you?''

Dana found she was holding her breath. There was an
air of mystery over the conversation, suddenly, and it
gripped her. She bent further over the menu card, but
she wasn't taking in one word of what was printed.

''He was successful, Sir John, in a manner of speaking—and flying by the seat of his pants, as usual.''

He spoke quietly. His voice now held a hint of humour that she hadn't been privileged to hear when he spoke to her. It was deep and strong, as compelling as the man. A voice an actor would kill for.

"You have it safe, then?" The old man was whispering now.

"I do."

"Tremendous! Well done, all of you! One might almost say, an omen."

"*Mash'Allah.*"

The two men sat, one on either side of her. Dana stared fixedly at the menu. She had never felt so unnerved by a situation. She reminded herself how many times in the past she had made conversation with awkward, difficult strangers, more or less successfully. There was no reason to feel as though there was a chasm in front of her.

Waiters were already circulating with trays of starters and pouring wine. Onstage the *tar* was being played with a heartrending virtuosity that no other instrument, she thought, ever achieved.

"Asparagus or tabbouleh?" the waiter asked her.

Dana loved the food of Bagestan; she had been raised on it. At sixteen she had stopped eating it, as a rejection of her father and all he stood for. That time of rebellion was long past; she was twenty-six now. But she found herself thrown back into that old, combative mind-set now.

She wanted to let Sheikh Ashraf Durran know that she was not to be judged by any of his rules. As she had her father.

"Asparagus, thank you," she said, and a plate of butter-soaked green spears was set before her. She took a sip of wine.

"Tabbouleh," Sheikh Durran firmly requested a moment later. She noticed that there was no wine in his wineglass. Well, she could have guessed that.

In the loud buzz of conversation that was going up all around the ballroom, it seemed to her that the silence between the two of them must be as obvious to everyone as their earlier disagreement. She wondered if gossip about them would find its way into the tabloids. Journalists often needed no more. Find a button and sew a coat onto it was their motto.

Dana glanced around the table in the hopes of finding a conversation to join. Somehow she had got put in with the political crowd. She recognized an academic who was often called in to discuss Bagestani affairs on a BBC current events program, and a television journalist who had made her name covering the Parvan-Kaljuk War and whose career was now devoted to reporting from one Middle East hot spot or another. Dana thought she would have enjoyed talking to them. But they were directly across the table from her, chatting quietly together.

Sir John Cross, too, was engaged with the person on his other side.

"You have no desire to see your father restored to his command, Miss Morningstar?" Sheikh Durran clearly had no reservations about picking up where they had left off.

Dana picked up a stalk of asparagus and turned her head. Up close she recognized the Parvan flag on one of his medals. He was a veteran of the Parvan-Kaljuk War, then, but she was no closer to knowing who he was.

"I have no *expectation* of seeing it," she returned, before biting into the tender, delicious tip.

"Why not?"

"My father is, after all, nearly sixty. Not very much younger than President Ghasib." She said the name deliberately, for in expat circles it wasn't the thing to give the dictator his title. Saying it on an occasion like this was tantamount to declaring herself on the Ghasib side.

She wasn't on the Ghasib side and never had been, not even in her days of wildest rebellion. But no way was she going to fall meekly in line with the sheikh's expectations.

She pushed the buttery stalk into her mouth. There was no change in the sheikh's expression, but suddenly she felt the phallic symbolism of it, almost as if he had pointed it out to her. *Dream on!* she wanted to snap. She chewed, then licked the butter from her fingertips before deliberately reaching for her wine again.

Sheikh Durran seemed to take no notice. He picked up a small lettuce leaf and used it to pinch up some of his tabbouleh salad.

"Do you think the only thing that will remove Ghasib from power is death from old age?"

She chose another stalk. She opened her mouth, wondering if she could unnerve him by sucking the butter from the tip. Her eyes flicked to his. His look was dry and challenging, and without any warning, heat flamed in her cheeks.

"Even granting the unlikely proposition that there was an al Jawadi heir," she said defiantly, "even granting that this mysterious person should at last reveal himself and, even more amazingly, make the risky attempt to take power, and then granting that he should be successful in restoring the monarchy in Bagestan—what are the odds that my father would be given his old job back by someone who wasn't even born at the time he held it?"

His eyebrows went up, but he made no answer.

"But the truth, if people would stop being excited by

newspaper reports as reliable as sightings of the Abominable Snowman, is that it's a mirage. No prince is going to come riding in on his white horse and wave his magic wand to make Ghasib disappear.''

''You know this?''

''Look—I got that nostalgia stuff at my daddy's knee. He talked of nothing else all through my childhood. When I was a kid, I believed it. I had a huge crush on the mysterious Crown Prince who was going to make it all happen. I wrote letters to him. I even had a dream that I was going to marry him when I grew up. But he never came, did he? Thirty years now.

''I paid my dues, Sheikh Durran. I believed the myth as firmly as I believed in Santa Claus. After my mother and father split Santa Claus never visited our house again, but I went on believing in him. And I went on believing in the al Jawadi restoration, too. But a dream like that only lasts so long. And then one day you wake up and realize—it's a fairy tale.''

''And at what age did you wake up?''

Dana tensed and wished she hadn't spoken so openly. She wasn't sure why she had. ''From the Santa Claus myth, eight. From the prince on a white horse fiction, sixteen,'' she said shortly, and applied herself to her meal.

''Sixteen,'' Sheikh Ashraf repeated consideringly. ''That's young to stop believing in justice.''

She supposed he was right. But she had had a very rude and sudden awakening.

Dana shrugged, demolished another spear of asparagus, and wiped her fingers on her napkin. He waited, and she felt forced to answer. She waved a hand at the room.

"What amazes me is the number of people who never wake up—who refuse to wake up."

"What happened at sixteen that took the stars from your eyes?"

I discovered that the father I adored was a monster and nothing he said was to be believed.

She shrugged and lied again. "Nothing in particular."

His gaze probed her for an uncomfortable moment, but to her relief he let it pass.

"And what happened to your letters?" he asked.

"What?" she asked blankly. She automatically leaned towards him as the waiter cleared her plate.

"The letters you wrote to the Crown Prince. What became of them?"

She really wished she hadn't told him about that. It wasn't a part of her past she confided very often. Something had knocked her off her centre tonight.

"I really don't know." Her tone said, *don't care.*

"They were never sent?"

"Where to? My father told me Crown Prince Kamil had escaped from the palace as a baby, with his mother carrying him in a load of Ghasib's dirty laundry. He said they got to Parvan, but no one knew any more than that, did they?"

He hesitated. "Some knew more."

She wasn't sure what made her ask, "Did you ever meet him?"

Again he hesitated. "Yes, I met him."

"He died fighting in the Kaljuk War, didn't he? Is that where you knew him?"

Sheikh Ashraf turned his head and lifted a hand as the waiter started to fill his glass with wine. "No, thank you."

When he turned back he seemed to have forgotten her

question. After a moment Dana nodded towards the row of medals on his chest.

"You were in the Kaljuk War?"

His eyelids came down as he nodded.

"Are you Parvani?" He didn't sound it.

"I was born in Barakat," he said. "I was in Prince Omar's Company."

The almost legendary Company of Cup Companions, led by Prince Omar of Central Barakat, who had gone to war on Prince Kavian's side. She had followed their fortunes while still at drama school. All her friends had had crushes on the Cup Companions and had plagued Dana with questions, feeling sure that, because of her background, she knew more than they did.

And she had, a little. At least she knew what the term Cup Companion meant. "In the old days, it used to mean the guys the king went on the prowl with. The sons of the aristocracy. They weren't supposed to know or care about politics or government, only wine and love and poetry." Cue for sighs. "But nowadays it's just the opposite. They're the prince's special advisors and stuff like that. By tradition he has twelve of them," she had explained.

There had been many more than the twelve in the Company, of course. Others recruited had been made Honorary Companions. So it wasn't foolish to ask, "Are you one of his Cup Companions?"

He replied with a little nod. She should have guessed before. But she'd forgotten until now that Cup Companions from Parvan and the Barakat Emirates were supposed to be attending tonight.

"What's your interest in the al Jawadis?" she pressed.

He eyed her consideringly for a moment. "Prince

Omar is related to the al Jawadi through the Durrani. I, too, am a Durrani.''

''And you want to help the al Jawadi back to the throne?''

His raised his eyebrows. ''Tonight we are here to raise money not for the al Jawadi, but for the victims of the drought which Ghasib's insane agricultural policies have created.''

''Maybe, on the surface, but you know and I know that tonight there are going to be lots of under-the-table donations to the al Jawadi campaign as well.''

''Do we?''

The waiter had refilled her wineglass and she took another sip. There was juice on the table for non-drinkers, but she noticed Sheikh Durran stuck to water. But refusing alcohol didn't prove he was a good man. No doubt her father was doing the same.

''Born in Barakat, you said. Are you Bagestani by blood?'' Not all the refugees from Ghasib's regime had fled to England or Canada, by any means. More had gone to Parvan and Barakat.

''I am half Barakati, half Bagestani,'' he said, after a pause in which he seemed to calculate.

''Ah! So you're one of those who never stopped believing in the fairy tale?''

His lips twitched again. ''You might say that. And you, Miss Morningstar—you do not believe anyone is capable of removing Ghasib from power?''

''Salmon or chicken?'' the waiter interrupted, and quickly set down what she asked for.

She chose automatically and scarcely noticed the interruption.

''Well, there's always the possibility that another ambitious nephew may one day be successful in some renewed assassination attempt, I suppose," she allowed, helping herself to the beautifully cooked vegetables offered. "Or the Islamic militants may pull it off. But Ghasib does seem to deal with both those possibilities in a very convincing way, doesn't he? I can't help feeling that anyone with their eyes on power, even a prince, if there is one, might be content to wait until natural causes win the day for them."

He concentrated on the vegetables for a moment. "You think the fear of death makes cowards of us all?"

His part of the conversation so far seemed to consist entirely of questions. "Maybe. It's the undiscovered country, isn't it? 'Thus conscience doth make cowards of us all,'" she recited.

His mouth went up on one side. It was the first smile she had had from him. "And who said that?"

"Hamlet. Isn't that who you were paraphrasing?"

This produced a small laugh. Humour transformed him, she found. The fire in his eyes turned to sparkle, and he suddenly seemed much younger. Now she would place him at well under thirty-five.

"I was not paraphrasing anyone." The flow to the new conversation was seamless as he pursued, "You know the play well?"

"I starred in a school production."

"Interesting—I thought the star part was Hamlet himself."

"It is the star part." She grinned, but still did not feel easy with him. "I was at a girls' school."

"And you were the tallest girl?"

It occurred to her suddenly that he did not know who she was. That was why he had called her by her father's name. Well, no surprise if a man like him didn't watch the soaps, and she hadn't yet landed a major film part.

She laughed. What did it matter? "Yes, I was the tallest girl by a long way," she said. "I was a natural for the part."

Three

―――

"**G**ood evening, ladies and gentlemen."

Dana and Sheikh Ashraf had chatted more amiably for a few minutes, and then, mercifully, the conversation had opened up and become general around the table. Now the meal, delicious by any standards and stupendous compared to the food served at most other charity functions she had attended, was finished. Coffee and liqueurs had been served.

Now it was down to business.

"We have a wonderful evening lined up for you tonight...."

Dana absently sipped her Turkish coffee and let the voice of the master of ceremonies wash over her. The organizer was introduced, an earnest, small man talking about the drought and the famine it had caused. And, knowing his audience, making much of President

Ghasib's deliberate mismanagement of Bagestan's agri-
culture and his habit of pocketing charity funds.

"But we have negotiated with Ghasib's government
to put our own representatives on the ground in Bagestan, and management of the funds raised tonight will
never leave our control until it is safe in the hands of
those who need it most...."

"I wonder if that's true," Dana murmured.

"Very difficult to manage, I should have thought,"
Sir John Cross agreed in a low voice. "However, what
else can one do? I think we must assume that some of
the money gets through to those who actually need it."

"And while we may hope and believe that we're getting closer by the day to the moment when Ghasib's
government will be history, our priority toni—"

The audience interrupted him with applause. Dana
shook her head and glanced towards Sheikh Ashraf. He
was looking very sober, leaning back in his chair, his
arms crossed. He was not applauding.

He turned his head and caught her eye with a dark,
level gaze that seemed to probe and assess, and made
her heart pound, but what he had gleaned from the examination, she couldn't guess.

The organizer wisely kept it short and then the real
star of the evening took the mike. Roddy Evans was a
well-known and popular comedian, always in demand
for events like this because of his ability to put people
into a generous, good-natured mood and then get bun-
dles of money out of them. Dana had always liked him.

"All right, I want every table to elect a captain,
please!" he said, when his warm-up had reduced everyone to cheers, laughter and applause. "Just choose one
person who'll keep the rest of you in line this evening

and take money from your wallets when instructed to do so...."

"I think it better be Dana!" someone announced. "If it comes to delivering money to the stage, she's the one they'll all want to see," and the rest of the table quickly agreed.

"Sheikh Durran looks like a much better bet," Dana protested, more out of curiosity to see how he would react than anything else. "He's at least big enough to make any threat stick."

"But one catches more flies with honey," he said smoothly, waving a hand, and they all laughed and agreed.

Dana gave in with a threat.

"You'll be sorry. Be afraid, be very afraid. I will *soak* you."

Being captain turned out to be a not very onerous duty. At intervals throughout the evening, on instruction, Dana had to get a five- or ten-pound note from each of the people seated at her table and pass the money on to one of the roving hostesses. Most people were familiar with the format and had come with a supply of folding money as well as their chequebooks. In the meantime there was plenty of nonsense to keep people laughing and donating.

After a while came what most of the paying guests considered the high point—the auction. Tonight there were some real prizes. Top of the list was an all-expense-paid first-class two-week holiday at the Hotel Sheikh Daud in West Barakat, sponsored by Prince Karim.

But that would come near the end, as would the brand-new Subaru donated by Ahmed Bashir Motors. Before that there was some very exciting and somewhat drink-inspired bidding for weekends at country hotels, meals in restaurants, books, celebrity memorabilia, theatre tickets—whatever the organizers had been able to screw out of donors. The organizers here had clearly been top rank, and there was a stream of the kind of prizes that were often the top prize at lesser events.

Sprinkled among them were half a dozen "personal appearance" donations. Certain celebrities had agreed to spend an evening at a restaurant with whoever bid the highest for the honour. In the ruthless way of the entertainment industry, these prizes, like the others, were graded according to ascending value through the evening, because of the excitement the increasing amounts of money generated from the guests.

It was always interesting, and often salutary for those concerned, to see which celebrities were expected to bring in only a low bid, and which were saved to the end—with the other best prizes. The celebrities usually hated the whole process.

Most of such celebrities were women, and tonight all were, which Dana supposed was a comment on the way society was still run. She was always asked to participate in such an auction, and sometimes did, though always disliking it. If a man got you for too little, he treated you with contempt. If he paid a lot, often he thought he should be able to expect a little more than your face over the dinner table. Or, worst of all, he invited a whole horde of his friends along and expected you to act as his hostess for the evening.

But good charity organizers were ruthless, and this one had been prime, and Dana had given in.

Her name hadn't been called yet. This was making her nervous, because although the early names didn't usually get up in front of the crowd during the auction, the later names were often asked to do so. This let you in for even more potential humiliation if your drawing power wasn't as strong as the organizers had assumed.

Jenny's name had come up early. She stayed in her seat, but she had got a very respectable two thousand pounds from a real estate agent whose company name was called out at least eight times during the prolonged bidding by the savvy Roddy. Dana had expected to be the next celebrity auctioned after an interval of theatre tickets and a year's membership to a top gym, but she wasn't.

Nor was she the next, nor the next.

She began to feel really uncomfortable. She was not a movie star, after all; they were the ones who pulled in the really big sums. She was a mere soap star with only a couple of film credits, and if she went up after high bids and scored much less than the previous celeb, it would be embarrassing.

Next up was a gorgeous, big-breasted but brain-dead television presenter, who was called up onstage for the auction and who, after a long and well-hyped bidding war between a Harley Street cosmetic surgeon and a new car dealer, pulled nearly five thousand pounds. It was a figure which impressed the whole room.

A set of golf clubs came next, but it was clear all the real emotional heat this time had become focussed on the human portion of the auction. A very well-known middle-aged movie actress who had been included in last year's Honours List and was now a Dame raised just over six thousand pounds. Dana started to feel very uncomfortable. Why had this woman been listed before her? It was ridiculous. Dana didn't have anything like her pulling power.

Maybe Dana's name had just been forgotten by the organizer. She certainly hoped so.

"It's a bit like a slave auction," the journalist across the table observed dispassionately, making Dana cringe even more. "I wonder why they do it?"

"Because we are made to feel, by whoever is pressuring us, that it is a small thing to ask and everyone else has agreed and we are selfish and smug if we refuse," Dana said clearly.

And just then Roddy cried, "...a dinner date at the fabulous Riverfront Restaurant with our very own favourite bitch, Reena! Otherwise known as *Brick Lane* star *Dana Morningstar!* And she's here tonight, ladies and gentlemen, so will you come up here, Reena, I mean, Dana, and let the folks take a look at the merchandise?"

Dana lifted her eyebrows at the journalist as one of the ever-present assistants dashed in to hold her chair and escort her to the stage amid an enthusiastic round of applause and cheers.

She smiled and twinkled her fingers as she stepped up under the lights, and wondered whether her dress was opaque or transparent at the moment.

"...and together you'll dine on caviar, lobster and champagne provided by the fabulous Riverfront Restaurant, which as you all know is one of London's most fabulous eateries! It's moored right on the Thames, and you'll be driven home afterwards in a chauffeur-driven Rolls-Royce provided by Launcelot Limos!

"So now, what am I bid for a delightful evening in Dana Morningstar's company? You might even learn from her the secret of Reena's demise before it's broadcast! Do I hear five hundred, ladies and gentlemen?"

"Five hundred!"

"Oooh, quick off the mark there, Harold. That's Harold McIntosh, ladies and gentlemen, not short of a bob or two when you run a Mayfair car dealership, now, are you? Five hundred, do I hear—''

''One thousand!''

''Ah, ha! Well, this promises to be a very exciting auction, ladies and gentlemen, not reticent at all, are we? That's a thousand bid from—''

''Ten thousand pounds.''

It wasn't a shout, but somehow the voice cut through the chatter and was heard by everyone. There was a collective gasp all over the room. Not only because of the enormous leap in the bidding, but because of the quality of the voice. Firm, assured, brooking no interference. And not at all the worse for drink.

Sheikh Ashraf Durrani's voice.

Dana felt her cheeks flame. She bit her lip. She had never had to work so hard to force a smile in her life, but she managed it. She even managed to fake a little wide-eyed, excited grimace.

''Ten thousand pounds, ladies and gentlemen! Well, now we're getting serious. And who is going to take that higher, I wonder? Jeremy, accountant to the stars, you're in this league, do I hear a raise on ten thousand for an evening with Dana Gorgeous Morningstar? What about you, George—''

''Ten thousand one hundred!'' cried a slightly inebriated voice.

''Ah ha! We're really cooking with—''

''Fifteen thousand pounds.''

It was the sheikh again, speaking as flatly as if he were giving an underling an order. The skin on Dana's body shivered into goose bumps. He was making it so obvious.

''Well, well, Sheikh Durran! I see you're pretty determined to get what you want. Do I hear any bids over fifteen thousand?'' cried Roddy, just a little nonplussed, because it suddenly was difficult to inject the humour and good-natured ribaldry he was such at expert at into the proceedings. The room was filled with an excited buzz. Dana, standing in a bright spot, just kept smiling.

It was a struggle. What on earth did the man think he was doing? To be the highest bidder was one thing. To carry on like this meant everyone would be talking! They'd be the subject of endless speculation, and the story would probably make it into the tabloids. They'd never get any peace if they appeared in public.

And yet part of her couldn't resist the lure of being thought so attractive. Fifteen thousand pounds in a couple of minutes! And such a powerful, influential man! It was like a fairy tale.

She saw Jenny and the others at the *Brick Lane* table gazing at her in blank, slightly reproachful astonishment, as if a secret part of her life had been revealed and they felt they should have known about it.

''...and gone! To Sheikh Ashraf Durran. I'm told you're one of Prince Omar of Central Barakat's most trusted advisors, Sheikh Durran, and I'm sure he'll agree you've shown excellent judgement tonight!''

The applause was thunderous as Dana was escorted back to her seat, a follow spot on her all the way.

''Whew!'' exclaimed Roddy, wiping the not-so-imaginary sweat from his brow. ''Ladies and gentlemen, what can we do to beat that? You'll have to work hard and bid high! And that won't be too difficult for our next prize—Prince Karim of West Barakat himself has actually donated this one, ladies and gentlemen. It's the one you've all been waiting for—well, except for a certain fairly obvious exception, who's already snaffled his prize! Here it is, a two-week holiday for two in the fabulous...''

''What on earth did you do that for?'' Dana hissed, as she sank into her chair. Everyone at the table was gazing at them in slightly stunned speculation. They must now believe one of two things—that Dana and the handsome sheikh already had a relationship, or that the sheikh was smitten and they were about to have one.

Nothing she could say was going to convince anyone otherwise, she was sure, but the moment she looked into his eyes she realized that it wasn't true. Whatever his reasons were, she knew damned well that Sheikh Ashraf Durran was anything but smitten with her. The expression in his eyes was anything but sexual interest.

A little seed of anger was born then.

He shrugged, and his next words confirmed her suspicions. ''Why not? That is what we are here for, to raise money.''

Inarguable. ''Well, after a display like that, I will not go out with you!'' she retorted childishly, in a low voice meant for his ears alone. ''We'd have every paparazzo in the city following us!''

He lifted his hands in a gesture that said it mattered not a jot whether she did or did not. ''Things are rarely what they promise to be. *Buyer Beware* I am sure is the first rule at such auctions.''

She could not get lighthearted about it. ''You have not bought me.''

He looked at her. ''No? But you were for sale, were you not? Or should we say for rent?''

That made her grit her teeth. ''I'll speak to the organizer, and you won't have to—''

He lifted a hand, cutting her off. ''Don't trouble, Miss Morningstar. I will not in any case be in the country beyond tomorrow. Take a friend and enjoy the lobster and the limousine without me.''

This made her even angrier, though she could dimly see that it shouldn't. She should have smiled graciously and said how generous he was and how the starving children in the Qermez Desert at least would benefit and that was what mattered. But she couldn't get the words past her teeth.

Maybe because she was gritting them.

''More coffee, Miss Morningstar?''

She was grateful for the excuse to turn her head. She nodded, and the waiter poured more sweet black sludge into her little cup. There was a plate of sugary Turkish delight which she had previously avoided, but now her irritation drove her to pick up a little cube. She bit it irritably in half. It was an unreal bright pink.

Meanwhile the holiday in Barakat was going for at least as much as it was probably worth.

She really couldn't have said why she was so irritated with him. To throw fifteen thousand pounds away like that—well, of course at first she had imagined it was because he was interested. And of course that had piqued her own interest. But why should she care if all he was interested in was making a show of his wealth while passing on money to charity?

The auction was over, but the wine was still flowing and there were more high jinks in store. People joined in with delight.

Not Dana. And not the stone-cold-sober Sheikh Ashraf. They stood up and sat down as instructed, and put their hands on their heads or their bums, and paraded around. But she noticed that when he turned out to be one of the group of men instructed to drop their trousers to their ankles and shuffle up onto the dance floor, he did not comply, and no one at the table even thought of challenging him on his dereliction.

But everybody else was having a marvellous time with all the nonsense, and the money was rolling in.

"Now, ladies and gentlemen, a little earlier in the evening, you were all handed out cards asking how much you would donate to Bagestan Drought Relief for the fun of a kiss. Yes? You were given the names of our six magic couples tonight—the men who bid for an evening with our lovely actress volunteers—and you voted for the couple you would most like to see kiss."

Dana felt a prickling of her skin, like a warning of doom. She flicked a glance at Sheikh Durran, and saw his mouth tighten. He knew, too. And was looking forward to it as much as she was.

"Now, while we've all been having such a fabulous good time, volunteers have been adding up all the votes and tallying them."

She had agreed to it—of course they wouldn't pull a thing like this without getting all the actresses' permission first. But she had agreed with a shrug, thinking it would be just one more thing. A one-in-six chance of having to kiss some smitten stranger in public—how bad could it be? No worse than the auction itself.

But it was going to be a whole lot worse.

"And ladies and gentlemen, at the risk of shattering some delicate egos, I can tell you, it was *no contest*. The pair you most want to see giving each other a kiss, ladies and gentlemen, is *Dana Morningstar and Sheikh Ashraf Durran!*"

The bright light of the follow spot fell on them. Sheikh Ashraf was sitting like a statue. Dana realized suddenly that *he* of course had not been consulted. For the sheikh this was coming totally out of left field.

And he liked it even less than she did. She knew that by his face. Sheikh Ashraf Durran looked like nothing so much as the masks of Hawk her Ojibwa grandfather carved.

But this was a pressure even the coldly disapproving sheikh would not be able to resist.

Four

"Now, first, I'm going to ask you all to put your money where your mouths are. Let's see how much you're willing to pay...."

Dana smiled. Sheikh Ashraf was still looking as though sparks would fly off if you hit him with a hammer.

She looked into his face and smiled deliberately at him. Everyone was watching. "It's inevitable," she murmured, her eyebrow giving a flirtatious flicker as if she were joking with him. "Let's just get it over with."

He hesitated. "We will look far less foolish if we give in gracefully," she warned him.

Meanwhile, Roddy was good-naturedly chivvying the audience into one last fit of generosity, reminding them of the starving children and the drought-stricken farms, making jokes about how poor old Sheikh Ashraf was going to have to kiss Dana, and what a terrible thing that was, while all the audience had to do was pay him to do it.

Someone drunkenly volunteered to stand in for the sheikh, and was speedily subdued by a witty rejoinder from Roddy that put off anyone else with that idea.

And the money buckets were going the rounds. At the edge of the stage someone was counting the cash and cheques and keeping Roddy advised as to the total.

Through it all the spotlight was on them. Dana smiled and laughed at the jokes. She no longer knew how Sheikh Ashraf was reacting, because although she smiled and flicked her eyes his way she didn't actually focus on him. Roddy was being decent, his patter was very lighthearted and without innuendo, and she didn't really understand why the whole thing was so hard to take.

Finally Roddy seemed to have milked them dry. He instructed the money-gatherers to pour all the money into a huge bucket at the front of the stage.

"Now, Dana, and Your Excellency, can I have you both up here on stage, please?"

Dana bit her lip and bent her head, taking a deep breath. Her blood was pounding in her head. She really didn't understand why. It was nothing. A quick kiss was all that was required. And yet...

She let the breath out on a sigh, lifted her head, and, as one of the waiters appeared behind her chair, prepared to stand.

A hand clamped on her arm, keeping her seated. Dana looked down stupidly, noting the strength in the square fingers that curled around her flesh, the tawny skin against the shimmery white fabric of her dress, the heat that burned through it.

"Wait here," he ordered softly.

He got to his feet, crossed the dance floor and moved

up onto the little stage. Such was his presence, his charisma, Dana noted with awe, that the rowdy audience fell immediately silent and expectant.

"You know me," he said, in his deep, firm voice. "You know who I am." She heard a gasp from a table behind her, and a murmur rustled through the room. He waited, looking around at the audience with the unsmiling, calm confidence of...she wasn't sure who she had ever seen with that kind of bone-deep authority.

The air seemed suddenly too heavy with expectation.

"I am Sheikh Ashraf Durran, Cup Companion to Prince Omar of Central Barakat. I am going to do what you want me to do, have no fear."

There was a massive roar of voices and applause, led, she saw, by the Bagestani contingent. He let it soar and peak, then cut it off with a raised hand.

"I am willing, even without your very generous donations." More cheers. "But this—" he gestured at the bucket of money at his feet with a flickering smile "—this is not by any means enough money to convince Miss Morningstar to make such a sacrifice as to kiss me."

She laughed along with everyone else. God, he should be a preacher! He was absolutely mesmerizing them! People began to shout and wave money and cheques, which the hostesses hurried to collect. Sheikh Durran stood with his arms folded, watching.

Roddy, she saw, was gazing at him in stunned admiration. He absently accepted a note passed to him by one of the hostesses, read it, then, with a glance at Sheikh Ashraf, put the mike to his lips.

"I have a note here from Ahmed Bashir of Ahmed Bashir Motors on the Edgware Road, pledging to double the amount raised! So come on, ladies and gentlemen, this is your chance to give double your money!"

Sheikh Ashraf looked and nodded towards the table where Ahmed Bashir was sitting, and another cheer went up. For a man who had started out looking as if he were carved in oak, he sure learned fast, Dana reflected.

"What does he do for Prince Omar?" someone at the table leaned to ask Dana.

It was a natural assumption, the way things had gone tonight. But there was too much noise for explanation, and she simply smiled and shook her head.

"Miss Morningstar," said Sheikh Ashraf from the stage, and Dana's head whipped around as if she were a puppet and he had caught her string. He put out a hand. In the room suddenly the sound of the air conditioning seemed loud.

"They give all this to the starving if you will kiss me, Dana. Do you agree?"

A waiter pulled out her chair. Dana got to her feet, feeling half hypnotized, and moved with swift grace towards him. Her heart was pounding, and the smile playing on her lips now was involuntary.

"Not everyone knows, I think, that Miss Morningstar herself has very close ties with Bagestan. Her father is Colonel Golbahn," said Sheikh Ashraf.

The Bagestanis in the audience were by now delirious. They screamed and cheered her up to the stage. Dana was totally bemused by the reaction.

"That is why—" They fell silent again, as if he held their strings, too. "That is why Miss Morningstar agrees to this blackmail. Because the money is going to a cause that is very close to all our hearts." Wild, almost hysterical applause. "The hungry, desperate children—all the hungry and desperate people—of Bagestan."

She reached the dais and lifted her hand. The platform was only a foot high, but Sheikh Ashraf seemed to tower over her. "You should take this kiss, therefore, as a symbol of our love for Bagestan, and our determination to fill the hungry ache of its people."

And with that he bent over her, wrapped his arms around her, lifted her bodily up against him, and clamped his mouth to hers with a passion and a thirst that made the world go black.

"You are *such* a sneak!" the voice carolled down the receiver.

Dana had answered the phone automatically, still half asleep. Now she rolled over and blinked at the clock. Seven thirty-eight. "Jenny, why are you calling at this hour?" she protested. Scraping her hair away from her ear, she punched a pillow into shape and slid up to a half sitting position in the bed.

"Oh, sorry, darling, I'm in Makeup! Are you in bed? I forgot how early it was," Jenny lied cheerfully.

"In a pig's eye," Dana muttered direfully.

"Is he there?" her friend hissed excitedly. "I really actually phoned thinking you wouldn't be home, to be honest."

"No, he is not here!" Dana told her indignantly. "Give me a break! I only met the man last night."

"Ha. That kiss had been building up steam for longer than a few hours. That kiss had History."

Dana shivered. "It didn't have steam at all," she protested weakly. "It was all set decoration, entirely for the multitude."

"Balls. Sorry, love, but you could see the heat rising. Everybody was absolutely entranced."

She had certainly *felt* the heat. Her whole body seemed to liquefy as his lips smothered hers, and then turn to scalding steam. She had never experienced such a transformation in her emotions in all her life before. She could barely remember now how they had got off the stage and back to their seats again. She could still hear the cheers, but why the crowd had got so excited by a kiss, she couldn't guess. Something to do with his magnetism, she supposed.

"It didn't make the morning editions, of course, but it'll be in the *Standard* and the *Mail* for sure," Jenny informed her gleefully. "I've already been called by both papers, for the background. They'll be calling you in a minute, I bet."

On cue, the phone gave the Call Waiting beep in Dana's ear. "Hell," she said mildly. "That's one of them now. What did they ask you?"

"Oh, the usual—how long you've been seeing each other. When you gave Mickey the push."

Dana rolled her eyes. "Oh, ouch!" This was a complication that hadn't occurred to her. "I suppose he'll be furious."

"It was open to him to get on his horse some time ago, as I recall," Jenny said pitilessly. "If it's now come to a point where he's made to look redundant, whose fault is that?"

Dana sighed. "I know, but what can a man do when he thinks persistence is a virtue?"

"Why didn't you just tell him about your rugged sheikh in the first place?" Jenny laughed. "I'm sure that would have scared him away."

"Jenny, I only met him last night. There was nothing to tell."

"I believe you, darling, but millions won't. If that's the truth, it's the most rampant case of passion at first sight since…since—Adam saw Eve, I suppose. That—"

"No, it wasn't." The Call Waiting signal was still

beeping. Most callers would have hung up by now. Definitely either a journalist or Mickey. "He was after something, for sure, but it wasn't me. Sheikh Ashraf was playing a deep game, as they say."

Jenny was surprised into silence. "Really?"

"Really. It may have looked good, but he made it very clear to me that—"

"Look good? That kiss steamed up every pair of glasses in the room. It looked as if it would melt marble!"

Dana couldn't help the little buzz that went through her bones, the smile that toyed with her lips. "I didn't say the man couldn't kiss."

Jenny whooped with delight. "I knew it! I knew—"

"Jenny."

"I knew you'd been keeping something from me! Tell me all about it! Ooooh, the way he said *fifteen thousand pounds* in that determined voice, as if daring anyone to overbid him!"

"Jenny, I came home in the limo alone. He told me he was leaving town today and that I should take a friend along for that evening at the Riverfront he paid for."

"Awwww!" Jenny cried. She was genuinely disappointed. Jenny was a rare person—she had no envy. She wanted what was best for her friends, never projecting her own needs onto the situation. "Aw, Dana, I thought you had it made! A gorgeous sheikh at your feet, who could ask for better than that?"

"Well, it ain't gonna happen," Dana said. "Look, darling, this phone is going crazy in my ear. I'll have to take the other call. Can we talk later?"

"Yes, I'm due on set in a few minutes anyway. I'll call you again when I get a break."

* * *

"It worked well, then," Ashraf Durran ibn Wafiq ibn Hafzuddin al Jawadi said, tossing the *Times* to one side and picking up the *Telegraph* as he reached lazily for his coffee cup.

"It worked like a dream," Gazi al Hamzeh concurred. The two men sat at opposite sides of a table in a private jet flying high above the English Channel. "We covered all the bases, something for every paper from the nationals right down to *News of the World*."

He pointed to the *Telegraph*'s front-page photo of Ashraf in the red jacket. Underneath was the caption *Sheikh Ashraf Durran was one of the dignitaries attending the Bagestani Drought Relief charity function in London last night. A Cup Companion to Prince Omar of Central Barakat, the sheikh is of mixed Bagestani and Barakati descent.*

Underneath was the small headline of a separate story: *Bagestan Living In The Hopes Of Discovering The Al Jawadi Heir.* The story mentioned Bagestan's unhappy plight under the monstrous dictator, President Ghasib, and how desperate the Bagestanis were to restore the monarchy through a direct descendant of ex-Sultan Hafzuddin al Jawadi. The problem was that after taking power in a military coup in 1969, Ghasib had embarked on a program of assassination of the al Jawadis. The entire family had been forced to live in exile under false names for three decades, and no one could say for certain whether any were still alive.

However, rumour was very strong within the expatriate Bagestani communities around the world that the al Jawadi family had successfully protected themselves except for the assassination of Sultan Hafzuddin's second son, Prince Wafiq, in the late seventies. Most Bagestanis believed that Wafiq had left two sons, now about thirty years old, and that one of them had been named Crown Prince by the old sultan before his death several years ago.

This man, it was rumoured, was now poised to take power from Ghasib. But who was he, and when would he show himself?

"Neat juxtapositioning," Ashraf remarked.

"Yeah," Gazi said. "It's absolutely textbook stuff. You can't say it straight up, so you run two stories side by side, and hope your readers are smart enough to get the drift. They certainly will be here. Not a Bagestani in town who won't put two and two together this morning.

"The upmarket afternoon tabloids will all carry the story of the outrageous bidding you did for Dana Morningstar—that's their kind of stuff—and the others will feature the kiss. Which, I have to say, was a powerful ad lib. For a minute there, even I thought you were going to come right out and declare yourself."

Ash shook his head. "Your campaign is too well thought out for me to fool with. Let's keep them guessing."

"Dana Morningstar played up well. She's a stunningly beautiful woman up close, isn't she?"

Ash's eye was caught by something in the paper and he didn't answer.

"Does she know?" Gazi pressed.

Ash shrugged, still reading. "She told me she thinks it's a fairy tale, and all the al Jawadi are dead."

"That's a bit odd, given the circumstances, isn't it?"

"It's possible she really doesn't know. Or maybe—" Ash lifted his head and eyed the public relations advisor thoughtfully. "She's estranged from her father, apparently. I wonder what's behind that."

The two men looked at each other for a pregnant moment while the implications sank in. "Hell!" Gazi exploded. "How is it we never found that out? She wouldn't be actually in the Ghasib camp, would she?"

Ash laughed and shook his head. "Stop worrying, Gazi. It was pretty obvious, when I thought of it, that she said what she said largely to irritate me. I overheard her say something and challenged her on it, and she's obviously a woman of spirit."

"It never even occurred to me to question whether the daughter of Colonel Golbahn was loyal to the cause. I should have. It should have been the first thing I checked."

"Well, it doesn't matter now if she isn't. The speculation will blow over in a few days, won't it?"

Gazi was staring gloomily into his cup. He shook his head. "It depends, Ash, doesn't it?"

"On what?"

"On what she does now. If she wants to pretend you're involved with her, she could say damned near anything about you, and after that show last night, she'll be believed."

"Forget it. She's not the type."

Gazi looked at him levelly. "Sure of that? She could wreck your chances with the religious, Ash. And you need the mullahs."

"She's got a grudge against her father, maybe, but if Dana Morningstar's actively rooting for Ghasib I am no judge of character."

"You are sure it's character you're focussed on, and not sex?" Gazi challenged him.

"Who says a man can only focus on one thing at a time?"

"When one of the things is sex, everybody. Remember, God gave man a brain and a penis, but only enough blood to run one at a time."

Ash laughed. "Dana Morningstar is not a traitor to the cause."

"All right, I hear you." Gazi shrugged. "Let's see what she does next."

Five

"**F**or God's sake!" Roxy cried, wriggling through the apartment door as soon as Dana cracked it open. "What is going *on?* I've been trying to phone you for three days!"

Dana shook her head at her younger sister, closed and locked the door. "So has everybody else in London."

"Who? Why? What do they want?"

Dana shrugged, turned and led the way to the sofa in front of an open glass-paned door. Outside was a small, sunny terrace overlooking nearby roofs. "Media people, mostly. They want to talk to me about a) my breakup with Mickey, and b) my hot affair with the handsome sheikh who might or might not be one of the al Jawadi grandsons. Not necessarily in that order." She waved Roxy into a chair as she spoke, went into the kitchen and returned with another cup.

Tossing aside the script she had been reading, she

sank into an armchair. She poured a cup of tea, passed it over, then sipped from her own cup and looked at Roxy over the rim. "And what do *you* want?"

Roxy had the grace to look a little embarrassed. It was true she didn't often visit just on the strength of sisterly love. Roxy spent money fast and furiously, and although usually their father covered her amazing deficits, there were times when she had a reason not to apply to him.

"Well, it's not money this time," she said mulishly. "Or at least, it is, but this isn't about borrowing anything."

"Good," Dana said clearly. "Because maybe you've noticed I'm unemployed as of last week."

"Yeah, I heard you're getting dropped from the show. That's too bad. What happened?"

"Partly the new producer thought I should be more grateful than I was when he told me he had plans for Reena to become a more important character. Partly just the demand for constant change."

Roxy stared at her, the second part of this speech lost on her. "Really? Oh, wouldn't Daddy hate that! He always said that was what would happen if you went into acting."

A cloud moved, and the afternoon sunlight suddenly poured into the room. Dana, wearing snug-fitting shorts and a three-quarter-sleeve top in soft jade brushed cotton, slung her long legs up over one arm of her chair and rested her back against the other.

"I know he did. So what?"

"Do you always say no to producers, Dana?"

Dana lifted eyebrows in the suddenly haughty expression that had always made her sister just a little afraid of her. "Yes, I always say no," she returned shortly. "Are you going to tell me what the problem is?"

The physical resemblance between the two sisters was not strong. Dana's build was long and slender, and her strong-boned face had a nobility that was quite unlike Roxy's prettily rounded, softly fleshed body and features. They had different mothers, and each took after her mother rather than their mutual father.

There was more than six years age difference between the two girls, too, so it was perhaps natural that soft, sweet Roxy should so often come to strong, proud Dana for help and advice.

"Daddy talks about you a lot," Roxy said suddenly, ignoring her cue. "He'd really love to see you."

Dana shrugged. "Six-thirty p.m. Monday to Thursday, and an omnibus edition on Sundays at three."

"Aren't you ever going to relent, Dana?"

"Roxy. You don't understand, you have never understood. You grew up with both your parents there and loving you. I was robbed of my mother's love for ten years and five months. You will never know what it means to a five-year-old to be told her mother doesn't love her or want her and to live with that for ten years before learning that it was a lie."

"I'm not saying what he did wasn't wrong. I'm only saying maybe—"

"I know what you're saying. You've said it before." Her face took on an untouchable look that always made her sister nervous. "Now, do you want to tell me your problem or not?"

It had been ten years since the day Dana had learned of her father's terrible, unspeakable betrayal of his wife and daughter. Ten years since a tall, beautiful woman with a tragically lined, oddly familiar face had come up to her table in the little bistro near the private girls' school she attended.

"Dana? Are you—Dana Golbahn?"

"That's right," Dana said with an enquiring smile. She wouldn't smile so freely again for a very long time.

"Dana, I'm—" The woman licked her lips and to Dana's amazement tears burst from her eyes. "I'm your mother. I've been looking for you every day for the past ten years."

He had kidnapped her. He had left his wife without a word and taken his daughter away without even a last goodbye kiss. He had lied to his daughter—"Mommy doesn't want you. Mommy's tired and wants to be by herself,"—but to her mother he had been even crueller than that. Not a word. Nothing. She had come back from shopping one calm Saturday afternoon to find that her husband, her daughter, and her life had disappeared.

"I was frantic. Out of my mind with worry. At first I thought you must have had an accident in the car—well, I went on wondering about that for years. Even after all the evidence was in that he had planned it all, had taken your passport…even after the divorce papers arrived, I still had nightmares about a car being found in a lake with you inside it."

"But *why?*" Dana cried. All the nights she had sobbed herself to sleep, wanting her mother, her beautiful mother, and the stories about Nanabush and the Bear, *Mishi-bizheu* the Lynx, and the Anishnabek people. To her it was utterly incomprehensible.

Her mother said, "Your father fell in love with me against his will. He wanted me to convert, but I wouldn't. But I agreed that our children should be brought up in his religion. I didn't realize then that he would consider my telling you Ojibwa stories and tales a violation of my promise. To your father, to talk about Bear and Fox was to set up partners with Allah, the worst kind of *shirk*."

And with those words a host of memories flooded back. Dana suddenly remembered her father asking her what grace she had said over her food. "I was thanking the salmon for giving up his life for mine," she had explained gravely. He had yanked her from the table, slapped her, sent her to bed. There were a dozen other moments like that—moments when he had tried to wipe all trace of her mother's influence from her life.

And he had almost succeeded.

Dana was sixteen when her mother finally found her, and going through a fairly normal teenage rebellion. The meeting with her mother pitchforked her into a complete rejection of her father and all he stood for. She refused to spend another holiday at his home, instead going back to Canada at every break to make up for lost time with her mother.

It was the beginning of a strong, rich relationship. After her loss, Alice Golbahn had returned to the reservation where she was born and begun to study with the medicine man there. Now she was a healer herself, and mother and daughter worked together to mend the rift in their lives during long walks through the forest while they gathered herbs for Alice's medicines, long chats while they dried and stored them.

Her relationship with her father suffered as that with her mother blossomed. Dana had listened to her father's explanations just long enough to establish that what her mother had told her was true. Then she had turned her back on him and all he stood for.

* * *

Roxy sat up and set her cup on the coffee table. "If I'm going to tell you I need something stronger than tea," she begged.

Dana nodded and got up to pour her a drink, her bare feet padding over the beautiful, hand-knotted Bagestani rug. The rug was only one of many signs in the apartment that Dana no longer turned her back completely on her Bagestani blood, however rarely she spoke to her father these days. "You kept me all to yourself for ten years," she had pointed out ruthlessly when she was sixteen. "Now it's my mother's turn."

She poured a glass of Roxy's usual chilled Australian Shiraz and handed it to her before sinking down into her armchair again. Then she waited.

Roxanna took a couple of healthy slugs and, staring down into the glass, muttered, "Well, you have to know. I got into debt at the casino again."

"Oh, Roxy!"

"I know, I know!"

"But *why?*"

"Because it's fun!" her sister snapped defiantly. "And because they encourage me, and because everyone else is doing it!"

"Everyone else is rich enough to lose. You aren't."

Roxy's chin set mulishly. Criticism was counterproductive with her. Dana shook her head. "How much have you lost?"

She couldn't believe her ears when she first heard the amount. The jolt brought her legs swinging around and she sat upright. She made Roxy repeat it, then stared at her.

"I don't believe this! Are you crazy? No one could lose that much money in a single night!"

Roxy began to cry. "It's bad, isn't it?"

"*Bad?* It's out of this world! It's utterly unbelievable!"

"I know, I know! Don't shout at me, I don't know how it happened! They just kept giving me more chips and I kept signing...."

"The casino must be cheating you. They faked some of the receipts or something."

Roxanna hiccupped on a sob. "No. The—the champagne's free, but all the signatures were mine. Oh, God, Dana, what am I going to do? You've got to help me!"

Dana stared at her blankly. "Help you? How? I don't begin to have money like that! Even if I sold this flat and the car—Roxy, what on earth do you imagine I can do about an amount like that? I doubt if even Dad could cover it."

The mention of their father made Roxy sob even louder. "This will kill Daddy! He can't find out! It will kill him!"

"Yes, I think it might," Dana said, because what was the point of mincing words? It wasn't just that their father had a weak heart. It wasn't just that gambling was forbidden by their religion. Roxy was his darling. The thought that she had been gambling again, after all his strictures, and had lost so dreadfully, would break him.

"But I don't see what choice you have, Roxy. He's got to be told. What else is there? You've got to raise the money somehow, or they'll— Dad told you before how dangerous those casino people are. He told you what they'd do."

Roxy sobbed more loudly.

"It will break him financially," Dana added, half to herself. "It'll take everything he has. He'll end up living in a council flat, if they give him one, on the state pension."

It was cruel, but she wasn't going to pretend. Roxy had been warned. And pretence would get them nowhere. This spelled ruin for their father, and quite possibly for Dana as well. But she at least had a career to turn to. Her father was retirement age.

"There *is* something else I can do," Roxy muttered when the spasm of crying had passed.

Dana heaved a breath. "They'll let you work in one of their brothels until you pay it off, I suppose. That's what Dad said, isn't it?"

"No, it's not that. They—they want two C U."

"They want what? What's a C U?"

Roxy got some strength from somewhere and lifted her head to look straight at her sister. "They want *to see you.*"

Dana went very still, staring at her sister, all puffy face and pleading eyes. "They want to see me?" she repeated slowly, weighting each word. A chill of prescient horror slithered down her spine.

Roxy sniffed, nodded, dropped her eyes again.

"What do you mean, they want to see me? What did they say?"

"'Bring Dana Morningstar to see us.'"

Her stomach heaved. "Why do they think you could arrange that?"

"They know we're sisters."

Dana's jaw set dangerously. "Who told them? You?"

Roxy sniffed and shook her head. "I don't know how they know. They just knew. They showed me your picture in the paper and said, *Bring your sister to see us immediately.*"

"Or what?"

"Or they'll tell...oh, Dana, please go and talk to them! They'll tell Daddy! And oh, Dana, I know it will kill him. It was bad enough you becoming an actress! If he knows I've been gambling again—oh, God! You don't love him, Dana, but I do! He's my father and he's never done anything bad to me and I love him and I don't want him to have another heart attack!''

Rage drove Dana to her feet. ''Why didn't you think of that when you were disobeying him? You say I don't love him—how can you pretend to love him when you do a thing like this? What did you think was going to happen? Did you imagine you'd win all the money back if you just went one more round? How many times did you think that before the truth finally sank in?''

Roxy started to sob again. ''Dana, I'm sorry! I'm sorry!''

''Dad warned you what those people were like! He told you they like to get upper class girls into prostitution that way! Why didn't you listen?''

''I don't know, Dana!''

''If they think *I* am going to prostitute for them, they can think again. And you, too! Why didn't you tell them I wasn't an option? Would you really be willing to have me do a thing like that in your place?''

Her sister's sobs increased to heartrending wails. ''No, no! I'm sure it's nothing like that! I'm sure of it!''

''How can you be sure? How can you begin to guess how minds like that work? For all you know I'll walk in the door and be chloroformed and—oh, God, Roxy, this is just too ugly! This is unbelievable!''

''You see, Miss Morningstar, it is very simple. Your friend, Sheikh Ashraf Durran, is an old, long-established customer of our casinos, here and elsewhere. And—''

''I don't think it's quite as simple as you imagine. I have told you, he is no friend of mine, and that is the truth. I met him once in my life and he kissed me because it was part of a charity function.'' Dana tossed aside the tabloid with the screaming headline and the photo of that kiss. ''It was an act.''

It looked like a very passionate clinch. Her arms were by her sides, one elbow half bent, in helpless protest or in the first beat of passion, or both. Her back was arched a little over his arms, one arm like a bar at her waist, the other on the bare skin of her upper back. Both their faces wore an expression of passionate abandon as her lips parted under his.

She remembered the kiss, the heat of his hand, the skill of his mouth, with a sudden, primitive immediacy that brought the blood to her cheeks. She had never in her life thought she was going to faint because of a kiss, but all the tension of the evening had seemed to surge back as she looked up at him, and his arms had been so passionately possessive she had stopped breathing on a gasp.

He had been talking about hunger, the hunger of the people, but her heart heard it as his, her, their mutual hunger. That strong mouth, those fierce eyes, and when his kiss smothered her she had felt devoured by his passion. Her mind knew it was fakery, but her body and soul had responded as if to a central truth.

Desire had erupted through her, a black, stunning jolt of electricity that blotted out all thought, leaving her at the mercy of pure sensation. Lightning had danced on her lips and skin, thunder rolled through blood and bones.

But she wasn't telling this man that. She fought down the heat in her blood and gazed at him in cool enquiry.

The man nodded. There was an inhuman aura which she found horrible, the stench of a rotting soul.

"You are an actress, Miss Morningstar, and I must allow you to be the expert on such matters as acting. But I am a man, and you in your turn must allow me to tell you that for the sheikh it was not an act. He was a man distracted by your beauty."

She couldn't quite place him or his accent. Wherever he had originated, and Bagestan was a possibility, he had clearly been living in the West for many years—but not in England. Australia or South Africa, she thought.

She shrugged, to hide the little whisper of echo in her that said it was true. He had not been unmoved by the kiss. "Much good may it do him, if you're right," she said.

The man nodded. "Let us not argue the matter. You are here because your sister foolishly gambled more than she had at the tables. If she does not pay her bill, I will approach your father and demand payment. It is of no moment to me, but I understand that your sister is reluctant for me to do this. You, too, or you would not have come."

Dana lifted a careless eyebrow. "It won't do you any good if you do—my father hasn't got money like that."

His gaze ran over her face with a knowing smile. "And of course your father has no friends to whom he could apply."

"Ask a friend to pay off his daughter's gambling debt? You don't know my father!" Dana said. He was making an insinuation that she didn't get, but she knew better than to let him see that it was so.

"Well, she preferred to go to you. Now, I'll be frank with you, Miss Morningstar. Large as it may seem to you and your sister, her debt is pocket change to us. We would be quite happy to write it off to experience—if we had a good reason to do so."

She flicked an eyebrow at him, but did not speak, and he went on, "There are other debts that aren't so small or so easy to write off. Sheikh Ashraf Durran ran up a debt here last winter that would make your hair stand on end. Millions of pounds. And then he ran out. He has not been in England long enough for us to get a bead on him since then. He has bodyguards, so none of our process servers has a chance in hell of getting close."

She was surprised, and a little disappointed, to find such a weakness in Sheikh Ashraf. But then her father had always been a morally upright man on the outside, too, and look what he had done. That was the worst of puritans, she thought. They lived a lie.

He lifted a finger and pointed at her. "That's where you come in."

Her eyebrows went up. It was all a game of bluff. "Really?" she said unconcernedly.

He leaned back in his chair, bent his arm and pointed at her again. "You could get close to him—no, don't tell me you don't know him, it may be the truth, I don't know and it's immaterial. The point is, you could get to know him. You could get under his skin."

"And then what?" Dana asked, with a coolness she was far from feeling. *You could get under his skin.*

"Then nothing. You just let us know where he's going to be one night, so we can serve a subpoena on him." He flattened his hands. "That's all. That's all there is to it. He's in the south of France at the moment.

"We'll set you up first class, Miss Morningstar, and send you out there, all expenses paid. We'll make sure you meet up with him again. All you have to do is let the attraction blossom."

Six

It hadn't been the most pleasant way to discover how much she still loved her father, Dana reflected two days later, stepping out onto the balcony of the world-famous hotel overlooking Cap d'Antibes' beautiful bay.

She had sat there, willing herself to say no and dare them to do what they could. But she knew, better than they, that they could do terrible damage. Roxanna was her father's darling; he doted on her.

He was a proud man. Dana had always known that she inherited her stubborn pride from her father. He would do whatever was necessary to wipe away Roxy's debt, but living with the consequences would break him. To be dependent on government handouts after a life of hard work and tragedy overcome…

All these things about her father she knew and had always known. What had surprised her had been her own heart's response. She couldn't do it. She couldn't let it happen to him.

Her agent had not been happy about the prospective open-ended holiday, until she learned where Dana would be going. "You're bound to meet people, Dana!" she'd enthused then. "Especially at the Eden Roc! Do some networking!"

They had told her she would get the star treatment, and she had. She had travelled first class, been met by a limousine. Her suite was utterly luxurious, on the third floor of the legendary Eden Roc Hotel, home to the stars.

They had insisted on supplying her with a wardrobe, saying she had to look the part, had to be able to mix with the rich and famous here. And once she had agreed in principle to their main demand, it seemed futile to waste energy arguing over details. They were right—she was an actress and she had to be costumed for the part she was playing.

She had no intention of fulfilling the spirit of the demands the casino owners had made on her. She had come here to save her father. But she was not going to try to insinuate herself into Sheikh Ashraf Durran's life or his bed.

She had to make it look good. The casino owner had hinted that he would have spies around her, and she didn't doubt that. So she was going to try to meet the sheikh again, all right. But what she planned to say to him wasn't on the casino owner's agenda.

The motor launch bucked over the swell under the shimmering afternoon sky and pulled up beside the megayacht. *Dhikra,* read the name on the bow, in large, lazy script, and underneath it, the same word in the more graceful Arabic alphabet. *Dhikra. Remembrance.*

Gazi al Hamzeh leapt out onto the landing platform and ran lightly up the steps to the deck above. "Where is he?" he asked of the nearest deckhand, who pointed aft.

He found Ash, barefoot and bare chested, sitting at a table spread with papers and books—documents, legal submissions, texts, and a Qu'ran. He had a yellow legal pad beside him and was making notes. When Gazi opened the door, he tossed down his pen and stood. The two men embraced and kissed cheeks in the Eastern manner.

"How's it going?" Gazi demanded.

Ash shrugged and stretched out the kinks of hours of paperwork. "Everything's looking good, Gazi. If we can trust the commitments we're getting, we've got it almost sewn up. The parliamentarians we pinpointed all look promising. As for the *ulema*—"

He lifted strong tanned fingers to rub his eyes.

"Giving you troubles?"

"They're making a lot of demands. They have agreed in principle to a secular government, but now they want the constitutional code of human rights we're drafting watered down in certain areas."

"Alcohol and women's rights," Gazi guessed, flinging himself down into a chair.

Ash nodded. "And a couple more, but those are the main ones." He gestured at the table. "I've been reading through legal and religious opinions of the past couple of centuries."

"Well, we know you aren't going to win over the extreme leaders," Gazi said. "But you don't need me to tell you you've got to have some of the moderates on board."

Ash grimaced. "No, you don't have to tell me. It's a

question of the minimum necessary compromise, isn't it? But I don't like it. As far as alcohol goes, I've tried to explain that too much of the economy currently is tourism-based. I've told them what would happen to the industry if the hotels and restaurants were suddenly forced to go dry, but—''

He broke off and looked more closely at Gazi's face, realizing this was not what had brought him here. "What is it?"

"There's been an unpleasant development on another front," said Gazi, looking a bit *I-told-you-so*.

"What front?"

"The daughter of Colonel Golbahn arrived last night. Dana Morningstar. Checked in to the Eden Roc."

Ash took it in silence, his eyes going slightly distant as he absorbed the implications. After a moment he nodded. "Right," he said.

"Too much of a coincidence, Ash," Gazi said sadly.

"She's an actress, Gazi, and this is the summer playground of movie people."

"There's more to it. She'll—uh—Lana Holding had a call from a press agent in London. Fed her some story about building up Morningstar's presence in advance of a film being released next month. Lana says that came across as eyewash. She owes the agent a favour and she says she should do it. She wanted to know how we felt about it."

"Should do what?" said Ash.

"Treat Morningstar as an A-list celebrity, which of course she isn't, not here in film star land. And include her in tomorrow's fund-raiser."

Dana's heart was thumping as she slipped out of the limousine, stepped onto the red carpet and glanced up.

A large red-and-green banner over the massive bronze
entry doors read *The Night of the Thousand and One
Books: The Parvan War Relief Celebrity Storytelling
Event.*

There were a few cheers and cries of "Reena" in
English voices from the crowds behind the barriers on
either side of the carpet as she mounted the broad steps
to the entrance, and that was more than she had expected. Most of the crowd here wouldn't recognize her.
An English soap star didn't rank very high in Cannes.
But there was plenty of speculative whispering as she
passed, probably because of her costume.

An official from the Parvan War Relief charity met
her at the door as eagerly as if she were a hot Hollywood
property. "Miss Morningstar! Dana!" she cried in a
warm voice, and the crowd shifted and began to wonder
if they should know her after all.

"I'm Lana Holding," the woman said, taking her arm
and leading her into the brilliantly lighted hall, and Dana
suddenly recognized her. Lana Holding al Khosravi was
the charity organizer who was almost as well-known as
the celebrities she regularly persuaded to take part in her
imaginative fund-raising events. These were for the benefit of the tiny kingdom of Parvan, whose three-year war
had so devastated the country. She was married to a
Parvani herself, and was the daughter of Jonathan Holding, the American computer mogul. She used her own
name professionally.

"You look terrific! Thank you so much for agreeing
to take part in this," Lana enthused. The slender redhead
escorted her down the length of the crowded foyer along
a cordoned-off path, explaining the event as they
walked.

"Of course no mingling with the audience before the

show," Lana explained when Dana asked. "Everyone is in the Green Room tonight. But if you'd mingle a bit in here afterwards, we'd be very grateful. That's really what they pay for."

A black-suited attendant opened a door with a flourish and Lana led her into the Green Room. All around the room famous people from different media and many countries, and in an interesting variety of costumes, were drinking, laughing and chatting.

Dana was wearing soft white deerskin, a long slender skirt with a fringed hem, a sleeveless top with an intricate beadwork design in turquoise and green, and matching dangly feather-and-bead earrings. A beadwork headband clasped her forehead and her hair streamed out over her shoulders. On her feet were matching beaded moccasins. It was an outfit one of her mother's friends had made for her. She looked like an Ojibwa princess.

Some of the celebrities had really taken the dictum "dress relevant to your performance piece" to heart; others had only given it the nod. One star dressed in tight shimmery black and outrageous feathers was fairly obviously going to be reading a story with a Wicked Queen in it, and an aging, rather alcoholic English stage actor was making a virtue of necessity: he'd be reading from *The Lost Weekend* or something similar, Dana guessed.

A Hollywood actor had come as Mark Twain, and an English actor, very predictably, was Shakespeare. A French actor she had always wanted to meet was, she guessed, meant to be the great fabulist La Fontaine.

Dana's heart gave an uncomfortable kick and there was Sheikh Ashraf Durran. It was the first time she had seen him since the night of the kiss; he had not been at this afternoon's brief rehearsal.

He was dressed like a fairy-tale caliph in a navy blue silk coat intricately embroidered in white, gold and red, a long gold-embroidered sash wrapped around his hips, flowing Middle Eastern trousers and curl-tip embroidered red leather slippers. A curved scimitar hung from his waist in an intricately decorated scabbard, and one dark hand rested negligently on the jewelled hilt. On his dark hair was a navy turban, tied with the ends falling over one shoulder.

Dana actually gasped as her eyes fell on him, as if some shock had been delivered deep to her system. He looked stunningly, exotically male. And powerful, Dana reflected, like a magician in a fairy tale. She slowed her steps as Lana Holding led her past him, and as if unconsciously drawn by her interest Sheikh Durran turned his head.

This might be a good time to talk to him, if only to say she had something to tell him and arrange to meet later.

She smiled, suddenly understanding how much she was looking forward to another meeting. She had not counted that as one of her reasons for giving in to the casino owner's demands, but perhaps, unconsciously, it had been.

"Hello again," she said, her voice warm.

His expression hardened as he recognized her. It showed no vestige of friendliness or even good humour. Dana caught her breath, wondering how she had offended him. His black gaze seemed to burn right through her.

"Oh, that's right, you two know each other!" Lana Holding exclaimed with a laugh.

"Ye—" Dana began, but Sheikh Ashraf's harsh voice overrode her.

"We have met. Hello." He nodded briefly at Dana and deliberately turned back to his companions.

Dana bit her lip and turned away, feeling humiliated and angry. He had treated her as if she were a starstruck fan who was always pestering him! Lana chatted brightly to cover the awkwardness and led her across the room to where several English actors were raucously laughing.

Dana knew most of them, one way or another, and she was welcomed into the group with loud bonhomie. It was balm to her hurt pride and, childishly, she hoped that Sheikh Durran noticed.

At eight o'clock they filed through a door onto the stage, where a large semicircle of sofas and armchairs around the perimeter defined the central space. Downstage centre were two large, comfortable armchairs, angled towards each other.

Lana Holding made a speech about the progress of the ongoing landmine clearance program in Parvan, to which the funds raised tonight would be devoted. Her speech was moving and short, proving her expertise at fund-raising, and she quickly passed the mike over to the night's MC.

"...We asked our celebrities to come with a favourite story or poem. They have chosen from all the spectrum of world literature. There will be stories you know by heart and stories you have never heard before, short stories and long stories, true stories and stories of wisdom, fairy tales and myths and legends. We ask you please not to applaud each individual story, but wait until the curtain falls at the interval and the end of the show before you show your appreciation. Now we're going to dim the lights...."

So it began. There were no introductions. Each storyteller simply got up and silently moved to sit in one of the chairs at centre stage as the person preceding them vacated it, just as they had rehearsed it. The soft light went alternately up and down on the two central chairs. The audience was obedient and there was no applause to slow the proceedings.

The timing was expert, the evening was beautifully organized, and soon the audience relaxed, trusting that they were in the hands of masters, and slipped into the childlike willingness to be entranced that was essential to a successful evening.

Some people simply read from books they had brought with them, a poem or a children's story or something taken from books like *Morte d'Arthur* or *The Canterbury Tales.* Some recited poetry by heart. When Dana's turn came, late in the first half of the program, she did not begin by opening a book and reading the title. Instead, as the lights came up on her, she began softly,

"Among the Anishnabek, my mother's people, storytelling is a very ancient tradition. But we do not read our stories from books. Each storyteller retells a story in their own words, so that a story is a little different every time it is told."

She paused. The silence in the hall was profound. "Tonight, I am going to tell you the story of Nanabush, Coyote Woman and the Duck Egg," she said.

She told the story simply, in her warm, deep voice, then got up and moved back to her seat, and the next story started. When the curtain came down at the interval the applause was warm and prolonged.

They all filed back into the Green Room, congratulating Lana Holding on a brilliant idea brilliantly organized. There was a photographer making the rounds asking people to go and pose where he had lighting set up in one corner.

When Dana entered the room, Sheikh Durran was almost directly opposite the doorway. He was talking to Lana Holding. Dana stood irresolute. She was torn between feeling she had to try again to talk to him, and a furious determination never to speak to him again.

She was angry with herself, too, for the naive arrogance of the plan she had half-formed. She had planned to tell Sheikh Ashraf the entire truth, and ask him to accept the subpoena.

In London, remembering the moment when he had kissed her, she had imagined that he might listen to her, might do what she asked. Well, she was miles from being able to do that, though she wouldn't understand the reasons for his attitude to her if she thought about it for a year.

But she couldn't just give up without making any effort at all. Khalid Abd al Darogh wouldn't accept failure from her easily.

She had to try. It infuriated her. She would rather be boiled in oil than try to speak to Sheikh Durran again. But she had to try, or let her father sink.

Dana was in a daze, and didn't realize it until the photographer's assistant came up and startled her with a request to pose. She turned to follow him to the corner where the photographer was snapping people in quick succession.

"I wonder if you'd mind—it'll make a great shot—" she heard, as the photographer guided her into position.

"What?" Dana asked, and turned to see Sheikh Durran coming towards her, shepherded by another of the photographer's assistants.

"Oh—but..." Dana began, in awkward refusal, not

wanting to be exposed to another public rebuff, but the sheikh was smiling and saying, "Of course."

She wondered if she was the only person who saw the glint of anger in his otherwise bland expression. He came and stood beside her, and she could feel his heat against her bare arm. She couldn't resist a glance towards his face. He was looking at her, and the contempt in his face burned her.

"This was not my doing!" she snapped before she could stop herself.

He only raised his eyebrows and turned his head obediently as the photographer cried, "This way, please!"

He was working fast, only a couple of clicks and whirrs and the assistant was thanking them and moving them out of the way for the next subject.

Dana suddenly realized it was now or never. She would not get near him again, his expression told her that. "I need to talk to you," she muttered. "There's something—"

To her fury, he smiled, bowed his head, and simply turned away without a word.

Seven

"**O**nce upon a time there was a king. His name was Malek."

Sheikh Ashraf Durran was the last speaker of the night, and Dana could see why. His stage presence was completely compelling. From the moment he had moved to centre stage, even when his chair was in shadow and the occupant of the other chair was reading, she couldn't keep her eyes away from him.

He had announced no title, given no introduction. He was sitting in a wide, easy lotus position in the chair, his scimitar resting across his knees, one hand lightly clasping it. He looked like a miniature painting of a Bagestani storyteller, painted on two inches of ivory, which was one of her father's treasures.

"Malek was not a great ruler, nor as wise as he should have been, but he was a good and honourable king. He ruled his people mildly and with as much justice as was possible in a troubled world. Nor was his kingdom a powerful one—there were many richer and more powerful kings in the world.

"In fact, one of King Malek's chief problems was how to maintain his nation's independence against the competing interests of two very powerful rival kings who were constantly trying to destroy each other. These kings were always looking for allies. They kept bringing other kings under their sway, and sometimes would urge these minor kings in their camps to fight. This was a cloak and a way to fight each other in limited war, for they were so powerful that to fight open war against each other would have destroyed them both.

"King Malek had, however, one source of wealth which these other kings envied and coveted. It was a mine of liquid gold. The two rival kings wanted this gold very much. They each tried everything to make the king declare his allegiance to one or the other and give them the gold.

"But the good king would not do so. He extended the hand of friendship, but he would not bend the knee of obeisance. And so the hearts of the powerful kings grew hard against him, and each suspected him of secretly conspiring with the other. And although neither king could risk taking Malek's tiny kingdom by force, for fear of what the other would do, they each waited for an opportunity.

"Now, King Malek took as one of his exemplars the great Caliph Haroun al Rashid. Imitating him, the king used to go out among his people in disguise, to see for himself how the kingdom was faring and how his appointed officials and others performed their duties. So the officers of the law and the judges of his courts and the dispensers of his charity were always fearful lest the person whom they treated unjustly or demanded a bribe of might prove to be King Malek himself.

"One day, while the king was walking in disguise in a street of poor homes, he saw a group of children playing. They were playing soldiers. One of the boys so impressed the king with his leadership and his grasp of military strategy that the king called the child to him and asked his name. He learned that Baltebani was an orphan, living in poverty with his uncle, who had no money to educate him or give him a trade.

"And so the king adopted the boy. Not as his heir, for Malek had sons of his own, one of whom would succeed him. Instead he educated the boy for the army. As the years passed he was rewarded with the youth's dedication and triumphs, for Baltebani lived up to every early expectation. And a deep trust and love developed in the king towards his adopted child, as strong as if Baltebani were his own son.

"When the boy had grown to manhood, the king created a new post, appointing him leader of all his armed forces, the first person other than the king himself to have this combined role, and thus the highest honour of his profession.

"I mentioned that the king had sons. He had three. One of them, Walid, the son of the king's favourite wife, Banu, grew up wise and true, and worthy to rule, and on his twenty-first birthday the king declared feasting throughout the kingdom. He named Walid Crown Prince in front of the people, declaring him his heir, and gave into his keeping a rose. That rose was the symbol of the family, and by tradition it passed into the guardianship and the responsibility of each Crown Prince on the day that he was appointed.

"Baltebani looked on at this ceremony, and envy was

born in his heart. He knew that he was as capable as
Crown Prince Walid, and he told himself that if he had
been in truth the king's son, Malek would have chosen
him rather than Walid to succeed him. He wondered in
his heart why blood should dictate the king's choice. For
it was no longer the fashion in the world for kings to
pass power to their sons. Some took power by force, and
some by the will of the people, but few by virtue of
blood.

"And the Commander of All the King's Forces asked
himself if he should not gain power by one of the other
methods."

The audience drew in a soft communal breath that
moved like a whisper of wind across a lake. The beginnings of understanding stirred in them. The sheikh's
voice was deeply compelling, and his story had drawn
them in so that the entire hall was wrapped in silent,
shared intimacy.

"I told you that King Malek had powerful enemies in
distant kingdoms, kings who pretended friendship for the
sake of the liquid gold, but who were waiting for opportunity. They saw it in Baltebani. The king himself
trusted his commander so far that he did not notice how
carefully Baltebani was choosing the men he appointed
to leadership within the forces. The man had, from the
earliest opportunity, and with the king's good will, been
bringing into the military members of his own family.
His brothers and cousins and even the friends from
childhood with whom he had played his battle games
had entered the army at his urging, and been promoted
by his orders.

"Now these men were being moved to the highest
positions in the armed forces, a fact which the foreign
kings noticed, but King Malek did not. One of the for-

eign kings began to meet secretly with Commander Baltebani, and to aid him with money and advice, on the understanding that if the commander succeeded in taking power he would give the king access to the liquid gold his soul craved.

"And the day came when Baltebani turned on his benefactor and drove him out of the kingdom and took the throne in his stead. Every unit of the armed forces followed the commander's orders, save one. The leader of the Palace Guard alone was a position still appointed by the king. Because this man remained loyal to his sovereign when the call came, the lives of the king and many members of his family were saved, and they escaped secretly to exile in neighbouring kingdoms.

"Crown Prince Walid was murdered, but his infant son survived, hidden in the palace. The Crown Princess disguised herself as a serving woman, and for a week she washed the laundry of the new ruler in the palace, before the leader of the Palace Guard helped her to escape, carrying her baby son in a load of laundry. He personally led her to safety in a neighbouring kingdom.

"What had happened was not approved by the people, who wanted their king back. King Malek appealed to his powerful friends, those distant kings, for support in regaining his throne, and it was then that he understood how deeply he had been betrayed.

"He knew he could not regain his throne when Baltebani had such a powerful ally to support him. All he could do was start a destructive war against Baltebani—like so many kings before him, he would be funded by one powerful rival king, and Baltebani by the other. The country would be destroyed. And this he could not bring himself to do.

"So Baltebani was king, as he had dreamed. But his

conscience did not allow him to sit easy on his stolen throne. Perhaps because he understood betrayal so intimately, he feared there would be an attempt to restore King Malek or one of his sons to the throne, and so he sent assassins out into the world to seek out and kill King Malek's family.

"One of Malek's surviving sons was brutally slain in a distant country, and then King Malek understood his protégé at last, saw what an evil heart beat in the one he had promoted to such power. He understood that Baltebani would never feel secure until all members of the royal family were dead.

"Then Malek ordered the family into hiding. They must live apart, and take different names to prevent the assassins finding them.

"But there was always someone to recognize a prince. After eight years, Malek's last surviving son was slain, almost breaking the old king's heart."

When the realization flowered fully in her, Dana saw that it had been growing for some time, the understanding that the story the sheikh was telling was true. It was the recent history of Bagestan, told in fairy-tale style. But she was still under the spell of his voice, and she didn't take in what that meant.

"By this time, the people in the kingdom were desperately unhappy. Baltebani had quickly grown into a monster. It was not only the royal family against whom he sent his assassins, but every citizen who expressed disagreement with his policies and methods. Those who spoke or wrote against his evil practices were thrown into prison, tortured, murdered, their families made destitute.

"Meanwhile, Amir, the son of Crown Prince Walid, lived and grew to manhood under a false name in a neighbouring country. And when he reached the age of twenty-one, Amir in his turn was named Crown Prince and given the rose by the ageing Malek, who never lost his belief that the faithless Baltebani would one day be overthrown by the will of the people, and the throne of his ancestors restored to the family.

"Then a separate tragedy befell Malek. The country to which Amir and his mother had fled, and whose king, knowing their secret history, had treated them well, was attacked and invaded by an enemy. Crown Prince Amir went to battle, and was killed.

"The rose was lost from the day Amir died. No one knew where he had kept it.

"This blow was the last. As they brought the body of his favourite grandson across the threshold, the old king was struck down and had to be carried to his bed. He remained there for the remainder of his days, which were short, never regaining his health.

"Malek had three other grandsons, and as he lay on his deathbed, he summoned them. With his last energy, the old king charged these men with the duty of continuing the struggle to regain the ancient throne of their forefathers, to unseat the hated and vicious Baltebani and free their people from terrible oppression.

"Malek named one of these three grandsons Crown Prince, and though he could not give him the rose, he charged him to find it if possible, and keep it to show to the people as a sign of legitimacy on the day he ascended the throne.

"The princes vowed, to the king and to each other, to do as their grandfather wished. They would work together to restore the throne of their forefathers. They knew that the rose was a powerful symbol of unity and hope for the people of the little kingdom. And so the first task they set themselves was—to find the rose.

"When they had the rose, they would declare themselves to the world, and with the people's help, drive the monster Baltebani from power.

"Of course Baltebani discovered their aspirations. He learned that they were seeking the lost rose, and he was determined to find the rose himself, and show it to the people as false evidence that he was the old king's chosen one.

"Another man, too, was seeking the rose, for his own purposes. And he was closest to it.

"But fate was on the side of the princes. The rose was hidden among other roses, and the agent of this third man was guided to the wrong flower. He plucked it and fled, with the agents of Baltebani in pursuit. And so the princes were left to pick the true rose in peace."

The auditorium was still mostly silent, but excitement was building in wild waves that flooded every heart and must soon erupt. Dana could feel it beating against her like a sea. Her own heart was thumping so hard she could hardly breathe.

God, was it him? Was he the one? A murmur broke out and was instantly shushed, because the sheikh was still speaking.

"And so the princes have the rose, the ancient sign of kingship of their family. Although they have been forced to live in other countries since the moment of their births, their love of their own nation is powerful in their hearts. They suffer with the sufferings of their grandfather's people.

"And with the help of the people, they are going to unseat the monster Baltebani and take back the throne of power, and restore peace and good government and above all *justice* to the kingdom at last."

Eight

"**D**ana, you have to *do* something!"

Dana sighed her exasperation into the phone. "Roxy, will you please listen to me? Things have changed. He's not just Sheikh Ashraf Durran, Cup Companion to Prince Omar, which was bad enough to begin with! He's one of the grandsons of ex-Sultan Hafzuddin, for all I know the Crown Prince-designate himself, and he as good as said they're involved right now in a campaign to unseat Ghasib!"

"I know, I know! It was all on the news." Roxy was momentarily diverted from her own concerns. "They said the audience rioted. Is that true?"

Dana smiled reflectively. Never had she seen an audience erupt with such excitement. She supposed she never would again. It was a once-in-a-lifetime thing. They exploded to their feet when the lights went down, cheering, howling, waving their arms. The wash of excitement that poured over the actors as they stood at the front of the stage taking their bows was as intoxicating as wine. She had never been so thrilled and moved to be a part of something.

"I guess you could call it a riot, yeah."

"Oh! Was it scary? Were you frightened?"

"No. It was the most thrilling moment of my career. If I never stand in front of another audience—well, I've had the ultimate moment. Nothing could ever match it."

"You always were the lucky one," Roxy said.

Envy was loud in her sister's tone, and Dana had always hated that.

"Look, what do you expect me to do now? They'll have guards all over him. I won't get within a mile of him."

"Dana you can't take these people's money and then do nothing in return! It's not right, and—"

This was going a bit far, even for her sister. Dana set her teeth. "Do not preach morals to me, Roxy. When it comes to taking money you have no right to, you have already won first prize, remember? That's why we're in this mess right now."

"Sorry!" Roxy said mulishly.

"I was willing to try, Roxy, but you have to see that this changes everything. Every journalist in the world will be trying to get an interview with him. Not to speak of all the expat Bagestanis desperate for a look at the man who may be their new sultan."

She suddenly remembered the way he had kissed her in London, and what he had said then. *You know who I am. I am going to do what you want me to do. The hungry, desperate people of Bagestan...* No wonder all the expats had been foaming at the mouth that night.

Half of them must have got it then. She couldn't believe she had been so slow herself.

"But you're so smart. You'll find a way."

"Roxy, has it occurred to you that I might get shot by his security guards?"

"That's ridiculous!"

"Is it? There are Ghasib's assassins to think of, and I am sure Sheikh Durran is thinking of them. They killed his father and two of his uncles, don't forget. He must be very twitchy right now. Come on! Even those madmen at the casino can't expect me to carry on after this."

But Roxy just didn't hear information that interfered with her wishes.

"But they *do*! They called me to ask how you were doing right after it was all on the news. They say they're going to tell Daddy the day after tomorrow. We've only got forty-eight hours, Dana. You've got to think of something!"

"Things are hotting up," Gazi said casually, flinging himself down onto his chair again. "That was Lana on the phone."

Ash, Harry and Najib looked at him. They were on board *Dhikra,* sitting on an aft deck in the bright Mediterranean sunshine. All around them was blue sea. No one had so far discovered that *Dhikra* belonged to him, though no doubt some enterprising journalist would find out soon enough.

"Apparently she's had a visit from a concerned Dana Morningstar. She has a message for you and has to deliver it to you personally."

Harry looked from Gazi to Ash and laughed. "I'll just bet she does! And the message is, *Here's some strychnine, love Ghasib.* Tell her no thanks."

But Ash shook his head. "No," he said. "I should have spoken to her before. We need to know what she wants. If she is from Ghasib and I send her away he may put in someone less obvious. If she's not from Ghasib, we need to know that, too."

Najib pulled his ear. "Could be risky, Ash. We don't know how he might be planning to use her."

"Warn her she'll be searched. Unless she swallows a bomb we'll be safe enough. But to be on the safe side, Naj and Harry better not be aboard. Nor you either, Gazi. I'll see her alone."

The helicopter touched down expertly on the yacht's upper deck, just behind a beautiful blue swimming pool, and waited only till Dana had clambered out and run clear before lifting off again. She stood for a moment gazing skyward at it, but when it moved into the sun she dropped her eyes and turned away.

Almost into Sheikh Ashraf Durran's arms.

"Good afternoon."

Dana's breath caught on a gasp of surprise and she put a hand to her chest in an unconscious bid to quiet her heart.

She was wearing white again—loose tie-waist cotton trousers and a man's shirt open over a tank top. Her slip-on espadrilles were white canvas. She had a drawstring bag slung over one shoulder, and white sunglasses held back her hair. The only colour in her outfit was a necklace of flat square wooden beads painted in bright colours against the warm skin of her throat, and matching square red earrings. Her lips were the same rich red.

She looked rich, expensive and successful, he thought. And very, very sexy.

"Good afternoon," she replied, a beat behind time as

she returned his gaze. He was looking very cool and masculine in a white kaftan with rolled sleeves and open at the neck. Her mouth stretched into a smile, which he sombrely did not return.

"This way," said Ashraf and turned to shepherd her down to a lower deck. At his bidding, she went down the stairs, through the luxurious yacht till they came to a stretch of open deck half shaded with an awning, where a manservant was waiting. Dana chose a seat in the shade and looked out over the glittering blue Mediterranean. In the distance, closer to shore, she could see other yachts, but save for one small launch there was nothing nearer than a few miles. They were heading out to sea. Ahead of them the water was empty.

A soft breeze blew. If paradise could be partly man-made, this was paradise.

"What will you have to drink?" Sheikh Ashraf asked politely. Suddenly she remembered the humiliation of their last meeting, and her heart hardened. More to spark a reaction than because she really wanted it, she asked for white wine and sparkling mineral water. The servant bowed and withdrew.

"You carry alcohol aboard?" she couldn't resist asking the sheikh.

He raised his eyebrows at her as he took the chair at an angle to hers. The day was hot, but Dana loved the sun. The breeze coming off the water was delicious, and in the shade she was perfectly comfortable.

"Why not?" he asked.

She shrugged. "But you don't drink yourself, do you?"

"I don't. Nor do I impose my views on my guests."

The servant returned with a tray and set it down on the table beside them. Sheikh Ashraf signalled him and he bowed and disappeared again. The sheikh picked up her spritzer and handed it to Dana. She took it with a murmur of thanks.

"Why don't you drink? Is it for religious reasons?"

"Alcohol dehydrates the brain. In hot countries its effect is intensified," he said, and Dana set the wineglass down beside her and wondered if she wouldn't be smarter keeping her wits about her today. "I don't drink because I don't feel the need for alcohol."

She discovered that she was fascinated by him. She really wanted to know what made him tick.

"Did you ever drink?" she pressed.

He sighed as if he found her questions tiresome but couldn't be bothered refusing to answer. "Yes, at two periods in my life I drank. The first was in my rebellious university days when, in common with many of my contemporaries, I believed in breaking every rule. The second was during the war when intervals of oblivion were necessary to maintain sanity."

The breath hissed between her teeth. The Parvan-Kaljuk War had been notorious for the atrocities committed by the Kaljuks against Parvan women and children.

"I'm sorry," she murmured.

Sheikh Ashraf poured himself a glass of mineral water.

"Tell me why you are here, Miss Morningstar." His voice was firm; he was a man used to command. Dana heaved a breath and took a sip of her drink.

"It's complicated. I don't really know where to begin."

He drank and sat holding his glass a moment between his knees, gazing down at it. Then he set it on the table and looked at her again. He didn't offer her any advice on where to start, she noticed. Many people would have said *begin at the beginning* or something like that. He merely looked patient.

She found herself alternately excited by his presence and irritated by his attitude. Trying to quell both responses, Dana took a deep breath and sighed it out.

"My sister," she began. Then paused and licked her lips. She didn't like having to expose Roxanna like this, but where was her story without that? He had to know. She looked up to find his dark gaze on her, an expression in his eyes she couldn't read. Her heart thumped.

How she wished she could have met him under better circumstances. She cursed herself for that stupid explosion at the charity ball in London—no wonder he didn't like her! All she had said about what fools people were to believe the al Jawadi would restore their throne, about how they were being taken in…! Bad enough in any case, but said to a man who was almost certainly one of the al Jawadi heirs… She wondered if he had thought she knew who he was when she spoke.

What a fool she was. What a man he was, but she would never get any closer to him than she was right now.

"My sister gambled away a fortune she didn't have at a London casino," she blurted out all at once. "The owner is now threatening to go to—to my father, and demand the money. It's so much money! My father could maybe pay it if—" she heaved a breath and gazed down into her drink "—if he sold absolutely everything he's got. But it's worse than that. Roxy—Roxanna had promised him she wouldn't do it again. He bailed her out last time, and he absolutely hated knowing that she had gambled. It's unIslamic and all that."

"How much is her debt?"

She told him, and he nodded, accepting it without a blink. "Fine," he said. His hand went out to an intercom beside his chair. He spoke into it in rapid Arabic that she didn't catch. It was a long time since she had spoken her father's language, and she suddenly regretted letting it get rusty.

"They called her in to talk to them—" Dana returned to her recital "—and my sister—"

She broke off as the manservant appeared with a small tray and set it down on the table in front of Sheikh Ashraf. On the tray were a pen and what looked like a chequebook. He picked up the fountain pen and unscrewed the lid.

"You need explain no further, Miss Morningstar," he said. "I will take care of it."

And under her astonished gaze, he filled out the cheque for the amount she had named. Dana stared at him in astonishment.

"What are you doing?" she choked.

"Shall I make it out to you, so that you can supervise your sister's repayment?"

She felt as though she had stepped into another dimension.

"What—what do you mean? Why are you...why should you pay for...?"

She ran out of steam and sat staring at him openmouthed.

Sheikh Ashraf looked at her. He ripped out the cheque and offered it to her. "Is not this why you came to me?"

"No! Why would I? Why would I even dream that you would pay—what do you...do you think I have some hold over you or something?" she babbled, horrified. "This isn't blackmail! I don't know anything about you!"

At this he tucked the cheque under the chequebook, screwed the cap back on his pen, and leaned back in his chair, watching her. "You can think of no reason why I would be willing to pay your sister's debt and relieve your father of such grief?"

Dana was quite certain that he thought the debt was her own. But that was beside the point. "None whatsoever," she said.

He took that with a thoughtful nod. "Then why have you come to me?"

"I was blackmailed into it," she said baldly.

Sheikh Ashraf didn't move, but she felt that his whole being was electrified by her words. "You were blackmailed," he repeated softly.

"The casino owner called my sister in to talk. He showed her a—" Dana dropped her head and spoke to her drink "—a newspaper with a photo of you and me at that charity thing. He...had jumped to conclusions, and he told Roxy to bring me to see him. I had no choice, I had to go."

"Yes, I see." His voice was so quiet and calm, and she realized suddenly that he would be the one you ran to in a crisis. Every time.

"They wouldn't believe there was nothing between us. They said, even if that was true, that I could—could start something if I wanted. They told me that you..."

"That I—?" he prompted, when she faded out.

"That you owe them a huge amount of money, ten times more than Roxy lost, and that you keep dodging when they try to serve you with a subpoena. They wanted me to come down here and get to know you, and then trick you into being someplace where they could come and serve you with whatever paper it is."

He laughed briefly. "Where were you to take me to receive these papers?"

"They didn't say anything about that. I got the idea that once I'd—established contact with you, they would let me know."

"What is the name of the casino?"

"Park Place," Dana told him, wondering how many casinos he owed money to.

"And what was in your mind when you did their bidding?"

"I had to pretend to agree. They threatened to go to my father and insist on being paid and...but I thought, if I could just tell you about it, maybe you could pay them what you owe them, or...or at least accept the subpoena...."

He was shaking his head long before she finished, and her heart sank.

"Miss Morningstar—Dana. I do not owe these men money. I do not gamble, at the Park Place casino or at any other. This was a story told you by men who have very different motives than the ones they pretended to reveal to you."

He spoke with complete conviction, and she believed him. She stared at him, licking dry lips. A whisper of danger seemed to hover in the air. "What motives?"

"Tell me the names of the men who spoke to you."

"Khalid Abd al Darogh and Fuad al Kadthib."

A shadow crossed his face, but he only nodded.

"What do they want?" she repeated, her voice croaking with dread.

He hesitated, then shook his head slightly, and she knew by the look on his face that he would not tell her anything more.

"The question is, what is now to be done?"

He reached for the mobile phone lying beside the intercom, picked it up and punched a couple of buttons. Then he stood up and moved out into the sun towards the stern. He lifted a hand as if in greeting.

"Harry," she heard him say, but then he bent his head and she could make out nothing more. As she watched him, she became aware that the yacht's engines had died, and the launch that had been trailing at a distance was now approaching them at speed. So they had been under surveillance all the time.

When Sheikh Ashraf closed the phone Dana got up to stand at the railing and watch two crew members drop the landing ladder. The other boat pulled alongside below and two men got out, moved quickly up the ladder and came aboard. They ran lightly to the aft deck.

"Ash!" one of them cried, with a certain degree of relief, giving his back a thump. He was as handsome as it got, and Dana smiled involuntarily. But she knew which face she preferred.

"This is Dana Morningstar," Sheikh Ashraf said. "Harry and Naj, Dana."

She had the funny feeling that she had met Naj before, but he didn't make any comment, and so she didn't mention it. But his face certainly looked familiar.

So did hers, apparently. "Hey, I've seen you on *Brick Lane!*" Harry told her with a grin. "It's a great show. That Reena, she's one *mean* woman!"

Dana smiled. "Well, she gets her comeuppance in a month or so, so stay tuned."

"She does? What happens?"

"I'm contractually bound not to tell you."

He lifted his hands to the bounding main. "Hey, we're in the middle of nowhere!"

She laughed and shook her head. "Sorry. We were

particularly warned about directional mikes being aimed at yachts in the middle of nowhere.''

''Dana has other interesting things to tell you about, however,'' Ashraf said, and they all sat down. Dana repeated her story for Harry and Naj.

The yacht rode gently on the swell as she spoke, the sun sparked from the creamy paint and the blue water, and the cooling breeze stirred her hair. The three men sat listening intently, and Dana had the sudden feeling of being in a dream. She couldn't quite understand how she had got here.

When she had finished her recital of the facts and answered a few questions, they all sat in silence, considering.

It was Harry who spoke first. ''Well, it would be easy enough to pay the debt and let Dana go back home.''

Dana longed to ask why that solution had occurred to him, but it didn't seem the moment. Ash merely gestured to the tray that was still resting on the table, with the cheque tucked under one corner.

''Yes.''

''But there's a more serious problem here. They probably won't stop trying to, ah...serve a subpoena on you just because they've lost Dana.''

The tone of his voice put the phrase ''serve a subpoena'' in quotes, and Dana mulled that over. The three men seemed to know something about Abd al Darogh and al Kadthib that she didn't, something so obvious it didn't have to be mentioned.

''Might be a good idea,'' Harry went on, ''to let them think this plan is working. They may not bother trying to come up with another.''

Naj nodded. ''It's the obvious solution.''

Then they all three turned and looked at her.

"Dana's exactly where she would be if she had done exactly what she was told, and been successful," Harry mused, and she could see that he was only voicing the thought that was in all their heads.

A nervous chill ran over her skin, ridiculous on so hot a day.

"What does that mean?" she asked.

"If the men who are blackmailing you believe that you've successfully seduced Ash, there are—" Naj began.

Dana jumped. "And how would I convince them of that?" she demanded nervously.

Naj lifted a hand. "There's no problem there, but let's leave that for a moment. There are two possible benefits," he continued, turning to the others. "First, we draw their fire. We discover what it is they're really after. Second, they won't be looking for another way of doing what Dana's already doing, so we'll have one less thing to worry about."

Harry and Ashraf agreed. She looked back and forth between them. "I thought you knew what they were really after."

"We have some informed guesses," Ashraf said. "The guesses boil down to variations on a couple of possibilities. One is—"

"Yes?" she prompted. She was feeling increasingly uncomfortable, without knowing why.

"That they are hoping to create some sort of scandal. If you establish a connection with me, it could be exploited in a dozen different ways. I am sure you can see that."

"Through my confessions in the tabloid press, I suppose," Dana offered dryly.

"Possibly. There are also the law courts. You might

accuse me of assault or rape, for example. That would certainly engage our energies at what is a critical time.''

"You're assuming they have reason to believe I'd go along with something like that.''

"They may consider that they have enough leverage on you to force your cooperation,'' he pointed out gently.

Dana had to accept the truth of this. She was sure in her own heart that she would never have agreed to take part in blackening anyone's character with a false accusation or exposé, but the men she had dealt with couldn't be expected to know that she would balk at such a thing. They had forced her to do their bidding once, why not twice?

"What's the other possibility?'' she asked.

The three men shifted and exchanged glances, and again she felt that whisper of dread touch her.

It was Ash who spoke. "They may want to kill me. Your role may have been—to set me up for assassination.''

Nine

"**N**o!" she cried, as the whisper of dread became a dank, heavy cloud and settled over her, reaching sickening, cold tendrils into the marrow of her bones. She had never felt such horror. It wasn't like the movies at all. It was dreadful. She had sat with those men, talked to them…and they had been forcing her to unknowingly conspire in—

"No! Assass—*murder?*"

"It is one very strong possibility."

She saw it all, as if it were playing out before her eyes. She would have told them that the sheikh was going to be at a certain place, at a certain time…it was not a subpoena, but death that they would have delivered.

"Oh, God!" Dana cried, her hands at her mouth, her eyes black and staring at Sheikh Ashraf. Chills were coursing up and down her back, her arms, from her toes to her scalp. "What if I hadn't told you? What if I'd just...done what they said?"

"*Alhamdolillah,* you did not choose that path."

"Who are those men?" she demanded, half seeing the answer as she spoke. "Who are they?"

Again, that exchange of glances among the three. It was Naj who spoke. "They are men who have a very good reason to want to keep Ghasib in power in Bagestan."

Dana shuddered. She felt dirty, covered in filth. "Do you mean I've been working for agents of Ghasib? For—for Ghasib himself?"

"Khalid Abd al Darogh and Fuad al Kadthib own sixty-five percent of all the casinos in Bagestan," Harry said. "They naturally want to keep him in power, but whether they are actively conspiring with him or not—" He shrugged. "We don't know."

"But I don't understand," Dana said, turning to Sheikh Ashraf. "My sister went to that casino before I ever met you at the charity thing. Why would they—"

"Some of it was probably a lucky chance for them," Ash said. "The Park Place casino is known for trapping young women of good family into heavy gambling losses. Then they offer to let them pay the debt through high-class prostitution. They fly them to wealthy clients in Bagestan and elsewhere. Either your sister fell by chance into that trap, or one of the women already trapped was instructed to entice her into it."

She stared at him. "Instructed to entice Roxy in particular? Why?"

"They might have felt that to have Colonel Golbahn's daughter in such a position would be useful to them."

Dana didn't see that. She shook her head uncomprehendingly. "And then I met you by chance and they changed tactics to suit?"

He lifted his well-shaped hands as if it were self-evident.

She had the feeling that the pieces didn't quite fit. But there was too much to take in for her to assess it all. She suddenly realized that she had been sitting forward in her seat, tense and anxious, for a long time. She leaned back in her chair, letting herself feel the heat and the breeze, her fabulous surroundings. The sun was low in the western sky, and it would be setting soon.

It was so beautiful. After a moment she took a deep, relaxed breath and picked up her drink, which the servant had refreshed without her noticing. She looked from one to the other of the men as they spoke. In the strong, slanting light of the sun now coming in under the awning, a subtle physical resemblance between them became visible.

Harry looked at his watch. "I've got to get back to *Ma Fouze* before dark."

"Right," Naj said, getting to his feet. He lifted a hand. "Nice meeting you, Dana."

Dana set her drink down and stood up to say goodbye. As the two men left she moved over to the railing and watched them go down. Sheikh Ashraf went with them to the main deck, then watched as they moved down to the landing platform.

When the launch had left, cutting a wide arc away from the yacht, and the deckhand was drawing the ladder up against the side of the yacht, Sheikh Ashraf started back up the stairs to where she was waiting at the top. He looked up as he came, and their eyes met, and Dana's heart contracted with sudden feeling. *I want to be the one who waits for you,* she thought.

As he stepped up the last step and came towards her his presence was overpowering. There was a kind of electricity surrounding him; she could feel it envelop her.

She tried to smile it away, but couldn't. "I suppose you'd better call the helicopter now."

Sheikh Ashraf frowned in surprise, putting a hand out to her elbow, then withdrawing it. "Helicopter?"

Her pulse kicked. "I should get back to the Eden Roc. Unless there's something else to discuss?"

His face was suddenly without expression. "There is nothing to discuss if you have already made your decision."

"What decision?" she said stupidly.

"Have you decided not to stay?" the sheikh pressed, with some impatience.

Her heart seemed to leap into her mouth. She had never felt so stupid. "Stay where?"

"But what is solved if you leave now?" he demanded impatiently, as if he had expected her to understand something. "Where will you go? Back to London? What will you tell the men who sent you?"

He was right. She had been so geared up to the task of meeting him and telling him her story that she hadn't thought beyond it. She had hoped that talking to him would solve Roxy's problems. But nothing was solved—unless she took that cheque he had offered her. And she couldn't do that. She was back at square one.

"I don't know." She licked her lips. "Uh—I'll have to think. I didn't actually think about it—I couldn't plan when I had no idea what you would say."

She felt at a huge disadvantage with him. He was powerfully masculine and attractive, and being near him didn't do her reasoning brain any favours. He was looking at her with a dark look that she found deeply sexy, though she was certain he didn't mean it that way.

"You still haven't heard what I am going to say."

"Haven't I?" She blinked. She turned her head in confusion and her eyes happened to fall on the cheque he had written, still lying tucked under his chequebook on the tray.

"I see," the sheikh said in a changed voice. "Yes, of course. In that case, there is nothing more to say."

He bent down, picked up the cheque, and straightened to hand it to her. "Thank you for coming to warn me. I will call for the helicopter. Can I offer you another drink while you are waiting?"

Fury overcame her. How dare he make such an assumption about her? She snatched the cheque from him and tore it three times in quick succession and, staring into his face, tossed the eight little ragged bits of paper down. They were instantly snatched by the breeze and scattered across the pristine teak deck.

"There is no need to speak to me in that tone of voice," she snapped furiously. "I have no intention of taking money from you, Sheikh Ashraf, now or ever! But I really don't see what else there is to talk about! What do you want from me?"

He laughed, and again she was struck by how laughter changed him. A treacherous little thought flickered across her mind—*you have too many cares. If I were your lover you would laugh more.* She shook her head impatiently.

"Of course there is something to talk about," he told her, his white teeth flashing against his warm skin. "Did you not understand the point Harry was making when he said you were in the very position you would have been in had you obeyed al Kadthib?"

"No." She had been too busy looking at them, perhaps, and hadn't concentrated on what they were saying.

"I have ordered dinner. Will you stay to dinner with me, Dana, and hear what I ask of you?"

Her heart pounding with a mixture of fear and anticipation, she agreed.

She was shown into a stateroom by Sheikh Ashraf, who opened the door on a closet that was hung with women's clothes.

"These belong to my brother's fiancée," he said. "She is much shorter than you, but she would be happy for you to make use of whatever you can. Most of these things are new."

"Where is she now?" Dana asked.

"On board the *Ma Fouze* with Harry. It is a sailing yacht, so doesn't have much closet space. In any case, Mariel says she doesn't need such clothes when they are sailing."

She was too aware of his presence in the bedroom, too conscious of the large bed. She was glad when he showed her quickly around and left.

In the bath the taps and fittings were gold, and Dana couldn't help laughing. She took a cooling shower, but ignored the closetful of clothes to dress again in her own. She wasn't sure what was going to be suggested tonight, but she didn't want to look as though she thought she was moving in.

When she emerged, night had fallen. Music was playing softly, a Middle Eastern instrumental number. A servant led her to the deck where dinner would be served, at a small, square table laid with candles underneath the stars. It was a heavenly night, and they were far enough away from the shore now for the stars to play in all their glory. There wasn't another boat in sight.

Sheikh Ashraf stood looking out over the black, moon-spangled water. He turned as she stepped out into the semi-darkness. He had changed into a short-sleeved shirt and cotton pants. He could wear both Western and Eastern clothes with equal ease, she saw, and thought that he would make an excellent sultan. Fully at home in both East and West. He would understand where both sides were coming from.

"Wine?" Ashraf asked her. "Or a cocktail?"

"Wine," she agreed. "And some ice in it, please."

The manservant handed her the glass and then slipped away, leaving them alone together with the night and the stars. There was silence and then another track of music started, a wailing, haunting woman's voice.

Dana sipped her wine and realized that it was a very expensive one, and that watering it down with ice was probably a terrible insult to it. But she wanted a clear head tonight. The air was heavy with unspoken meaning.

"Was Prince Wafiq your father?" she asked, when they had stood in silence for a few minutes gazing into the darkness. She turned and leaned back against the railing, her glass resting on it at her side, her elbows back.

"He was."

"Yours and Harry's."

He inclined his head.

"Does Ghasib know that you were the one named as your grandfather's heir?"

It was obvious to her now that Sheikh Ashraf was the one named by his grandfather as Crown Prince-designate of Bagestan. She should have realized it the moment she noticed the family resemblance between the three men this afternoon, but it was only later, when Ashraf said Harry was his brother, that the penny had finally dropped. Amongst the Bagestani expat community, Prince Wafiq was widely rumoured to have had two sons. And Dana had finally clicked on why Naj looked familiar—his recent romantic reunion with his wife and son had been all over television and the papers. He had been revealed as Najib al Makhtoum, Hafzuddin al Jawadi's grandson.

So she had been talking to the three grandsons. There could be no doubt that Ashraf was the leader among them. His authority, both in himself and with the other two, was unmistakable. They had consistently deferred to him.

"We don't know for a certainty what Ghasib knows, or guesses, about us. But since the storytelling, we have to assume that he has come to the correct conclusion."

"That would be why they put the screws on Roxy the next morning," Dana guessed, and he nodded.

A servant arrived with a tray, and they sat down at the table. They were served with a beautifully presented starter of roasted vegetables, and at a sign from the sheikh were left alone to enjoy it.

"This is delicious!" Dana said, for once in her life finding silence unnerving. "Is your chef Bagestani?"

"By birth, but he was raised in Paris and trained there," Sheikh Ashraf said. They talked about food, and then about Bagestani culture and what had happened to it over the past three decades. The meal progressed, and each course seemed more spectacular than the last.

But Dana couldn't quite relax. The subject they did not speak of hovered over the conversation. What did he want of her, and what would it entail?

"Do you like the sea? Are you a good sailor?" he

asked her at last, when little cups of Turkish coffee had been served, and a plate of bite-sized morsels of fresh fruit in the centre of the table was all that remained of the meal.

"I haven't done all that much sailing. I like boats, yes. Why?"

"I wondered if you would enjoy a holiday at sea."

"Is that what you want me to do? Stay aboard?"

The breeze was warm but gusting strongly now, and the candle flames were caught by it, even inside the protective globes. Ash looked at her in the flickering darkness and wished she were less beautiful. Or that he could send her away till it was over rather than do what he had to—ask her to stay in close proximity.

"We may gain something, as Harry said, if Fuad al Kadthib and his partner believe you to be successfully obeying orders," he told her. "If they have assassination in mind, they may see you as a possible means. If it is disgrace that they plan, again, they can't hope to send in another woman when you are with me."

"Starting when?"

"Effectively, now. Tonight it will be best, I think, if you return to the Eden Roc. In the morning you can check out. For you to simply disappear and have strangers collect your luggage will attract too much attention."

"And then what?"

"We do not know where Ghasib's spies are, or how much he knows. It would not be good enough for you merely to say you are with me. You would have to be actually with me here."

"You mean, to convince them that I'm in position and can be activated whenever they choose," Dana said flatly.

He bent his head.

Dana was furious suddenly. "And what do I say when they give me a vial of poison to feed you, or ask me to take you to such and such a place so they can use you for target practice? What if they trick me? What if they've already tricked me? What if there's a bomb in my suitcase or a...an inhalant poison in my perfume or something?"

He looked at her. *Not poison, but intoxication,* he thought. *And just as dangerous to my concentration.*

"These are mostly unfounded fears," he told her gently.

"I—"

"And they can be counteracted by a thorough examination of your luggage before you bring it aboard. What arrangement did you make with these men for contacting them?"

"None. I'm supposed to keep in touch with Roxy. I have no idea how often she talks to them. Too often, probably."

"Suppose you phone your sister tonight and tell her that I have invited you to stay with me at a secret location. Do not mention the *Dhikra,* or let her know that you are at sea at all. Say that the phone will be monitored where you are going and you will not call her again for a week or more, but that after that time I have promised to take you to Paris and London."

"On a shopping trip," she suggested, one corner of her mouth tilting.

Ashraf laughed, getting the joke at once. "On a shopping trip," he agreed. "Tell her that your rich Arab lover has promised to deck your beauty in the precious jewels it deserves."

His voice roughened at the end, as if he had started out joking and then lost his grip. Their eyes met for a moment over the candle flames, and her pulse raced as if his gaze were a physical touch.

"Roxy will love that," she said, for something to say.

"And you, Dana—what do you love?" he asked. The words seemed to come from him unwillingly, and her heart responded with even more wild thudding. Before she could answer, his lips tightened and he dragged his eyes away from her. "I apologize," he said.

"What?"

"I want you to feel secure with me, Dana. If you agree to these plans, do not be afraid that I will be unable to keep to my part of the bargain."

"Which is—what?" Dana said, her heart choking her.

"You are a beautiful, deeply attractive woman. In the nature of things we must be often alone together while you are here. But I will not take advantage of this situation, or your cooperation."

Dana pressed her lips together, wondering how to answer this. At last she asked, "Are you married?"

His eyes narrowed at her. After a moment he said slowly, "I am not married. No."

"Engaged? Involved?"

Ash saw the direction of her thoughts. He shook his head protestingly, closing his eyes. Took a deep breath.

"Dana…" he began.

"Who told you that I wanted to be protected from you?" she asked softly. "Or haven't you noticed that you are also handsome and deeply attractive?"

"Dana," he said, in a different voice, shoved his chair back and stood. He looked at her with eyes that were as black and as deep as the sky behind his head.

Ten

He drew her to her feet and wrapped his arms securely around her back. She lifted her own arms around his neck, and they stood there for a moment, with the music playing softly around them, gazing into each other's face. A thousand wordless messages seemed to pass between them.

Her blood took heat from his body, so that she was burning up from the inside. The touch of his mouth was electric on her lips, brushing softly, softly over the fullness till she was crazy for the firm pressure of hunger. She understood that she had been waiting for this every moment since that first kiss.

His hunger at last grew too much for him, and he pressed one hand into her hair, cupping her head and turning her chin helplessly up before his mouth came down with a loss of control that thrilled her to her bones.

His arms tightened almost painfully, drawing her

against his body. Blood thundered in her ears and brain, drowning out the soft music, making her dizzy. She opened her mouth to his, hungrier than she had ever been for a man, and her hands pressed his neck and tangled in his hair. Of its own volition her body arched into his, responsive to the pressure of his demanding hands, making demands of its own.

His hands were inside her shirt, slipping underneath her tank top, his skin rough and warm against her bare skin. She trembled and melted at the incredible intimacy of the touch.

He drew his mouth away and they gazed into the magical night in each other's dark eyes. She was meltingly, wildly hungry for him. He bent to press his lips against her throat and she closed her eyes and felt herself half-fainting. Her blood thundered in her ears, and she saw light behind her eyelids, and suddenly Ashraf's hands gripped her upper arms and she was being held away from his warmth.

"You drive me to the edge," he muttered.

The clamour in her blood abated, but the swooping thunder was still in her ears. Dana understood suddenly, and with a little gasp looked up.

The helicopter, its bright searchlight beaming down, was slowly lowering onto the deck above their heads. She stared at it uncomprehendingly for a moment, and then said huskily, "Is that for me?"

Ashraf drew back out of her arms, set her away from him. "To take you back to the hotel," he said. "There is someone to accompany you. Sharif Azad al Dauleh. He will examine your luggage, and assist you wherever necessary. Tomorrow he will bring you back again."

She brushed the back of one hand over her kiss-swollen lips. "All right," she said. He had better control than she did—she didn't think she would have been able to pull back from the brink like that for any money.

"I guess you don't get to be considered sultan material without a larger than usual dose of self-discipline," she muttered.

"Not as much as I need," he said roughly.

She supposed he had chewed her lipstick all over her face. She turned to reach for her handbag, on a lounge chair. The helicopter was just touching down on the upper deck, and she knew she should be up there already. The pilot had explained to her on the way in how tricky such a landing was.

"Good night," she said tonelessly, tossing the bag over her shoulder as she crossed to the stairs.

He said nothing as he followed her up to the top deck. He bent double and ran towards the chopper, and she followed suit.

"Till tomorrow," he said, when she had clambered into the empty seat and strapped herself in, and that was all they had time for. He bent and ran back the way he had come, and the helicopter lifted off. A moment later the brightly lighted yacht was only a shape in the surrounding sea of blackness.

"Oh, you are so lucky!" Roxy's voice came enviously down the wire.

"I've got a sister with a very short memory, if you call that luck," Dana responded. Roxy seemed to have wiped recent events from her mind. She was reacting a little as though Dana had stolen some excitement that was rightfully hers.

"Don't tell me you're not enjoying yourself. I wouldn't believe you!" she accused.

"Snap!"

"What does that mean?" Roxy demanded petulantly.

"You enjoy pulling strings and manipulating people," Dana told her, suddenly seeing the truth of this herself clearly for the first time. "You especially have always enjoyed watching me bust my ass to pull things out of the fire that you have deliberately tossed in. And you're enjoying it now."

"I am *not*. I don't know how you can say that, Dana!"

"I can say it because it's true."

"It is not!"

"Then listen up, and stop oohing and aahing as if you think that if it weren't for me you'd be here playing footsie with a sheikh yourself. If it weren't for me, you'd be explaining to Dad why you felt the thrill of a few hours' gambling was worth everything he's worked for in life and then some."

Roxy subsided into sullen silence. But for once, she wasn't sure why, Dana wasn't impressed. Maybe it was the contrast: she had sensed a ruthless self-honesty in Ashraf Durran, and it was a deeply attractive trait. She was sure he was a man who never tried to blind himself as to his own motives.

The problem with people who played games with themselves was that, if you loved them, you ended up playing the games too. You sold out the truth to soothe them.

And maybe that was what had enabled Roxy to go on in the irresponsible path she had apparently chosen in life. Dana had not only fixed things for her, but had always reassured her that what she had done wasn't very important in the scheme of things.

Who did she have to blame if it had now come to

this—Roxy, believing she had forced her sister into prostitution, was now pretending to envy her.

"Tell them I am going away with Sheikh Durran," Dana said concisely. "He hasn't said where, only that we'll be there a week or so. And then he'll bring me back to London and Paris. I won't call you again till we arrive in London, because we'll be somewhere I can't use the phone."

She didn't say anything about having told the sheikh the truth. Roxy just couldn't be trusted to carry it off if she knew. But Dana would have loved to be able to ask her sister if she knew of any reason why Sheikh Durran should have offered to pay off the full amount Roxy owed, no questions asked.

Sharif Azad al Dauleh checked every inch of her luggage and pronounced it clean, and by eleven the next morning was escorting her back to the *Dhikra* by helicopter. It was a longer ride than last night's, so the yacht must have been sailing through the night.

Dana had phoned no one except Roxy. Mostly she was comfortable with this, but from time to time she was struck by doubt. Gut instinct told her Sheikh Ashraf Durran was a man to be trusted. Logic warned her that she might be mistaken. What if she sailed off with him and never returned? Would Roxy be believed if she told her story?

In the end she had gone to the hotel's cyber café, briefly noted the facts and sent the document to her own e-mail address. No one else had her password, but she supposed that if she went missing the police would get it soon enough. And that would have to do.

The sheikh was not there to meet her when she arrived on board. A stewardess showed Dana to a different stateroom than the one she had borrowed last night. It was a suite consisting of sitting room, bath and bedroom with two huge empty closets, and a small study with a computer and several shelves of books.

Most of the books were worn with use, but one shelf was filled with what looked like new purchases. Dana scanned the titles and saw that they were a mix of recently published literary and popular books, and some classics. A biography of Byron sat side by side with half a dozen paperback romances and the latest John Grisham. There was a history of Bagestan.

A smile pulled the corners of her mouth as she noticed a beautiful Moroccan leather-bound four-volume set. *The Complete Works of William Shakespeare. Comedies. Histories. Tragedies. Poems and Sonnets.*

So he had not just said, *Get her a few books to keep her from boredom.* He had thought about one, at least.

"Where is Sheikh Ashraf?" she asked the stewardess, a Frenchwoman named Adile who told Dana that she had come aboard early this morning.

"He is in a meeting in the boardroom, madame," she replied.

"A meeting?"

"With some men who flew in an hour ago," Adile explained. "His Excellency asks that you excuse him. They will take lunch together in the large dining room. And when would you like your own lunch to be served, madame?"

So she wasn't going to be asked to act as his hostess, Dana understood with a little pang of disappointment. Then she told herself she was being a fool. Why should she be?

A few minutes later, wearing a tankini swimsuit under a matching knee-length green shirt, her hair tied back with its own knot, Dana went out to the aft deck for a bottle of water. She found one of the deckhands there, snipping the wires off the thick stack of newspapers that had been dropped off by the helicopter pilot. There were two copies of everything, and the deckhand was dividing them into two piles. When he had finished, he pulled the old papers out of the newspaper rack and slipped one new stack in. He tossed the old papers down behind the serving bar before disappearing inside with the second stack of new ones.

Dana paused to glance through the headlines. There were several of today's English broadsheets, as well as yesterday afternoon's tabloids, papers from France, Germany, Italy and elsewhere in Europe, and one or two of yesterday's papers from North America.

Al Jawadi Flings Down The Gauntlet, cried one splash headline on a Canadian paper. Dana suddenly realized that she had missed yesterday's reporting of the Night of the Thousand and One Books and went and retrieved the papers from behind the bar.

"Madame?"

It was the drinks waiter, who appeared a little ruffled, not having realized she was out here.

Message To Ghasib—Get Out! one of the tabloids screamed. Dana glanced up at the waiter with a preoccupied smile. "May I have a bottle of mineral water to take up to the pool with me?" she asked.

He frowned at her. "You go to pool? Swimmink?" He made motions for the sake of clarity.

"Yeah," Dana said lightly. She had picked up an olive from a bowl behind the bar and was absently munching it.

Are You Our Sultan?

"You go up, we brink," the man told her sternly. He pointed to the intercom on the bar. "You say what."

"Well, I'm here now," Dana began, then gave up. His English wasn't good enough for an explanation—she would just confuse him. "All right, mineral water and lime, then, please."

She had to wait while he laboriously showed her two bottles, and she pointed to the sparkling variety. Then, tucking several papers, new and old, under her arm, Dana made her way up to the swimming pool and sank into a comfortable lounger under a striped umbrella.

It was heaven. The sea stretched for miles around, a beautiful, empty blue.

She was followed a few minutes later by Adile, bearing a tray with a bottle of water in an ice bucket, a tub of ice, a glass, a plate of sliced lime, and several bowls of tidbits. She arranged everything neatly on the little table beside Dana's lounger.

"Anything else, madame?" she asked, straightening.

Dana smiled at her. "Thanks, that's fine. Adile, why did you bring this up, instead of Abdulahad?"

"Because I am your personal maid, madame. I have been instructed by His Excellency to look after you personally in everything, as far as possible."

She sounded as though death would have to intervene before she defaulted on her sworn duty, and Dana, hearing the hero worship behind the tone, thought that with charisma like this Ashraf couldn't possibly fail.

"I see. Well, thank you," she said, a bit helplessly.

Adile nodded and left her to the perusal of the papers.

Where Is Our Sultan?

Several papers had photographs of the demonstrations taking place in Medinat al Bostan, the capital of Bagestan. According to the story, it was illegal in Bagestan to

congregate for the purposes of political discussion, and
Ghasib routinely punished any infraction with extreme
measures. It was also illegal for crowds to gather in front
of Ghasib's grotesque New Palace.

So the demonstrations were taking place in the city's
central square in front of the elegant Old Palace—which
had once been the home of the al Jawadis—and they had
been completely silent.

Dana gasped when she read that. Thousands of people
standing silently together for hours—what a will they
must have! They deserved Ashraf as a sultan. No lesser
man would do.

She swam and read, and ate a late lunch where she
was, and wondered how long he would be stuck in his
meeting, and when he would be free to come to her. She
dozed and dreamed of him, and awoke and read more
journalists' informed guesses as to whether Sheikh Ashraf Durran was himself the sultan-in-waiting, or merely
his messenger.

It is widely believed that, when the sultan-
designate announces himself publicly, he will produce the al Jawadi Rose—the fabulous sixty-three-
carat pink diamond ring that has been passed from
the reigning sultan to his designated successor for
generations.

The jewel is a potent symbol for most Bagestanis, even though it has not been seen by anyone
outside the family since Prince Nazim was named
Crown Prince thirty-three years ago. The belief has
been given great impetus by Sheikh Ashraf Durran's clear mention of the Rose during his remarkable performance at the Cannes charity function.

She dozed again and woke to the noise of the helicopter's landing. She watched as several men in crumpled summer suits clambered aboard and it took off again, leaving the sheikh standing on the landing pad. The chopper dropped quickly astern as it climbed. Ashraf turned, saw her on the lounger and came towards her.

Her thighs melted with anticipation, and her blood came suddenly alive. She felt both electrically alive and lazily sensuous at the same time.

"Good afternoon," he said, as Dana swung her long legs off the lounger and sat up, pulling on her shirt.

"Isn't it, though?" she agreed with a smile. "Can I pour you something to drink?" She had long ago asked Adile to bring a second glass up. She scooped some half-melted ice cubes into it and drew the dripping bottle of water out of the ice bucket.

"Thank you," he said after a beat, and sank down into a chair opposite her. He was wearing Western clothes today—casual, loose-fitting trousers in navy cotton with a neat braided belt, a white polo-neck shirt, and bare feet in deck shoes. His skin looked clean and healthy, his hair glowed. His chin was dark with beard shadow, which only made him sexier.

She passed him the glass, offered him the bowl of olives, watched in satisfaction as he took a long drink and popped a couple of the green globes into his mouth.

"How did your meeting go?"

He lifted his shoulders, getting the kinks out. "Long-winded, but about as productive as could be expected."

"Who were they?"

"Representatives of a multinational which has an established presence in Bagestan. They naturally want to be reassured that they are not going to be the losers if Ghasib goes.''

''What does that mean?''

''They won't want to see me on the throne if it means their profits are reduced.''

''And you have to reassure them?''

One eyebrow went up, and he drank again. ''Yes, and no. On the one hand they have a very sweet deal with Ghasib—he gives them pretty wide latitude in return for their support. On the other hand, they have lately been getting flak back home because of their collusion with his regime, and it's becoming harder and harder for them to pretend they aren't involved in the atrocities against protesters and the wanton environmental pollution.

''They can only threaten me at the moment, because they know that if it were proven that they were actively conspiring to keep Ghasib in power their share price would drop. And they can't be sure that I don't have the evidence.''

She was sickened. ''I can't believe you have to do deals with people like that!''

He gestured at a newspaper folded open on the photo of a demonstration. ''The more the people of Bagestan go out on the streets, the less I'll have to compromise— with everyone. But I have no genie in a bottle. Nothing happens in a vacuum, not even the sultan riding in on his white horse.''

She saw suddenly how tired he was, how sick of dealing with people who thought of nothing but their profits. ''Are you finished for the day?'' she asked.

He shook his head. ''I have briefing papers to read in advance of another meeting tomorrow.'' He looked at his watch. ''And the helicopter will bring back our public relations advisor.''

"Have a swim first," she urged him. "It's so hot and the pool's lovely and cool."

"I have been in an air-conditioned room," he pointed out humorously.

"Take a break," she pleaded.

And suddenly the air between them was singing with meaning. Sensation rushed over her skin, so that she shivered in the heat.

Ashraf watched her without speaking for a pregnant moment, dropped his eyes to his glass, lifted it and finished the water in it.

"Baleh," he said. He slipped out of his shoes where he sat, pulled his polo shirt out of his pants and over his head. She watched the tanned skin emerge, firm with muscle, and almost fainted with the rush of desire that assailed her. His forearms and his chest were dark with hair.

He stood up, his hands going to his belt, and for one crazy moment, thinking he was going to strip and swim naked, she felt her heart stop. But he was wearing a neat pair of swim trunks. He stepped over to the edge of the pool and dived neatly in.

Dana slipped out of her own shirt. She was wearing a dark green tankini top with a thong. The outfit suited her long, neatly muscled body, the small, firm breasts, her skin all a pale mocha shade. She kicked off green sandals and followed Ashraf into the pool.

It wasn't a large pool, ten metres long at most, not something you could get a real workout in. But it was cooling and relaxing, and best of all, filled with sea water, so she didn't have to worry about chlorine on her hair.

Dhikra's colours were dark green and navy. There were stacks of towels in these colours on a cart beside the freshwater shower at one side of the pool. When he had done a dozen quick lengths, Ashraf pulled himself out and rinsed down in the shower before grabbing a towel.

He turned to see Dana coming towards him, water beaded on her long, slender body, her breasts tight under her top, the thong clinging to her mound, outlining the thickly curling hair. She had slim, straight shoulders, smoothly curved arms, a dancer's muscled legs, a neat rump. She passed him, stroking the salt water from her eyelashes, and stepped under the shower. He felt a wave of psychic heat as she went past.

The sun was hot. The air was perfumed—either by the flowering plants on the deck below, or by her passing, he did not know which. In the shower she was turning her face up to the spray exactly as she had lifted her mouth for his kiss last night.

Ashraf turned, slung the towel around his neck, strode to the other end of the deck and went down the stairs.

Eleven

She didn't see him again until dinner, when he introduced her to Gazi al Hamzeh, his public relations advisor. They ate on deck again, under the stars. Ashraf was very silent, and Gazi did most of the talking, explaining to Dana how a public relations campaign was managed.

"So basically you're saying you could make anybody at all famous for nothing at all," she laughed.

For dinner she had dressed in a rose red raw silk dress that was slim and sleeveless, with a high Japanese collar. It fell below the knee, slit for a couple of inches on each side seam. Her hair was clipped casually up on top of her head with diamanté clips.

"Not literally anybody, but close enough," he said. "Even twenty years ago it wouldn't have been all that difficult, but today?" Gazi waved a hand.

She was interested, but her interest was given focus

by her determination to suppress her response to Ashraf's presence. And he seemed determined to all but ignore her.

"Would you like the treatment?" Gazi asked.

She grinned. "You're offering to make me a celebrity?"

"In England, of course, you already are. It would be an easy thing to spread the word and make you more of a name internationally. It could boost your career."

Still smiling, she shook her head.

"Why not? Consider it our thank-you for coming to Ashraf with the truth."

"I don't particularly like addictive substances," she said. Gazi raised his eyebrows, and she gestured at her glass of wine. "Like alcohol, a little fame goes a long way. It's one thing if it comes as a by-product of something I've achieved. It would be another thing completely if it were the result of nothing more than media manipulation."

Gazi laughed as if she had won a point. He had an attractive birthmark patch all around one eye. He looked like a pirate, and she thought that, in some ways, he was one.

"You and my wife would get along," he said. "You'd like her."

She saw Ashraf watching her with dark eyes, but the expression in them was unreadable.

The helicopter came to take Gazi away, and as usual, Ashraf went up to the landing pad to see him off. He returned to where Dana was sitting, his steps slow, and she heard reluctance in the tread. Her heart contracted with sadness, because what could it mean except that he did not, after all, find her as attractive as she found him?

Part of her cried that he did. He must. How was it she

could feel so much, so quickly, if he did not feel an answering passion? It wasn't possible!

She had moved from the dining table to a lounger, and was sitting with her feet up looking out over the stern, watching the helicopter's lights disappear, watching starlight flicker and break on *Dhikra*'s wake.

She felt him pause behind her, but did not turn her head. *Don't let him go,* she begged. *Let him stay with me.*

He moved silently past her to stand at the rail. For a moment he stood looking out over the black sea. The moon hadn't risen. There was no visible horizon line, just a depth of star-speckled darkness.

He turned, and she felt his movement brush her, though he was at a distance of five feet. "Dana," he said.

She closed her eyes, for the tone in his voice was not the one she wanted to hear. It was the voice of a man who was going to tell her why he couldn't love her.

She sighed and opened her eyes again. There was a little wine left in her glass, and she drained it and leaned over to set the empty glass on a table. Resting her elbows on the arms of the chair, she folded her hands over her abdomen.

"All right," she said.

"Dana, you know what work I have ahead of me. I don't think I have to argue with you over its importance, as we did in London, because I know now you didn't really believe what you said that night. I think you accept that what we plan is vital to the lives and happiness of many more than ourselves."

The last thing she had expected him to broach tonight was politics. A kind of disappointed fury shook her. Did he really not understand what she was feeling?

"And why is it important that I accept that?"

His eyes searched hers in the dark. "Dana, you could derail me. And if me, then the whole project."

She gasped. For a moment, neither spoke. Her surprise hung in the silence between them.

"I have never been so drawn to a woman, Dana. Never been so disturbed by a woman's presence."

Her heart protested with three heavy jolts. "Ashraf," she whispered.

"Let me finish. I know, or perhaps I desire it so much it feels like certainty, that you, too, are drawn to me. I think you believe, expect—that we should become lovers tonight."

His voice was like butterfly wings over her skin, causing shiver after shiver of sensation.

"My heart craves such a simple solution. My body begs for it."

"Then what—" she began, but broke off. Her voice was drowned in her own ears by the clamorous song of her blood.

"Dana, I can't do it. I am engaged in the most important endeavour of my life—the most important endeavour in three generations of my family's history. I have to remain focussed. I have to maintain a clear head. The smallest slip could bring disaster on us all. Do you understand?"

Since he had knocked her brain reeling with his first words, understanding wasn't exactly what she would call her state of mind at the moment. She swallowed.

"Um…" she tried. She licked her lips and tried again. "Uh—"

"I am out of my depth with you. If I allow myself to make love to you now I know that I will drown. You are not a woman whose bed a man leaves and forgets. You are—''

His throat closed and his voice grated to a halt.

''What am I?'' she whispered.

''You said half an hour ago to Gazi that fame was an addictive substance. I look at you and I know that you are that to me, Dana. You have the potential to absorb my every waking thought. If I spent the next month nowhere else but in your bed it would be only the beginning. I knew it the first moment I set eyes on you. I knew nothing about you, except that I had met my destiny. A moment too soon.''

She sobbed with reaction and relief and got to her feet. ''Oh, Ashraf!'' she whispered, reaching for him.

He could not resist her when her cheeks were wet with tears. Ashraf wrapped his arms savagely around her and took her mouth with a wildness that made them drunk. She entwined her hands in his hair and pressed him closer, as hunger for his closeness swamped her.

But when her body arched against him with deep, flooding yearning, he lifted his lips and, looking into her eyes, shook his head. Then he kissed her eyes with a gentleness that made more tears flow.

''I cannot do it without your cooperation,'' he murmured. ''If you push me, now or in the days to come, I will crack, Dana.''

''Well, then—''

''But I will regret it. Even as we make love my heart will whisper that I steal my own pleasure at the expense of the happiness of many. I do not want guilt to lie between us in the bed, Dana. I ask you to accept my decision. We will not have to wait long.''

Faced with that, what argument could she muster? She thought he was wrong, she was convinced he was only making things harder on himself. How she would love to wrap her arms around him and convince him she was right! But the choice had to be his. He was only suggesting a delay in their pleasures, after all. And she had to accept that he knew himself better than she did.

She lifted her hand to his cheek and smiled. "Delaying gratification is supposed to be a sign of maturity, and now I know why," she said ruefully.

She felt the tension go out of him, and realized that he had feared her opposition. He caught her hand in his and kissed the palm, then straightened and set her away from him.

"I will do my best to make it up to you," he said, with a lazy, promising smile that took her already over-heated blood up another couple of degrees. They walked back to the table.

"I am going to have coffee while I work," Ash said. "Will you have some with me?"

She wished she could help him. "Is there anything I can do? Who's on the agenda for tomorrow?"

"There is nothing you can do, except to sit with me while I work. Tomorrow we have a meeting with the oil company executives."

"Oh! Are they on your side?"

He looked at her. "They are on the side of their profits, in Bagestan as anywhere, Dana. What do they care about national politics? They financed Ghasib's coup against my grandfather thirty years ago because my grandfather stood up to them, refusing to let them take all the profits out of the country. They only look to me because they know that Ghasib's power base is eroding and they are more afraid of the Islamic militants than of me."

"Do you need them to succeed?"

He lifted both hands in an eloquent shrug. "Who knows what we need or don't need? We are trying to hold off from all firm commitments, especially with these villains. But I do not dare to show my hand too soon. If the oil companies actively moved against us—"

Abdulahad arrived with more Turkish coffee. Ashraf flicked on a reading light, lifted a briefcase onto a small side table, opened it, chose a thick document, and sank into one of the loungers. Dana went to her suite, collected the Bagestan history book from the shelf there, and came back on deck.

Conquest to Coup: The History of Bagestan from Cyrus the Great to President Ghasib. Dana settled on a lounger beside Ashraf's and cracked the cover. It looked very densely written. She glanced over at him, and sensing her eyes on him, he looked up.

"You are sure that this is the way you want it?" she asked, with a rueful grimace.

He only gave her a look that melted her bones, shook his head a little, and turned back to business.

For the next two days she hardly saw him. There were others staying on the yacht now, his brother and cousin among them, and although she dined with them in the evenings, there was no small talk. It was all business.

She spent the hot, lazy days reading by the pool while the helicopter came and went and the meetings went on and on. The newspapers, particularly the English and Italian tabloids, were getting daily more excited about the subject of Bagestan's "Sultan-in-Hiding." They speculated, they agonized, they recapped history, all in a bid to blind the reader to the fact that they had no firm evidence as to who the sultan was, and not an idea in hell where to find him.

One paper ran a murky photo of a palatial, if unidentifiable, building, and suggested that the sultan-in-waiting was holding his meetings there. Another hinted that he was actually within the borders of Bagestan, very dangerously, waiting to lead an uprising.

Ghasib, meanwhile, was reported to have gone to ground inside the hideous New Palace compound. Dana wondered where he really was. Meanwhile, one thing was certain—the silent protests were growing larger by the hour, were extending into all-night vigils, and neither the army nor the police were moving to break them up.

On the second night, as on the previous one, Ash, his brother, Haroun, their cousin Najib, Gazi al Hamzeh, Prince Omar and a couple of assistants sat discussing the day just past, and the one to come.

"It's my feeling we can get away with a very light nod on the alcohol question," Ashraf said, and the others agreed. "A ban on actual alcohol production within the country I think would do it, in addition to what's already in place. What do we have in production in the country? How many jobs would a ban affect?"

Someone pulled out a sheet of statistics and they discussed how the businesses affected could be protected.

"But it looks like we're going to run aground on the *hejab* question."

Dana, who by this time had left the table and was on a lounger, reading, with her back to them, pricked up her ears. *Hejab* meant veil. It meant women covering their hair according to Islamic rules.

"I don't think they're going to give way on that."

"Well, let's give it another try. It would be a very unpopular move. Who's closest to compromise there?"

They were speaking in English half the time and Bagestani Arabic the other half, and Dana found it very difficult to follow the thread. If they had settled into Arabic she might have got her bearings, but the constant switch confused her ear.

"They have to see how difficult a curfew is to police...."

When the discussion was over at last and they were refreshing their coffees and slipping into ordinary conversation, Dana got up and slowly approached the table. They all looked up as she sank into her vacant seat.

"Who's coming tomorrow?" She reached for the coffee pot and poured herself another cup.

"The *ulema* are due for another round of argument," Ash told her dryly.

The *ulema* were the religious leaders in Bagestan.

"Do you have their support?" she asked.

He rubbed the back of his neck. "The extreme leaders of course will not back me, they're behind the Islamic movement. The moderates coming in the morning have—like the multinationals—got to the point of demanding concessions from us."

Although he had turned the Central Mosque into a museum, Ghasib had not completely suppressed religion in Bagestan, Dana knew. But there was total separation of mosque and state. No religious precept was enshrined in the law of the nation. What Ashraf was telling her was that the mullahs were hoping to force him to change that.

"And are you going to give in?"

"On as few points as possible."

"Are you going to give in on the question of *hejab?*" she pressed, stirring her coffee.

"Not unless we absolutely have to," Ash said.

"What does that mean—absolutely have to? You're

talking about the freedom of half your subjects. Why would you *have* to compromise their rights?''

They were all watching her now.

Gazi said, ''I understand your concerns, Dana, but Ashraf has got to get some religious leaders behind him. However moderate they are, the vast majority of the citizens are Muslim, and if the mullahs start preaching against Ashraf now…it could be critical.''

''So after thirty years of a dictator, the men of Bagestan will be free, but the women will just switch to a different kind of oppression,'' she said levelly.

''We are working on it,'' Ash said. ''Of course we don't want—''

She interrupted him without apology. ''It was your grandfather who created the separation of mosque and state,'' she reminded him, having just learned this fact from the history book she had been reading. ''Not Ghasib. Hafzuddin made all the women in his government abandon the veil. He let women run for parliament. He started with those reforms almost fifty years ago.''

''Times change, Dana.''

''Do they? I don't think so,'' she snapped. ''Not when it comes to women. People always complain that religion oppresses women, but it's not really religion, is it? It's men! Men will pick up any handy tool and use it to beat women down! Religion is just a convenient tool.''

''I am not using religion or any other tool to beat women down,'' Ash said stiffly.

'' 'Women hold up half the sky'—who said that?''

''I don't know,'' Ash said stiffly.

''Chairman Mao,'' Harry supplied.

''Right! About fifty years ago. And who said this one—'women are the twin-halves of men'?''

They all knew. ''Dana…''

"The Prophet Mohammad," she told them anyway. "Fourteen hundred years ago. Is anybody listening yet?"

"Dana, in a situation like this we can't act exactly the way we want to, or even the way we should. It's just a—"

"If you don't act the way you should, Ashraf, how are you different from Ghasib? If you're prepared to sell out women in order to gain power, what does that say about you? Who are you liberating from Ghasib's yoke? Women as well as men are counting on you, as I am sure you know.

"Look at the photographs in the papers—at least half of the people who are staging the demonstrations that you're counting on to bring you to power are women. You're going to imprison those women further in order to free the men. What kind of sultan will you make if that's the kind of 'freedom' you bring?"

They all sat silent and uncomfortable, looking at her or into their coffee cups. "Dana, nothing's perfect in this world. I will do my best, but—" He left it hanging.

Dana shook her head in disgust, shoved her cup away from her, stood, and left them.

She was so angry she thought she would explode. She arrived back in her stateroom and slammed the door in a bid to release her feelings, but it didn't have much effect.

She was angriest because she loved him and admired him, and this proved him to have clay feet up to the hips. She couldn't believe he had said what she'd heard him say. The same tired old arguments that had been used for decades.

She had been right the first time she'd set eyes on him. Ashraf al Jawadi was a man just like her father.

Twelve

She made no attempt to join them for breakfast in the dining room next morning, instead waiting until she heard the helicopter arrive with the mullahs and then going to the aft deck for a solitary breakfast.

She rubbed her head where a headache was just settling in behind her temples. She hadn't slept well last night; she was drinking too much coffee too late at night, she told herself. And crying herself to sleep didn't help.

After breakfast, as was becoming her habit, Dana took a few of the newly arrived papers and a book and went up to the pool.

But she couldn't settle. The bloom had gone off the situation. She had not minded the enforced idleness over the past couple of days because she felt she was at least contributing to good. What did she have to console her now? Ashraf was down there selling out the women of Bagestan to men whose whole sense of self-importance seemed to derive from telling others how to behave, how to live their religion.

The day was long and tedious. She swam a little, but without much satisfaction. A few strokes and she was at the other end of the pool. And then the Med got choppy, and the water started slapping around in the pool as the yacht negotiated the waves.

As the sea got rougher, Dana wondered how they were managing in the boardroom. Ashraf and the others on his team were experienced sailors, but she doubted if the mullahs were. As if in response to her thoughts, Dana felt the engines slow and went to the railing to look out forward.

They were approaching a small island, with a beautiful half-moon bay. Several other boats were also seeking refuge there, and she soon saw why. Once inside the arms of the half-moon, the water became tranquil again.

She had no idea where they were or what country the island belonged to. She watched as the anchor went down, and then there was silence as the engines were shut off.

This was her first chance to swim in the Med itself, and, her shirt billowing behind her, Dana went quickly down the staircase to ask one of the deckhands to lower the ladder. Pausing only to take a towel, she went down to the landing platform, stripped off her beach shirt, and dived in.

The water was fabulous—clear, clean, a rich blue-green. The island had sandstone cliffs, and one or two tiny islands of sandstone punctured the water of the bay closer in to shore. She struck out for one of them, her body grateful for the freedom after her days of confinement.

She landed on the first rock. Sandstone had been harvested from it at some time in the past, and it still retained the shape of the building blocks that had been removed from it. She swam on to the next and then saw snorkellers a short distance away, trawling back and forth over a confined area, and swam to take a look. But instead of the coral bed she half expected, what met her eyes was an underwater ruin—a sunken city.

Dana headed back to the yacht, where she was supplied with a snorkel and flippers, and spent the next hour contentedly swimming over the remains of the underwater rooms of the long-dead city. Late in the day she saw the helicopter arrive to take the mullahs off, and she headed back to the yacht. She wondered if the mullahs had got their way. She wondered if Ashraf would tell her.

She was sitting at the dressing table wearing only her beach shirt, brushing the day's tangles from her hair, when she heard a second helicopter arrive and depart. Ashraf's team must be leaving for the night, too. A moment later, just as the yacht's engines were starting up, there was a knock on her door. Not Adile's gentle tap, but the strong, firm rap of impatient knuckles.

She turned in her chair, brush in hand, and gazed at the door for a moment, with a slight sense of foreboding. "Come in," she cried.

Ashraf opened the door and stepped inside, looking very Bagestani in a kaftan and *keffiyeh*. No doubt he had put them on to make the mullahs feel at home.

She couldn't help the smile that came to her lips when she saw him, angry though she might be. She got to her feet and stepped towards him as he entered and closed the door.

Then his eyes moved to meet hers, but his gaze was

not a friendly one. It was black with anger and disapproval. Dana stopped where she was, halfway across the room from him, feeling she had hit a stone wall.

"Ashraf!"

He crossed his arms and stood looking at her. "What did you hope to gain by today's display, Dana?"

She blinked uncomprehendingly. "What?"

"Did you just want to make us all acutely uncomfortable, or were you hoping to sabotage today's talks completely?"

"What on *earth* are you talking about?"

He pointed at her body. "I am talking about you running around the yacht all but naked in full view of the boardroom windows. You knew who we were in discussion with today, so don't tell me it was an accident. It was deliberate, and I would like to know what you hoped to achieve!"

"All but naked?" Dana's fury, never slow to ignite, erupted with an engulfing swoosh. "Who do you think you're talking to?" she cried. "Don't you speak to me in that tone of voice! You're not sultan yet, and even if you were I wouldn't accept that from you!"

"I think I'm talking to someone who puts her own opinion above everyone else's, whatever is at stake!" he said, in a low, gravelly voice. "Whether you want to accept it from me or not, I'm here to tell you that today's display was an outrage. You know perfectly well the mullahs are deeply religious men who—"

"Who what?" she demanded. "Who what, Ash? Who can't look at a woman's legs without their passions becoming ignited by the sight? What kind of crap is that? They can see naked women on *billboards!* What do they do about that?"

"Billboards are one thing. On my yacht is something

else. Is it asking too much of you to dress more appropriately when such men are my guests?''

She stared at him, her pulse beating in her throat, her temples. ''I am not in a mosque, Ash, or even the middle of a city,'' she said levelly. ''I am on a boat in the Mediterranean, and I was swimming. My dress is *entirely* appropriate to that. A lot of women would have been topless. I didn't realize that I could be seen from the boardroom. I don't even know where the boardroom is. But if I had known, it wouldn't have occurred to me to button my shirt to spare the blushes of men who, after all, are supposed to have had some training and experience in self-control. If it bothered them to see me, why didn't you offer them blindfolds?''

''What?'' he exploded, outraged.

''If they didn't like seeing my body, why is that *my* problem? It's *their* problem!'' she expounded, stabbing the air with a forefinger. ''So let them deal with it. The one solution men always come up with when there's a question of men not being able to control their passions is that *women* should be forced to correct this weakness. *Women* should hide. Why don't they ever think that if a man is so weak he can't control himself, he *ought to be forced to wear a blindfold?*''

''You're being—''

''Or isn't it a question of men's unbridled passions at all? Is it maybe just an excuse for exerting control over women? Well, I am not going to give in to that, for your sake or anyone else's. I was born a free citizen of a free country. Don't ever think you're going to take that away from me without a battle.''

''I am not trying to take away your freedom! But—''

''You *are!* Not only my freedom of the person, but my freedom of religion! *'La ikraa fi uddin,'''* she quoted

suddenly from the Qu'ran, and then with pointed delib-
eration, measuring her words, translated it. "'There is
no compulsion in religion.' Did you quote that to your
mullahs, when they complained about your girlfriend's
bathing suit?''

"No, I did not," he said flatly. "And they did not
co—"

"You did not. Let me guess. You sat there being embarrassed—embarrassed because there you were, a man
wanting to rule a country, and you couldn't even keep
your own woman in line. Is that about it?"

"No, that is not about it!"

"Well, good! Because leaving aside the fact that I am
not your woman, why should you be keeping your
woman in line, Ashraf? Why do men—"

But as if her words had unleashed some rage that he
had been keeping in uneasy check, with two steps he
was standing before her. His hands wrapped her upper
arms.

"Not my woman? You are my woman!" he growled
at her, and with no more warning than a gasp, she was
in his arms, being painfully held, and fiercely kissed.

Her blood roared up in answer, fast, hot and filled with
thunder. Her mouth opened to receive the hungry thrust
of his tongue, her body pressed against the sudden hard
searching of his.

One hand released her arm to encircle her naked waist
under her open shirt, his hand hot against her spine. The
other slid up to cup her neck. She was melting with the
passion of wanting him. The suddenness of his cracking
overwhelmed her.

His kiss was almost cruel with passionate hunger. He
lifted his mouth only to cast a burning look into her eyes
and then smother her lips again.

Dana almost wept with the relief of holding him and touching him after an age of yearning. Waves of delight so strong it was almost pain swept her. When he lifted his mouth at last, she pressed her lips against his strong, brown throat and planted little kisses from his chin to the neck of his kaftan. She felt him kiss her ear, her temple, felt his fingers thread her damp hair.

He was murmuring her name as if the sound intoxicated him. The passion in his arms, his body, his voice made her weak with desire. With trembling fingers he drew the shirt away from her shoulders, down her arms, let it fall to the floor. He pulled off his *keffiyeh* and she heard the shoosh of its landing by her feet.

For a moment his hands were tight on her waist, and then he turned and led her to the bed. She sank down onto it as Ashraf lifted his kaftan over his head and tossed it aside. He was naked underneath, and she watched his magnificent body for a moment of delight before he reached for the light switch. His hand moved and darkness descended around them.

The lamp on the dressing table cast a small double circle of soft light, itself and its reflection in the mirror. Then Ashraf came between her eyes and the glow, and pushed her down on the bed. And then there was nothing but shadow and delight.

Hours later she lay in the circle of his arms, purring with contentment, his hand gently stroking her skin. What a lover he was! She had never experienced anything so thorough as the pleasure he had given her.

"Do you feel guilty?" she asked.

There was a smile on his lips which she had longed to put there. "Guilty? No. I feel reluctant to leave you, as I soon will have to."

"More meetings tomorrow?"

He nodded. "I must prepare."

Suddenly the world came rushing back. "Is it the mullahs again?"

He moved his lips. "No. We'll meet for further talks when I get back to London."

"Are you going to cut a deal with them?"

His hand stroked her back. "Dana, the future of Bagestan depends upon my coming to some agreement with them."

She sat up, all the lazy honey he had set adrift in her system with his lovemaking drying up with a suddenness that shocked her.

"Bull," she said. She turned to look down at him in the shadows. "*Bull,* Ashraf! That is just not true. If you let those men help you to the throne, you've won the battle but lost the war. If they get a grip on you now, you will never be free of them." She reached for the light by the bed and flicked it on. She knelt on their love-tossed bed and bent over him.

"Look at the papers. The people of Bagestan are standing in the streets, more of them every day, tens of thousands of them by now. Silently, just watching. Waiting. What more do you need? How much of an invitation do they have to give you? What do they have to do to prove that they're behind you, and no mullah, no matter how popular, or how rabid, will sway them?"

"Of course they—"

But the passion of truth was urgent in her. "You don't need the oil companies, either, Ash. You don't need to sell out your reign to anyone. The people are your strength, and they won't be asking for concessions. All they want is to be free to live their lives as they judge right. And if that's not your first priority, what's the point of the whole exercise?''

''There is more to a coup than riding through the streets on a white horse,'' he told her, in bitter imitation of her own words. ''If there is no stability afterwards, if the economy descends into chaos, where are we? I have to achieve stability before anything else can be achieved. If the *ulema* and the oil companies and other nations of the world are not behind me, tossing Ghasib out is no more than a gesture. That is why we play these games with the Western press. To make the world aware of the situation, so that informed public opinion is on our side.

''The people want freedom, you say. But they also want a functioning economy. Look at Russia. Do you think the people are happier there today than they were under Communism? The rouble drops every day. The economy is in the hands of gangsters. The people yearn for the stability of former times! And why? Because the country was left to drift after the overthrow. Because the West did not come to Russia's aid during the transition period. I do not want this to happen in Bagestan. Bad as Ghasib is, he nevertheless represents a certain stability. I cannot sacrifice that stability in the name of liberty.''

''All right, you have to have them on your side! But that's afterwards,'' she said. ''What is the point of dealing with these people—any of them—when you have no real authority yet and they know it? Of course they'll push you for the hardest possible deal when you're weak.

''You can get the authority of the people behind you first. You don't need the oil companies and the *ulema* and the multinationals to do it. You're looking at it backwards. What you need is the people behind you—to help you deal with the oil companies and the multinationals and the mullahs. Not the other way around.''

He lay thoughtfully watching her. ''This is fine as an ideal. But there are practicalities to consider, Dana.''

She sighed and shook her head, then got up and stood looking down at him. ''How much are you going to give way on women's rights?''

He watched how anguish shadowed her eyes even as the lamplight shadowed her beautiful body, and wished he did not have to answer. ''I have told you. As little as possible.''

She shook her head, turned away, and went to the bathroom. When she came back he was gone.

Their dinner *à deux* was strained. She seemed to have waited forever to have him to herself again, and now she was too hurt to enjoy it. She thought bitterly that he was right—they should not have made love while he was involved so deeply with this. But even as she thought it, her body melted with gratitude for his lovemaking and the need for more.

The food, as always, was delicious. They tried to talk about other things as they ate—about her television experiences, about Shakespeare, even about the Night of the Thousand and One Books. But there was always a tiny frown of preoccupation in his eyes, and of unhappiness in hers.

''You don't think William Shakespeare wrote the plays of Shakespeare?'' he repeated in surprise.

''I think the name *William Shake-speare* was a pseudonym,'' she said. ''And I think the man William Shakspere of Stratford on Avon was hired to front for someone who couldn't admit he was the playwright.''

''Who would that someone be?''

But though it was a favourite hobbyhorse of hers, she couldn't get excited by the subject tonight.

"Are you—devoted to your acting career?" Ashraf asked her a moment later.

She shrugged. "I don't even know. Sometimes I think I only went into acting because it was the thing my father would hate most. Even when I was a young teenager people were always saying I should be an actor or a model, but my father always said categorically that it was something I would never do, and I didn't mind much. Then when I was sixteen—well, that was when I suddenly saw how desperately in love with the theatre I was. And I auditioned for RADA and got in. And that was that."

He looked as though he could understand more than she was saying. "Why sixteen? This is the second time you have mentioned that age. What happened at sixteen, Dana, to turn your life upside down?"

She took a tiny bite of food and chewed it. Then she said quietly, "I learned that my father had stolen me from my mother and kept us apart for ten years. All the while she tore the world apart looking for me, and I cried myself to sleep at nights wishing she had loved me enough to stay with us. He told me she didn't. He didn't tell her anything at all. He just disappeared with me one day. For weeks she thought we must be dead in some accident. Then she discovered he had taken out a passport for me."

Ashraf gazed at her throughout the recital, deeply disturbed. "That's a tragic, desperate story," he said. "What grief must have been caused you both."

She felt the ready tears spring to her eyes, more easily because her emotions were so near the surface tonight.

"Yes," she said, her voice tight. "But he was happy,

so that made it all right. He got married again, and had another daughter, to a Muslim woman who didn't put her daughter's soul in danger with tales of Coyote and Bear and Gitchi Manitou. He was protecting me, of course," she pointed out with dry sarcasm. "He wasn't thinking selfishly at all. He had to save me from my mother and her paganism."

He seemed to have no reply for this. They sat and ate in silence for a while.

"And how did you find your mother? Did your father tell you at last?" he asked.

"Oh, no! I don't think he would ever have done that. My mother tracked me down. She'd spent most of the ten years trying to get information in Bagestan and Barakat, because my father had left a false trail. I don't know what clue suddenly made her start to look in England." She paused. "I swore not to speak to my father for ten years, so that he could taste a little of her experience."

Ashraf looked shocked. "And you—you kept your oath?"

She nodded. "But not for the full ten years. I was at boarding school, and then drama school, and I spent all my holidays with my mother for five or six years and hardly saw him. After that I relaxed a bit. I never visited him, but if he came to see me I didn't throw him out, either. Sometimes he came to the theatre when I was in a show. He must have hated that."

Ashraf said, "Your father had suffered much. It is no surprise if grief and stress made him a little mad. Have you not been able to take the past into account and forgive him? Even now?"

"What past? Bagestan suffered a coup, and in common with many other Bagestanis, he fled and started his life again in Canada.''

"But your father had a wife, a son and daughter in Bagestan. They were killed by Ghasib's murder squad. You do not consider this grounds for special grief?''

Dana set down her fork and stared at him. ''What? Who told you this?''

"You do not know it?''

"I've never heard a word of it!''

He twisted his head. "It is true, nonetheless.''

"How can it be? And how do you happen to know?''

"All my family knows the history of Colonel Loghatullah. It was taught to us in our cradles, so that we should never forget the service he performed or the debt we owe.''

"My father's name is Golbahn,'' she pointed out, with a curious look.

"That is the name he took when he escaped to the West. In Parvani, it means, *Protector of the Rose*. Are you really aware of none of this?''

She was staring at him in a mixture of astonishment and horror. ''No one has ever said a word to me about...'' Dana faded off, as vague memories surfaced. The Bagestanis who were always in and out of their flat, smiling at her with damp eyes, and saying things like, *You have a very brave, wonderful father.*

She remembered something else, too.

"Is *this* why you tried to give me a cheque that day?''

He lifted his hands in acknowledgement.

"What service did he perform for your family?'' she demanded.

Ashraf looked curiously at her. ''But you are half Bagestani. Does the name Colonel Loghatullah mean nothing to you?''

She shook her head emphatically. "The only Colonel Loghatullah I ever heard of all my life long is the courageous Colonel Loghatullah who led the Palace Guard resistance and saved the lives of the royal...oh, my *God!*" She dropped her fork and clapped her hands over her mouth.

"Are you—Ashraf, are you telling me that...that my father...?"

Ashraf smiled gently. "Is the great hero of the Bagestani coup. Yes. The man who carried the Crown Princess and her son to safety in Parvan, and for payment saw his own wife and children murdered. The man without whom my entire family would have been slaughtered on the first day of the coup.

"I would not be sitting here with you today, were it not for your father, Dana. I would never have been born were it not for his great courage, and his sacrifice."

Thirteen

The candles on the table seemed to darken. Dana rested her head in her hand as nausea gripped her. Hot tears sprang to her eyes and spilled down her cheeks.

"My father—*Allah,* is it possible? Why didn't he *tell* me?"

"Perhaps he felt that you were too young to keep the secret. He, too, was in danger from Ghasib's hit squads. And when you were older..."

When she was older he had had no opportunity. She sniffed and wiped her eyes with her fingers, staring at him. "You've just explained so much in my life!" she told him. "Oh, God, his utter obsession with the restoration—he made me obsessed, too. I told you I used to write letters to the Crown Prince! And then—oh!" She sighed. She squeezed her eyes shut, wiped tears from her cheeks again. "All those people, always coming and talking about the good old days...oh, it all makes sense!''

She sat back in her chair, propping her chin in her hand, as the tears burned their way down her cheeks. She looked at Ashraf again. ''His wife and children were killed?''

''It was Ghasib's revenge. When your father led Princess Hana and the infant Prince Kamil to safety in Parvan, word followed him of what had happened. He never went back.''

Of course she had heard the story, in the past. But then it had been the story of a distant hero, not her own father's life.

It was long before she could feel she had absorbed it, and she knew that it would be a lot longer than tonight before all the repercussions had settled in her psyche. They finished dinner, still talking it over, and took their coffee cups to the loungers.

At length, he said, ''Dana, do you understand a little better my anger this afternoon? The mullahs were informed that the daughter of Colonel Loghatullah would be on the yacht. I was hoping to introduce you to them. I had told them...''

He broke off, as if thinking better of what he had been going to say.

She turned curiously. ''What?''

There was a silence as he considered his course of action. Then he said quietly, ''I told them that I hoped to marry you. They—they drew from this the inference that we were already engaged. I didn't correct that misapprehension.''

She stared at him, her heart beating hard. ''Marry! What—why did you tell them that?''

''Because it is true. I want to marry you, Dana.''

She opened her mouth for air. Her heart was full to bursting; there was too much feeling for her to hold it all. "But you're...Ash!" she exploded disbelievingly. "You're going to be the Sultan of Bagestan!"

"Yes. It will be a great endeavour," he said simply. "And I ask you to be my partner in this endeavour, Dana."

Her heart was melting with love and need. She smiled and pressed her lips together, then bit her lower lip and looked at the stars, trying not to cry again. "Ash—" she began, knowing suddenly that there was nothing she wanted more than to be his wife. But—

"Ash, that would mean living in Bagestan."

"Would it be so terrible a fate?" he asked, with a suppressed anguish in his tone, as if he feared what her answer would be.

She stood up, went and leaned over the railing to look into the darkness and the stars. Her world was completely unrecognizable from what it had been two weeks ago. Everything was changed. She groped for a rudder in the stormy sea of her life.

He let her stand there for several minutes, then got up to stand beside her. She looked out at the sea. It looked so tranquil, but then, so did this moment. And under the surface all kinds of things were stirring and in turmoil.

"Ash, you're going to meet with the mullahs in a few days in order to barter with women's rights. You're asking me to be a wife in a *hejab*," she said.

"Dana—"

"A second-class citizen, whose rights are to be dictated by the whim of a lot of old men using God for their own ends."

"It may not come to that," he said urgently. "I may—"

"You may be able to convince them to go easy on women?" She shook her head. "Ash, don't you see that you've already given in? Just the idea that you *may* convince them—you've given them the power. What right have you got—no, but I've said it all."

She heaved a deep, trembling sigh. "No, Ash. No. If you want a lover for those times when the Sultan of Bagestan visits the West, I'm your woman. But don't ask me to go and be the sultana of a country where my sex has been sold down the river. I won't do it."

He was turning her to him, drawing her into his hold with ruthless passion. "What are you saying? I want a wife, not a lover when I am in the West!" he cried angrily. "Why do you taunt me like this? I looked on you and loved you, don't you understand? You are the only woman I will ever want! Please. Whatever arrangement we come to with the *ulema,* it will not be onerous, Dana. It will sit lightly on most women, I promise. I will not agree to anything very restrictive."

She looked at him. "I was born free," she said simply.

"You could use your talents and experience in Bagestan. There is much to be done revitalizing the old culture, the arts—you could make a great contribution, Dana."

She was shaken, but she knew she was right. She couldn't live like that. It would drive her crazy. "If your bid fails, Ashraf, I'll marry you like a shot. As long as you agree to live in the West. I couldn't say no. But until and unless women in Bagestan have the same civil, social and economic rights as men—I won't cross the border. Think what you're asking, Ash, and then ask yourself if it's love to ask that sacrifice of me."

* * *

"Hi, Roxy."

"Dana? Are you back in London?"

"Yes. I'm still—"

"Oh, they told me he was coming back today, and that you'd be with him!" Roxy exclaimed.

"Did they? Who?"

"Khalid Abd al Darogh. He said he wants to see you as soon as possible."

"Does he," Dana said flatly. "I wonder why he thinks he can dictate to me like that?"

"Dana, you have to go! Please—I'm scared. He's—last time he said something about Daddy. I didn't understand it, but it sounded like some kind of threat to hurt him."

"And you want me to go and face him, huh? What gets me, Roxy, is the surprise in your voice, as if you had no idea people could be so nasty. But Dad told you all about these men last time you got into trouble, didn't he? So I'm wondering why you are so amazed to come up against it now."

She was being hard, but her softness in the past, she could see now, had done her sister no favours. If Roxy had the feeling that there were no consequences to her actions, who had assisted her to come to that conclusion?

"You don't always believe everything Daddy says!" Roxy exploded.

"Right. So the position is, they're threatening to do some physical violence against Dad, so you want me to go and see them instead," Dana said dryly.

"No!—well, yes, but...look, Dana, I've been thinking. Don't you think it would be easier to just ask Sheikh Ashraf for the money to pay them off? I mean, if he's really a sultan, he must be loaded."

"And why would he give me such a huge amount of money?" Dana had to scotch this, because Ashraf and his team wanted to learn what the casino owners planned.

"Well, you...I mean, after all—"

"I'm sorry, I'm not in a position to ask the sheikh to pay my sister's gambling debts."

"No, but I thought—couldn't you pretend they were your own?"

She drew a long, deep breath. "No," Dana said flatly. "Not to them, and not to you."

"You see," Roxy said sulkily, "when I do try to protect you, you won't listen."

Dana laughed with real amusement. "That's how you see it, is it? Well, I'm sorry to reject your deep consideration for my continued good health, Roxy. However, I will meet with them and find out what they want. So suppose you arrange that?"

Ashraf was sitting in the main room of their hotel suite with Naj, Harry and several advisors—two of whom, she noted with surprise, were women. They all looked up as she entered, but it was Ash's gaze she returned. He put out his hand and she came around to the empty chair next to him.

"Any trouble?" he asked.

"No, they didn't threaten me or anything, or even ask to search me." Which was just as well, because she had been miked up to the bodyguards Ashraf had had tailing her.

Everyone was silent, waiting. She heaved a breath. "They want me to insist on taking that prize dinner at the Riverfront you bid £15,000 for. I'm supposed to book a table in the conservatory. Someone is going to

walk up and say your name, and then hand you a subpoena. I should just play ignorant.''

Everyone exchanged glances. There was no need to
repeat the obvious—that it was going to be an assassination attempt, not a newspaper exposé, not an accusation of brutality.

''When?'' Ash asked.

''Five days from now,'' she said.

A helicopter took them to a beautiful estate on the
coast of Cornwall belonging to Sir John Cross, the former ambassador to Bagestan and Parvan, who had sat
beside her at the Drought Relief fund-raiser.

There the meetings began again.

Sometimes, when they were alone, they fought. He
wanted her to say she would marry him, to trust him to
deal with the *ulema*'s demands in a reasonable way. She
tried to make him understand why she could not.

''What *good* does it do them, anyway, to force women
to obey a religious diktat, even if it was prescribed in
the Qu'ran?'' she demanded once.

''What do you mean?''

''It's not going to improve *my* soul, or my relationship
with God, if I only obey the rules because I'm forced
to! And it's not going to do their souls any good, because nowhere does it say you get a reward for forcing
someone else to be good! So what's the point, from a
religious perspective?''

''You are asking me to get inside the mind of a religious leader. I do not know the answer to this.''

''There's no law anywhere forcing people to fast during Ramadan, is there?'' Dana went on wildly. ''Why
not?''

''I don't—''

"You know why not! Because religion is meant to be a matter of conscience! But somehow, that fact gets lost when it comes to a question of women's duties!"

"Why do you put these arguments to me, when you know that I agree with you? I am faced with a political problem—how to take over with the least possible disruption in the country. To do this, I have explained to you—"

"You have to compromise! Well, that's your choice made, then, Ashraf! And that's fine. But don't expect *me* to agree to the selling of my rights and freedom just because you choose to do it. You are making a choice for your life that includes being Sultan of Bagestan, but excludes having me as your wife. That's it."

Always they parted with bitterness.

He would not make love to her. When she tried to soothe her hurt in his arms, he held her, but would not give in to her passionate longing.

"I want a wife, not a lover," he told her again. "If I have to live without you, Dana, what good will it do me to have fed my need of you with lovemaking? You are already in my blood. Do you think I am not tortured by the desire to leave the country to its fate? To say to my brother, let it be you who rules? To have you and damn the world?

"I cannot do it. My duty has been marked out for me since the moment of my cousin Kamil's death. But even before that, I knew that my life would be circumscribed by the family's duty to Bagestan. You force a choice on me that gives me unending torment. Well, I must live with that. But I will not voluntarily increase my pain by learning all the ways of your body and my own pleasure, knowing all the while that it is not to be mine."

She was weeping when he finished.

Dana wandered the estate during the hot August days, trying to see some way out of her dilemma. She loved him, she wanted to marry him. But he was destined to be the Sultan of Bagestan. He could not give that up for her sake, but nor could she make the sacrifice of her rights, however desperately her love tore at her heart and pleaded with her that no sacrifice was too great when such love as this was at stake.

They had separate bedrooms. She was always awake when he came upstairs at night, after a late meeting, and she always waited and hoped for the sound of his footsteps to pause outside her door. But he never came to her. And she would not go to him.

"Good afternoon, ladies and gentlemen. Thank you for coming today," said Ashraf Durran ibn Wafiq ibn Hafzuddin al Jawadi.

The lawn was crammed with reporters. A helicopter seemed to have arrived every five minutes for the past two hours to disgorge more. In front of the house the cars were lined up for a mile down both sides of the pretty, narrow lane.

Bleachers of a sort had been arranged on the lawn, providing three levels, so that those at the back would not have their view blocked. Dana hadn't seen so many television cameras in one place except in movies.

Ashraf, with Harry, Najib and Gazi al Hamzeh around him, was standing on the terrace in front of a microphone stand. There were so many microphones it looked like a bunch of giant grapes.

"I think—" Ashraf smiled a little ruefully at the crowd out on the lawn "—that some of you may have guessed what I am here to say."

A murmur of appreciation rippled through his audience.

"So let me say it." He lifted his right hand. "This ring is the al Jawadi Rose. It has been passed from the reigning monarch to his nominated heir in Bagestan for many, many generations. Even in my family, no one knows who was the first monarch to wear the Rose."

The clicking and whirring of cameras was almost deafening as photographers angled to get a shot of Prince Ashraf with his hand lifted, and do justice to the magnificent pink diamond that glowed on his forefinger.

"My grandfather was Sultan Hafzuddin al Jawadi. This ring tells you that I am my grandfather's nominated heir for the throne of Bagestan. And I call on President Ghasib to heed the will of the people, which is being expressed daily in the streets of Medinat al Bostan and throughout Bagestan. I call upon President Ghasib to resign his ill-gotten place, and leave the country for wherever he may find a safe haven. I ask him to do this immediately and peacefully. And I expect to take back the throne of my family within the next few days."

It was no more than they had come for, but Ashraf's charisma added an unexpected element to the equation. There was excitement in the air, and not just because they knew they had a story that was going to give them front page copy for days, if not weeks.

"I know that there are representatives here from the media in Bagestan. I ask them to take this message back to the people of Bagestan," Ash continued. He turned his head and looked straight into two cameras which had been put in a privileged position just to one side, and began to speak in Bagestani Arabic.

With all her listening practice lately, Dana could just about follow his speech. "...I know that you have suf-

fered much under the cruel hand that has had you in its
grip for the past thirty years and more. The sight of your
sufferings was a grief to my honoured grandfather and
to my father after him, and it continues a grief to me.

"But if you wish it, your suffering is at an end. If you
desire it, I will restore the throne of the al Jawadi, who
have ruled you in good times and bad, but always with
your happiness at heart...."

"His Excellency will take a few questions if you
wish." Gazi stepped to the mike when Ashraf had finished; Gazi was the stage manager of the press conference.

A hundred hands snapped into the air. Gazi pointed
first to a reporter from Bagestan. The question was asked
and answered in Arabic.

Gazi's management of the conference was virtually
flawless. There were reporters from all around the world
in attendance, and he was managing to take one question
from each of two dozen different nations. And although
the majority of the questions were put in English, Ashraf
also answered with fair fluency those that were asked in
French and Parvani, and even managed a brief response
in Japanese, which everyone applauded.

He answered with an intelligence and a grasp of world
affairs that clearly impressed everyone, jaded as they
might be. His personality and charisma came over amazingly, Dana saw. They might have come expecting
someone very different, but they quickly grasped the fact
that Ashraf was no fool.

"What is the import of the title His Excellency?"
someone called at the end. "Is that the traditional address for the sultan?"

"It is the address used to the Cup Companions of the
Barakat Emirates, a position His Excellency still holds.

He will not use the titles reserved for the Sultan of Bagestan until he is actually on the throne.''

That was the last question. Ashraf bowed and turned back inside, while the assembled burst into applause.

''Stage One complete,'' said Gazi.

Fourteen

"**I**'m going to outline the overall arrangements now for everyone," Naj said. "Each of you has had a particular briefing already."

The room, the sitting room of a huge suite at the top of one of London's most famous and expensive hotels, was filled with men and women, all listening attentively.

"As most of you know, we'll have a very strong presence in the Riverfront Restaurant tonight. Some of you are going to be busboys, some patrons. Just under half the tables are full, including our agents and the ordinary patrons of the place.

"You've all been given individual schedules that tell you when to arrive. Ash's booking is for nine o'clock, and most of you will be in position by that time....

"Ash will sit in the conservatory. Three of you dressed in similar clothes will also be seated there.

Amina's standing in for Dana—she'll keep her headscarf over her face as far as she can.''

Dana had argued and argued for the right to go as herself. Some inner conviction told her she should be there. But Ashraf and the others had rejected the idea completely. She was to stay safe in the hotel till it was all over. She had barely managed to convince Ash to let her come up to London to help with her stand-in's disguise.

"They warned me I'd have to wear platforms to get the extra height," Amina complained to her a short time later, in the dressing room that led off Dana's bedroom. Dana was helping the agent to dress in some of her own clothes. Amina had stripped to her underwear and was walking around in a pair of platform heels, getting used to them. "They don't really let you connect to the ground, do they?"

Dana only shook her head. "I've never worn platforms."

Amina looked at her and laughed. "Well, at five-eleven I guess you wouldn't. Where's that vest?"

Dana lifted the bulletproof vest and held it up for her. It was heavy, but not as bulky as she'd imagined. Amina slipped her arms in, pulled the flap between her legs and up over her abdomen, pressed all the fasteners.

Dana next held up a pair of *shalwar* in a black silk-linen mix, then the embroidered black tunic. It was an outfit she had chosen to Najib's instructions—the pants were drawstring, and the *kamees* was full, to disguise the thickness of the protective vest. The outfit was completed with a black-and-silver scarf which she helped the agent pin securely in her long, dark hair—the only thing in which she really resembled Dana—and draped it around her lower face.

"Right!" said Amina, consulting her watch. "Zero hour. Wish me luck."

"Good luck," Dana said with a smile, moving backwards out of the dressing room. She drew the door closed behind her, and turned the key to lock it. "Sorry," she called through the panels, as Amina gave a cry of surprise. "But you understand, I have to be there."

She had purchased a brand of perfume she had never worn before, and moving quickly now she sprayed it liberally on her hair and skin. Then from the bed she picked up the peach scarf that matched her own silky outfit, and sprayed that before wrapping it carefully around her face and head.

As she left the room she could hear Amina start to pound the door, but the hotel was one of the old, solidly built kind, and when she closed the bedroom door the sound died.

One of the bodyguards was waiting for her in the hall.

"Come," he said. "We are two minutes behind time. The others have gone down."

This was a piece of luck! Dana relaxed and knew suddenly that it was going to work. She had been most worried about Ash recognizing her in the elevator.

Three limousines were waiting in the hotel drive. Ash, wearing a flowing white djellaba and luxurious *keffiyeh* with gold ropes, was standing at one side talking to Harry. Dana went past without looking towards him, hiding her hands under her scarf as she held it over her face.

Suddenly she was almost laughing. Only a few days ago she had told him she would never put on *hejab* for his sake, and here she was, as terrified of showing her face as the most downtrodden of women!

The door of the second limo was opened for her and Dana slipped inside and drew back into the corner. The bodyguard followed, and sat facing her on the pull-down seat. A moment later Ash and another bodyguard got in and the first limousine moved out into the street. Their own followed, and behind them came the third.

They sat mostly silent in the darkness, each of them thinking about the task ahead. Dana said nothing at all, just kept as far from Ash as she could. Fortunately the limousine had a pull-down arm between their seats.

Her heart was pumping hard, but didn't really start to thunder until they pulled up at the Riverfront Restaurant. There, wrapping her scarf very securely around her face, as Amina would have done, Dana followed the bodyguard out of the car.

The bodyguard led the way down the gangplank into the restaurant, Dana following, then Ashraf, then the second bodyguard. It seemed little enough protection, but she reminded herself that the restaurant itself was filled with agents, and probably so was the street.

"Good evening, Miss Morningstar, good evening, Your Excellency. What a great pleasure." The maître d' smiled a welcome as Ashraf stopped just behind her. She felt Ash's firm grip on her upper arm.

"What the hell do you think you're doing?" he hissed in her ear. She turned and smiled at him, and saw by the shock on his face that he could hardly believe his eyes.

She turned to follow after the maître d', and Ash had to let her go. He could not create a scene for fear of triggering some reaction in the agents.

"It's Reena!" she heard the whispers as she moved past various tables, and she felt the strangeness of being in that old world suddenly, when all her concentration was in the new one.

The front deck of the old ship had been enclosed with a large bubble of glass, giving a beautiful view of the Thames. The massive Ferris wheel called the London Eye dominated the skyline on the other side of the river.

"What the devil are you doing here?" he demanded in an undervoice when they were seated at a table alone, the two bodyguards ostentatiously placed at a table nearby. That was to convince anyone watching that these two were all there were.

"You know this would all be jeopardized without me," Dana returned, unapologetically, talking into her menu. "Why did you try to prevent me?"

"Order a meal, and then get up and go to the ladies' room and stay there," he ordered her furiously.

"Don't let the headscarf fool you," Dana said sweetly. "It hasn't changed anything. I'm still a free woman. And I make my own choices."

The drinks waiter arrived with a bottle of the best champagne in the house. It was all part of the prize for which Ashraf had paid fifteen thousand pounds. Ash let him pop the cork and pour the champagne, watched as the attentive waiter set the bottle in an ice bucket beside the table. Then he quietly ordered water in addition.

Dana had no intention of drinking alcohol tonight, but she picked up her glass nevertheless. "Pick it up and toast me," she said. "Otherwise we are going to look all wrong."

Furious as he was, he knew she was right. He picked up his glass and saluted her, then replaced it on the table without making any pretence of drinking. Dana smiled and pretended to sip, but she didn't taste a drop. Tonight was the night for a completely clear head.

Another waiter was coming towards them, with a small tray and two glasses on it. Dana blinked and felt a buzz of alarm. There was some anomaly which her subconscious mind had picked up, but she couldn't get consciously. She stared at him.

"Ash," she said warningly, and then it clicked—there was no bottle of water on the tray....and she had seen the man before. In Fuad al Kadthib's office at the casino, the second time she had met him.

Ash reacted instantly to the change in her tone. He lifted his arm and looked at his watch in the prearranged signal of trouble.

The waiter came towards the table, a tray clasped in one hand, balanced over the other. And for Dana the world suddenly went into slow motion. She saw the man lift the tray slightly, saw the dull glint of metal under it. Watched her own hand go out to the ice bucket and wrap the neck of the champagne bottle.

Ash, meanwhile, put both hands on the edge of the table and shoved.

The champagne bottle, spilling its foamy contents in a wide arc, smashed down on the metal tray with a whang to wake the world, just as the table smacked into the man's groin. He made a strangled sound.

For Dana time returned to normal.

Someone shouted. The gun exploded three times in quick succession, a nasty little *pfutt! pfutt! pfutt!* as the assassin staggered back. The first hit the table, the second hit Ash, the third hit the glass of the conservatory behind his head.

"*Ash!*" Dana screamed. His chair went over backwards under the blow, and as he went down on the floor she flung herself out of her own chair and across his head and body in instinctive protection. "Ash! Ash!"

Over her head there was uproar as agents erupted from half the tables in the room and converged on the man with the gun. Men and women screamed and shouted, some falling to the floor, others frozen in their seats, still others running this way or that.

Then suddenly there was stillness.

"Ash!" Dana sobbed again, scrabbling to her knees to look down at him. He was lying with his face contorted, his hand clutching his ribs. "Oh, God, Ash, are you hit?"

He opened his eyes and grinned at her. "Yes, I'm hit," he said. "*Allah,* a bullet packs a wallop, even when you're wearing body armour!"

The first rays of the summer morning were coming up over the green hills as the helicopter rose away from the lawn and the peace of the Cornish countryside enveloped them. The butler let them into the otherwise still sleeping house and, Ash's arm around Dana's waist, they went upstairs.

Her bedroom door was reached first, but Ash simply ignored it, drawing Dana past it and along to his own room. Her heart kicked with reaction, and she looked a smile up at him. The expression she saw in his eyes melted her.

It was a beautiful room, with wide windows open onto the green lawn and the forest, and a large antique four-poster bed. The oak floor glowed with the polish of centuries under Bagestani and Parvani rugs spread as if at random.

They walked over to one of the windows beside the bed and stood looking out for a moment. A deer stood in the protection of the trees at the edge of the lawn, flicking her ears, watching. They waited in silence, let-

ting the peace sink into their bones, as the beautiful creature at last stepped out onto the lush grass and, with
another flick of her delicate ears, bent to eat.

He turned to her and lifted one strong hand to her
cheek and temple, looking into her face, and thinking
how like the deer she was—elegant, graceful, beautiful,
but quick and strong. The eyes she watched him with
were like the deer's, too. Wide, dark, and slanting, and
full of a mystery that had captured him with that first,
challenging glance.

She laid her hands flat against his chest and tilted her
head for his kiss, and he realized that he could never
have resisted her. His mouth took the offering with a
hunger and a passion that made them both moan. Then
he held her head in his hands and kissed her cheek, her
ear, and down the long graceful line of her neck.

After endless, tenderly passionate kisses, he led her to
the bed and slowly slipped the pale silk of her clothes
from her body, till she was standing in only a tiny pair
of briefs. He caressed the long line of her naked back
while she busied herself unbuttoning his shirt.

She gasped when she pulled it open, for the place
where the bullet had slammed into him was now marked
with a huge, black bruise. Just under his heart.

She bent and kissed it with feather kisses, murmuring
her concern.

Ashraf laughed and drew her face back up to his.
"That is not the worst wound I have had in my life,"
he told her. "Not by any means."

She bit her lip. "Really?"

"I was hit with a fatal shot the first time you looked
at me. And I was wearing no protective armour then. It
went straight to my heart." She gasped. "It is still there,
in my heart. You will be always there."

Dana smilingly shook her head. ''The first time I looked at you,'' she accused him, ''you were looking daggers at me! I've never seen such disapproval.''

He touched her cheek. ''I was angry with you then. You came into the room, and it was as if you brought beauty and nobility with you. There was a glow around you. I know you are a famous actress, but I had never seen you. I didn't know anything about you, except that I was destined to win you and you were destined to be mine.

''And then—you turned, and your dress became transparent. At first I thought you could not know, but I soon saw by your face that you did. I was so angry with you!'' He smiled and drew the warmth of his hands down her back, around and up her abdomen and stomach until his hands rested just under the swell of her breasts. ''I thought, she is mine, how does she show the world what is mine?''

Dana's heart melted, even as she shook her head. ''Oh, Ashraf!''

''That was when you looked at me. And your look said—*I do not accept your judgement of what I do!*''

A little burst of laughter escaped her because of the truth of it.

''And then I knew that I would make you mine, but that the road to your love would not be an easy one for me. And I was right.''

They lay on the bed then, naked and entranced with each other's body. His hands were perfect on her skin. There had never been a touch that thrilled her so. He made her melt and freeze and melt again, till she could do no more than whimper his name.

Then he rose up over her, slipped his legs between her helplessly spread thighs, and pushed into the connection they both needed. They cried out together, and smiled, already tasting the joy to come, and knew that this was what their souls had yearned for.

"Dana, I love you," he said later, as they lay in each other's arms in the wide bed. "Tell me you love me."

"I love you, Ash, oh, I love you!" she cried. "But please don't ask—"

He put his fingers to her lips and stilled her anguish. "Shh!" he commanded. "Have no more fears. I understand you, Dana. I did not see it so clearly before. You are a woman as brave as Nusaybah. And—"

"Nusaybah?"

"She was a warrior. Before the Battle of Uhud she asked the Prophet's permission to bear arms as a warrior. He gave her that permission. And when the day went against him, and the enemy broke through, Nusaybah was among those who circled him, and stood between the Prophet and death. His life was saved."

Dana propped herself up on one arm and looked down at him with a surprised smile. "I've never heard that before!"

"It is recorded in certain biographies. I do not know why it is not more known. It is a clear lesson."

Dana sighed, and happiness seemed to flow through her. "Is it?"

"The Prophet allowed Nusaybah to follow the dictates of her own heart. If he had not done so, who can say whether he would have survived the disaster of Uhud? Why should ordinary men do otherwise? Are we so much wiser than the Prophet that we can instruct women in their religion?"

She was silent, but her heart was full to bursting.

"You saved my life last night, Dana."

"Mash'Allah," she murmured. *It was God's will.* And that was no more than the truth. She had not acted entirely from herself. She had been inspired.

"I was a fool to gainsay your determination to go to the restaurant with me. But I am not a Prophet, and wisdom comes slowly to men. I am grateful that you refused to substitute my judgement for your own, and I hope I will never again ask such a thing of you. And I see that you are right in what you said. I cannot allow myself to rule over a nation where any woman's conscience is dictated by the law.

"On those terms, Dana, I ask you to marry me. To be my wife and my sultana. To be the mother of my children, and to govern my people beside me."

She was weeping too hard to answer.

"Assalaamu aleikum," Ashraf said, as the bearded, turbaned men clambered out of the helicopter, their robes flapping in the wind that the slowly beating rotors stirred up.

"Waleikum assalaam."

They exchanged formal greetings and bows, and he led them across the green lawn towards the sprawling manor house.

He stopped a few yards short of the door, and stretched out one arm to the left. Obediently they turned their eyes in the direction he pointed. There was nothing to see but the shrubbery surrounding the lawn. But before they could ask, he turned and led them inside the house and along a wide hall.

Again, Prince Ashraf stopped and pointed, this time towards the end of the hall. Again their eyes followed the direction of his finger. An antique oak dresser with a small inlaid mirror and a potted plant. Above it, something framed. Nothing of note, and the men wondered and exchanged mystified glances.

Inside the formal dining room, equipped now as a boardroom, they quickly dispersed to the chairs allotted to them. Prince Ashraf's team, men and women, were interspersed among the mullahs, rather than on the opposite side of the table, as a way of reducing confrontation. Ashraf went to the head of the table, where he remained on his feet.

When they were all settled and looking his way, he pointed again, at a corner of the ceiling. Murmuring with confusion now, the men nevertheless could not resist looking in the direction indicated by his clenched fist, his strong finger. There was nothing there.

When they looked back at him in bewilderment, he was holding a Qu'ran in his hand. "What is it you wish us to look at, Prince Ashraf?" one of the religious men asked.

"At my hand, of course," he said. He held it up.

"Your hand!"

"But you were pointing at something!"

"What?" he asked.

Now there were murmurs of disquiet and confusion. "You have been pointing as if to show us something."

Ashraf stared. "Do you mean that if I hold up my hand and point, you look not at my hand but in the direction to which I am pointing my finger?"

"But of course!" a bearded one cried, impatient. "This is true everywhere. A man points at what he wishes to draw one's attention to!"

Prince Ashraf looked around them in bewilderment. "Do you all agree with this idea?"

They were confused, disturbed, even angry. "Certainly," they muttered. "What else?"

"Each of you says the same thing?"

"Of course! Everyone knows it!"

Prince Ashraf smiled and lifted up the book in his hand. "Wise sirs," he said softly, "this Holy Qu'ran is the pointing finger of Allah. You all agree on the meaning of a pointing finger. Yet your focus is entirely fixed upon the book, and not on the direction in which it points."

They sat in astonished, bewildered silence, looking at Prince Ashraf, and at one another.

"If Allah allows men to act in a certain way, not because that way is right, but because He knows too well that mankind is weak, is it right for the faithful to carry on acting in that way, once they have discovered, through their own God-given wits, that it is wrong?"

They were speechless.

"If Mohammad, peace and blessings upon him, tells us that the greater jihad is not the battle against the infidel, but the battle to subdue the self, is it right for the faithful to neglect any aspect of the self which needs to be subdued?

"Today I give you notice that as Sultan of Bagestan I will ask you to turn your gaze in the direction to which the Holy Qu'ran points us. There are many hints within it that Allah expected us to travel further along the road that He had pointed out to us, rather than remaining exactly where He found us in the days of the Prophet.

"I say to you that it is no longer appropriate for men to consider the latitude Allah allowed to the ignorant and unruly men of earlier times as our guide. I will ask you for a new interpretation of Islamic law. In particular, as that law pertains to man's treatment of woman, to marriage, and to women's rights. But also in many other areas.

"I will ask you to consider the fact that the only instructions as to dress in the Holy Qu'ran are those given to the wives of the Prophet, and that until all men behave with the perfection of the Prophet, it is inappropriate to force all women to emulate the perfection of the Prophet's wives.

"These and many other considerations will be on the agenda.

"I say to you that the Door of *Ijtihad* must be opened again, and a fresh understanding of God's word discovered, which is appropriate for our own times."

He paused and looked into their amazed, chagrined, curious faces. "I tell you now so that you may be prepared for such discussions on the day when, *insha'Allah!* I become sultan in Bagestan."

Fifteen

"**M**assive demonstrations have been taking place tonight in Medinat al Bostan, the capital of Bagestan. President Ghasib is reported to have fled. And Crown Prince Ashraf al Jawadi is said to be on his way to the country, where he expects to take command. With that story and more, here's Michael Druid."

"Good evening. Hundreds of thousands of people are massing around the walls of the New Palace in Medinat al Bostan tonight, as reports of the attempted assassination of Crown Prince Ashraf al Jawadi, which took place in London last night, reached the streets of Bagestan early today. We have no pictures yet, but John Sarwah is there, and he's on the line live from Bostan's Freedom Square. Hello, John."

"Hello, Michael. Well, there has never been anything like this, Michael, this is one of the most exciting moments of history I've witnessed. I'm in Freedom Square at the moment, opposite the main gate of the compound. The people are massed in absolutely unbelievable numbers all around the perimeter wall of the New Palace, filling not only the square, which is a massive space, but also all the streets leading to it, on all sides.

"Is it a silent vigil, John?"

"They're no longer silent. You can probably hear them in the background. They're screaming, they're chanting, they're demanding Ghasib's resignation. And they're also singing the underground song *Aina al Warda?* 'Where is the Rose?' That's been the song of the anti-Ghasibists, or rather the pro-Jawadi-ists, for a couple of decades now, but you'd better believe it hasn't been sung in public in Bagestan before."

"What sort of police presence is there?"

"None at all. That's one of the most remarkable things about it. There has been no police or military presence whatsoever, and since Ghasib has always had such close ties with the military, that fact alone tells the story."

"What's the mood of the crowd, John?"

"I would say angry and determined. They're battering the gates with logs and driving at them with a bus, and it's only a matter of minutes before those impregnable gates go down. But there's no mob hysteria."

"We've heard here that President Ghasib may no longer even be in the New Palace. What do you know about that?"

"Yes, that's the rumour circulating here, too. He may have already fled the country. People are also saying that Ashraf al Jawadi—well, there go the gates, John, can you hear the cheer going up around me? They are smashing through the gates, and the crowd is streaming into the compound. And there's not a sign of a guard, no shot has been fired in defence. There won't be much left of the noble New Palace by morning.

"I think that whatever happens now, John, we can say that this moment marked the end of President Ghasib's power in Bagestan."

"Well, Marta, it's a great day for Bagestan."

"Yes, Barry, thrilling times lately for the people of Bagestan, and just to recap—it's only six weeks since they stormed the New Palace to bring down the dictator Ghasib, and welcomed their new sultan's arrival, but that six weeks has brought tremendous change already, and today produces maybe the most exciting change of all.

"Will any of us ever forget the sight of the massive crowds who welcomed Sultan Ashraf al Jawadi as he rode *on horseback* through the streets of Medinat al Bostan to the Old Palace? The same crowds who stood in silent vigil for so many days in protest against Ghasib—who would have thought they would be cheering so loudly, and dancing in the streets, in so short a time? Here's some library film of those wild hours when a sultan came home again."

"We loof heem! We loof our sultaan!" a dark, heavy-set man screamed into a microphone, waving a banner, his eyes streaming with tears. He grabbed the Western reporter who stood beside him smiling bemusedly, and exuberantly kissed him. The camera drew back to show a long chain of dancing men and women, their arms twined around each other's shoulders, kicking their legs to the music of the song *Aina al Warda?*

"Djes! Djes!" a woman cried. "He brink us freedom, and good happiness, and we wont heem very much, for lonk time! And now he come!"

An aerial shot showed two thick ribbons of crowd,

lining either side of a boulevard that stretched for miles through the city, and then cut to the sight of handsome Sultan Ashraf al Jawadi, on a spirited white horse, riding slowly among the delirious crowds, accompanied by a dozen men also on horseback. He lifted his right hand at intervals, to show them the al Jawadi Rose on his finger. The cheers were deafening.

"It did the heart good, didn't it, Marta?" said Barry, as the camera returned to the studio.

"Yes, oh, it did," said Marta, wiping a corner of her eye. "It still makes me cry, even though I suppose that white horse was a bit of deliberate stage management. I guess I'm a sucker for that hero stuff."

"You and millions of excited Bagestanis, Marta. And who knows? Maybe it's really true."

"Let's hope so. Well, Barry, and then just three days ago we had the wonderful spectacle of the wedding of Sultan al Jawadi to his fiancée, the actress Dana Morningstar, who saved his life during that assassination attempt in London. And that's a day to remember, too."

The library film showed Dana and Ashraf standing under a magnificent arched doorway covered in painted green tile. "And there's another source of happiness for the majority of Bagestanis," a reporter was saying softly. "The wedding of their new sultan and sultana is the first ceremony to take place in the newly restored Central Mosque. For almost thirty years, it has been a museum, and an army of craftspeople and artisans has been working day and night for weeks to restore it to its original use. And here they come."

The film showed Ashraf and Dana stepping out into the bright sunlight and waving at the cheering crowds. Dana was wearing a beautiful, flowing, pure white *shal-*

war kamees, with white flowers in her long dark hair. Ashraf wore a turquoise silk high-necked jacket.

"The bride deliberately chose not to wear any kind of veil, as a signal that there will be no dress laws in the new Bagestan. It's a symbol of the equal freedom and rights that women will share with men in Bagestan under the new government. Sultan Ashraf is known to have asked religious leaders throughout the country to work together on a new interpretation of Qu'ranic law for the modern world...."

The film gave way to the studio talking heads again.

"And now, Marta, after three days of wedding celebrations, the Bagestanis are taking to the streets again to celebrate the formal coronation of their sultan and sultana. This is the first joint rule of a husband and wife in the history of Bagestan," said Barry.

"Yes, it's a resoundingly historic moment to add to all the other historic moments in Bagestan. I am sure this year will be a landmark year in the Bagestani calendar for decades to come. And Andrea is at the ceremony which is just about to take place in the Throne Room of the Old Palace...Andrea, are you there?"

"Yes, Marta, we're just outside the Throne Room waiting for the ceremony to begin. Through the doors behind me is the room where for centuries the Sultans of Bagestan held court for ordinary citizens, and that is where the ceremony will take place. Inside, for the first time in history, are two thrones. The new monarchs will be crowned by the Nazim al Zaman, the former Grand Wazir of Sultan Ashraf's grandfather, who is now eighty-eight years old.

"We've still got quite a long wait, so let me remind the viewers that after the ceremony Bagestan is going to be indulging in one massive, country-wide party that will last another three days. And when it's over Bagestanis will have been celebrating for a week in all. A very traditional period of celebration in Bagestan.

"Through the doors in the other direction are several interconnecting rooms, through all of which the royal procession will pass on the way to the Throne Room. And each of those rooms is filling up with the wedding guests, who are now arriving in large numbers. There will be representatives of governments and monarchies from around the world who have come to witness this historic occasion, including all the princes of the Barakat Emirates and their wives.

"Every city and town in the country has sent one representative, chosen by lot. Also invited to share the celebration, we are told, are all those who assisted the al Jawadi family in their campaign to regain the throne. Among the guests on his own merits is the new sultana's father. General Loghatullah is a hero in his own right. He is credited with single-handedly saving the royal family from extinction back in 1969."

"It must run in the blood, Andrea."

"Yes, the new sultana is going to find herself very popular with her people, from all that I've heard in the streets. That photograph of her on the floor of the restaurant, protecting a wounded Ashraf al Jawadi, has been blazoned all over the front pages here...."

It was another half hour before the trumpets announced to those who waited that the pageant was about to begin, and silence fell. There was a long pause, with absolute quiet. Then a voice called out something indecipherable, and there was a loud rapping, and two pages stepped from their posts to open two massive, arched double doors.

Two more opened the next doors, and two more the next, until there was a passage, carpeted in red, leading through a dozen rooms of the palace from an antechamber all the way to the Throne Room. Each of the rooms was lined with rows of seats and crowded with spectators.

The trumpets sounded again. Then an old man in white robes stepped through the door of the antechamber and set out along the passage. He carried a richly jewelled and decorated Qu'ran open on his two outspread hands. Behind him came a dozen men and a dozen women in fabulous costumes of bright silks and jewels. They walked in two rows, and first in line were Najib al Makhtoum and Haroun al Jawadi, carrying two circlets of gold on purple velvet cushions.

The magnificent procession moved slowly along the red carpet that ran from room to room, towards the Throne Room and the raised dais within.

Behind them, side by side, walking slowly under the weight of their cloaks, came Sultana Dana Morningstar Loghatullah and Sultan Ashraf Durran ibn Wafiq ibn Hafzuddin al Jawadi.

The sultana wore a lustrous heavy cloth-of-gold cloak, luxuriously ruched and latticed with thousands of pearls and caught over her shoulders with a double rope of gleaming pearls. Her hair was woven into a heavy chignon threaded with pearls and diamonds, and massive pearl drops hung from her ears. Her simply cut shimmering dress was also cloth of gold, as were the slippers that peeped out from under its hem. Behind her stretched a train several yards long.

Beside her, the dark-haired handsome sultan also wore a suit of cloth of gold, with high-necked jacket. Strings of luscious pearls were looped across his chest from shoulder to waist, held in place by a giant emerald on his breast. His cloth-of-gold cloak was purfled with pearls and diamonds, and his train matched the length of hers.

And on his hand, the diamond ring called the al Jawadi Rose glittered and glowed with a magic few could believe.

Four pages dressed in white and gold walked on either side of the long trains.

As they passed from room to room among the silently standing guests, the sun falling through the tall windows caught the gold so that the royal couple glowed in the centre of a shimmering halo, giving a touch of unreality to the scene.

For those watching, it was a once-in-a-lifetime experience. For many, it was their first taste of such splendour, and they would be forever changed by the moment.

In one room, a woman reached for the hand of an elegant, white-haired old man, and clutched it for as long as the golden vision lasted. When the royal procession had moved through the doors into the next chamber, she continued in silence for a long, breathless moment, staring up at the monitor which showed its further progress. Then she sighed, turned her head a little and whispered in French, "Oh, Monsieur Saint-Julien! Who would have imagined it? Can you believe that this is not a dream? Did you see the ring? Is it not magnificent? And to think that we contributed, even so little, to this wonderful occasion."

The old man whispered back, "Marthe, we are in danger of becoming the worst bores in the region. We will tell the story until we have one foot in the grave, and even on our deathbeds we will say, *You know, I was once of material assistance to the Sultan of Bagestan's brother, when he was on a most important mission to find the ring they called the al Jawadi Rose. Did I ever tell you about the coronation...?''*

When the procession reached the Throne Room, the aged Grand Wazir climbed three shallow steps to the first level of the dais and turned to face the long passage. One step above was the platform where the thrones sat.

Twelve women and ten men filed along the sides of the dais on the first two steps, but Haroun al Jawadi and Najib al Makhtoum, carrying the crowns, climbed up and stood one on each side of the Grand Wazir.

Then, with the trumpets sounding triumphantly, the royal couple stepped through the entrance to the Throne Room and moved along the carpet towards the dais, and then up the first three steps. There they knelt.

"Bismullah arrahman arrahim," intoned the old wazir.

In the streets, too, there was silence, as people stood watching the ceremony on the large public television screens that were relics of the old, hated regime. Cars slowed and pulled over, their drivers stopping to listen as the magic of the day translated even over the radio waves.

In the Throne Room, after more than thirty years, the crown was at last placed on the head of an al Jawadi again, and, for the first time in history, on his wife's head. Then the newly crowned sultan and sultana rose, and moving up the last step together, turned and sat on the thrones. The band played the old national anthem, and all the assembled sang so loudly the domed roof seemed to lift.

When the anthem was finished, the palace erupted with cheering.

Then there was the procession of various officials,

who marched to the throne to bend their knee in a sign of allegiance.

And then, as the sultan and sultana still sat side by side, smiling at the assembled and at each other, and the guests sank to their seats, an old woman, who was among the representatives of all the cities and towns of the country, remained standing, and walked forward to the throne. She held up one hand, and one of the sultan's newly appointed Cup Companions leapt forward, but the sultan's hand on his shoulder arrested him.

"Ya Sultan!" cried the old woman in a country patois. "I come to you from the troubled citizens of Skandar!" And then everyone saw that what she held up was a roll of paper. "I bring a petition to the sultan! Please help us in our troubles!" And she bent and placed the little scroll on a step of the dais.

She had not returned to her seat before a man followed her. He, too, held up a paper and begged for it to be read. And then all eyes were turned to the red carpet, for along it were coming others, and still others, until a steady stream of those who had suffered under Ghasib's yoke came forward to offer petitions in the Throne Room, exactly as their forebears had done in times past.

The room was silent with astonished awe.

Many of the petitioners laid their petitions specifically before the Sultana, begging her intercession. And at the end of an hour, there was a mound of papers, some torn and dirty and almost illiterate, some neat and scrupulously written, some in envelopes, some rolled, some flat, some tied with bits of ribbon, before each of the thrones.

The sultan and the sultana sat and waited until everyone who wished to leave a petition had been able to do so. Then, at a signal, the newly appointed Cup Companions of each of them stepped forward and gathered up every petition.

Only then did the sultan and sultana, their golden crowns around their temples, rise from their seats and step down from the dais and walk back along the red carpet, leading the guests to the great banqueting hall where a feast awaited them.

Late that night, when the feasting and celebration were over for the day, Ashraf and Dana were alone again. Dana, her hair spread out around her shoulders, and wearing a tiny slip of silk, lay across the wide bed on her stomach, a neat leather box beside her, reading from a paper.

Ash stood at a window, looking out over the courtyard where his father had played as a child, and his father before him, for so many generations. The great tree that his father had told him about when he was a child, against all expectations, was still there.

It's done, Grandfather, he whispered to the old man. *Now I must hope to be granted the wisdom to do it well.*

"I don't believe it!" Dana muttered, frowning at the paper she was reading. "What does this word mean— *manba?*"

"It means a well."

"I thought so! It's appalling! One of Ghasib's functionaries was insulted by some member of this community, and in revenge he slaughtered some animals and threw the carcasses in their *well*. To deliberately poison it! And they haven't been able to clear it, and for two years they've had to walk miles to the next village to get the water there, and…Ash, what would it take? A crane?"

"We'll have to send an engineer to assess the situation."

Shaking her head, Dana set the petition back in the box, and got to her feet. She approached the window and stood beside him. A full moon was riding high in a cloudless sky. Below, the courtyard was in darkness.

"What are you looking at?" she murmured, as his mood stole over her.

"Do you see that tree out there?"

"That big one?"

He nodded. "My father used to get up inside that tree to hide from his tutors. And none of them ever discovered his hiding place."

She caught her lip between her teeth and smiled. "And it's still there!"

"It's still there."

"You never got a chance to do that," she said softly.

"No."

"Maybe your sons will."

He turned to face her, his hands lifting to her shoulders. She looked fearlessly into his eyes, ready for their shared future. And he knew that she was the wife every man dreams of—a partner for the good times and the bad. Who would face both troubles and successes with the same confident strength.

"Yes," he said, "*insha'Allah,* our sons will. And our daughters, too."

And he drew his wife into his arms and set his mouth on hers.

*   *   *   *   *

THE SHEIKH'S
CHOSEN WIFE

Michelle Reid

Michelle Reid grew up on the southern edges of Manchester, the youngest in a family of five lively children. But now she lives in the beautiful county of Cheshire with her busy executive husband and two grown-up daughters. She loves reading, the ballet, and playing tennis when she gets the chance. She hates cooking, cleaning, and despises ironing! Sleep she can do without and produces some of her best written work during the early hours of the morning.

Don't miss Michelle Reid's new novel,
The Markonos Bride, out in May 2008
from Mills & Boon® Modern™!

CHAPTER ONE

DRESSED to go riding, in knee-length black leather boots, buff pants, a white shirt and a white *gutrah* held to his dark head by a plain black *agal*, Sheikh Hassan ben Khalifa Al-Qadim stepped into his private office and closed the door behind him. In his hand he held a newly delivered letter from England. On his desk lay three more. Walking across the room, he tossed the new letter onto the top of the other three then went to stand by the grilled window, fixing his eyes on a spot beyond the Al-Qadim Oasis, where reclaimed dry scrubland had been turned into miles of lush green fig groves.

Beyond the figs rose the sand-dunes. Majestic and proud, they claimed the horizon with a warning statement. Come any closer with your irrigation and expect retaliation, they said. One serious sandstorm, and years of hard labour could be turned back into arid wasteland.

A sigh eased itself from his body. Hassan knew all about the laws of the desert. He respected its power and its driving passion, its right to be master of its own destiny. And what he would really have liked to do at this very moment was to saddle up his horse, Zandor, then take off for those sand-dunes and allow them to dictate his future for him.

But he knew the idea was pure fantasy. For behind him lay four letters, all of which demanded he make those decisions for himself. And beyond the relative sanctuary of the four walls surrounding him lay a palace in waiting; his father, his half-brother, plus a thousand and one other people, all of whom believed they owned a piece of his so-called destiny.

So Zandor would have to stay in his stable. His beloved sand-dunes would have to wait a while to swallow him up. Making a half-turn, he stared grimly at the letters. Only one had been opened: the first one, which he had tossed aside with the contempt it had deserved. Since then he had left the others sealed on his desk and had tried very hard to ignore them.

But the time for burying his head in the sand was over.

A knock on the door diverted his attention. It would be his most trusted aide, Faysal. Hassan recognised the lightness of the knock. Sure enough the door opened and a short, fine-boned man wearing the traditional white and pale blue robes of their Arabian birthright appeared in its arched aperture, where he paused and bowed his head, waiting to be invited in or told to go.

'Come in, Faysal,' Hassan instructed a trifle impatiently. Sometimes Faysal's rigid adherence to so-called protocol set his teeth on edge.

With another deferential bow, Faysal moved to his master's bidding. Stepping into the room, he closed the door behind him then used some rarely utilised initiative by walking across the room to come to a halt several feet from the desk on the priceless carpet that covered, in part, the expanse of polished blue marble between the desk and the door.

Hassan found himself staring at the carpet. His wife had ordered it to be placed there, claiming the room's spartan appearance invited no one to cross its austere threshold. The fact that this was supposed to be the whole point had made absolutely no difference to Leona. She had simply carried on regardless, bringing many items into the room besides the carpet. Such as the pictures now adorning the walls and the beautiful ceramics and sculptures scattered around, all of which had been produced by gifted artists native to the small Gulf state of Rahman. Hassan had soon found he could no longer lift his eyes without having them settle on an example of local enterprise.

Yet it was towards the only western pieces Leona had brought into the room that his eyes now drifted. The low table and two overstuffed easy chairs had been placed by the other window, where she would insist on making him sit with her several times a day to enjoy the view while they drank tea and talked and touched occasionally as lovers do...

Dragging the *gutrah* from his head with almost angry fingers, Hassan tossed it aside then went to sit down in the chair behind his desk. 'Okay,' he said. 'What have you to tell me?'

'It is not good news, sir.' Faysal began with a warning. 'Sheikh Abdul is entertaining certain...factions at his summer palace. Our man on the inside confirms that the tone of their conversation warrants your most urgent attention.'

Hassan made no comment, but his expression hardened fractionally. 'And my wife?' he asked next.

'The Sheikha still resides in Spain, sir,' Faysal informed him, 'working with her father at the new resort of San Estéban, overseeing the furnishing of several villas about to be released for sale.'

Doing what she did best, Hassan thought grimly—and did not need to glance back at the two stuffed chairs to conjure up a vision of long silken hair the colour of a desert sunset, framing a porcelain smooth face with laughing green eyes and a smile that dared him to complain about her invasion of his private space. 'Trust me,' he could hear her say. 'It is my job to give great empty spaces a little soul and their own heartbeat.'

Well, the heartbeat had gone out of this room when she'd left it, and as for the soul...

Another sigh escaped him. 'How long do you think we have before they make their move?'

The slight tensing in Faysal's stance warned Hassan that he was not going to like what was coming. 'If you will forgive me for saying so, sir,' his aide apologised, 'with Mr Ethan Hayes also residing at her father's property, I would say that the matter has become most seriously urgent indeed.'

Since this was complete news to Hassan it took a moment for the full impact of this information to really sink in. Then he was suddenly on his feet and was swinging tensely away to glare at the sand-dunes again. Was she mad? he was thinking angrily. Did she have a death wish? Was she so indifferent to his feelings that she could behave like this?

Ethan Hayes. His teeth gritted together as an old familiar jealousy began mixing with his anger to form a much more volatile substance. He swung back to face Faysal. 'How long has Mr Hayes been in residence in San Estéban?'

Faysal made a nervous clearing of his throat. 'These seven days past,' he replied.

'And who else knows about this…? Sheikh Abdul?'

'It was discussed,' Faysal confirmed.

With a tight shifting of his long lean body, Hassan returned to his seat. 'Cancel all my appointments for the rest of the month,' he instructed, drawing his appointments diary towards him to begin scoring hard lines through the same busy pages. 'My yacht is berthed at Cadiz. Have it moved to San Estéban. Check that my plane is ready for an immediate take-off and ask Rafiq to come to me.'

The cold quality of the commands did nothing to dilute their grim purpose. 'If asked,' Faysal prompted, 'what reason do I give for your sudden decision to cancel your appointments?'

'I am about to indulge in a much needed holiday cruising the Mediterranean with my nice new toy,' Sheikh Hassan replied, and the bite in his tone made a complete mockery of the words spoken, for they both knew that the next few weeks promised to be no holiday. 'And Faysal…' Hassan stalled his aide as he was about to take his leave '…if anyone so much as whispers the word adultery in the same breath as my wife's name, they will not breathe again—you understand me?'

The other man went perfectly still, recognising the responsibility that was being laid squarely upon him. 'Yes, sir.' He bowed.

Hassan's grim nod was a dismissal. Left alone again, he leaned back in his chair and began frowning while he tried to decide how best to tackle this. His gaze fell on the small stack of letters. Reaching out with long fingers, he drew them towards him, picked out the only envelope with a broken seal and removed the single sheet of paper from inside. The content of the letter he ignored with the same dismissive contempt he had always applied to it. His interest lay only in the telephone number printed beneath the business logo. With an expression that said he resented having his hand forced like this, he took a brief glance at his watch, then was lifting up the telephone, fairly sure that his wife's lawyer would be in his London office at this time of the day.

The ensuing conversation was not a pleasant one, and the following conversation with his father-in-law even less so. He had just replaced the receiver and was frowning darkly over what Victor Frayne had said to him, when another knock sounded at the door. Hard eyes lanced towards it as the door swung open and Rafiq stepped into the room.

Though he was dressed in much the same clothes as Faysal was wearing, there the similarity between the two men ended. For where Faysal was short and thin and annoyingly effacing, Rafiq was a giant of a man who rarely kowtowed to anyone. Hassan warranted only a polite nod of the head, yet he knew Rafiq would willingly die for him if he was called upon to do so.

'Come in, shut the door, then tell me how you would feel about committing a minor piece of treason?' Hassan smoothly intoned.

Below the white *gutrah* a pair of dark eyes glinted. 'Sheikh Abdul?' Rafiq questioned hopefully.

'Unfortunately, no.' Hassan gave a half smile. 'I was in fact referring to my lovely wife, Leona...'

Dressed for the evening in a beaded slip-dress made of gold silk chiffon, Leona stepped into a pair of matching beaded mules then turned to look at herself in the mirror.

Her smooth russet hair had been caught up in a twist, and diamonds sparkled at her ears and throat. Overall, she supposed she looked okay, she decided, giving the thin straps at her shoulders a gentle tug so the dress settled comfortably

over her slender frame. But the weight she had lost during
the last year was most definitely showing, and she could have
chosen a better colour to offset the unnatural paleness of her
skin.

Too late to change, though, she thought with a dismissive
shrug as she turned away from her reflection. Ethan was already waiting for her outside on the terrace. And, anyway,
she wasn't out to impress anyone. She was merely playing
stand-in for her father who had been delayed in London due
to some urgent business with the family lawyer, which had
left her and her father's business partner, Ethan, the only
ones here to represent Hayes-Frayne at tonight's promotional
dinner.

She grimaced as she caught up a matching black silk shawl
and made for her bedroom door. In truth, she would rather
not be going out at all tonight having only arrived back from
San Estéban an hour ago. It had been a long day, and she
had spent most of it melting in a Spanish heatwave because
the air-conditioning system had not been working in the villa
she had been attempting to make ready for viewing. So a
long soak in a warm bath and an early night would have
been her idea of heaven tonight, she thought wryly, as she
went down the stairs to join Ethan.

He was half sitting on the terrace rail with a glass in his
hand, watching the sun go down, but his head turned at her
first step, and his mouth broke into an appreciative smile.

'Ravishing,' he murmured, sliding his lean frame upright.

'Thank you,' she replied. 'You don't look so bad yourself.'

His wry nod accepted the compliment and his grey eyes
sparkled with lazy humour. Dressed in a black dinner suit
and bow tie, he was a tall, dark, very attractive man with an
easy smile and a famous eye for the ladies. Women adored
him and he adored them but, thankfully, that mutual adora-
tion had never raised its ugly head between the two of them.

Leona liked Ethan. She felt comfortable being with him.
He was the Hayes in Hayes-Frayne, architects. Give

Ethan a blank piece of paper and he would create a fifty-storey skyscraper or a whole resort complete with sports clubs, shopping malls and, of course, holiday villas to die for, as with this new resort in San Estéban.

'Drink?' he suggested, already stepping towards the well stocked drinks trolley.

But Leona gave a shake of her head. 'Better not, if you want me to stay awake beyond ten o'clock,' she refused.

'That late? Next you'll be begging me to take you on to an all-night disco after the party.' He was mocking the fact that she was usually safely tucked up in bed by nine o'clock.

'Do you disco?' she asked him curiously.

'Not if I can help it,' he replied, discarding his own glass to come and take the shawl from her hand so he could drape it across her shoulders. 'The best I can offer in the name of dance is a soft shoe shuffle to something very slow, preferably in a darkened room, so that I don't damage my ego by revealing just how bad a shuffler I am.'

'You're such a liar.' Leona smiled. 'I've seen you dance a mean jive, once or twice.'

Ethan pulled a face at the reminder. 'Now you've really made me feel my age,' he complained. 'Next you'll be asking me what it was like to rock in the sixties.'

'You're not that old.' She was still smiling.

'Born in the mid-sixties,' he announced. 'To a free-loving mother who bopped with the best of them.'

'That makes you about the same age as Hass...'

And that was the point where everything died: the light banter, the laughter, the tail end of Hassan's name. Silence fell. Ethan's teasing grey eyes turned very sombre. He knew, of course, how painful this last year had been for her. No one mentioned Hassan's name in her presence, so to hear herself almost say it out loud caused tension to erupt between the both of them.

'It isn't too late to stop this craziness, you know,' Ethan murmured gently.

Her response was to drag in a deep breath and step right away from him. 'I don't want to stop it,' she quietly replied.

'Your heart does.'

'My heart is not making the decisions here.'

'Maybe you should let it.'

'Maybe you should mind your own business!'

Spinning on her slender heels Leona walked away from him to go and stand at the terrace rail, leaving Ethan behind wearing a rueful expression at the severity with which she had just slapped him down.

Out there at sea, the dying sun was throwing up slender fingers of fire into a spectacular vermilion sky. Down the hill below the villa, San Estéban was beginning to twinkle as it came into its own at the exit of the sun. And in between the town and the sun the ocean spread like satin with its brand-new purpose-built harbour already packed with smart sailing crafts of all shapes and sizes.

Up here on the hillside everything was so quiet and still even the cicadas had stopped calling. Leona wished that she could have some of that stillness, put her trembling emotions back where they belonged, under wraps, out of reach from pain and heartache.

Would these vulnerable feelings ever be that far out of reach? she then asked herself, and wasn't surprised to have a heavy sigh whisper from her. The beaded chiffon shawl slipped from her shoulders, prompting Ethan to come and gently lift it back in place again.

'Sorry,' he murmured. 'It wasn't my intention to upset you.'

I do it to myself, Leona thought bleakly. 'I just can't bear to talk about it,' she replied in what was a very rare glimpse at how badly she was hurting.

'Maybe you need to talk,' Ethan suggested.

But she just shook her head, as she consistently had done since she had arrived at her father's London house a year ago, looking emotionally shattered and announcing that her five-year marriage to Sheikh Hassan ben Khalifa Al-Qadim was over. Victor Frayne had tried every which way he could think of to find out what had happened. He'd even travelled out to Rahman to demand answers from Hassan, only to meet the same solid wall of silence he'd come up against with his daughter. The one thing Victor could say with any certainty was that Hassan was faring no better than Leona, though his dauntingly aloof son-in-law was more adept at hiding his emotions than Leona was. 'She sits here in London, he sits in Rahman. They don't talk to each other, never mind to anyone else! Yet you can feel the vibrations bouncing from one to the other across the thousands of miles separating them as if they are communicating by some unique telepathy that runs on pure pain! It's dreadful,' Victor had confided to Ethan. 'Something has to give some time.'

Eventually, it had done. Two months ago Leona had walked unannounced into the office of her family lawyer and had instructed him to begin divorce proceedings, on the grounds of irreconcilable differences. What had prompted her to pick that particular day in that particular month of a very long year no one understood, and Leona herself wasn't prepared to enlighten anyone. But there wasn't a person who knew her who didn't believe it was an action that had caused a trigger reaction, when a week later she had fallen foul of a virulent flu bug that had kept her housebound and bedridden for weeks afterwards.

But when she had recovered, at least she'd come back ready to face the world again. She had agreed to come here to San Estéban, for instance, and utilise her design skills on the completed villas.

She looked better for it too. Still too pale, maybe, but overall she'd begun to live a more normal day to day existence.

Ethan had no wish to send her back into hiding now she had come out of it, so he turned her to face him and pressed a light kiss to her brow. 'Come on,' he said briskly. 'Let's go and party!'

Finding her smile again, Leona nodded her agreement and

tried to appear as though she was looking forward to the evening. As they began to walk back across the terrace she felt a fine tingling at the back of her neck which instinctively warned her that someone was observing them.

The suspicion made her pause and turn to cast a frowning glance over their surroundings. She could see nothing untoward, but wasn't surprised by that. During the years she had lived in an Arab sheikhdom, married to a powerful and very wealthy man, she had grown used to being kept under constant, if very discreet, surveillance.

But that surveillance had been put in place for her own protection. This felt different—sinister. She even shivered.

'Something wrong?' Ethan questioned.

Leona shook her head and began walking again, but her frown stayed in place, because it wasn't the first time she'd experienced the sensation today. The same thing had happened as she'd left the resort site this afternoon, only she'd dismissed it then as her just being silly. She had always suspected that Hassan still kept an eye on her from a distance.

A car and driver had been hired for the evening, and both were waiting in the courtyard for them as they left the house. Having made sure she was comfortably settled, Ethan closed the side door and strode around the car to climb in beside her. As a man she had known for most of her adult life, Ethan was like a very fond cousin whose lean dark sophistication and reputed rakish life made her smile, rather than her heart flutter as other women would do in his company.

He'd never married. 'Never wanted to,' he'd told her once. 'Marriage diverts your energy away from your ambition, and I haven't met the woman for whom I'm prepared to let that happen.'

When she'd told Hassan what Ethan had said, she'd expected him to say something teasing like, May Allah help him when he does, for I know the feeling! But instead he'd looked quite sombre and had said nothing at all. At the time, she'd thought he'd been like that because he'd still been harbouring jealous suspicions about Ethan's feelings for her.

It had been a long time before she'd come to understand that the look had had nothing at all to do with Ethan.

'The Petronades yacht looks pretty impressive.' Ethan's smooth deep voice broke into her thoughts. 'I watched it sail into the harbour tonight while I was waiting for you on the terrace.'

Leandros Petronades was the main investor in San Estéban. He was hosting the party tonight for very exclusive guests whom he had seduced into taking a tour of the new resort, with an invitation to arrive in style on his yacht and enjoy its many luxurious facilities.

'At a guess, I would say it has to be the biggest in the harbour, considering its capacity to sleep so many people,' Leona smiled.

'Actually no, it wasn't,' Ethan replied with a frown. 'There's another yacht tied up that has to be twice the size.'

'The commercial kind?' Leona suggested, aware that the resort was fast becoming the fashionable place to visit.

'Not big enough.' Ethan shook his head. 'It's more likely to belong to one of Petronades' rich cronies. Another heavy investor in the resort, maybe.'

There were enough of them, Leona acknowledged. From being a sleepy little fishing port a few years ago, with the help of some really heavyweight investors San Estéban had grown into a large, custom-built holiday resort, which now sprawled in low-rise, Moorish elegance over the hills surrounding the bay.

So why Hassan's name slid back into her head Leona had no idea. Because Hassan didn't even own a yacht, nor had he ever invested in any of her father's projects, as far as she knew.

Irritated with herself, she turned her attention to what was happening outside the car. On the beach waterfront people strolled, enjoying the light breeze coming off the water.

It was a long time since she could remember strolling anywhere herself with such freedom. Marrying an Arab had brought with it certain restrictions on her freedom, which

were not all due to the necessity of conforming to expectations regarding women. Hassan occupied the august position
of being the eldest son and heir to the small but oil-rich Gulf
state of Rahman. As his wife, Leona had become a member
of Rahman's exclusive hierarchy, which in turn made everything she said or did someone else's property. So she'd
learned very quickly to temper her words, to think twice
before she went anywhere, especially alone. Strolling just for
the sake of just doing it would have been picked upon and
dissected for no other reason than interest's sake, so she had
learned not to do it.

This last year she hadn't gone out much because to be
seen out had drawn too much speculation as to why she was
in London and alone. In Rahman she was known as Sheikh
Hassan's pretty English Sheikha. In London she was known
as the woman who gave up every freedom to marry her
Arabian prince.

A curiosity in other words. Curiosities were blatantly
stared at, and she didn't want to offend Arab sensibilities by
having her failed marriage speculated upon in the British
press, so she'd lived a quiet life.

It was a thought that made Leona smile now, because her
life in Rahman had been far less quiet than it had become
once she'd returned to London.

The car had almost reached the end of the street where the
new harbour was situated. There were several large yachts
moored up—and Leandros Petronades' elegant white-hulled
boat was easy to recognise because it was lit up like a show-
boat for the party. Yet it was the yacht moored next to it that
caught her attention. It was huge, as Ethan had said—twice
the length and twice the height of its neighbour. It was also
shrouded in complete darkness. With its dark-painted hull, it
looked as if it was crouching there like a large sleek cat,
waiting to leap on its next victim.

The car turned and began driving along the top of the
harbour wall taking them towards a pair of wrought iron

gates, which cordoned off the area where the two yachts were tied.

Climbing out of the car, Leona stood looking round while she waited for Ethan to join her. It was even darker here than she had expected it to be, and she felt a distinct chill shiver down her spine when she realised they were going to have to pass the unlit boat to reach the other.

Ethan's hand found her arm. As they walked towards the gates, their car was already turning round to go back the way it had come. The guard manning the gates merely nodded his dark head and let them by without a murmur, then disappeared into the shadows.

'Conscientious chap,' Ethan said dryly.

Leona didn't answer. She was too busy having to fight a sudden attack of nerves that set butterflies fluttering inside her stomach. Okay, she tried to reason, so she hadn't put herself in the social arena much recently, therefore it was natural that she should suffer an attack of nerves tonight.

Yet some other part of her brain was trying to insist that her attack of nerves had nothing to do with the party. It was so dark and so quiet here that even their footsteps seemed to echo with a sinister ring.

Sinister? Picking up on the word, she questioned it impatiently. What was the matter with her? Why was everything sinister all of a sudden? It was a hot night—a beautiful night—she was twenty-nine years old, and about to do what most twenty-nine-year-olds did: party when they got the chance!

'Quite something, hmm?' Ethan remarked as they walked into the shadow of the larger yacht.

But Leona didn't want to look. Despite the tough talking-to she had just given herself, the yacht bothered her. The whole situation was beginning to worry her. She could feel her heart pumping unevenly against her breast, and just about every nerve-end she possessed was suddenly on full alert for no other reason than—

It was then that she heard it—nothing more than a whispering sound in the shadows, but it was enough to make her go perfectly still. So did Ethan. Almost at the same moment the darkness itself seemed to take on a life of its own by shifting and swaying before her eyes.

The tingling sensation on the back of her neck returned with a vengeance. 'Ethan,' she said jerkily. 'I don't think I like this.'

'No,' he answered tersely. 'Neither do I.'

That was the moment when they saw them, first one dark shape, then another, and another, emerging from the shadows until they turned themselves into Arabs wearing dark robes, with darkly sober expressions.

'Oh, dear God,' she breathed. 'What's happening?'

But she already knew the answer. It was a fear she'd had to live with from the day she'd married Hassan. She was British. She had married an Arab who was a very powerful man. The dual publicity her disappearance could generate was in itself worth its weight in gold to political fanatics wanting to make a point.

Something she should have remembered earlier, then the word 'sinister' would have made a lot more sense, she realised, as Ethan's arm pressed her hard up against him.

Further down the harbour wall the lights from the Petronades boat were swinging gently. Here, beneath the shadow of the other, the ring of men was steadily closing in. Her heart began to pound like a hammer drill. Ethan couldn't hold her any closer if he tried, and she could almost taste his tension. He, too, knew exactly what was going to happen.

'Keep calm,' he gritted down at her. 'When I give the word, lose your shoes and run.'

He was going to make a lunge for them and try to break the ring so she could have a small chance to escape. 'No,' she protested, and clutched tightly at his jacket sleeve. 'Don't do it. They might hurt you if you do!'

'Just go, Leona!' he ground back at her, then, with no more warning than that, he was pulling away, and almost in the same movement he threw himself at the two men closest to him.

It was then that all hell broke loose. While Leona stood there frozen in horror watching all three men topple to the ground in a huddle, the rest of the ring leapt into action. Fear for her life sent a surge of adrenaline rushing through her blood. Dry-mouthed, stark-eyed, she was just about to do as Ethan had told her and run, when she heard a hard voice rasp out a command in Arabic. In a state of raw panic she swung round in its direction, expecting someone to be almost upon her, only to find to her confusion that the ring of men had completely bypassed her, leaving her standing here alone with only one other man.

It was at that point that she truly stopped functioning— heart, lungs, her ability to hear what was happening to Ethan—all connections to her brain simply closed down to leave only her eyes in full, wretched focus.

Tall and dark, whip-cord lean, he possessed an aura about him that warned of great physical power lurking beneath the dark robes he was wearing. His skin was the colour of sun-ripened olives, his eyes as black as a midnight sky, and his mouth she saw was thin, straight and utterly unsmiling.

'Hassan.' She breathed his name into the darkness.

The curt bow he offered her came directly from an excess of noble arrogance built into his ancient genes. 'As you see,' Sheikh Hassan smoothly confirmed.

CHAPTER TWO

A BUBBLE of hysteria ballooned in her throat. 'But—why?' she choked in strangled confusion.

Hassan was not given the opportunity to answer before another fracas broke out somewhere behind her. Ethan ground her name out. It was followed by some thuds and scuffles. As she turned on a protesting gasp to go to him, someone else spoke with a grating urgency and Hassan caught her wrist, long brown fingers closing round fleshless skin and bone, to hold her firmly in place.

'Call them off!' she cried out shrilly.

'Be silent,' he returned in a voice like ice.

It shocked her, really shocked her, because never in their years together had he ever used that tone on her. Turning her head, she stared at him in pained astonishment, but Hassan wasn't even looking at her. His attention was fixed on a spot near the gates. With a snap of his fingers his men began scattering like bats on the wing, taking a frighteningly silent Ethan with them.

'Where are they going with him?' Leona demanded anxiously.

Hassan didn't answer. Another man came to stand directly behind her and, glancing up, she found herself gazing into yet another familiar face.

'Rafiq,' she murmured, but that was all she managed to say before Hassan was reclaiming her attention by snaking an arm around her waist and pulling her towards him. Her breasts made contact with solid muscle; her thighs suddenly burned like fire as they felt the unyielding power in his. Her eyes leapt up to clash with his eyes. It was like tumbling into oblivion. He looked so very angry, yet so very—

20

'Shh,' he cautioned. 'It is absolutely imperative that you do exactly as I say. For there is a car coming down the causeway and we cannot afford to have any witnesses.'

'Witnesses to what?' she asked in bewilderment.

There was a pause, a smile that was not quite a smile because it was too cold, too calculating, too—

'Your abduction,' he smoothly informed her.

Standing there in his arms, feeling trapped by a word that sounded totally alien falling from those lips she'd thought she knew so well, Leona released a constricted gasp then was totally silenced.

Car headlights suddenly swung in their direction. Rafiq moved and the next thing that she knew a shroud of black muslin was being thrown over her head. For a split second she couldn't believe what was actually happening! Then Hassan released his grasp so the muslin could unfurl right down to her ankles: she was being shrouded in an *abaya*.

Never had she *ever* been forced to wear such a garment! 'Oh, how could you?' she wrenched out, already trying to drag the *abaya* off again.

Strong arms firmly subdued her efforts. 'Now, you have two choices here, my darling.' Hassan's grim voice sounded close to her ear. 'You can either come quietly, of your own volition, or Rafiq and I will ensure that you do so—understand?'

Understand? Oh, yes, Leona thought painfully, she understood fully that she was being recovered like a lost piece of property! 'I'll never forgive you for this,' she breathed thickly.

His response was to wedge her between himself and Rafiq and then begin hustling her quickly forward. Feeling hot, trapped and blinded by the *abaya*, she had no idea where they were taking her.

Her frightened gasp brought Hassan's hand to cup her elbow. 'Be calm,' he said quietly. 'I am here.'

His reassurance was no assurance to Leona as he began urging her to walk ahead of him. The ground beneath her

feet gave way to something much less substantial. Through
the thin soles of her shoes she could feel a ridged metal
surface, and received a cold sense of some dark space yawn-
ing beneath it.

'What is this?' she questioned shakily.

'The gangway to my yacht,' Hassan replied.

His yacht, she repeated, and thought of the huge dark vessel squatting in the darkness. 'New toy, Hassan?' she hit out
deridingly.

'I knew you would be enchanted,' he returned. 'Watch
your step!' he cautioned sharply when the open toe of her
flimsy shoe caught on one of the metal ridges.

But she couldn't watch her step because the wretched
abaya was in the way! So she tripped, tried to right herself,
felt the slender heel of her shoe twist out from beneath her.
Instinct made her put out a hand in a bid to save herself. But
once again the *abaya* was in the way and, as she tried to
grapple with it, the long loose veil of muslin tangled around
her ankles and she lurched drunkenly forward. The sheer
impetus of the lurch lost Hassan his guiding grip on her arm.
As the sound of her own stifled cry mingled with the rough-
ness of his, Leona knew she hadn't a hope of saving herself.
In the few split seconds it all took to happen, she had a
horrible vision of deep dark water between the boat and the
harbour wall waiting to suck her down, with the wretched
abaya acting as her burial shroud.

Then hard hands were gripping her waist and roughly
righting her; next she was being scooped up and crushed hard
against a familiar chest. She curled into that chest like a
vulnerable child and began shaking all over while she listened to Hassan cursing and swearing beneath his breath as
he carried her, and Rafiq answering with soothing tones from
somewhere ahead.

Onto the yacht, across the deck, Leona could hear doors
being flung wide as they approached. By the time Hassan
decided that it was safe to set her down on her own feet
again, reaction was beginning to set in.

Shock and fright changed to a blistering fury the moment her feet hit the floor. Breaking free, she spun away from him, then began dragging the *abaya* off over her head with angry, shaking fingers. Light replaced darkness, sweet cool air replaced suffocating heat. Tossing the garment to the floor, she swung round to face her two abductors with her green eyes flashing and the rest of her shimmering with an incandescent rage.

Both Hassan and Rafiq stood framed by a glossy wood doorway, studying her with differing expressions. Both wore long black tunics beneath dark blue cloaks cinched in at the waist with wide black sashes. Dark blue *gutrahs* framed their lean dark faces. One neatly bearded, the other clean-shaven and sleek. Both held themselves with an indolent arrogance that was a challenge as they waited to receive her first furious volley.

Her heart flipped over and tumbled to her stomach, her feeling of an impossible-to-fight admiration for these two people, only helping to infuriate her all the more. For who were they—*what* were they—that they believed they had the right to treat her like this?

She began to walk towards them. Her hair had escaped from its twist and was now tumbling like fire over her shoulders, and somewhere along the way she had lost her shawl and shoes. Without the help of her shoes, the two men towered over her, indomitable and proud, dark brown eyes offering no hint of apology.

Her gaze fixed itself somewhere between them, her hands closed into two tightly clenched fists at her side. The air actually stung with an electric charge of anticipation. 'I demand to see Ethan,' she stated very coldly.

It was clearly the last thing either was expecting her to say. Rafiq stiffened infinitesimally, Hassan looked as if she could not have insulted him more if she'd tried.

His eyes narrowed, his mouth grew thin, his handsome sleek features hardened into polished rock. Beneath the dark robes, Leona saw his wide chest expand and remain that way as, with a sharp flick of a hand, he sent Rafiq sweeping out of the room.

As the door closed them in, the sudden silence stifled almost as much as the *abaya* had done. Neither moved, neither spoke for the space of thirty long heart-throbbing seconds, while Hassan stared coldly down at her and she stared at some obscure point near his right shoulder.

Years of loving this one man, she was thinking painfully. Five years of living the dream in a marriage she had believed was so solid that nothing could ever tear it apart. Now she couldn't even bring herself to focus on his face properly in case the feelings she now kept deeply suppressed inside her came surging to the surface and spilled out on a wave of broken-hearted misery. For their marriage was over. They both knew it was over. He should not have done this to her. It hurt so badly that he could treat her this way that she didn't think she was ever going to forgive him for it.

Hassan broke the silence by releasing the breath he had been holding onto. 'In the interests of harmony, I suggest you restrain from mentioning Ethan Hayes in my presence,' he advised, then simply stepped right past her to walk across the room to a polished wood counter which ran the full length of one wall.

As she followed the long, lean, subtle movement of his body through desperately loving eyes, fresh fury leapt up to save her again. 'But who else would I ask about when I've just watched your men beat him up and drag him away?' she threw after him.

'They did not beat him up.' Flicking open a cupboard door, he revealed a fridge stocked with every conceivable form of liquid refreshment.

'They fell on him like a flock of hooligans!'

'They subdued his enthusiasm for a fight.'

'He was defending me!'

'That is my prerogative.'

Her choked laugh at that announcement dropped scorn all

over it. 'Sometimes your arrogance stuns even me!' she informed him scathingly.

The fridge door shut with a thud. 'And your foolish refusal to accept wise advice when it is offered to you stuns me!'

Twisting round, Hassan was suddenly revealing an anger that easily matched her own. His eyes were black, his expression harsh, his mouth snapped into a grim line. In his hand he held a bottle of mineral water which he slammed down on the cabinet top, then he began striding towards her, big and hard and threatening.

'I don't know what's the matter with you,' she burst out bewilderedly. 'Why am I under attack when I haven't done anything?'

'You dare to ask that, when this is the first time we have looked upon each other in a year—yet all you can think about is Ethan Hayes?'

'Ethan isn't your enemy,' she persisted stubbornly.

'No.' Thinly said. Then something happened within his eyes that set her heart shuddering. He came to a stop a bare foot away from her. 'But he is most definitely yours,' he said.

She didn't want him this close and took a step back. 'I don't know what you mean,' she denied.

He closed the gap again. 'A married woman openly living with a man who is not her husband carries a heavy penalty in Rahman.'

'Are you daring to suggest that Ethan and I *sleep* together?' Her eyes went wide with utter affront.

'Do you?'

The question was like a slap to the face. 'No we do not!'

'Prove it,' he challenged.

Surprise had her falling back another step. 'But you know Ethan and I don't have that kind of relationship,' she insisted.

'And, I repeat,' he said, 'prove it.'

Nerve-ends began to fray when she realised he was being serious. 'I can't,' she admitted, then went quite pale when she felt forced to add, 'But you know I wouldn't sleep with him, Hassan. You *know* it,' she emphasised with a painfully thickening tone which placed a different kind of darkness in his eyes.

It came from understanding and pity. And she hated him for that also! Hated and loved and hurt with a power that was worse than any other torture he could inflict.

'Then explain to me, please,' he persisted nonetheless, 'when you openly live beneath the same roof as he does, how I convince my people of this certainty you believe I have in your fidelity?'

'But Ethan and I haven't spent one night alone together in the villa,' she protested. 'My father has always been there with us until he was delayed in London today!'

'Quite.' Hassan nodded. 'Now you understand why you have been snatched from the brink of committing the ultimate sin in the eyes of our people. There,' he said with a dismissive flick of the hand. 'I am your saviour, as is my prerogative.'

With that, and having neatly tied the whole thing off to his own satisfaction, he turned and walked away— Leaving Leona to flounder in his smooth, slick logic and with no ready argument to offer.

'I don't believe you are real sometimes,' she sent shakily after him. 'Did it never occur to you that I didn't want *snatching from the brink*?'

Sarcasm abounding, Hassan merely pulled the *gutrah* from his head and tossed it aside, then returned to the bottle of water. 'It was time,' he said, swinging the fridge door open again. 'You have had long enough to sulk.'

'I wasn't sulking!'

'Whatever,' he dismissed with a shrug, then chose a bottle of white wine and closed the door. 'It was time to bring the impasse to an end.'

Impasse, Leona repeated. He believed their failed marriage was merely stuck in an *impasse*. 'I'm not coming back to you,' she declared, then turned away to pretend to take an

interest in her surroundings, knowing that his grim silence
was denying her the right to choose.

They were enclosed in what she could only presume was
a private stateroom furnished in subtle shades of cream faced
with richly polished rosewood. It was all so beautifully designed that it was almost impossible to see the many doors
built into the walls except for the wood-framed doors they
had entered through. And it was the huge deep-sprung divan
taking pride of place against a silk-lined wall, that told her
exactly what the room's function was.

Although the bed was not what truly captured her attention, but the pair of big easy chairs standing in front of a
low table by a set of closed cream velvet curtains. As her
heart gave a painful twist in recognition, she sent a hand
drifting up to her eyes. Oh, Hassan, she thought despairingly,
don't do this to me...

She had seen the chairs, Hassan noted, studying the way
she was standing there looking like an exquisitely fragile,
perfectly tooled art-deco sculpture in her slender gown of
gold. And he didn't know whether to tell her so or simply
weep at how utterly bereft she looked.

In the end he chose a third option and took a rare sip at
the white wine spritzer he had just prepared for her. The
forbidden alcohol content in the drink might be diluted but
he felt it hit his stomach and almost instantly enter his blood-
stream with an injection of much appreciated fire.

'You've lost weight,' he announced, and watched her chin
come up, watched her wonderful hair slide down her slender
back and her hand drop slowly to her side while she took a
steadying breath before she could bring herself to turn and
face him.

'I've been ill—with the flu,' she answered flatly.

'That was weeks ago,' he dismissed, uncaring that he was
revealing to her just how close an eye he had been keeping
on her from a distance. The fact that she showed no surprise
told him that she had guessed as much anyway. 'After a virus
such as influenza the weight recovery is usually swift.'

'And you would know, of course,' she drawled, mocking the fact that he had not suffered a day's illness in his entire life.

'I know *you*,' he countered, 'and your propensity for slipping into a decline when you are unhappy…'

'I was *ill*, not unhappy.'

'You missed me. I missed you. Why try to deny it?'

'May I have one of those?' Indicating towards the drink he held in his hand was her way of telling him she was going to ignore those kind of comments.

'It is yours,' he explained, and offered the glass out to her.

She looked at the glass, long dusky lashes flickering over her beautiful green eyes when she realised he was going to make her come and get the drink. Would she do it? he wondered curiously. Would she allow herself to come this close, when they both knew she would much rather turn and run?

But his beautiful wife had never been a coward. No matter how she might be feeling inside, he had never known her to run from a challenge. Even when she had left him last year she had done so with courage, not cowardice. And she did not let him down now as her silk stockinged feet began to tread the cream carpet until she was in reach of the glass.

'Thank you.' The wine spritzer was taken from him and lifted to her mouth. She sipped without knowing she had been offered the glass so she would place her lips where his lips had been.

Her pale throat moved as she swallowed; her lips came away from the glass wearing a seductively alluring wine glossed bloom. He watched her smother a sigh, watched her look anywhere but directly at him, was aware that she had not looked him in the face since removing the *abaya*, just as she had stopped looking at him weeks before she left Rahman. And he had to suppress his own sigh as he felt muscles tighten all over his body in his desire to reach out, draw her close and make her look at him!

But this was not the time to play the demanding husband. She would reject him as she had rejected him many times a year ago. What hurt him the most about remembering those bleak interludes was not his own angry frustration but the grim knowledge that it had been herself she had been denying.

'Was the Petronades yacht party an elaborate set-up?' she asked suddenly.

A brief smile stretched his mouth, and it was a very self-mocking smile because he had truly believed she was as concentrated on his close physical presence as he was on hers. But, no. As always, Leona's mind worked in ways that continually managed to surprise him.

'The party was genuine.' He answered the question. 'Your father's sudden inability to get here in time to attend it was not.'

At least his honesty almost earned him a direct glance of frowning puzzlement before she managed to divert it to his right ear. 'But you've just finished telling me that I was snatched because my father was—'

'I know,' he cut in, not needing to hear her explain what he already knew—which was that this whole thing had been very carefully set up and co-ordinated with her father's assistance. 'There are many reasons why you are standing here with me right now, my darling,' he murmured gently. 'Most of which can wait for another time to go into.'

The *my darling* sent her back a defensive step. The realisation that her own father had plotted against her darkened her lovely eyes. 'Tell me now,' she insisted.

But Hassan just shook his head. 'Now is for me,' he informed her softly. 'Now is my moment to bask in the fact that you are back where you belong.'

It was really a bit of bad timing that her feet should use that particular moment to tread on the discarded *abaya*, he supposed, watching as she looked down, saw, then grew angry all over again.

'By abduction?' Her chin came up, contempt shimmering along her finely shaped bones. 'By plots and counter-plots and by removing a woman's right to decide for herself?'

He grimaced at her very accurate description. 'We are by nature a romantic people,' he defended. 'We love drama and poetry and tragic tales of star-crossed lovers who lose each other and travel the caverns of hell in their quest to find their way back together again.'

He saw the tears. He had said too much. Reaching out, he caught the glass just before it slipped from her nerveless fingers. 'Our marriage is a tragedy,' she told him thickly.

'No,' he denied, putting the hapless glass aside. 'You merely insist on turning it into one.'

'Because I hate everything you stand for!'

'But you cannot make yourself hate the man,' he added, undisturbed by her denunciation.

Leona began to back away because there was something seriously threatening about the sudden glow she caught in his eyes. 'I left you, remember?'

'Then sent me letters at regular intervals to make sure I remembered you,' he drawled.

'Letters to tell you I want a divorce!' she cried.

'The content of the letters came second to their true purpose.' He smiled. 'One every two weeks over the last two months. I found them most comforting.'

'Gosh, you are so conceited it's a wonder you didn't marry yourself!'

'Such insults.' He sighed.

'Will you stop stalking me as if I am a hunted animal?' she cried.

'Stop backing away like one.'

'I do not want to stay married to you.' She stated it bluntly.

'And I am not prepared to let you go. There,' he said. 'We have reached another impasse. Which one of us is going to win the higher ground this time, do you think?'

Looking at him standing there, arrogant and proud yet so much her kind of man that he made her legs go weak, Leona knew exactly which one of them possessed the higher ground. Which was also why she had to keep him at arm's length at all costs. He could fell her in seconds, because he was right; she didn't hate him, she adored him. And that scared her so much that when his hand came up, long fingertips brushing gently across her trembling mouth, she almost fainted on the sensation that shot from her lips to toe tips.

She pulled right away. His eyebrow arched. It mocked and challenged as he responded by curling the hand around her nape.

'Stop it,' she said, and lifted up her hand to use it as a brace against his chest.

Beneath dark blue cotton she discovered a silk-smooth, hard-packed body pulsing with heat and an all-too-familiar masculine potency. Her mouth went dry; she tried to breathe and found that she couldn't. Helplessly she lifted her eyes up to meet with his.

'Seeing me now, hmm?' he softly taunted. 'Seeing this man with these eyes you like to drown in, and this nose you like to call dreadful but usually have trouble from stopping your fingers from stroking? And let us not forget this mouth you so like to feel crushed hotly against your own delightful mouth.'

'Don't you dare!' she protested, seeing what was coming and already beginning to shake all over at the terrifying prospect of him finding out what a weak-willed coward she was.

'Why not?' he countered, offering her one of his lazily sensual, knowing smiles that said he knew better than she did what she really wanted—and he began to lower his dark head.

'Tell me first.' Sheer desperation made her fly into impulsive speech. 'If I am here on this beautiful yacht that belongs to you—is there another yacht just like it out there somewhere where your second wife awaits her turn?'

In the sudden suffocating silence that fell between them Leona found herself holding her breath as she watched his face pale to a frightening stillness. For this was provocation of the worst kind to an Arab and her heart began pounding madly because she just didn't know how he was going to respond. Hassan possessed a shocking temper, though he had never unleashed it on her. But now, as she stood here with her fingers still pressed against his breastbone, she could feel the danger in him—could almost taste her own fear as she waited to see how he was going to respond.

What he did was to take a step back from her. Cold, aloof, he changed into the untouchable prince in the single blink of an ebony eyelash. 'Are you daring to imply that I could be guilty of treating my wives unequally?' he responded.

In the interim wave of silence that followed, Leona stared at him through eyes that had stopped seeing anything as his reply rocked the very axis she stood upon. She knew she had prompted it but she still had not expected it, and now she found she couldn't breathe, couldn't even move as fine cracks began to appear in her defences.

'You actually went and did it, and married again,' she whispered, then completely shattered. Emotionally, physically, she felt herself fragment into a thousand broken pieces beneath his stone-cold, cruel gaze.

Hassan didn't see it coming. He should have done, he knew that, but he had been too angry to see anything but his own affronted pride. So when she turned and ran he didn't expect it. By the time he had pulled his wits together enough to go after her Leona was already flying through the door on a flood of tears.

The tears blinded what was ahead of her, the *abaya* having prevented her from taking stock of her surroundings as they'd arrived. Hassan heard Rafiq call out a warning, reached the door as Leona's cry curdled the very air surrounding them and she began to fall.

What he had managed to prevent by the skin of his teeth only a half-hour before now replayed itself before his helpless eyes. Only it was not the dark waters of the Mediterranean she fell into but the sea of cream carpet that ran from room to room and down a wide flight of three shallow stairs that led down into the yacht's main foyer.

CHAPTER THREE

CURSING and swearing in seething silence, Hassan prowled three sides of the bed like a caged tiger while the yacht's Spanish medic checked her over.

'No bones broken, as far as I can tell,' the man said. 'No obvious blow to the head.'

'Then why is she unconscious?' he growled out furiously.

'Shock—winded,' the medic suggested, gently laying aside a frighteningly limp hand. 'It has only been a few minutes, sir.'

But a few minutes was a lifetime when you felt so guilty you wished it was yourself lying there, Hassan thought harshly.

'A cool compress would be a help—'

A cool compress. 'Rafiq.' The click of his fingers meant the job would be done.

The sharp sound made Leona flinch. On a single, lithe leap Hassan was suddenly stretched out across the bed and leaning over her. The medic drew back; Rafiq paused in his step.

'Open your eyes.' Hassan turned her face towards him with a decidedly unsteady hand.

Her eyes fluttered open to stare up at him blankly. 'What happened?' she mumbled.

'You fell down some stairs,' he gritted. 'Now tell me where you hurt.'

A frown began to pucker her smooth brow as she tried to remember.

'Concentrate,' he rasped, diverting her mind away from what had happened. 'Do you hurt anywhere?'

She closed her eyes again, and he watched her make a mental inventory of herself then give a small shake of her head. 'I think I'm okay.' She opened her eyes again, looked directly into his, saw his concern, his anguish, the burning fires of guilt—and then she remembered *why* she'd fallen.

Aching tears welled up again. From coldly plunging his imaginary knife into her breast, he now felt it enter his own. 'You really went and did it,' she whispered.

'No, I did not,' he denied. 'Get out,' he told their two witnesses.

The room emptied like water down a drain, leaving them alone again, confronting each other again. It was dangerous. He wanted to kiss her so badly he could hardly breathe. She was his. He was hers! They should not be in this warring situation!

'No—remain still!' he commanded when she attempted to move. 'Don't even breathe unless you have to do so! Why are females so *stupid*?' he bit out like a curse. 'You insult me with your suspicions. You goad me into a response, and when it is not the one you want to hear you slay me with your pain!'

'I didn't mean to fall down the stairs,' she pointed out.

'I wasn't talking about the fall!' he bit out, then glared down into her confused, hurt, vulnerable eyes for a split second longer. 'Oh, Allah give me strength,' he gritted, and gave in to himself and took her trembling mouth by storm.

If he had kissed her in any other way Leona would have fought him with her very last breath. But she liked the storm; she *needed* the storm so she could allow herself to be swept away. Plus he was trembling, and she liked that too. Liked to know that she still had the power to reduce the prince in him to this vulnerable mass of smashed emotion.

And she'd missed him. She'd missed feeling his length lying alongside her length, had missed the weight of his thighs pressing down on her own. She'd missed his kiss, hungry, urgent, insistent…wanting. Like a banquet after a year of long, hard fasting, she fed greedily on every deep, dark, sensual delight. Lips, teeth, tongue, taste. She reached for his chest, felt the strong beat of his heart as she glided her palms beneath the fabric of his top robe where only the thin cotton of his tunic came between them and tightly muscled, satin-smooth flesh. When she reached his shoulders her fingers curled themselves into tightly padded muscle then stayed there, inviting him to take what he liked.

He took her breasts, stroking and shaping before moving on to follow the slender curve of her body. Long fingers claimed her hips, then drew her against the force of his. Fire bloomed in her belly, for this was her man, the love of her life. She would never, ever, find herself another. What he touched belonged to him. What he desired he could have.

What he did was bring a cruelly abrupt end to it by rising in a single fluid movement to land on his feet beside the bed, leaving her to flounder on the hard rocks of rejection while he stood there with his back to her, fighting a savage battle with himself.

'Why?' she breathed in thick confusion.

'We are not animals,' he ground back. 'We have issues to deal with that must preclude the hungry coupling at which we already know we both excel.'

It served as a dash of water in her face; and he certainly possessed good aim, Leona noted as she came back to reality with a shivering gasp. 'What issues?' she challenged cynically. 'The issue of what we have left besides the excellent sex?'

He didn't answer. Instead he made one of her eyebrows arch as he snatched up her spritzer and grimly downed the lot. There was a man at war with himself as well as with her, Leona realised, knowing Hassan hardly ever touched alcohol, and only then when he was under real stress.

Sitting up, she was aware of a few aches and bruises as she gingerly slid her feet to the floor. 'I want to go home,' she announced.

'This is home,' he replied. 'For the next few weeks, anyway.'

Few weeks? Coming just as gingerly to her feet, Leona stared at his rigid back—which was just another sign that

Hassan was not functioning to his usual standards, because no Arab worthy of the race would deliberately set his back to anyone. It was an insult of the worst kind.

Though she had seen his back a lot during those few months before she'd eventually left him, Leona recalled with a familiar sinking feeling inside. Not because he had wished to insult her, she acknowledged, but because he had refused to face what they had both known was happening to their marriage. In the end, she had taken the initiative away from him.

'Where are my shoes?'

The surprisingly neutral question managed to bring him swinging round to glance at her feet. 'Rafiq has them.'

Dear Rafiq, Leona thought wryly, Hassan's ever-loyal partner in crime. Rafiq was an Al-Qadim. A man who had attended the same schools, the same universities, the same everything as Hassan had done. Equals in many ways, prince and lowly servant in others. It was a complicated relationship that wound around the status of birth and the ranks of power.

'Perhaps you would be kind enough to ask him to give them back to me.' Even she knew you didn't *command* Rafiq to do anything. He was a law unto himself—and Hassan. Rafiq was a maverick. A man of the desert, yet not born of the desert; fiercely proud, fiercely protective of his right to be master of his own decisions.

'For what purpose?'

Leona's chin came up, recognising the challenge in his tone. She offered him a cool, clear look. 'I am not staying here, Hassan,' she told him flatly. 'Even if I have to book into a hotel in San Estéban to protect your dignity, I am leaving this boat now, tonight.'

His expression grew curious, a slight smile touched his mouth. 'Strong swimmer, are you?' he questioned lazily.

It took a few moments for his taunt to truly sink in, then she was moving, darting across the room and winding her way between the two strategically placed chairs and the accompanying table to reach for the curtains. Beyond the glass, all she could see was inky darkness. Maybe she was on the seaward side of the boat, she told herself in an effort to calm the sudden sting of alarm that slid down her spine.

Hassan quickly disabused her of that frail hope. 'We left San Estéban minutes after we boarded.'

It was only then that she felt it: just the softest hint of a vibration beneath the soles of her feet that told of smooth and silently running engines. This truly was an abduction, she finally accepted, and turned slowly back round to face him.

'Why?' she breathed.

It was like a replay of what had already gone before, only this time it was serious—more serious than Leona had even begun to imagine. For she knew this man—knew he was not given to flights of impulse just for the hell of it. Everything he did had to have a reason, and was always preceded by meticulous planning which took time he would not waste, and effort he would not move unless he felt he absolutely had to do.

Hassan's small sigh conveyed that he too knew that this was where the prevarication ended. 'There are problems at home,' he informed her soberly. 'My father's health is failing.'

His father... Anger swiftly converted itself into anxious concern for her father-in-law. Sheikh Khalifa had been frail in health for as long as she had known him. Hassan doted on him and devoted most of his energy to relieving his father of the burdens of rule, making sure he had the best medical attention available and refusing to believe that one day his father would not be there. So, if Hassan was using words like 'failing', then the old man's health must indeed be grave.

'What happened?' She began to walk towards him. 'I thought the last treatment was—'

'Your interest is a little too late in coming,' Hassan cut in, and with a flick of a hand halted her steps. 'For I don't recall you showing any concern about what it would do to his health when you left a year ago.'

That wasn't fair, and Leona blinked as his words pricked a tender part of her. Sheikh Khalifa was a good man—a kind man. They had become strong, close friends while she had lived at the palace. 'He understood why I felt I needed to leave,' she responded painfully.

You think so? Hassan's cynical expression derided. 'Well, I did not,' he said out loud. 'But, since you decided it was the right thing for you to do, I now have a serious problem on my hands. For I am, in effect, deemed weak for allowing my wife to walk away from me, and my critics are making rumbling noises about the stability of the country if I do not display some leadership.'

'So you decided to show that leadership by abducting me, then dragging me back to Rahman?' Her thick laugh poured scorn over that suggestion, because they both knew taking her back home had to be the worst thing Hassan could possibly do to prove that particular point.

'You would prefer that I take this second wife who makes you flee in pain when the subject appears in front of you?'

'She is what you need, not me.' It almost choked her to say the words. But they were dealing with the truth here, painful though that truth may be. And the truth was that she was no longer the right wife for the heir to a sheikhdom.

'I have the wife I want,' he answered grimly.

'But not the wife you *need*, Hassan!' she countered wretchedly.

His eyes flicked up to clash with her eyes. 'Is that your way of telling me that you no longer love me?' he challenged.

Oh, dear God. Lifting a trembling hand up to cover her eyes, Leona gave a shake of her head in refusal to answer. Without warning Hassan was suddenly moving at speed down the length of the room.

'Answer me!' he insisted when he came to a stop in front of her.

Swallowing on a lump of tears, Leona turned her face away. 'Yes,' she whispered.

His sudden grip on her hand dragged it from her eyes. 'To my face,' he instructed, 'You will tell me this to my face!'

Her head whipped up, tear darkened eyes fixing painfully on burning black. 'Don't—' she pleaded.

But he was not going to give in. He was pale and he was hurt and he was furiously angry. 'I want to hear you state that you feel no love for me,' he persisted. 'I want you to tell that wicked lie to my face. And then I want to hear you beg forgiveness when I prove to you otherwise! Do you understand, Leona?'

'All right! So, I love you! Does that make it all okay?' she cried out. 'I love you but I will not stay married to you! I will *not* watch you ruin your life because of me!'

There—it was out. The bitter truth. On voicing it, she broke free and reeled away, hurting so much it was almost impossible to breathe. 'And your life?' he persisted relentlessly. 'What happens to it while you play the sacrificial lamb for mine?'

'I'll get by,' she said, trying to walk on legs that were shaking so badly she wasn't sure if she was going to fall down.

'You'll marry again?'

She shuddered and didn't reply.

'Take lovers in an attempt to supplant me?'

Harsh and cruel though he sounded, she could hear his anguish. 'I need no one,' she whispered.

'Then you mean to spend the rest of your life watching me produce progeny with this second wife I am to take?'

'Oh, dear heaven.' She swung around. 'What are you trying to do to me?' she choked out tormentedly.

'Make you see,' he gritted. 'Make you open your eyes and *see* what it is you are condemning us both to.'

'But I'm not condemning you to anything! I am giving you my blessing to do what you want with your life!'

If she'd offered to give him a whole harem he could not have been more infuriated. His face became a map of hard angles. 'Then I will take what I want!' It was a declaration of intent that propelled him across the space between them. Before Leona knew what was coming she was locked in his arms and being lifted until their eyes were level. Startled green irises locked with burning black passion. He gave her one small second to read their message before he was kissing her furiously. Shocked out of one kind of torment, she found herself flung into the middle of another—because once again she had no will to fight. She even released a protesting groan when her feet found solid ground again and he broke the urgent kiss.

Her lips felt hot, and pulsed with such a telling fullness that she had to lick them to try and cool them down. His breath left his body on a hiss that brought her eyes flickering dazedly up to his. Thick dark lashes rested over ebony eyes that were fixed on the moist pink tip of her tongue. A slither of excitement skittered right down the front of her. Her breasts grew tight, her abdomen warming at the prospect of what all of this meant.

Making love. Feeling him deep inside her. No excuses, no drawing back this time. She only had to look at Hassan to know this was it. He was about to stake his claim on what belonged to him.

'You will regret this later,' she warned unsteadily, because she knew how his passions and his conscience did not always walk in tandem—especially not where she was concerned.

'Are you denying me?' he threw back in a voice that said he was interested in the answer, but only out of curiosity.

Well, Leona asked herself, are you?

The answer was no, she was not denying him anything he wanted to take from her tonight. Tomorrow was another day, another war, another set of agonising conflicts. Reaching up, she touched a gentle finger to his mouth, drew its shape, softened the tension out of it, then sighed, went up on tiptoe and gently joined their mouths.

His hands found the slender frame of her hips and drew her against him; her hands lifted higher to link around his neck so her fingers could slide sensually into his silk dark hair. It was an embrace that sank them into a long deep loving. Her dress fell away, slithering down her body on a pleasurable whisper of silk against flesh. Beneath she wore a dark gold lace bra, matching high-leg briefs and lace-topped stockings. Hassan discovered all of this with the sensual stroke of long fingers. He knew each pleasure point, the quality of each little gasp she breathed into his mouth. When her bra fell away, she sighed and pressed herself against him; when his fingers slid beneath the briefs to cup her bottom she allowed him to ease her into closer contact. They knew each other, *loved* each other—cared so very deeply about each other. Fight they might do—often. They might have insurmountable problems. But nothing took away the love and caring. It was there, as much part of them as the life-giving oxygen they took into their lungs.

'You want me,' he declared.

'I've always wanted you,' she sadly replied.

'I am your other half.'

And I am your broken one, Leona thought, releasing an achingly melancholy sigh.

Maybe he knew what she was thinking, because his mouth took burning possession that gave no more room to think at all. It came as an unwelcome break when he lowered her down onto the bed then straightened, taking her briefs with him. Her love-flooded eyes watched his eyes roam over her. He was no longer being driven by his inner devils, she realised as she watched him removing his own clothing. Her compliance had neutralised the compelling need to stake his claim.

So she watched him follow her every movement as she made a sensual love-play out of removing her stockings from her long slender legs. His dark robe landed on the floor on top of her clothing; the tunic eventually went the same way. Beneath waited a desert-bronzed silk-smooth torso, with a muscled structure that set her green eyes glowing with pleasure and made her fingers itch to touch. Those muscles rippled and flexed as he reached down to grasp the only piece of clothing he had left to remove. The black shorts trailed away from a sexual force that set her feminine counterpart pulsing with anticipation.

He knew what was happening, smiled a half-smile, then came to lean over her, lowering his raven head to place a kiss there that was really a claim of ownership. She breathed out a shivering breath of pleasure and he was there to claim that also. Then she had all of him covering her. It was the sweetest feeling she had ever experienced. He was her Arabian lover. The man she had seen across a crowded room long years ago. And she had never seen another man clearly since.

He seduced her mouth, he seduced her body, he seduced her into seducing him. When it all became too much without deeper contact, he eased himself between her thighs and slowly joined them.

Her responsive groan made him pause. 'What?' he questioned anxiously.

'I've missed you so much.' She sighed the words out helplessly.

It was a catalyst that sent him toppling. He staked his claim on those few emotive words with every driving thrust. She died a little. It was strange how she did that, she found herself thinking as the pleasure began to run like liquid fire. They came as one, within the grip of hard, gasping shudders and afterwards lay still, locked together, as their bodies went through the pleasurable throes of settling back down again.

Then nothing moved, not their bodies nor even their quiet breathing. The silence came—pure, numbing, unbreakable silence.

Why?

Because it had all been so beautiful but also so very empty. And nothing was ever going to change that.

Hassan moved first, levering himself away to land on his feet by the bed. He didn't even spare her a glance as he walked away. Sensational naked, smooth and sleek, he touched a finger to the wall and a cleverly concealed door sprung open. As he stepped through it Leona caught a glimpse of white tiling and realised it was a bathroom. Then the door closed, shutting him in and her completely out.

Closing her eyes, she lifted an arm up to cover them, and pressed her lips together to stop them from trembling on the tears she was having to fight. For this was not a new situation she was dealing with here. It had happened before—often— and was just one of the many reasons why she had left him in the end. The pain had been too great to go on taking it time after time. His pain, her pain—she had never been able to distinguish where one ended and the other began. The only difference here tonight was that she'd somehow managed to let herself forget that, until this cold, solitary moment.

Hassan stood beneath the pulsing jet of the power shower and wanted to hit something so badly that he had to brace his hands against the tiles and lock every muscle to keep the murderous feeling in. His body was replete but his heart was grinding against his ribcage with a frustration that nothing could cure.

Silence. He hated that silence. He hated knowing he had nothing worth saying with which to fill it in. And he still had to go back in there and face it. Face the dragging sense of his own helplessness and—worse—he had to face hers.

His wife. His woman. The other half of him. Head lowered so the water sluiced onto his shoulders and down his back, he tried to predict what her next move was going to be, and came up with only one grim answer. She was not going to stay. He could bully her as much as he liked, but in the end she was still going to walk away from him unless he could come up with something important enough to make her stay.

Maybe he should have used more of his father's illness, he told himself. A man she loved, a man she'd used to spend hours of every day with, talking, playing board games or just quietly reading to him when he was too weak to enjoy anything else.

But his father had not been enough to make her want to

stay the last time. The old fool had given her his blessing, had missed her terribly, yet even on the day he'd gone to see him before he left the palace he had still maintained that Leona had had to do what she'd believed was right.

So who was in the wrong here? Him for wanting to spend his life with one particular woman, or Leona for wanting to do what was right?

He hated that phrase, *doing what was right*. It reeked of duty at the expense of everything: duty to his family, duty to his country, duty to produce the next Al-Qadim son and heir.

Well, I don't need a son. I don't need a second wife to produce one for me like some specially selected brood mare! I need a beautiful red-haired creature who makes my heart ache each time I look at her. I *don't* need to see that glazed look of emptiness she wears after we make love!

On a sigh he turned round, swapped braced hands for braced shoulders against the shower wall. The water hit his face and stopped him breathing. He didn't care if he never breathed again—until instinct took over from grim stubbornness and forced him to move again.

Coming out of the bathroom a few minutes later, he had to scan the room before he spotted her sitting curled up in one of the chairs. She had opened the curtains and was just sitting there staring out, with her wonderful hair gleaming hot against the pale damask upholstery. She had wrapped herself in a swathe of white and a glance at the tumbled bed told him she had dragged free the sheet of Egyptian cotton to wear.

His gaze dropped to the floor by the bed, where their clothes still lay in an intimate huddle that was a lot more honest than the two of them were with each other.

'Find out how Ethan is.'

The sound of her voice brought his attention back to her. She hadn't moved, had not turned to look at him, and the demand spoke volumes as to what was really being said. Barter and exchange. She had given him more of herself than she had intended to do; now she wanted something back by return.

Without a word he crossed to the internal telephone and found out what she wanted to know, ordered some food to be sent in to them, then strode across the room to sit down in the chair next to hers. 'He caught an accidental blow to the jaw which knocked him out for a minute or two, but he is fine now,' he assured her. 'And is dining with Rafiq as we speak.'

'So he wasn't part of this great plan of abduction you plotted with my father.' It wasn't a question, it was a sign of relief.

'I am devious and underhand on occasion but not quite that devious and underhand,' he countered dryly.

Her chin was resting on her bent knees, but she turned her head to look at him through dark, dark eyes. Her hair flowed across her white-swathed shoulders, and her soft mouth looked vulnerable enough to conquer in one smooth swoop. His body quickened, temptation clawing across flesh hidden beneath his short robe of sand-coloured silk.

'Convincing my own father to plot against me wasn't devious or underhand?' she questioned.

'He was relieved I was ready to break the deadlock,' he informed her. 'He wished me well, then offered me all the help he could give.'

Her lack of comment was one in itself. Her following sigh punctuated it. She was seeing betrayal from her own father, but it just was not true. 'You knew he worried about you,' he inserted huskily. 'Yet you didn't tell him why you left me, did you?'

The remark lost him contact with her eyes as she turned them frontward again, and the way she stared out into the inky blackness beyond the window closed up his throat, because he knew what she was really seeing as she looked out there.

'Coming to terms with being a failure is not something I wanted to share with anyone,' she murmured dully.

'You are not a failure,' he denied.

'I am infertile!' She flashed out the one word neither of them wanted to hear.

It launched Hassan to his feet on a surge of anger. 'You are not infertile!' he ground out harshly. 'That is not what the doctors said, and you know it is not!'

'Will you stop hiding from it?' she cried, scrambling to her feet to stand facing him, with her face as white as the sheet she clutched around her and her eyes as black as the darkness outside. 'I have one defunct ovary and the other one ovulates only when it feels like it!' She spelt it out for him.

'Which does not add up to infertility,' he countered forcefully.

'After all of these years of nothing, you can still bring yourself to say that?'

She was staring up at him as if he was deliberately trying to hurt her. And, because he had no answer to that final charge, he had to ask himself if that had been his subconscious intention. The last year had been hell to live through and the year preceding only marginally better. Married life had become a place in which they'd walked with the darkness of disappointment shadowing their past and future. In the end, Leona had not been able to take it any more so she'd left him. If she wanted to know what failure really felt like then she should have trodden in his shoes as he'd battled with his own failure to relieve this woman he loved of the heavy burden she was forced to carry.

'We will try other methods of conception,' he stated grimly.

If it was possible her face went even whiter. 'My eggs harvested like grains of wheat and your son conceived in a test tube? Your people would never forgive me for putting you through such an indignity, and those who keep the Al-Qadim family in power will view the whole process with deep suspicion.'

Her voice had begun to wobble. His own throat closed on

the need to swallow, because she was right, though he did not want her to be. For she was talking about the old ones, those tribal leaders of the desert who really maintained the balance of power in Rahman. They lived by the old ways and regarded anything remotely modern as necessary evil to be embraced only if all other sources had been exhausted. Hassan had taken a big risk when he'd married a western woman. The old ones had surprised him by deciding to see his decision to do so as a sign of strength. But that had been the only concession they had offered him with regard to his choice of wife. For why go to such extremes to father a son he could conceive as easily by taking a second wife?

Which was why this subject had always been so sensitive, and why Leona suddenly shook her head and said, 'Oh, why did you have to bring me back here?' Then she turned and walked quickly away from him, making unerringly for the bathroom he had so recently used for the same purpose—to be alone with her pain.

CHAPTER FOUR

Two hours, Leona noticed, as she removed her slender gold watch from her wrist with badly trembling fingers and laid it on the marble surface along with the diamonds from her ears and throat. Two hours together and already they were tearing each other to pieces.

On a sigh she swivelled round to sink down onto the toilet seat and stare dully at her surroundings. White. Everything was white. White-tiled walls and floor, white ceramics—even the sheet she had discarded lay in a soft white heap on the floor. The room needed a bit of colour to add some—

She stopped herself right there, closing her eyes on the knowledge that she had slipped into professional mode and knowing she had done it to escape from what she should really be thinking about.

This situation, this mad, foolish, heart-flaying situation, which was also so bitter-sweet and special. She didn't know whether to laugh at Hassan's outrageous method of bringing them together, or sob at the unnecessary agony he was causing the both of them.

In the end she did both, released a laugh that turned into a sob and buried the sound in her hands. Each look, each touch, was an act of love that bound them together. Each word, each thought, was an act of pain that tore them apart at the seams.

Then she remembered his face when he had made the ultimate sacrifice. Chin up, face carved, mouth so flat it was hardly a mouth any more. When the man had had to turn himself into a prince before he could utter the words, 'We will try other methods of conception,' she had known they had nothing left to fight for.

What was she supposed to have done? Made the reciprocal sacrifice to their love and offered to remain his first wife while he took a second? She just could not do it, could not live with the agony of knowing that when he wasn't in her bed he would be lying in another. The very idea was enough to set her insides curling up in pained dismay while her covered eyes caught nightmare visions of him trying to be fair, trying to pretend it wasn't really happening, that he wasn't over the moon when the new wife conceived his first child. How long after that before his love began to shift from her to this other woman with whom he could relax—enjoy her without feeling pain every time he looked at her?

'No,' she whispered. 'Stop it.' She began to shiver. It just wasn't even an option, so she must stop thinking about it! He knew that—he *knew it*! It was why he had taunted her with the suggestion earlier. He had been angry and had gone for the jugular and had enjoyed watching her die in front of him! It had always been like this: exploding flashes of anger and frustration, followed by wild leaps into sensual forgetfulness, followed by the low-of-low moments when neither could even look at the other because the empty truth was always still waiting there for them to re-emerge.

Empty.

On a groan she stood up, and groaned again as tiny muscles all over her body protested at being forced into movement. The fall, the lovemaking, or just the sheer stress of it all? she wondered, then wearily supposed it was a combination of all three.

So why do it? Why put them both back into a situation they had played so many times before it was wretched? Or was that it? she then thought on a sudden chill that shot down her backbone. Had he needed to play out the scene this one last time before he could finally accept that their marriage was over?

Sick. She felt sick. On trembling legs she headed quickly for the shower cubicle and switched the jet on so water sluiced over her body. Duty. It was all down to duty. His

duty to produce an heir, her duty to let him. With any other
man the love would be enough; those *other methods of conception* would be made bearable by the strength of that love.
But she'd fallen in love with a prince not a man. And the
prince had fallen in love with a barren woman.

Barren. How ugly that word was. How cold and bitter and
horribly cheap. For there was nothing barren about the way
she was feeling, nor did those feelings come cheap. They
cost her a part of herself each time she experienced them.
Like now, as they ate away at her insides until it was all she
could do to slide down into a pathetic huddle in the corner
of the shower cubicle and wait for it all to recede.

Where was she? What was she doing in there? She had been
shut inside the bathroom for half an hour, and with a glance
at his watch, Hassan continued to pace the floor on the vow
that if she didn't come out in two minutes he was going in
there after her.

None of this—*none* of it—was going the way he had
planned it. How had he managed to trick himself into diluting
just how deep their emotions ran, how painful the whole
thing was going to be? He hit his brow with the palm of his
hand, then uttered a few choice curses at his arrogant belief
that all he'd needed to do was hook her up and haul her back
in for the rest to fall into place around them.

All he'd wanted to do was make sure she was safe, back
here where she belonged, no matter what the problems. So
instead he'd scared the life out of her, almost lost her to the
depths of the ocean, fought like the devil over issues that
were so old they did not need raking over! He'd even lied
to score points, had watched her run in a flood of tears,
watched her fly through the air down a set of stairs he now
wished had never been put there. Shocked, winded and dazed
by the whole crazy situation, he had then committed his
worst sin and had ravished her. Now she had locked herself
away behind a bathroom door because she could not deal

with him daring to make an offer they both knew was not, and never had been, a real option!

What was left? Did he unsheath his ceremonial scabbard and offer to finish them both off like two tragic lovers?

Oh, may Allah forgive him, he prayed as his blood ran cold and he leapt towards the bathroom door. She wouldn't. She was made of stronger stuff, he told himself as he lifted a clenched fist to bang on the door just as it came open.

She was wearing only a towel and her hair was wet, slicked to her beautiful head like a ruby satin veil. Momentarily shocked by the unexpected face-to-face confrontation, they both just stared at each other. Then he bit out, 'Are you all right?'

'Of course,' she replied. 'Why shouldn't I be?'

He had no answer to offer that did not sound insane, so he took another way out and reached for her, pulled her into his arms and kissed her—hard. By the time he let her up for air again she was breathless.

'Hassan—'

'No,' he interrupted. 'We have talked enough for one night.'

Turning away, he went over to the bed to retrieve the pearl-white silk robe he had laid out ready for her. During her absence the room had been returned to its natural neatness, at his instruction, and a table had been laid for dinner in the centre, with the food waiting for them on a heated trolley standing beside it.

He saw her eyes taking all of this in as he walked back to where she was standing. She also noticed that the lights had been turned down and candles had been lit on the table. She was no fool; she knew he had set the scene with a second seduction in mind and he didn't bother to deny it.

'Here,' he said, and opened the robe up between his hands, inviting her to slip into it.

There was a pause where she kept her eyes hidden beneath the sweep of her dusky lashes. She was trying to decide how to deal with this and he waited in silence, more than willing to let the decision be hers after having spent the previous few minutes listing every other wrong move he had made until now.

'Just for tonight,' she said, and lifted those lashes to show him the firmness of that decision. 'Tomorrow you take me back to San Estéban.'

His mouth flexed as the urge to say, Never, throbbed on the end of his tongue. 'Tomorrow we—talk about it,' he offered as his only compromise, though he knew it was no compromise at all and wondered if she knew it too.

He suspected she did, suspected she knew he had not gone to all of this trouble just to snatch a single night with her. But those wonderful lashes fluttered down again. Her soft mouth, still pulsing from his kiss, closed over words she decided not to say, and with only a nod of her head she lost the towel, stepped forward and turned to allow him to help feed her arms into the kimono-type sleeves of the robe.

It was a concession he knew he did not deserve. A concession he wanted to repay with a kiss of another kind, where bodies met and senses took over. Instead, he turned her to face him, smoothed his fingers down the robe's silken border from slender shoulders to narrow waist, then reached for the belt and tied it for her.

His gentle ministrations brought a reluctant smile to her lips. 'The calm before the storm,' she likened dryly.

'Better this than what I really want to do,' he very ruefully replied.

'You mean this?' she asked, and lifted her eyes to his to let him see what was running through her head, then reached up and kissed him, before drawing away again with a very mocking smile.

As she turned to walk towards the food trolley she managed to trail her fingers over that part of him that was already so hard it was almost an embarrassment. The little vixen. He released a soft laugh. She might appear subdued on the surface, but underneath she still possessed enough spirit to play the tease.

They ate poached salmon on a bed of spinach, and beef stroganoff laden with cream. Hassan kept her glass filled with the crisp dry white wine she liked, while he drank sparkling water. As the wine helped mellow her mood some more, Leona managed to completely convince herself that all she wanted was this one wonderful night and she was prepared to live on it for ever. By the time the meal was finished and he suggested a walk on the deck, she was happy to go with him.

Outside the air was warm and as silken as the darkness that surrounded them. Both in bare feet, dressed only in their robes, they strolled along the deck and could have been the only two people on board it was so quiet and deserted.

'Rafiq is entertaining Ethan—up there,' Hassan explained when she asked where everyone else was. Following his gaze, Leona could see lights were burning in the windows of the deck above.

'Should we be joining them?'

'I don't think they would appreciate the interruption,' he drawled. 'They have a poker game planned with several members of the crew, and our presence would dampen their—enthusiasm.'

Which was really him saying he didn't want to share her with anyone. 'You have an answer for everything, don't you?' she murmured.

'I try.' He smiled.

It was a slaying smile that sent the heat of anticipation burning between the cradle of her hip-bones, forcing her to look away so he wouldn't see just how susceptible she was even to his smile. Going to lean against the yacht's rail, she looked down to watch the white horses chase along the dark blue hull of the boat. They were moving at speed, slicing through the water on slick silent power that made her wonder how far they were away from San Estéban by now.

She didn't ask, though, because it was the kind of question that could start a war. 'This is one very impressive toy, even for an oil-rich sheikh,' she remarked.

'One hundred and ninety feet in length,' he announced, and came to lean beside her with his back against the rail. 'Twenty-nine feet across the beam.' His arm slid around her waist and twisted her to stand in front of him so she could follow his hand as he pointed. 'The top deck belongs mainly to the control room, where my very efficient captain keeps a smoothly running ship,' he said. 'The next down belongs to the sun deck and main reception salons designed to suitably luxurious standards for entertaining purposes. We stand upon what is known as the shade deck, it being cast mostly in the shade of the deck above,' he continued, so smoothly that she laughed because she knew he was really mocking the whole sumptuous thing. 'One half is reserved for our own personal use, with our private staterooms, my private offices etcetera,' he explained, 'while the other half is split equally between outer sun deck, outer shade deck, plus some less formal living space.'

'Gosh, you're so lucky to be this rich.' She sighed.

'And I haven't yet finished this glorious tour,' he replied. 'For below our feet lies the cabin deck, complete with six private suites easily fit for the occupation of kings. Then there is the engine room and crew's quarters below that. We can also offer a plunge pool, gymnasium and an assortment of nautical toys to make our weary lot a happier one.'

'Does it have a name, this sheikh's floating palace?' she enquired laughingly.

'Mmm. *Sexy Lady*,' he growled, and lowered his head so he could bury his teeth in the side of her neck where it met her shoulder.

'You're joking!' she accused, turning round in his arms to stare at him.

'Okay.' He shrugged. 'I am joking.'

'Then what is she called?' she demanded, as her heart skipped a beat then stopped altogether because he looked so wonderful standing here with his lean dark features relaxed and smiling naturally for the first time. She loved him quite desperately—how could she not? He was her—

The laughter suddenly died on her lips, his expression telling her something she didn't want to believe. 'No,' she breathed in denial. He couldn't have done—he *wouldn't*...

'Why not?' he challenged softly.

'Not in this case!' she snapped at him, not knowing quite what it was that was upsetting her. But upset she was; her eyes felt too hot, her chest too tight, and she had a horrible feeling she was about to weep all over his big hard beautiful chest!

'It is traditional to name a boat after your most cherished loved-one,' he pointed out. 'And why am I defending myself when I could not have paid you a better compliment than this?'

'Because...' she began shakily.

'You don't like it,' he finished for her.

'No!' she confirmed, then almost instantly changed her mind and said. 'Yes, I like it! But you shouldn't have! Y-you—'.

His mouth crushed the rest of her protest into absolute oblivion, which was where it belonged anyway, because she didn't know what she was saying, only that a warm sweet wave of love was crashing over her and it was so dangerously seductive that—

She fell into it. She just let the wave close over her head and let him drown her in the heat of his passion, the power of his arms and the hunger of his kiss.

'Bed?' he suggested against her clinging mouth.

'Yes,' she agreed, then fed her fingers into his hair and her tongue between his ready lips. A groan broke low in his throat; it was husky and gorgeous; she tasted it greedily. A hand that knew her so very well curved over her thighs, slid up beneath her wrap, then cupped her bottom so he could bring her into closer contact with his desire. It was all very hot and very hungry. With a flick of a few scraps of silk they could be making love right here against the yacht's rail and in front of however many unseen eyes that happened to be glancing this way.

Hassan must have been thinking similarly because he suddenly put her from him. 'Bed,' he repeated, two dark streaks of colour accentuating his cheekbones and the fevered glitter in his eyes. 'Can you walk, or do I carry you?'

'I can run,' she informed him candidly, and grabbed hold of his hand, then turned to stride off on long slender legs with his husky laugh following as she pulled him behind her.

Back in their stateroom, now magically cleared of all evidence that they had eaten, they parted at the end of the bed, one stepping to one side of it, one to the other. Eyes locking in a needle-sharp, sensual love game, they disrobed together, climbed into the bed together and came together.

Hot, slow and deep, they made love into the night and didn't have to worry about empty spaces in between because one loving simply merged into another until—finally—they slept in each other's arms, legs entwined and faces so close on the pillows that the sleep was almost a long kiss in itself.

Leona came awake to find the place beside her in the bed empty and felt disappointment tug at her insides. For a while she just lay there, watching the sunlight seeping in through the window slowly creep towards her across the room, and tried not to let her mind open up to what it was bringing with it.

After a night built on fantasy had to come reality, not warm, like the sun, but cold, like the shadow she could already feel descending upon her even as she tried to hold it back for a little while longer.

A sound caught her attention. Moving her head just a little she watched Hassan walk out of the bathroom wearing only a towel, his sun-brown skin fashioned to look almost like skillfully tanned leather. For such a dark man he was surprisingly free of body hair, which meant she could watch unhindered each beautifully toned muscle as he strode across to one of the concealed doors in the wall and sprung it open at a touch to reveal a wardrobe to provide for the man who had everything. A drawer was opened and he selected a pai of white cotton undershorts, dropped the towel to give her a glimpse of lean tight buttocks before he pulled the shorts on. A pair of stone-washed outer shorts followed. Zipped and buttoned, they rested low on a waist that did not know the meaning of spare flesh to spoil his sleek appearance. A casual shirt came next, made of such fine white Indian cotton she could still see the outline of his body through it.

'I can feel you watching me,' he remarked without turning.

'I like to look at you,' Leona replied. And she did; rightly or wrongly in their present situation, he was a man to watch whatever he was doing, even fastening buttons as he was doing now.

Shirt cuffs left open, he turned to walk towards the bed. The closer he came the faster her heart decided to beat. 'I like to look at you, too,' he murmured, bracing his hands on either side of head so he could lean down and kiss her.

He smelt clean and fresh and his face wore the smooth sheen of a wet razor shave. Her lips clung to his, because she was still pretending, and her arms reached up so she could clasp them round the back of his neck. 'Come back to bed with me,' she invited.

'So that you can ravish me? No way,' he refused. 'As the wise ones will tell you, my darling, too much of a good thing is bad for you.'

He kissed her again to soften the refusal, and his mouth was smiling as he straightened away, but as his hands reached up to gently remove her hands she saw the toughening happening behind his eyes. Hassan had already made contact with reality, she realised.

With that he turned away and strode back to the wall to spring open another set of doors which revealed clothes for the woman who wanted for nothing—except her man. And already she felt as if he had moved right out of her reach.

'Get up and get dressed,' he instructed as he walked towards the door. 'Breakfast will be served on the sun deck in fifteen minutes.'

As she watched him reach for the door handle the shadow

of reality sank that bit deeper into her skin. 'Nothing has changed, Hassan,' she told him quietly. 'When I leave this room I won't be coming back to it again.'

He paused, but he did not turn to glance back at her. 'Everything has changed,' he countered grimly. 'You are back where you belong. This room is only part of that.' Then he was gone, giving her no chance to argue.

Leona returned to watching the sun inch its way across the cream carpet for a while. Then, on a sigh, she slid out of the bed and went to get herself ready to face the next round of argument.

In another room not that far away Hassan was facing up to a different opponent. Ethan Hayes was standing there in the clothes he had arrived in minus the bow tie, and he was angry. In truth Hassan didn't blame him. He was wearing a bruise on his jaw that would appal Leona if she saw it, and he had a thick head through being encouraged to imbibe too much alcohol the night before.

'What made you pull such a crazy stunt?' he was demanding.

Since Hassan had been asking himself the same thing, he now found himself short of an adequate answer. 'I apologise for my men,' he said. 'Their…enthusiasm for the task got the better of them, I am afraid.'

'You can say that again.' Ethan touched his bruised jaw. 'I was out for the count for ten minutes! The next thing I know I am stuck on a yacht I don't want to be on, and Leona is nowhere to be seen!'

'She's worried about you, too, if that is any consolation.'

'No, it damn well isn't,' Ethan said toughly. 'What the hell was wrong with making contact by conventional methods? You scared the life out of her, not to mention the life out of me.'

'I know, and I apologise again.' Not being a man born to be conciliatory, being forced to be so now was beginning to grate, and his next cool remark reflected that. 'Let it be said that you will be generously compensated for the… disruption.'

Ethan Hayes stiffened in violent offence. 'I don't want compensation,' he snapped. 'I want to see for myself that Leona is okay!'

'Are you daring to imply that I could harm my wife?'

'I don't know, do I?' Ethan returned in a tone deliberately aimed to provoke. 'Overenthusiasm can be infectious.'

Neither man liked the other, though it was very rare that either came out from behind their polite masks to reveal it. But, as the sparks began to fly between the two of them, this meeting was at risk of being one of those times. Leona might prefer to believe that Ethan Hayes was not in love with her. But, as a man very intimate with the symptoms, Hassan knew otherwise. The passion with which he spoke her name, the burn that appeared in his eyes, and the inherent desire to protect her from harm all made Ethan Hayes' feelings plain. And, as far as Hassan was concerned, the handsome Englishman's only saving grace was the deep sense of honour that made him respect the wedding ring Leona wore.

But knowing this did not mean that Hassan could dismiss the other man's ability to turn her towards him if he really set his mind to it. He had the build and the looks to turn any woman's head.

Was he really afraid of that happening? he then asked himself, and was disturbed to realise that, yes, he was afraid. Always had been, always would be, he admitted, as he fought to maintain his polite mask because, at this juncture, he needed Ethan Hayes' cooperation if he was going to get him off this boat before Leona could reach him.

So, on a sigh which announced his withdrawal from the threatening confrontation, he said grimly, 'Time is of the essence,' and went on to explain to the other man just enough of the truth to grab his concern.

'A plot to get rid of her?' Ethan was shocked and Hassan could not blame him for being so.

'A plot to use her as a lever to make me concede to certain

issues they desire from me,' he amended. 'I am still holding onto the belief that they did not want to turn this into an international incident by harming her in any way.'

'Just snatching her could do it,' Ethan pointed out.

'Only if it became public property,' Hassan responded. 'They would be betting on Victor and myself holding our silence out of fear for Leona's safety.'

'Does she know?' Ethan asked.

'Not yet,' Hassan confessed. 'And not at all if I can possibly get away with it.'

'So why does she think she's here?'

'Why do you think?' Hassan countered, and gained some enjoyment out of watching Ethan stiffen as he absorbed the full masculine depth of his meaning. 'As long as she remains under my protection no one can touch her.'

Ethan's response took him by surprise because he dared to laugh. 'You've no chance, Hassan,' he waged. 'Leona will fight you to the edge and back before she will just sit down and do what you want her to do simply because you've decided that is how it must be.'

'Which is why I need your support in this,' Hassan replied. 'I need you to leave this boat before she can have an opportunity to use your departure as an excuse to jump ship with you.'

He got it. In the end, and after a bit more wrangling, he watched Ethan Hayes turn to the door on a reluctant agreement to go. And, oddly, Hassan admired him for trusting him enough to do this, bearing in mind the year that had gone before.

'Don't hurt her again.' Almost as if he could read his thoughts, Ethan issued that gruff warning right on cue.

'My wife's well-being is and always has been of paramount importance to me,' Hassan responded in a decidedly cooler tone.

Ethan turned, looked him directly in the eye, and for once the truth was placed in the open. 'You hurt her a year ago. A man gets only one chance at doing that.'

The kid gloves came off. Hassan's eyes began to glint. 'Take a small piece of advice,' he urged, 'and do not presume to understand a marital relationship until you have tried it for yourself.'

'I know a broken-hearted woman when I see one,' Ethan persisted.

'And has she been any less broken-hearted in the year we have been apart?'

Game, set and match, Hassan recognised, as the other man conceded that final point to him, and with just a nod of his head Ethan went out of the door and into the capable hands of the waiting Rafiq.

At about the same time that Rafiq was escorting Ethan to the waiting launch presently tied up against the side of the yacht, Leona was slipping her arms into the sleeves of a white linen jacket that matched the white linen trousers she had chosen to wear. Beneath the jacket she wore a pale green sun top, and she had contained her hair in a simple pony-tail tied up with a green silk scarf. As she turned towards the door she decided that if she managed to ignore the throbbing ache happening inside her then she was as ready as she ever could be for the battle she knew was to come with Hassan.

Stepping out of the stateroom, the first person she saw was a bearded man dressed in a long white tunic and the usual white *gutrah* on his head.

'Faysal!' Her surprise was clear, her smile warm. Faysal responded by pressing his palms together and dipping into the kind of low bow that irritated Hassan but didn't bother Leona at all simply because she ignored it. 'I didn't know you were here on the boat. Are you well?' she enquired as she walked towards him.

'I am very well, my lady,' he confirmed, but beneath the beard she had a suspicion he was blushing uncomfortably at the informal intimacy she was showing him.

'And your wife?' she asked gently.

'Oh, she is very well,' he confirmed with a distinct softening in his formal tone. 'The—er—problem she suffered has gone completely. We are most grateful to you for taking the trouble to ensure she was treated by the best people.'

'I didn't do anything but point her in the right direction, Faysal.' Leona smiled. 'I am only grateful that she felt she could confide in me.'

'You saved her life.'

'Many people saved her life.' Daring his affront, she crossed the invisible line Arab males drew between themselves and females and reached out to press her hands against the backs of his hands. 'But you and I were good conspirators, hmm, Faysal?'

'Indisputably, my lady.' His mouth almost cracked into a smile but he was too stressed at having her hands on his, and in the end she relented and moved away.

'If you would come this way...' he bowed '...I am to escort you to my lord Hassan.'

Ah, my lord Hassan, Leona thought, and felt her lighter mood drop again as Faysal indicated that she precede him down the steps she had taken a tumble on the night before. On the other side of the foyer was a staircase which Leona presumed led up to the deck above.

With Faysal tracking two steps behind her, she made her way up and into the sunlight flooding the upper deck, where she paused to take a look around. The sky was a pure, uninterrupted blue and the sea the colour of turquoise. The sun was already hot on her face and she had to shade her eyes against the way it was reflecting so brightly off the white paintwork of the boat.

'You managed to make Faysal blush, I see,' a deep voice drawled lazily.

Turning about, she found that Faysal had already melted away, as was his habit, and that Hassan was sitting at a table laid for breakfast beneath the shade of a huge white canvas awning, studying her through slightly mocking eyes. Her heart tried to leap in her breast but she refused to let it.

'There is a real human being hiding behind all of that strict protocol, if you would only look and see him.'

'The protocol is not my invention. It took generations of family tradition to make Faysal the man he is today.'

'He worships you like a god.'

'And you as his angel of mercy.'

'At least he felt I was approachable enough that he could bring his concerns to me.'

'After I had gently suggested it was what he should do.'

'Oh,' she said; she hadn't realised that.

'Come out of the sun before you burn.'

It was hot, and he was right, but Leona felt safer keeping her distance. She had things to say, and she began with the one subject guaranteed to alter his mellow mood into something else entirely. 'I was hoping that Ethan would be here with you,' she said. 'Since he isn't, I think I will go and look for him.'

Like a sign from Allah that today was not going to be a good day, at that moment the launch powered up and slipped its ties to the yacht.

Attention distracted, Leona glanced over the side, then went perfectly still.

Hassan knew what she was seeing even before he got up to go and join her. Sure enough, there was Ethan standing on the back of the launch. As the small boat began to pick up speed he glanced up, saw them and waved a farewell.

'Wave back, my darling,' he urged smoothly. 'The man will appreciate the assurance that all is well.'

'You rat,' she whispered.

'Of the desert,' he dryly replied, then compounded his sins by bringing an arm to rest across her stiff shoulders and lifting his other to wave.

Leona waved also, he admired her for that because it showed that, despite how angry she was feeling, she was—as always—keeping true to her unfailing loyalty to him.

In the eyes of other people, anyway. He extended that statement as the two of them stood watching Ethan and his passage away from them decrease in size, until the launch was nothing more than an occasional glint amongst many on the ocean. By then Leona was staring beyond the glint, checking the horizon for a glimpse of land that was not there. She was also gripping the rail in front of them with fingers like talons and wishing they were around his throat, he was sure.

'Try to think of it this way,' he suggested. 'I have saved us the trouble of yet another argument.'

CHAPTER FIVE

'WE HAVE to put into port some time,' Leona said coldly. She twisted out from beneath his resting arm then began walking stiffly towards the stairs, so very angry with him that she was quite prepared to lock herself in the stateroom until they did exactly that.

Behind the rigid set of her spine, she heard Hassan release a heavy sigh. 'Come back here,' he instructed. 'I was joking. I know we need to talk.'

But this was no joke, and they both knew it. He was just a ruthless, self-motivated monster, and as far as she was concerned, she had nothing left to— Her thoughts stopped dead. So did her feet when she found her way blocked by a giant of a man with a neat beard and the hawklike features of a desert warrior.

'Well, just look what we have here,' she drawled at this newly arrived target for her anger. 'If it isn't my lord sheikh's fellow conspirator in crime.'

Rafiq had opened his mouth to offer her a greeting, but her tone made him change his mind and instead he dipped into the kind of bow that would have even impressed Faysal, but only managed to sharpen Leona's tongue.

'Don't you dare efface yourself to me when we both know you don't respect me at all,' she sliced at him.

'You are mistaken,' he replied. 'I respect you most deeply.'

'Even while you throw an *abaya* over my head?'

'The *abaya* was an unfortunate necessity,' he explained, 'For you sparkled so brilliantly that you placed us in risk of discovery from the car headlights. Though please accept my apologies if my actions offended you.'

65

He thought he could mollify her with an apology? 'Do you know what you need, Rafiq Al-Qadim?' she responded. 'You need someone to find you a wife—a real harridan who will make your life such a misery that you won't have time to meddle in mine!'

'You are angry, and rightly so,' he conceded, but his eyes had begun to glint at the very idea of anyone meddling with his life. 'My remorse for the incident with the *abaya* is all yours. Please be assured that if you had toppled into the ocean I would have arrived there ahead of you.'

'But not before me, I think,' another voice intruded. It was very satisfying to hear the impatience in Hassan's tone. He was not a man who liked to be upstaged in any way, which was what Leona had allowed Rafiq to do. 'Leona, come out of the sun,' he instructed. 'Allowing yourself to burn because you are angry is the fool's choice.'

Leona didn't move but Rafiq did. In two strides he was standing right beside her and quite effectively blocking her off from the sun with his impressive shadow.

Which only helped to irritate Hassan all the more. 'Your reason for being up here had better be a good one, Rafiq,' he said grimly.

'Most assuredly,' the other man replied. 'Sheikh Abdul begs an urgent word with you.'

Hassan's smile was thin. 'Worried, is he?'

'Protecting his back,' Rafiq assessed.

'Sheikh Abdul can wait until I have eaten my breakfast.' Levering himself away from the yacht's rail, he walked back to the breakfast table. 'Leona, if you are not over here by the time Rafiq leaves you will not like the consequences.'

'Threats now?' she threw at him.

'Tell the sheikh I will speak to him later,' he said, ignoring her remark to speak to Rafiq.

Rafiq hesitated, stuck between two loyalties and clearly unsure which one to heed. He preferred to stay by Leona's side until she decided to leave the sun, but he also needed to deliver Hassan's message; so a silence dropped and tension rose. Hassan picked up the coffee pot and poured himself a cup while he waited. He was testing the faith of a man who had only ever given him his absolute loyalty, and that surprised and dismayed Leona because, tough and cold though she knew Hassan could be on occasion, she had never known him to challenge Rafiq in this way.

In the end she took the pressure off by stepping beneath the shade of the awning. Rafiq bowed and left. Hassan sent her a brief smile. 'Thank you,' he said.

'You didn't have to challenge him like that,' she admonished. 'It was an unfair use of your authority.'

'Perhaps,' he conceded. 'But it served its purpose.'

'The purpose of reminding him of his station in life?'

'No, the purpose of making you remember yours.' He threw her a hard glance. 'We both wield power in our way, Leona. You have just demonstrated your own by giving Rafiq the freedom to leave with his pride intact.'

He was right, though she didn't like being forced to realise it.

'You can be so cruel sometimes.' She released the words on a sigh. To her surprise Hassan countered it with a laugh.

'You call me cruel when you have just threatened him with a wife? He has a woman,' he confided, coming to stand right behind her. 'A black-haired, ruby-eyed, golden-skinned Spaniard.' Reaching round with his hands, he slipped free the single button holding her jacket shut, then began to remove the garment. 'She dances the flamenco and famously turns up men's temperature gauges with her delectably seductive style.' His lips brushed the slender curve of her newly exposed shoulder. 'But Rafiq assures me that nothing compares to what she unleashes when she dances only for him.'

'You've seen her dance?' Before she could stop herself, Leona had turned her head and given him just what he had been aiming for, she realised, too late to hide the jealous green glow in her eyes.

A sleek dark brow arched, dark eyes taunting her with his

answer. 'You like to believe you can set me free but you are really so possessive of me that I can feel the chains tightening, not slackening.'

'And you are so conceited.' She tried to draw back the green eyed monster.

'Because I like the chains?' he quizzed, and further disarmed her.

It wasn't fair, Leona decided; he could seduce her into a mess of confusion in seconds: Ethan, the launch, her sense of righteous indignation at the way she was being manipulated at just about every turn; she was in real danger of becoming lost in the power he had over her. She tried to break free from it. From *her* chains, she recognised.

'I prefer tea to coffee,' she murmured, aiming her concentration at the only neutral thing she could find, which was the table set for breakfast.

The warm sound of his laughter was in recognition of her diversion tactics. Then suddenly he wasn't laughing, he was releasing a gasp of horror. 'You are bruised!' he claimed, sending her gaze flittering to the slight discolouring to her right shoulder that she had noticed herself in the shower earlier.

'It's nothing.' She tried to dismiss it.

But Hassan was already turning her round and his black eyes were hard as they began flashing over every other exposed piece of flesh he could see. 'Me, or the fall?' he demanded harshly.

'The fall, of course.' She frowned, because she couldn't remember a single time in all the years they had been together that Hassan had ever marked her, either in passion or anger, yet he had gone so pale she might have accused him of beating her.

'Any more?' he asked tensely.

'Just my right hip, a little,' she said, holding her tongue about the sore spot at the side of her head, because she could see he wasn't up to dealing with that information. '—Hassan, will you stop it?' she said gasping when he dropped down in front of her and began to unfasten her white trousers. 'It isn't that bad!'

He wasn't listening. The trousers dropped, his fingers were already gently lifting the plain white cotton of her panty line out of the way so he could inspect for himself. 'I am at your feet,' he said in pained apology.

'I can see that,' she replied with a tremor in her voice that had more to do with shock than the humour she'd tried to inject into it. His response was so unnecessary and so very enthralling. 'Just get up now and let me dress,' she pleaded. 'Someone might come, for goodness' sake!'

'Not if they value their necks,' he replied, but at least he began to slide her trousers back over her slender hip-bones.

It had to be the worst bit of timing that Faysal should choose that moment to make one of his silent appearances. Leona was covered—just—but it did not take much imagination for her to know what Faysal must believe he was interrupting. The colour that flooded her cheeks must have aided that impression. Hassan went one further and rose up like a cobra.

'This intrusion had better be worth losing your head for!' he hissed.

For a few awful seconds Leona thought the poor man was going to prostrate himself in an agony of anguish. He made do with a bow to beat all bows. 'My sincerest apologies,' he begged. 'Your most honourable father, Sheikh Khalifa, desires immediate words with you, sir.'

Anyone else and Hassan would have carried out his threat, Leona was sure. Instead his mouth snapped shut, his hands took hold of her and dumped her rudely into a chair.

'Faysal, my wife requires tea.' He shot Leona's own diversion at the other man. Glad of the excuse to go, Faysal almost ran. To Leona he said, 'Eat,' but he wasn't making eye contact, and the two streaks of colour he was wearing on his cheekbones almost made her grin because it was so rare that anyone saw Sheikh Hassan Al-Qadim disconcerted.

'You dare,' he growled, swooping down and kissing her

twitching mouth, then he left quickly with the promise to return in moments.

But moments stretched into minutes. She ate one of the freshly baked rolls a white liveried steward had brought with a pot of tea, then drank the tea—and still Hassan did not return.

Eventually Rafiq appeared with another formal bow and Hassan's apologies. He was engaged in matters of state.

Matters of state she understood having lived before with Hassan disappearing for hours upon end to deal with them.

'Would you mind if I joined you?' Rafiq then requested.

'Orders of state?' she quizzed him dryly.

His half-smile gave her an answer. Her half-smile accompanied her indication to an empty chair. She watched him sit, watched him hunt around for something neutral to say that was not likely to cause another argument. There was no such thing, Leona knew that, so she decided to help him out.

'Tell me about your Spanish mistress,' she invited.

It was the perfect strike back for sins committed against her. Rafiq released a sigh and dragged the *gutrah* from his head, then tossed it aside. This was a familiar gesture for a man of the Al-Qadim household to use. It could convey many things: weariness, anger, contempt or, as in this case, a relayed throwing in of the towel. 'He lacks conscience,' he complained.

'Yet you continue to love him unreservedly, Rafiq, son of Khalifa Al-Qadim,' she quietly replied.

An eyebrow arched. Sometimes, in a certain light, he looked so like Hassan that they could have been twins. But they were not. 'Bastard son,' Rafiq corrected in that proud way of his. 'And you continue to love him yourself, so we had best not throw those particular stones,' he advised.

Rafiq had been born out of wedlock to Sheikh Khalifa's beautiful French mistress, who'd died giving birth to him. The fact that Hassan had only been six months old himself at the time of Rafiq's birth should have made the two half-brothers bitter enemies as they grew up together, one certain of his high place in life, the other just as certain of what would never be his. Yet in truth the two men could not have been closer if they'd shared the same mother. As grown men they had formed a united force behind which their ailing father rested secure in the knowledge that no one would challenge his power while his sons were there to stop them. When Leona came along, she too had been placed within this ring of protection.

Strange, she mused, how she had always been surrounded by strong men for most of her life: her father, Ethan, Rafiq and Hassan; even Sheikh Khalifa, ill though he now was, had always been one of her faithful champions.

'Convince him to let me go,' she requested quietly.

Ebony eyes darkened. 'He had missed you.'

So did green. 'Convince him,' she persisted.

'He was lonely without you.'

This time she had to swallow across the lump those words helped to form in her throat before she could say, 'Please.'

Rafiq leaned across the table, picked up one of her hands and gave it a squeeze. 'Subject over,' he announced very gently.

And it was. Leona could see that. It didn't so much hurt to be stonewalled like this but rather brought it more firmly home to her just how serious Hassan was.

Coming to his feet, Rafiq pulled her up with him. 'Where are we going?' she asked.

'For a tour of the boat in the hopes that the diversion will restrain your desire to weaken my defences.'

'Huh,' she said, for the day had not arrived when anyone could weaken Rafiq in any way involving his beloved brother. But she did not argue the point about needing a diversion.

He turned to collect his *gutrah*. The moment it went back on his head, the other Rafiq reappeared, the proud and remote man. 'If you would be so good as to precede me, my lady. We will collect a hat from your stateroom before we begin...'

Several hours later she was lying on one of the sun loungers on the shade deck, having given in to the heat and changed into a black and white patterned bikini teamed with a cool white muslin shirt. She had been shown almost every room the beautiful yacht possessed, and been formally introduced to Captain Tariq Al-Bahir, the only other Arab as far as she could tell in a twenty-strong crew of Spaniards. This had puzzled her enough to question it. But 'Expediency,' had been the only answer Rafiq would offer before it became another closed subject.

Since then she had eaten lunch with Rafiq and Faysal, and had been forced, because of Faysal's presence, to keep a lid on any other searching questions that might be burning in her head, which had been Rafiq's reason for including the other man, she was sure. And not once since he'd left her at the breakfast table had she laid eyes on Hassan—though she knew exactly where he was. Left alone to lie in the softer heat of the late afternoon, she was free to imagine him in what would be a custom built office, dealing with *matters of state*.

By phone, by fax, by internet—her mouth moved on a small smile. Hyped up, pumped up and doing what he loved to do most and in the interim forgetting the time and forgetting her! At other times she would have already been in there *reminding* him that there was a life other than *matters of state*. Closing her eyes, she could see his expression: the impatient glance at her interruption; the blank look that followed when she informed him of the time; the complaining sigh when she would insist on him stopping to share a cup of coffee or tea with her; and the way he would eventually surrender by reaching for her hand, then relaxing with a contented sigh...

In two stuffed chairs facing the window in his palace office—just like the two stuffed chairs strategically placed in the yacht's stateroom. Her heart gave a pinch; she tried to ignore what it was begging her to do.

*   *   *

Hassan was thinking along similar lines as he lay on the lounger next to hers. She was asleep. She didn't even know he was here. And not once in all the hours he had been locked away in his office had she come to interrupt.

Had he really expected her to? he asked himself. The answer that came back forced him to smother a hovering sigh because he didn't want to make a noise and waken her. They still had things to discuss, and the longer he put off the evil moment the better, as far as he was concerned, because he was going to get tough and she was not going to like it.

Another smothered sigh had him closing his eyes as he reflected back over the last few hours in which he had come as close as he had ever done to causing a split between the heads of the different families which together formed the Arabian state of Rahman.

Dynastic politics, he named it grimly. Al-Qadim and Al-Mukhtar against Al-Mahmud and Al-Yasin, with his right to decide for himself becoming lost in the tug of war. In the end he had been forced into a compromise that was no compromise at all—though he had since tried to turn it into one with the help of an old friend.

Leona released the sigh he had been struggling to suppress, and Hassan opened his eyes in time to see her yawn and stretch sinuously. Long and slender, sensationally curved yet exquisitely sleek. The colour of her hair, the smoothness of her lovely skin, the perfectly proportioned contours of her beautiful face. The eyes he could not see, the small straight nose that he could, the mouth he could feel against his mouth merely by looking at it. And—

Be done with it, he thought suddenly, and was on his feet and bending to scoop her into his arms.

She awoke with a start, saw it was him and sent him a sleepy frown. 'What are you doing?' she protested. 'I was comfortable there—'

'I know,' he replied. 'But I wish to be comfortable too, and I was not.'

He was already striding through the boat with a frown that

was far darker than hers. Across the foyer, up the three shallow steps. 'Open the door,' he commanded and was surprised when she reached down and did so without argument. He closed it with the help of a foot, saw her glance warily towards the bed. But it was to the two chairs that he took her, set her down in one of them, then lowered himself into the other with that sigh he had been holding back for so long.

'I suppose you have a good reason for moving me here,' she prompted after a moment.

'Yes,' he confirmed, and turned to look into those slumber darkened green eyes that tried so hard to hide her feelings from him but never ever quite managed to succeed. The wall of his chest contracted as he prepared himself for what he was about to say. 'You have been right all along.' He began with a confession. 'I am being pressured to take another wife...'

She should have expected it, Leona told herself as all hint of sleepy softness left her and her insides began to shake. She had always *known* it, so why was she feeling as if he had just reached out with a hand and strangled her heart? It was difficult to speak—almost impossible to speak—but she managed the burning question. 'Have you agreed?'

'No,' he firmly denied. 'Which is why you are here with me now—and more to the point, why you have to stay.'

Looking into his eyes, Leona could see that he was not looking forward to what he was going to say. She was right.

'A plot was conceived to have you abducted,' he told her huskily, 'the intention being to use your capture as a weapon with which to force my hand. When I discovered this I decided to foil their intentions by abducting you for myself.'

'Who?' she whispered, but had a horrible feeling she already knew the answer.

'Did the plotting? We are still trying to get that confirmed,' he said. 'But whoever it was they had their people watching your villa last night, waiting for Ethan and your father to leave for the party on the Petronades yacht. Once they had assured themselves that you were alone they meant to come in and take you.'

'Just like that,' she said shakily, and looked away from him as so many things began to fall into place. 'I felt their eyes on me,' she murmured. 'I knew they were there.'

'I suspected that you would do,' Hassan quietly commended. 'It is the kind of training we instilled into you that you never forget.'

'But this was different.' She got up, wrapped her arms around her body. 'I *knew* it felt different. I should have heeded that!'

'No—don't get upset.' Following suit, Hassan stood up and reached for her. She was as pale as a ghost and shaking like a leaf. 'My people were also there watching over you,' he assured. 'The car driver was my man, as was the man at the gate. I had people watching their people. There was not a single moment when you were not perfectly safe.'

'But to dislike me so much that they should *want* to take me!' Hurt beyond belief by that knowledge, Leona pushed him away, unwilling to accept his comfort. It had been hard enough to come to terms with it, when she'd believed he had snatched her back for his own purposes. But to discover now that he had done it because there was a plot against her was just too much to take. 'What is it with you people that you can't behave in a normal, rational manner?' she threw at him, eyes bright, hurt and accusing. 'You should have phoned *me* not my father!' she cried. 'You should have agreed to a divorce in the first place, then none of this would have happened at all!'

The *you people* sent Hassan's spine erect; the mention of divorce hardened his face. 'You are one of *my people*,' he reminded her curtly.

'No, I am not!' she denied with an angry shake of her head. 'I am just an ordinary person who had the misfortune to fall in love with the *extra*ordinary!'

'At least you are not going back to denying you love this

extraordinary person,' he noted arrogantly. 'And stop glaring at me like that!' he snapped. 'I am not your enemy!'

'Yes, you are!' Oh, why had she ever set eyes on this man? It would have been so much easier to have lived her life without ever having known him! 'So what happens now?' she demanded. 'Where do we go from here? Do I spend the rest of my days hiding from dark strangers just because you are too stubborn to let me go?'

'Of course not.' He was standing there frowning impatiently. 'Stop trying to build this into more than it actually is—'

More? 'Don't you think it is enough to know that I wasn't safe to be walking the streets in San Estéban? That my life and my basic human rights can be reduced to being worth nothing more than a mere pawn in some wretched person's power game?'

'I am sorry it has to come to this—'

Well, that just wasn't good enough! 'But you are no better yourself!' she threw at him angrily. 'Up to now you've used abduction, seduction and now you've moved onto intimidation to bring the wayward wife into line.' She listed. 'Should I be looking for the hidden cameras you are using so that you can show all of Rahman what a strong man you can be? Do I need to smile now?' she asked, watching his face grow darker with the sarcasm she tossed at him—and she just didn't care! 'Which way?' she goaded. 'Do I need to let Rafiq shroud me in an *abaya* again and even go as far as to abase myself at your exalted feet just to save your wretched face?'

'Say any more and you are likely to regret it,' he warned very grimly.

'I regret knowing you already!' Her eyes flashed, her body shook and her anger sparkled in the very air surrounding her. 'Next I suppose you will have me thrown into prison until I learn to behave myself!'

'This is it—' he responded, spreading his arms out wide in what was an outright provocation. 'Your prison. Now stop shouting at me like some undignified fishwife,' he snapped. 'We need to—'

'I want my life back without you in it!' Leona cut loudly across him.

What she got was the prince. The face, the eyes, his mood and his manner changed with the single blink of his long dark eyelashes. When his shoulders flexed it was like a dangerous animal slowly raising its hackles, and the fine hairs on her body suddenly became magnetised as she watched the metamorphosis take place. Her breathing snagged; her throat grew tight. He was standing perhaps three yards away from her but she could suddenly feel his presence as deeply as if he was a disturbing inch away.

'You want to live your life without me, then you may do so,' he announced. 'I will let you go, give you your divorce. There, it is done. *Inshallah*.' With a flick of the hand he strode across the room and calmly ordered tea!

It was retaliation at its most ruthless and it left her standing there utterly frozen with dismay. *Inshallah*. She couldn't even wince at what that single word represented. The will of Allah. Acceptance. A decision. The end. Hassan was agreeing to let her go and she could neither move nor breathe as the full power of that decree made its stunning impact.

She had not deserved that, Hassan was thinking impatiently as he stood glaring down at the telephone. She had been shocked, angry, hurt. Who would not be when they discovered that people they cared about, people they had tried to put before themselves, had been plotting to use them ruthlessly in a nasty game called politics? She had every right to vent her feelings—he had expected it! It was the reason why he had found them privacy before telling her the truth!

Or part of the truth, he then amended, all too grimly aware that there was yet more to come. But the rest was going to have to wait for a calmer time, for this moment might be silent but it certainly was not calm, because—

Damn it, despite the sensible lecture he was angry! There

was not another person on this planet who dared to speak to
him as she had just done, and the hell if he was going to
apologise for responding to that!

He flicked a glance at her. She hadn't moved. If she was
even breathing he could see no evidence of it. Her hair was
untidy. Long silken tendrils had escaped from the band she'd
had it tied up in all day and were now caressing her nape,
framing her stark white profile to add a vulnerability to her
beauty that wrenched hard on his heart-strings. Her feet were
bare, as were her slender arms and long slender legs. And
she was emulating a statue again, only this time instead of
art-deco she portrayed the discarded waif.

He liked the waif. His body quickened; another prohibited
sigh tightened his chest. Curiosity replaced anger, though
pride held his arrogant refusal to be the first one to retract
his words firmly in place. She moved him like no other
woman. She always had done. Angry or sad, hot with searing
passion or frozen like ice as she was now.

Inshallah. It was Allah's will that he loved this woman
above all others. Let her go? Not while he had enough breath
in his body to fight to hold onto what was his! Though he
wished he could see evidence that there was breath inside
hers.

He picked up an ornament, measured the weight of the
beautifully sculpted smooth sandstone camel then put it back
down again to pick up another one of a falcon preparing to
take off on the wing. And all the time the silence throbbed
like a living pulse in the air all around them.

Say something—talk to me, he willed silently. Show me
that my woman is still alive in there, he wanted to say. But
that pride again was insisting he would not be the one to
break the stunning deadlock they were now gripped in.

The light tap at the door meant the ordered tea he didn't
even want had arrived. It was a relief to have something to
do. She didn't move as he went to open the door, still hadn't
moved when he closed it again on the steward he'd left

firmly outside. Carrying the tray to the low table, he put it down, then turned to look at her. She still hadn't moved.

Inshallah, he thought again, and gave up the battle. Walking over to her, he placed a hand against her pale cheek, stroked his thumb along the length of her smooth throat then settled it beneath her chin so he could lift her face up that small inch it required to make her look at him.

Eyes of a lush dark vulnerable green gazed into sombre night-dark brown. Her soft mouth parted; at last she took a breath he could hear and see. 'Be careful what you wish for,' she whispered helplessly.

His legs went hollow. He understood. It was the way it had always been with them. 'If true love could be made to order, we would still be standing here,' he told her gravely.

At which point the ice melted, the gates opened and in a single painfully hopeless move she coiled her arms around his neck, buried her face into his chest and began to weep.

So what do you do with a woman who breaks her heart for you? You take her to bed. You wrap her in yourself. You make love to her until it is the only thing that matters any more. Afterwards, you face reality again. Afterwards you pick up from where you should never have let things go astray.

The tea stewed in the pot. Evening settled slowly over the room with a display of sunset colours that changed with each deepening stage of their sensual journey. Afterwards, he carried her into the shower and kept reality at bay by loving her there. Then they washed each other, dried each other, touched and kissed and spoke no words that could risk intrusion for as long as they possibly could.

It was Leona who eventually approached reality. 'What now?' she asked him.

'We sail the ocean on our self-made island, and keep the rest of the world out,' he answered huskily.

'For how long?'

'As long as we possibly can.' He didn't have the heart to

tell her he knew exactly how long. The rest would wait, he told himself.

It was a huge tactical error, though he did not know that yet. For he had not retracted what he had decreed in a moment of anger. And, although Leona might appear to have set the words aside, she had not forgotten them. Nor had she forgotten the reason she was here at all: there were people out there who wanted to harm her.

But for now they pretended that everything was wonderful. Like a second honeymoon in fact—if an unusual one with Rafiq and Faysal along for company. They laughed a lot and played like any other set of holidaymakers would. Matters of state took a back seat to other more pleasurable pursuits. They windsurfed off the Greek islands, snorkelled over shipwrecks, jet-skied in parts of the Mediterranean that were so empty of other human life that they could have had the sea to themselves.

One week slid stealthily into a second week Leona regained the weight she had lost during the empty months without Hassan, and her skin took on a healthy golden hue. When matters of state refused to be completely ignored, Rafiq was always on hand to help keep up the pretence that everything was suddenly and miraculously okay.

Then it came. One heat-misted afternoon when Hassan was locked away in his office, and Faysal, Leona and Rafiq were lazing on the shade deck sipping tall cool drinks and reading a book each. She happened to glance up and received the shock of her life when she saw that they were sailing so close to land it felt as if she could almost reach out and touch it.

'Oh, good grief,' Getting up she went to stand by the rail. 'Where are we, Rafiq?'

'At the end of our time here alone together,' a very different voice replied.

CHAPTER SIX

LEONA turned to find Hassan was standing not far away and Rafiq was in the process of rising to his feet. One man was looking at her; the other one was making sure that he didn't. Hassan's words shimmered in the air separating them and Rafiq's murmured, 'Excuse me, I will leave you to it,' was as revealing as the speed with which he left.

The silence that followed his departure pulsed with the hurried pace of her heartbeat while Leona waited for Hassan to clarify what he had just said.

He was still in the same casual shorts and shirt he had been wearing when she had last seen him, she noticed. But there, the similarity between this man and the man who had kissed the top of her head and strolled away to answer Faysal's call to work a short hour ago ended. For there was a tension about him that was almost palpable, and in his hand he held a gold fountain pen which offered up an image of him getting up from his desk to come back here at such speed that he hadn't even had time to drop the pen.

'We arrived here sooner than I had anticipated,' he said, confirming her last thought.

'It would be helpful for me to know where *here* is,' she replied in a voice laden with the weight of whatever it was that was about to come at her.

And come it did. 'Port Said,' he provided, saw her startled response of recognition and lowered his eyes on an acknowledging grimace that more or less said the rest.

Port Said lay at the mouth of the Suez Canal, which linked the Mediterranean with the Red Sea. If they were coming into the port, then there could only be one reason for it:

81

Hassan was ready to go home and their self-made, sea-born
paradise was about to disintegrate.

He had noticed the pen in his hand and went to drop it on
the lounger next to the book she had left there. Then he
walked over to the long white table at which they had eaten
most of their evening meals over the last two weeks. Pulling
out a chair, he sat down, released a sigh, then put up a hand
to rub the back of his neck as if he was trying to iron out a
crick.

When he removed it again he stretched the hand out towards her. 'Join me,' he invited.

Leona shook her head and instead found her arms crossing
tightly beneath the thrust of her breasts. 'Tell me first,' she
insisted.

'Don't be difficult,' he censured. 'I want you here, within
touching distance when I explain.'

But she didn't want to be within touching distance when
he said what she knew he had to say. 'You are about to go
home, aren't you?'

'Yes,' he confirmed.

It was all right challenging someone to tell you the truth
when you did not mind the answer, but when you did mind
it— 'So this is it,' she stated, finding a short laugh from
somewhere that was not really a laugh at all. 'Holiday
over...'

Out there the sun glistened on the blue water, casting a
shimmering haze over the nearing land. It was hot but she
was cold. It was bright but she was standing in darkness. The
end, she thought. The finish.

'So, how are you going to play it?' she asked him. 'Do
you drop me off on the quay in the clothes I arrived in and
wave a poignant farewell as you sail away. Or have I earned
my passage back to San Estéban?'

'What are you talking about?' Hassan frowned. 'You are
my wife, yet you speak about yourself as a mistress.'

Which was basically how she had been behaving over the

ast two weeks, Leona admitted to herself. '*Inshallah*,' she murmured.

The small sarcasm brought him back to his feet. As he strode towards her she felt her body quicken, felt her breasts grow tight and despised herself for being so weak of the flesh that she could be aroused by a man who was about to carry out his promise to free her. But six feet two inches of pedigree male to her five feet seven was such a lot to ignore when she added physical power into the equation, then included mental power and sexual power. It really was no wonder she was such a weakling where he was concerned.

And it didn't stop there, because he came to brace his hands on the rail either side of her, then pushed his dark face close up to hers. Now she could feel the heat of him, feel his scented breath on her face. She even responded to the ever-present sexual glow in his eyes though it had no right to be there—in either of them.

'A mistress knows when to keep her beautiful mouth shut and just listen. A wife does her husband the honour of hearing him out before she makes wildly inaccurate claims,' he said.

'You've just told me that our time here is over,' she reminded him with a small tense shrug of one slender shoulder. 'What else is there left for you to say?'

'What I said,' he corrected, 'was that our time here *alone* was over.'

The difference made her frown. Hassan used the moment to shift his stance, grasp both of her hands and pry them away from the death grip they had on her arms. Her fingers left marks where they had been clinging. He frowned at the marks and sighed at her pathetically defiant face. Then, dropping one of her hands, he turned and pulled her over to the table, urged her down into the chair he had just vacated and, still without letting go of her other hand, pulled out a second chair upon which he sat down himself.

He drew the chair so close to her own that he had to spread his thighs wide enough to enclose hers. It was a very effective way to trap his audience, especially when he leaned forward and said, 'Now, listen, because this is important and I will not have you diverting me by tossing up insignificant comments.'

It was automatic that she should open her mouth to question that remark. It was predictable, she supposed, that Hassan should stop her by placing his free hand across her parted lips. 'Shh,' he commanded, 'for I refuse to be distracted yet again because the anguish shows in your eyes each time we reach this moment, and your words are only weapons you use to try and hide that from me.'

'Omniscient' was the word that came to mind to describe him, she thought, as her eyes told him she would be quiet. His hand slid away from her face, leaving its warm imprint on her skin. He smiled a brief smile at her acquiescence, then went so very serious that she found herself holding onto her breath.

'You know,' he began, 'that above all things my father has always been your strongest ally, and it is for him that I am about to speak...'

The moment he mentioned Sheikh Khalifa her expressive eyes clouded with concern.

'As his health fails, the more he worries about the future of Rahman,' he explained. 'He frets about everything. You, me, what I will do if the pressures currently being brought to bear upon me force me to make a decision which could change the rule of Rahman.'

'You mean you have actually considered giving up your right to succession?' Leona gasped out in surprise.

'It is an option,' he confessed. 'And one which became more appealing after I uncovered the plot involving you, which was aimed to make me do as other people wish,' he added cynically. 'But for my father's sake I assured him that I am not about to walk away from my duty. So he decided to fret about my happiness if I am forced to sacrifice you for the sake of harmony, which places me in a frustrating no-win situation where his peace of mind is concerned.'

'I'm sorry,' she murmured.

'I don't want your sympathy, I want your help,' he stated with a shortness that told her how much he disliked having to ask. 'He loves you, Leona, you know that. He has missed you badly since you left Rahman.'

'I didn't completely desert him, Hassan.' She felt pushed into defending herself. 'I've spoken to him every day via the internet.' Even here on the yacht she had been using Faysal's computer each morning to access her e-mail. 'I even read the same books he is reading so that we can discuss them together. I—'

'I know,' Hassan cut in with a wry smile. 'What you say to him he relays to me, so I am fully aware that I am a bully and a tyrant, a man without principle and most definitely my father's son.'

'I said those things to tease a laugh out of him,' she defended.

'I know this too,' he assured her. 'But he likes to make me smile with him.' Reaching up, he stroked a finger along the flush of discomfort that had mounted her cheeks. 'And let me face it,' he added, removing the finger, 'your communication with him was far sweeter than your communication with me.'

He was referring to the letters he'd received from her lawyer. 'It was over between us. You should have left it like that.'

'It is not over between us, and I *cannot* leave it like that.'

'Your father—'

'Needs you,' he grimly inserted. '*I* need you to help me ease his most pressing concerns. So I am asking you for a full and open reconciliation of our marriage—for my father's sake if not for yours and mine.'

Leona wasn't a fool. She knew what he was *not* saying here. 'For how long?'

He offered a shrug. 'How long is a piece of string?' he posed whimsically. Then, because he could see that the answer was not enough, he dropped the whimsy, sat right back

in his seat and told her curtly, 'The doctors give him two
months—three at most. In that period we have been warned
to expect a rapid deterioration as the end draws near. So I
ask you to do this one thing for him and help to make his
passage out of this world a gentle one...'

Oh, dear heaven, she thought, putting a hand up to her
eyes as the full weight of what he was asking settled over
her. How could she refuse? She didn't even want to refuse.
She loved that old man as much as she loved her own father.
But there were other issues here which had not been aired
yet, and it was those that kept her agreement locked inside.

'The other wife they want for you,' she prompted, 'am I
to appear to accept her imminent arrival also?'

His expression darkened. 'Do me the honour of allowing
me some sensitivity,' he came back. 'I have no wish to sacrifice your face for my own face. And I find it offensive that
you could suspect that I would do.'

Which was very fine and noble of him but— 'She is still
there, hovering in the shadows, Hassan,' Leona said heavily.
She could even put a name to the woman, though he probably didn't know that she could. 'And taking me back to
Rahman does not solve your problems with the other family
leaders unless you take that other wife.'

'The old ones and I have come to an agreement,' he informed her. 'In respect for my father, they will let the matter
ride while he is still alive.'

'Then what?'

'I will deal with them when I have to, but for the next
few months anyway, my father's peace of mind must come
first.'

And so, he was therefore saying, should it for her. 'Will
you do this?'

The outright challenge. 'Did you really think that I would
not?' She sighed, standing up and pushing her chair away so
that she could step around him.

'You're angry.' His eyes narrowed on her sparkling eyes
and set expression.

Anger didn't nearly cover what she was really feeling. 'In principle I agree to play the doting wife again,' she said. 'But in fact I am now going to go away and *sulk* as you like to call it. Because no matter how well you wrap it all up in words of concern, Hassan, you are as guilty for using me in much the same way my foiled abductors intended to use me, and that makes you no better than them, does it?'

With that she turned and walked away, and Hassan allowed her to, because he knew she was speaking the truth so had nothing he could offer in his own defence.

Within seconds Rafiq appeared with a question written into the hard lines of his face.

'Don't ask,' he advised heavily. 'And she does not even know the half of it yet.'

'Which half does she not know,' Rafiq asked anyway.

'What comes next,' Hassan replied, watching his half-brother's eyes slide over his left shoulder. He spun to see what he was looking at, then began cursing when he saw how close they were to reaching their reserved berth in Port Said. 'How long?' he demanded.

'You have approximately one hour before the first guests begin to arrive.'

A small hour to talk, to soothe, to plead yet again for more charity from a woman who had given enough as it was. 'You had better prepare yourself to take my place, Rafiq,' he gritted. 'Because, at this precise moment, I am seriously considering jumping ship with my wife and forgetting I possess a single drop of Al-Qadim blood.'

'Our father may not appreciate such a decision,' Rafiq commented dryly.

'That reminder,' Hassan turned to snap, 'was not necessary.'

'I was merely covering for myself,' his half brother defended. 'For I have no wish to walk in your shoes, my lord Sheikh.'

About to go after Leona, Hassan paused. 'What do you wish for?' he questioned curiously.

'Ah.' Rafiq sighed. 'At this precise moment I wish fo
midnight, when I should be with *my* woman in
hotel room in Port Said. For tonight she flies in to dance fo
visiting royalty by special request. But later she will danc
only for me and I will worship at her feet. Then I will wor
ship other parts of her until dawn, after which I will reluc
tantly return here, to your exalted service, my lord sheikh,
he concluded with a mocking bow.

Despite the weight of his mood, Hassan could not resist
smile. 'You should change your plans and bring her to din
ner,' he suggested. 'The sheer sensation she would caus
would be a diversion I would truly appreciate.'

'But would Leona?' Rafiq pondered.

Instantly all humour died from Hassan's face. 'Leona,' h
predicted. 'is in no frame of mind to appreciate anything.'

And on that grim reminder, he went off to find *his* woman
while half wishing that he was the one treading in Rafiq'
shoes.

He found her without difficulty, shut behind the bathroom
door and hiding in the steam being produced by the shower
The fact that she had not bothered to lock the door spok
volumes as to her mood. Hassan could visualise the angr
way she would have walked in here, throwing the door shu
behind her then taking the rest of her anger out on the hea
of clothes he could see tossed onto the floor.

So what did he do now? Go back to the bedroom and wai
for her to reappear, or did he throw caution to the wind, stri
off and just brave her fiery den?

It was not really a question since he was already takin
off his clothes. For this was no time to be feeble. Leona ha
agreed *in principle*, so now she was about to learn the con
sequences of that. With a firming of his mouth he opene
the shower-cubicle door, stepped inside and closed it again

She was standing just out of reach of the shower jets wit
her head tipped back as she massaged shampoo into her hair
Streams of foaming bubbles were sliding over wet gold skin
collecting around the tips of her tilted breasts and snaking

through the delightful valley in between to pool in the perfect oval of her navel, before spilling out to continue their way towards the chestnut cluster marking the apex with her slender thighs.

His body awoke; he allowed himself a rueful smile at how little it took to make him want this beautiful creature. Then she realised he was there and opened her eyes, risking soap burn so that she could kill him with a look.

'What do you want now?' she demanded.

Since the answer to that question was indubitably obvious, he didn't bother with a reply. Instead he reached for the container of foaming body soap, pumped a generous amount into the palm of his hand and began applying it to her skin. Her hands dropped from her hair and pressed hard against his chest in an effort to push him away.

'Thank you,' he said, and calmly pumped some soap onto his own chest as if it was a foregone conclusion that she would wash him. 'Sharing can turn the simplest of chores into the best of pleasures, do you not think?'

The green light in her eyes took on a distinctly threatening gleam. 'I think you're arrogant and hateful and I want you to get out of here,' she coldly informed him.

'Close your eyes,' he advised. 'The shampoo is about to reach them.'

Then, even as she lifted a hand to swipe the bubbles away, he reached up and directed the shower head at her so that the steamy spray hit her full in the face. While gasping at the shock, he made his next move, turned the spray away and replaced it with his mouth.

For a sweet, single moment he allowed himself to believe he'd made the easy conquest. It usually worked. On any other occasion it would have worked as a tasty starter to other ways of forgetfulness. But this time he received a sharp dig in the ribs for his optimism, and a set of teeth closed threateningly on his bottom lip until he eased the pressure and lifted his head. Her eyes spat fire and brimstone at him.

He arched an eyebrow and glided a defiant hand down to the silken warmth of her abdomen.

'You are treading on dangerous ground, Sheikh,' she warned him.

'I am?'

She ignored the message in his tone. 'I have nothing I want to say to you. So why don't you leave me alone?'

'But I was not offering to talk,' he explained, and boldly slid the hand lower.

'You are not doing *that* either!' Squirming away like a slippery snake, she ended up pressed against the corner of the cubicle, eyes like green lasers trying their best to obliterate him. One arm was covering her breasts, the other hand was protecting other parts. She looked like some sweet, cowering virgin, but he was not fooled by the vision. This beautiful wife of his possessed a temper that could erupt without warning. At the moment it was merely simmering.

'Okay.' With an ease that threw her into frowning confusion, he conceded the battle to her, pumped more soap onto his chest and began to wash while trying to ignore the obvious fact that a certain part of him was as hard as a rock and begging he do something about it. 'We did not really have time, anyway. Our guests arrive in less than an hour...'

'Guests?' she looked up sharply. 'What guests?'

'The guests we are about to transport to Rahman to attend the anniversary of my father's thirtieth year of rule, which will take place in ten days' time,' he replied while calmly sluicing the soap from his body as if he had not dropped yet another bomb at her feet. 'Here.' He frowned. 'Wash the shampoo from your hair before you really do hurt your eyes.' And he stepped back to allow her access to the spray.

Leona didn't move; she didn't even notice that he had. She was too busy suffering from one shock too many. 'How long have you known you were taking on guests?'

'A while.' Reaching up to unhook the shower head from the wall, he then pulled her towards him to began rinsing the shampoo from her hair for himself.

'But you didn't feel fit to tell me before now?'

'I did not feel fit to do anything but enjoy being with you.'
Pushing up her chin, he sent the slick, clean pelt of her hair
sliding down her spine with the help of the shower jet.
'Why?' He asked a question of his own. 'Would knowing
have had any bearing on your decision to come back to
Rahman with me?'

Would it? Leona asked herself, when really she did not
need to, because she knew her answer would have been the
same. He was rinsing the rest of her now and she just stood
there and let him do it. Only a few minutes ago his smallest
touch had infused her with that need to feel him deep inside
her, now she could not remember what the need felt like. As
he waited for him to finish administering to her wooden
form, she noticed that his passion had died too.

'I suppose I had better know if there is anything else you
haven't bothered to tell me,' she murmured eventually.

His pause before speaking could have been a hesitation
over his answer, or it could have been a simple pause while
he switched off the shower. 'Just the names of our guests,'
he said. 'And that can wait until we have dealt with the more
urgent task of drying ourselves and getting dressed.'

With that he opened the shower door and stepped out to
collect a towel, which he folded around her before offering
her another one for her hair. For himself he reached for a
towelling bathrobe, pulled it on and headed for the door.

'Hassan...' she made him pause '...the rest of this trip
and your father's celebration party—am I being put on public
show for a specific purpose?'

'Some people need to be shown that I will not be coerced
in any way,' he answered without turning. 'And my father
wants you there. This will be his last anniversary. I will deny
him nothing.'

At Hassan's request, she was wearing a calf-length white
silk tunic studded with pearl-white sequins that shimmered
when she moved. In accordance with Arabian tradition, the
tunic had a high neckline, long sleeves and a pair of match-

ing slender silk trousers that covered her legs. On her hea
she had draped a length of fine silk, and beneath it her hai
had been carefully pleated into a glossy, smooth coronet. He
make-up was so understated you could barely tell it was ther
except for the flick of black mascara highlighting the lengt
of her eyelashes and the hint of a gloss to her soft pin
mouth.

Beside her stood the Prince. Dressed in a white silk tuni
and gold silk top robe, on his head he wore a white *gutra*
ringed by three circles of gold. To her other side and on
short pace behind stood Rafiq, dressed almost exactly th
same as his brother only without the bands of gold. And a
they waited in the boat's foyer, Leona was in no doubt tha
the way they were presented was aimed to make a specifi
statement.

Sheikh Hassan ben Khalifa Al-Qadim and his wife th
Sheikha Leona Al-Qadim—bestowed upon her at her re
quest, for the woman of Arabia traditionally kept their fa
ther's name—were ready to formally receive guests, whethe
those guests were friends or foes.

Rafiq was their guardian, their protector, their most re
spected brother and trusted friend. He possessed his own ti
tle, though he had never been known to use it. He possesse
the right to wear the gold bands of high office, but no on
had ever seen them circling his head. His power rode on th
back of his indifference to anything that did not interest him
His threat lay in the famed knowledge that he would la
down his life for these two people standing in front of him
plus the father he loved without question.

His presence here, therefore, made its own loud statement
come in friendship and be at peace; come in conflict an
beware.

Why? Because the first person to tread the gangway ont
the yacht was Sheikh Abdul Al-Yasin and his wife, Zafina
Hassan and Rafiq knew that Sheikh Abdul was behind th
plot to abduct Leona, but the sheikh did not know the broth
ers knew. Which was why he felt safe in taking the bai

handed out for this trip—namely a meeting of the chiefs during a cruise on the Red Sea, in which his aim was to beat Hassan into submission about this second wife he was being so stubborn in refusing.

What none of them knew was that Leona suspected it was Sheikh Abdul who had planned her abduction. Because she knew about Nadira, his beautiful daughter, who had been held up to her many times as the one chosen to take that coveted place in Sheikh Hassan's life as his second wife.

'Ah—Hassan!' The two men greeted and shook hands pleasantly enough. 'You will be pleased to know that I left your father in better sorts than of late. I saw him this morning before I caught my flight to Cairo.'

'I must thank you for keeping him company while we have been away,' Hassan replied.

'No thanks—no thanks.' Sheikh Abdul refused them. 'It was my privilege—Leona...' He turned towards her next, though offered no physical contact as was the Arab way. He bowed instead. 'You have been away too long. It is good to see you here.'

'Thank you.' She found a smile, wished she dared search for the comfort of Hassan's hand, but such shows of weakness would be pounced upon and dissected when she was not there to hear it happen.

'Rafiq.' His nodded greeting was distinctly wary. 'You made a killing with your stock in Schuler-Kleef, I see.'

'My advice is usually sound, sir,' Rafiq replied respectfully. 'I take it you did not buy some for yourself?'

'I forgot.'

Through all of this, Sheikh Abdul's wife, Zafina, stood back in total silence, neither stepping forward to follow the line of introduction nor attempting to remind her husband of her presence. It was such a quiescent stance, one that Leona had grown used to from the women of Rahman when they were out in the company of their men.

But it was a quiescence that usually only lasted as long as it took them to be alone with the other women. Then the real personalities shot out to take you by surprise. Some were soft and kind, some cold and remote, some alive with fun. Zafina was a woman who knew how to wield her power from within the female ranks and had no hesitation in doing so if it furthered her own particular cause. It was due to her clever machinations that her son had married another sheikh's most favoured daughter.

She'd had Hassan marked for her daughter, Nadira, from the day the child had been born. Therefore, in her eyes, she had every reason to dislike Leona. And, tranquil though she might appear right now, Leona could feel resentment flowing towards her in waves.

'Zafina.' She stepped forward, deciding to take the polite stand. 'You are well, I trust? Thank you for taking time out of your busy life to join us here.'

'The pleasure is all mine, Sheikha,' the older woman replied. But then her husband was listening and so was the coveted Sheikh Hassan. 'You have lost weight, I think. But Sheikh Khalifa tells me you have been sick?'

Someone had told her at any rate, but Leona suspected it was not Hassan's father. Thankfully other guests began to arrive. Sheikh Jibril Al-Mahmud and his timid wife, Medina, who looked to her husband before she dared so much as breathe.

Sheikh Imran Al-Mukhtar and his youngest son, Samir, arrived next. Like a light at the end of a tunnel, Samir put the first genuine smile on everyone's face because he broke right through every stiff convention being performed in the yacht's foyer, and headed directly for Leona. 'My princess!' he greeted, picked her up in his arms then swung her around.

'Put her down,' his father censured. 'Rafiq has that glint in his eye.'

'Not Hassan?' Samir questioned quizzically.

'Hassan knows what belongs to him, Rafiq is merely overprotective. And everyone else simply disapproves of your loose ways.'

And there it was, tied up in one neat comment, Hassan

noted as he watched Leona laugh down into Samir's handsome young face. Al-Qadim and Al-Mukhtar set apart from Al-Mahmud and Al-Yasin. It promised to be an interesting trip. For the first time in two weeks they used the formal dining room on the deck above. White-liveried stewards served them through many courses, and the conversation around the table was pleasant and light, mainly due to Samir, who refused to allow the other men to sink into serious discussion, and even the other women unbent beneath his boyish charm.

But Leona was quiet. From his end of the table Hassan watched her speak when spoken to, smiling in all the right places. He watched her play the perfect hostess in that easy, unassuming way he remembered well, where everyone's needs were predicted and met before they knew they were missing something. But occasionally, when she thought no one was attending her, he watched the corners of her mouth droop with short releases of the tension she was experiencing.

Sad. Her eyes were sad. He had hurt her with his drippingtap method of feeding information to her. Now here she sat, having to pretend everything was perfect between them, when really she wanted to kill him for waiting until the last minute to spring all of this.

His heart clenched when he caught sight of her impulsive grin as she teasingly cuffed Samir for saying something outrageous. She had not laughed with him like that since the first night they'd been together again. No matter how much she had smiled, played, teased—loved him—during the last two weeks, he had been aware of an inner reserve that told him he no longer had all of her. Her spirit was missing, he named it grimly. It had been locked away out of his reach.

I love you, he wanted to tell her. But loving did not mean much to a woman who felt that she was trapped between a rock and a hard place.

A silence suddenly reigned. It woke him up from his own thoughts to notice that Leona was staring down at the plate

in front of her and Samir had frozen in dismay. What had
he missed? What had been said? Muscles began tightening
all over him. Rafiq was looking at him for guidance. His skin
began to crawl with the horrible knowledge that he had just
missed something supremely important, and he could not
think of a single thing to say!

His half-brother took the initiative by coming to his feet.
'Leona, you will understand if I beg to leave you now,' he
petitioned as smooth as silk, while Hassan, who knew him
better than anyone, could see him almost pulsing with rage.

Leona's head came up as, with a flickering blink of her
lashes, she made the mammoth effort to pull herself together.
'Oh, yes, of course, Rafiq,' she replied, having absolutely no
idea, Hassan was sure, why Rafiq was excusing himself halfway through dinner, and at this precise moment she didn't
care. It was a diversion. She needed the diversion. It should
have been himself who provided it.

'I need a word before you leave,' he said to Rafiq, and
got to his feet. 'Samir, do the honours and replenish my
wife's glass with wine.'

The poor young man almost leapt at the wine bottle, relieved to have something to do. As Rafiq walked past Hassan, with a face like fury, Hassan saw Leona reach out and
gently touch Samir's hand, as if to assure him that everything
was all right.

'What did I miss in there?' he rapped out at Rafiq as soon
as they were out of earshot.

'If I did not like Samir I would strangle him,' Rafiq responded harshly. 'Leona asked him how his mother was. He
went into a long and humorous story about her sitting in wait
for his sister to give birth. Leona dealt with that. She even
laughed in all the right places. But then the fool had to suggest it was time that she produced your son and heir.'

'He cannot have known what he was saying,' Hassan said
angrily.

'It was not the question which threw Leona, it was the
resounding silence that followed it and the bleak expression

upon your face! Where were you, man?' Rafiq wanted to know. It was so rare that he used that tone with Hassan, that the censure in it carried twice the weight.

'My mind had drifted for a few seconds,' he answered tensely.

'And the expression?'

'Part of the drift,' he admitted heavily.

'You were supposed to be on the alert at all times for attacks of this kind.' Rafiq was not impressed. 'It was risk enough to bring onto this boat the man who wishes her ill, without you allowing your mind to drift.'

'Stop spitting words at my neck and go to your dancer,' Hassan snapped back impatiently. 'You know as well as I do that neither Abdul or Jibril would dare to try anything when they are here for the specific purpose of talking me round!'

It's okay, Leona was telling herself. I can deal with it. I've always known that deep inside he cared more than he ever let me see. So, he had been caught by surprise and showed the truth to everyone. *I* was caught by surprise and showed it myself.

'Samir,' she murmured gently. 'If you pour me any more wine I will be sozzled and fall over when I have to stand up.'

'Hassan wants your glass kept full.' He grimly kept on pouring.

'Hassan was attempting to fill an empty gap in the conversation, not put me under the table,' she dryly pointed out.

Samir sat back with a sigh. 'I want to die a thousands deaths,' he heavily confessed.

Hassan arrived back at the table. Leona felt his glance sear a pointed message at her down the table's length. She refused to catch his eye, and smiled and smiled until her jaw ached.

After that, the rest of the dinner passed off without further incident. But by the time the ladies left the men alone and removed to the adjoining salon Leona was in no mood for a

knife-stabbing session. So she was actually relieved that
Medina and Zafina chose to stab at her indirectly by discussing Zafina's daughter, Nadira, whose beauty, it seemed,
had multiplied during the last year. And as for her grace and
quiet gentle ways—she was going to make some lucky man
the perfect wife one day.

At least they didn't prose on about how wonderful she
was with children, Leona thought dryly, as the conversation
was halted when Hassan brought the men through within
minutes of the ladies leaving them.

The evening dragged on. She thought about the other days
and nights still to come and wondered if she was going to
get through them all in one piece. Eventually the other two
women decided they were ready to retire. A maid was called
and within minutes of them leaving Leona was happy to
follow suit. As she stepped outside, Hassan joined her. It was
the first time he had managed to get her alone since the
incident at the dinner table.

'I am at your feet,' he murmured contritely. 'I was miles
away and had no idea what had taken place until Rafiq explained it to me.'

She didn't believe him, but it was nice of him to try the
cover-up, she supposed. 'Samir wins hands down on apologies,' she came back. 'He wants to die a thousands deaths.'

With that she walked away, shaking inside and not really
sure why she was. She got ready for bed and crawled between the cool cotton sheets, sighed, punched the pillow,
then attempted to fall asleep. She must have managed it,
because the next thing she knew a warm body was curling
itself in behind her.

'I don't recall our new deal involving having to share a
bed,' she said coldly.

'I don't recall offering to sleep elsewhere,' Hassan coolly
returned. 'So go back to sleep.' The arm he folded around
her aimed to trap. 'And, since I am as exhausted as you are,
you did not need the silk pyjamas to keep my lecherous
desires at bay…'

'I really hate you sometimes.' She wanted the last word.

'Whereas I will love you with my dying breath. And when they lay us in our final resting place in our crypt of gold it will be like this, with the scent of your beautiful hair against my face and my hand covering your lying little heart. There,' he concluded, 'is that flowery enough to beat Samir's one thousand deaths?'

Despite not wanting to, she giggled. It was her biggest mistake. The exhausted man became an invigorated man. His lecherous desires took precedence.

Did she try to stop him? No, she did not. Did she even want to? No, again. Did he know all of that before he started removing the pyjamas?' Of course he did. And there was something needle-piercingly poignant in this man losing touch with everything but this kind of loving as he came inside her, cupped her face with his hands and held her gaze with his own, as he drove them towards that other resting place.

CHAPTER SEVEN

MORNING came too soon, to Leona's regret. Although here shut inside this room and wrapped in the relative sanctuary of Hassan's arms, she could let herself pretend for a little while longer that everything was perfect.

He was perfect, she observed tenderly as she studied the lean smooth lines of his dark golden face. He slept quietly—he always had done—lips parted slightly, black lashes lying still against the silken line of his cheekbones. Her heart began to squeeze and her stomach muscles joined in. This deep-rooted attraction he had always inspired in her had never diminished no matter what else had come in between.

She released a sigh that feathered his face and made his nose twitch. And it was such a nose, she thought with a smile, irresistibly reaching up to run a fingertip down its long silken length.

'Life can have its perfect moments,' a sleepy voice drawled.

Since she had been thinking much the same herself, Leona moved that bit closer so she could brush a kiss on his mouth.

Eyelashes drifted upward, revealing ebony irises packed with love. 'Does the kiss mean you have forgiven me for dropping all of this on you?'

'Shh,' she whispered, 'or you will spoil it.'

'Kiss me again, then,' he insisted. So she did. Why not, she asked herself. This was her man. Rightly or wrongly he was most definitely hers here and now.

It was a shame the ring of the telephone beside the bed had to intrude, or one thing would have led to another before they should have needed to face reality again. As it was, Hassan released a sigh and reached out to hook up the re-

100

ceiver. A few seconds later he was replacing it again and reaching out to touch her kiss-warmed mouth with a look of regret.

'Duty calls,' he murmured.

Ah, duty, Leona thought, and flopped heavily onto her back. Perfect moment over, pretence all gone. Stripped clean to his smooth dark golden skin, it was the prince who rose up from the bed and without saying another word disappeared into the bathroom.

He came out again ten minutes later, wrapped in fluffy white cotton and looking as handsome as sin. Wishing his pull wasn't as strong on her senses, she got up with a definite reluctance to face the day mirrored on her face, pulled on her wrap and went to take her turn in the bathroom.

But Hassan stopped her as she walked past him, his hand gently cupping her chin. He smelt of soap and minted toothpaste as he bent to kiss her cheek. 'Fifteen minutes, on the sun deck,' he instructed as he straightened again. 'For breakfast with an added surprise.'

The 'added surprise' made Leona frown. 'You promised me you had no more surprises waiting to jump out at me,' she protested.

'But this one does not count,' he said with a distinctly worrying gleam in his eye. 'So hurry up, wear something deliciously stylish that will wow everyone, and prepare yourself to fall on my neck.'

'Fall on his neck,' Leona muttered to herself as she showered. She had developed a distinct aversion to surprises since arriving on this wretched boat so she was more likely to strangle him.

In a pale blue sundress made of a cool cotton, and with her red hair floating loose about her shoulders—because she felt like wearing it as a banner, which made a statement about...something, though she wasn't absolutely sure what—Leona walked out onto the sun deck to find Rafiq there but no Hassan.

He looked up, smiled, then stood to pull out a chair for

her. He was back in what she called his off-duty clothes, loose-fitting black chinos and a white V-neck tee shirt that did things to his muscled shape no one saw when he was covered in Arab robes.

'Was your mother an Amazon, by any chance?' she enquired caustically, because his father was a fine boned little man and Rafiq had to have got his size from someone.

The waspishness in her tone earned her a sharp glance. 'Did you climb out of bed on the wrong side, by any chance?' he threw back.

'I *hate* surprises,' she announced as she sat down.

'Ah,' Rafiq murmured. 'So you have decided to take it out on me because I am unlikely to retaliate.'

He was right, and she knew it, which didn't help this terrible, restless tension she was suffering from. 'Where is Hassan?' She strove for a nicer tone and managed to half succeed. 'He said he would be here.'

'The pilot who will guide us through the Suez Canal has arrived,' Rafiq explained. 'It is an expected courtesy for Hassan to greet him personally.'

Glancing outwards, Leona saw Port Said sprawling out in front of them like a vast industrial estate. It was not the prettiest of views to have with your breakfast, even though they seemed to have got the best of the berths, moored way off to one side in a separate harbour that looked as if it was reserved for the luxury private crafts.

'And the rest of our guests?' she enquired next, aware that she probably should have asked about them first.

'Either still asleep or breakfasting in their suites.'

Mentioning sleep had a knock-on effect on him, and in the next moment Rafiq was stifling a yawn. It was only then that Leona recalled his slick retreat from the fray the evening before.

'Up all night?' The spike was back in her voice.

He didn't reply, but the rueful way his mouth tilted suddenly made her think of Spanish dancers. 'I hope she was good.' She took a tart stab in the dark.

'Delightful.' He smiled. It was yet another blow to her fragile ego that her one solid ally had deserted her last night for another woman. 'Here,' he said gently, and began to pour her out a cup of tea. 'Maybe this will help soothe your acid little tongue.'

Something needed to, Leona silently admitted as she picked up the cup. She had never felt so uptight and anxious, and it all was down to Hassan and surprises she did not want and people she did not want to be with and a marriage she did not—

The slightly sweet scent of Earl Grey suddenly turned her stomach. She must have gone pale because Rafiq began frowning. 'What is the matter?' he demanded.

'I think the milk must be off,' she explained, hastily putting the cup back on its saucer then pushing it away.

The sickly sensation left her almost as suddenly as it had hit. Problem solved in her mind, she wasn't convinced when Rafiq picked up the jug to sniff at the milk and announced, 'It seems fine to me.'

But he rose anyway and went to replace the milk with fresh from the cartons kept in the refrigerator situated just inside the salon. Then Hassan appeared and the incident was forgotten because, after dropping a kiss on her forehead, he went to pull out the chair next to Rafiq, who was just returning to the table with the fresh jug of milk. For a moment Leona was held captivated by how much alike the two men were. Even their clothes were similar, only Hassan wore beige chinos and a black tee shirt.

Men of beauty no matter what clothes they were wore, she mused a trifle breathlessly, knowing that she would be hard put to it to find two more perfect specimens. So why do I love them both so differently? she asked herself as she watched them sit down. Life would certainly have been a whole lot simpler if she'd fallen in love with Rafiq instead of Hassan. No strict calls to duty, no sheikhdom to rule, no onus to produce the next son and heir to his vast power and untold fortune.

But she loved Rafiq as a brother, not as a lover—just as he loved her as a sister. Plus, he had his mysterious dancer, she added wryly, as she poured herself another cup of tea in a clean cup, then reached for a slice of toast.

'You look pale. What's wrong?' Glancing up, she found Hassan's eyes were narrowed on her profile.

'She hates surprises.' Rafiq offered a reply.

'Ah. So I am out of favour,' Hassan drawled. 'Like the milk and the butter…' he added with the sharp eyes that should have been gold, like a falcon's, not a bottomless black that made her feel as if she could sink right into them and never have to come back out again.

'The milk was off, it turned my stomach, so I decided not to risk it or the butter,' she said, explaining the reason why she was sipping clear tea and nibbling on a piece of dry toast.

Keeping dairy produce fresh was an occupational hazard in hot climates, so Hassan didn't bother to question her answer—though Leona did a moment later when a pot of fresh coffee arrived for Hassan and the aroma sent her stomach dipping all over again.

Hassan saw the way she pushed her plate away and sat back in the chair with the paleness more pronounced, and had to ask himself if her pallor was more to do with anxiety than a problem with the milk. Maybe he should not be teasing her like this. Maybe no surprise, no matter how pleasant was going to merit putting her through yet more stress. He glanced at his watch. Ten more minutes. Was it worth him hanging on that long?

'You look stunning,' he murmured.

She turned her head, her wonderful hair floating out around her sun-kissed shoulders and the perfect heart-shape of her face. Her eyes were like emeralds, to match the one she wore on her finger, glowing with a passion she could never quite subdue no matter how low she was feeling. Kiss me, her small, soft, slightly sulky mouth seemed to say.

'I am *de trop*.' Rafiq broke through the moment and rose

to his feet. 'I will go and awaken Samir and drag him to the gym for an hour before I allow him breakfast.'

Neither bothered to answer even if they heard him, which Rafiq seriously doubted as he went to leave. Then a sound beyond the canvas awning caught his attention, diverting him towards the rail. A car was coming down the concrete quay towards them, its long black sleekly expensive lines giving him a good idea as to who was inside it.

This time he made sure he commanded attention by lightly touching Hassan's shoulder. 'Your surprise is arriving,' he told him, then left as Hassan stirred himself and Leona blinked herself back from wherever she had gone to.

Getting up, Hassan went to capture one of her hands and urged her out of her chair. 'Come,' he said, and keeping hold of her hand walked them down the stairs, across the foyer, out onto the shade deck and to the rail beside the gangway, just in time to watch a beautiful creature with pale blonde hair step out of the car and onto the quayside.

Beside him he felt Leona's breath catch on a gasp, felt the pulse in her wrist begin to race. 'Evie,' she whispered. 'And Raschid,' she added as Sheikh Raschid Al-Kadah uncoiled his long lean body out of the car.

'They're sailing with us?' Now her eyes were shining with true pleasure, Hassan noted with deep satisfaction. Now she was looking at him as if he was the most wonderful guy in the world, instead of the most painful to be around.

'Will their presence make your miserable lot easier to bear?'

Her reply was swift and uninhibited. She fell upon him with a kiss he would have given half of his wealth for. Though it did not need wealth, only the appearance of her closest friend and conspirator against these—arrogant Arabian men, as she and Evie liked to call Raschid and himself.

'After six years, I would have expected the unrestrained passion to have cooled a little,' a deep smooth, virtually accent-free voice mocked lazily.

'Says the man with his son clutched in one arm and his daughter cradled in the other,' mocked a lighter, drier voice.

Son and daughter. Hassan stiffened in shock, for he had not expected the Al-Kadahs to bring along their children on this cruise. Leona, on the other hand, was pulling away from him, turning away from him—hiding away from him? Had his pleasant surprise turned into yet another disaster? He turned to see what she was seeing and felt his chest tighten so fiercely it felt as if it was snapping in two. For there stood Raschid, as proud as any man could be, with his small son balanced on his arm while the beautiful Evie was in the process of gently relieving him of his small pink three-month-old daughter.

They began walking up the gangway towards them, and it was his worst nightmare unfolding before his very eyes, because there were tears in Leona's as she went to meet them. Real tears—bright tears when she looked down at the baby then up at Evangeline Al-Kadah before, with aching description, she simply took the other woman in her arms and held her.

Raschid was watching them, smiling, relaxed while he waited a few steps down the gangway for them to give him room to board the boat. He saw nothing painful in Leona's greeting, nor the way she broke away to gently touch a finger to the baby girl's petal soft cheek.

'I didn't know,' she was saying softly to Evie. 'Last time I saw you, you weren't even pregnant!'

'A lot can happen in a year,' Raschid put in dryly, bringing Leona's attention his way.

The tableau shifted. Evie moved to one side to allow her husband to step onto the deck so he could put his son to the ground, leaving his arms free to greet Leona properly. 'And aren't you just as proud as a peacock?' She laughed, defying the Arab male-female don't-touch convention by going straight into Raschid's arms.

What was wrong with Hassan? Leona wondered, realising that he hadn't moved a single muscle to come and greet their atest guests. She caught his eye over one of Raschid's broad shoulders, sent him a frowning look that told him to pull himself together. By the time he was greeting Evie Leona was squatting down to say hello to the little boy who now clutched his mother's skirt for safety. Dark like his father; golden-eyed like his father. The fates had been kind to these two people by allowing them to produce a son in Raschid's image and a daughter who already looked as if she was going to be a mirror of her mother.

'Hello, Hashim.' She smiled gently. They had met before but she was sure the small boy would not remember. 'Does that thumb taste very nice?'

He nodded gravely and stuck the thumb just that quarter inch further between sweetly pouting lips.

'My name is Leona,' she told him. 'Do you think we can be friends?'

'Red,' he said around the thumb, looking at her hair. 'Sunshine.'

'Thank you.' She laughed. 'I see you are going to be a dreadful flirt, like your papa.'

Mentioning his papa sent the toddler over to Raschid, where he begged to be picked up again. Raschid swung him up without pausing in his conversation with Hassan, as if it was the most natural thing in the world for him to have his son on his arm.

Tears hit again. Leona blinked them away. Hassan gave a tense shift of one shoulder and in the next moment his arm was resting across her shoulders. He was smiling at Evie, at her baby, at Raschid. But when Leona noticed that he was not allowing himself to so much as glance at Raschid's son it finally hit her what was the matter with him. Hassan could not bear to look at what Raschid had, that which he most coveted.

Her heart dropped to her stomach to make her feel sick again. The two men had been good friends since—for ever. Their countries lay side by side. And they shared so many similarities in their lives that Leona would have wagered everything that nothing could drive a wedge between their friendship.

But a desire for what one had that the other did not, in the shape of a boy-child, could do it, she realised, and had to move away from Hassan because she just couldn't bear to be near him and feel that need pulsing in him.

'May I?' she requested of Evie, holding out her arms for the baby.

Evie didn't hesitate in handing the baby over. Soft and light and so very fragile. It was like cradling an angel. 'How old is she?' she asked.

'Three months,' Evie supplied. 'As quiet as a mouse, as sweet as honey—and called Yamila Lucinda after her two grandmothers, but we call her Lucy because it's cute.'

At the sound of her mother's voice, Lucy opened her eyes to reveal two perfect amethysts the same as Evie's, and Leona found herself swallowing tears again.

You're so lucky, she wanted to say, but remarks like that were a potential minefield for someone in her situation. So she contented herself with lifting the baby up so she could feel her soft cheek against her own and hoped that no one noticed the small prick of tears she had to blink away.

A minute later and other guests began appearing on the shade deck to find out who else had joined them. Sheikh Raschid earned himself looks of wary surprise from some. From all he was awarded the respect accorded to a man who held absolute rule in his own Gulf state of Behran. His children brought down other barriers; the fact that Evie had achieved what Leona had not, in the shape of her small son, earned her warm smiles instead of stiffly polite ones that conveyed disapproval. Still, most of the tension from the evening before melted away in the face of the newcomers, and Leona was deeply grateful to them for succeeding in neutralising the situation.

When it was decided that they would move up to the sun deck, with its adjoining salon, to take refreshment and talk in comfort, Leona quickly shifted herself into hostess mode and led the way upstairs with her small bundle in her arms and her husband walking at her shoulder.

He didn't speak, and she could sense the same mood about him he had donned when he'd come face to face with Raschid and his son. It hurt. Though she strove not to show it. But his manner made such a mockery out of everything else he had said and done.

They arrived on the upper deck as the yacht slipped smoothly from its moorings and began making its way towards the mouth of the Suez Canal. Medina Al-Mahmud suddenly appeared in front of Leona and politely begged to hold the baby. She was a small, slight woman with nervous eyes and a defensive manner, but as Leona placed the little girl in her arms Medina sent her a sympathetic look which almost broke her composure in two.

She did not want people's pity. Oh, how she had come to hate it during her last year in Rahman when the rumours about her had begun flying. With a desperate need of something else to do other than stand here feeling utterly useless, she walked into the salon to pick up the internal phone and order refreshments.

It was really very bad timing for Hassan to follow her. 'I must offer you my deepest apologies,' he announced so stiffly it was almost an insult. 'When I arranged this surprise for you I did not expect the Al-Kadahs to bring their children with them.'

She was appalled to realise that even Hassan believed her an object of such pity. 'Oh, stop being so ultra-sensitive,' she snapped. 'Do you really believe that I could resent them their beautiful children because I cannot have them for myself?'

'Don't say that!' he snapped back. 'It is not true, though you drive me insane by insisting it is so!'

'And you stop burying your head in the sand, Hassan,' she returned. 'Because we both know that you know it is you who lies to yourself!'

With that she stalked off, leaving him to simmer in his

own frustration while she went to check that the accommodation could stretch to two more guests than they had expected. Faysal already had the matter in hand, she discovered, finding several people hurriedly making ready a pair of adjoining suites, while others unpacked enough equipment, brought by the Al-Kadahs, to keep an army of young children content.

On her way back upstairs she met Rafiq and Samir. Rafiq studied her narrowly, his shrewd gaze not missing the continuing paleness in her face. He was probably questioning whether one sniff at suspect milk could upset her stomach for so long when in actual fact it had never been the milk, she had come to realise, but sheer anxiety and stress.

Samir, on the other hand, noticed nothing but a target for his wit. By the time the three of them had joined the others, Samir had her laughing over a heavily embroidered description of himself being put through the agonies of hell in the gym by a man so fit it was a sin.

After that she played the circulating hostess to the hilt and even endured a whole ten minutes sitting with Zafina listening to her extol the virtues of her daughter, Nadira. Then Evie rescued her by quietly asking if she would show her to their room, because the baby needed changing.

With Hashim deciding to come with them, they went down to the now beautifully prepared twin cabins and a dark-eyed little nurse Evie had brought with them appeared, to take the children into the other room. The moment the two women were alone Evie swung round on Leona and said, 'Right, let's hear it. Why did Hassan virtually beg and bribe us to come along on this trip?'

At which point; Leona simply broke down and wept out the whole sorry story. By the time she had hiccuped to a finish they were curled up on the bed and Evie was gently stroking her hair.

'I think you are here to make me feel better.' She finally answered Evie's original question. 'Because anyone with eyes can see that the Al-Mahmuds and the Al-Yasins wish me on another planet entirely. Hassan doesn't know that I've always known that Nadira Al-Yasin is the people's preferred wife for him.'

'I've been there. I know the feeling,' Evie murmured understandingly. 'I suppose she's beautiful, biddable and loves children.'

Leona nodded on a muffled sob. 'I've met her once or twice. She's quite sweet,' she reluctantly confessed.

'Just right for Hassan, I suppose.'

'Yes,'

'And, of course, you are not.'

Leona shook her head.

'So why are you here, then?' Evie challenged.

'You tell me,' she suggested, finding strength in anger and pulling herself into a sitting position on the bed. 'Because I don't know! Hassan says I am here for this reason, then he changes it to another. He is stubborn and devious and an absolute expert at plucking at my heart strings! His father is ill and I adore that old man so he uses him to keep me dancing to his secret tune!'

'Raschid's father died in his arms while I held Raschid in my arms,' Evie told her sadly. 'Wretched though it was, I would not have been anywhere else. He needed me. Hassan needs you too.'

'Oh, don't defend him,' Leona protested, 'It makes me feel mean, yet I know I would have gone to his father like a shot with just that request. I didn't need all of this other stuff to make me do it.'

'But maybe Hassan needed this other stuff to let him make you do it.'

'I'm going to sit you at the dinner table between Mrs Yasin and Mrs Mahmud tonight if you don't stop trying to be reasonable,' Leona said warningly.

'Okay, you've made your point,' Evie conceded. 'You need a loyal champion, not a wise one.' Then, with a complete change of manner, 'So get yourself into the bathroom and tidy yourself up before we go and fight the old dragons together.'

Leona began to smile. 'Now you're talking,' she enthused, and, stretching out a long leg, she rose from the bed a different person than the one who'd slumped down on it minutes ago. 'I'm glad you're here, Evie,' she murmured huskily.

It was a remark she could have repeated a hundred times over during the following days when everyone did try to appear content to simply enjoy the cruise with no underlying disputes to spoil it.

But in truth many undercurrents were at work. In the complicated way of Arab politics, there was no natural right to succession in Rahman. First among equals was the Arab way of describing a collective of tribe leaders amongst which one is considered the most authoritative. The next leader did not necessarily have to be the son of the one preceding him, but choice became an open issue on which all heads of the family must agree.

In truth everyone knew that Hassan was the only sensible man for the job simply because he had been handling the modern thrusts of power so successfully for the last five years as his father's health had begun to fail. No one wanted to tip the balance. As it stood, the other families had lived well and prospered under Al-Qadim rule. Rahman was a respected country in Arabia. Landlocked though it was, the oil beneath its desert was rich and in plenty, and within its borders were some of the most important oases that other, more favourably placed countries, did not enjoy.

But just as the sands shifted, so did opinions. Al-Mahmud and Al-Yasin might have lived well and prospered under thirty years of Al-Qadim rule, but they had disapproved of Hassan's choice of wife from the beginning. Though they could not fault the dedication Hassan's wife had applied to her role, nor ignore the respect she had earned from the Rahman people, she was frail of body. She had produced no sons in five years of marriage, and then had made Hassan appear weak to his peers when she'd walked away from him of her own volition. Divorce should have followed swiftly. Hassan had refused to discuss it as an option. Therefore, a second wife should have been chosen. Hassan's refusal to pander to what he called the ways of the old guard had incensed many. Not least Sheikh Abdul Al-Yasin who had not stopped smarting from the insult he'd received when Hassan had not chosen his daughter, Nadira, who had been primed from birth to take the role.

With Hassan's father's health failing fast, Sheikh Abdul had seen an opportunity to redress this insult. All it required was for Hassan to agree to take on a second wife in order to maintain the delicate balance between families. It was that simple. Everyone except Hassan agreed that his marriage to Nadira Al-Yasin would form an alliance that would solve everyone's problems. Hassan could keep his first wife. No one was asking him to discard this beautiful but barren woman. But his first son would come from the womb of Nadira Al-Yasin, which was all that really mattered.

The alternatives? Sheikh Jibril Al-Mahmud had a son who could be considered worthy of taking up the mantle Hassan's father would leave vacant. And no one could afford to ignore Sheikh Imran Al-Mukhtar and his son, Samir. Samir might be too young to take on the mantle of power but his father was not.

This, however only dealt with the male perspective. As the sheikhs fought their war with words on each other during long discussions, ensconced in one of the staterooms, the women were waging a similar war for their own reasons. Zafina Al-Yasin wanted Leona out and her daughter, Nadira, in. Since Hassan was not allowing this, then she would settle for her daughter taking second place. For the power lay in the sons born in a marriage, not the wives. So critical remarks were dropped at every opportunity to whittle away at Leona's composure and a self-esteem that was already fragile due to her inability to give Hassan what he needed most in this world.

In the middle of it all stood Sheikh Raschid and his wife, Evie offering positive proof that west could successfully join with east. For Behran had gone from strength to strength since their marriage and was fast becoming one of the most influential States in Arabia. But they had a son. It was the cog on which everything else rotated.

It took two days to navigate the Suez Canal, and would take another five to cross the Red Sea to the city of Jeddah on the coast of Saudi Arabia. By the time they had reached the end of the Canal, battle lines had been clearly marked for those times when the war of words would rage or a truce would be called. Mornings were truce times, when everyone more or less did their own thing and the company could even be called pleasant.

In the afternoons most people took a siesta, unless Samir grew restless and chivvied the others towards more enjoyable pursuits.

'Just look at them,' Evie murmured indulgently one afternoon as they stood watching Samir, Rafiq, Raschid and Hassan jet-skiing the ocean like reckless idiots, criss-crossing each other's wash with a daring that sometimes caught the breath. 'They're like little boys with exciting new toys.'

They came back to the boat, refreshed, relaxed—and ready to begin the first wave of strikes when the men gathered to drink coffee in one of the staterooms while the women occupied another.

Dinner called a second truce. After dinner, when another split of the sexes occurred, hostilities would resume until someone decided to call it a day and went to bed.

Bed was a place you could neither describe as a place of war nor truce. It gave you a sanctuary in which you had the chance to vent all of the things you had spent the day suppressing. But when the person in the bed with you saw you as much the enemy as every one else did, then you were in deep trouble. As Hassan acknowledged every time he slid into bed beside Leona and received the cold shoulder if he so much as attempted to touch her or speak.

She was angry with him for many reasons, but angriest most for some obscure point he had not managed to expose. He was aware that this situation was difficult, that she would rather be anywhere else other than trapped on this yacht right now. He knew she was unhappy, that she was only just managing to hide that from everyone else. That she was eating little and looking contradictorily pale when in truth her skin was taking on a deeper golden hue with every passing day. He knew that Zafina and Medina used any opportunity presented to them to compare her situation unfavourably with Evie's. And he wished Raschid had shown some sensitivity to that prospect when he'd made the decision to bring his children along!

The children were a point of conflict he could not seem to deal with. This evening, for instance, when Raschid had brought his son into the salon to say goodnight to everyone, Hashim had run the length of the room with his arms open wide in demand for a hug from Leona. She had lifted him up in her arms and received all of his warm kisses to her face with smiles of pleasure while inside, Hassan knew, the ache of empty wishes must be torture for her.

When she hurt, he hurt. When he had no remedy to ease that pain, he had to turn away from its source or risk revealing to her the emptiness of helplessness he suffered whenever he saw her hugging a son that was not their own.

But in trying to protect Leona from himself he had forgotten the other pairs of eyes watching him. The Al-Mahmuds and the Al-Yasins had seen, read and drawn their own conclusions.

'A sad sight, is it not?' Abdul had dared to say.

Leona had heard him, had known what he'd been referring to, and had been shunning Hassan ever since.

'Talk to me, for Allah's sake.' He sighed into the darkness.

'Find another bed to sleep in.'

Well, they were words, he supposed, then sighed again, took the bull by the horns and pushed himself up to lean over her, then tugged her round to face him. 'What is it that you want from me?' he demanded. 'I am trying my best to make this work for us!'

Her eyes flicked open; it was like gazing into pools of broken ice. 'Why go to all this trouble when I am still going to leave you flat the first moment I know I can do it without hurting your father?'

'Why?' he challenged.

'We've already been through the *whys* a hundred times! They haven't changed just because you have decided to play the warlord and win the battle against your rotten underlings without giving an inch to anyone!'

'Warlord?' His brow arched. 'How very pagan.' He made sure she knew he liked the sound of that title in a very physical way.

'Oh, get off me,' she snapped, gave a push and rolled free of him, coming to her feet by the bed. Her hair floated everywhere, and the cream silk pyjamas shimmied over her slender figure as she walked down the room and dumped herself into one of the chairs, then dared to curl up in it as if he would allow her to sleep there!

'Come back here, Leona,' he commanded wearily.

'I regret ever agreeing to be here,' she answered huskily.

Husky meant tears. Tears made him want to curse for making a joke of what they had been talking about when any fool would have known it was no time for jokes! On yet another sigh he got out of the bed, then trod in her footsteps and went to squat down in front of her.

'I'm sorry,' he said, 'that this situation is so difficult for you. But my father insisted that the family heads must talk to each other. I have no will to refuse him because in truth his reasons are wise. You know I have no automatic right to succession. I must win the support of the other family leaders.'

'Stop being so stubborn and just let me go and you would not have to win over anyone,' she pointed out.

'You know...' he grimaced '...I think you are wrong

there. I think that underneath all the posturing they want me to fight this battle and win, to prove the strength of my resolve.'

She brushed a tear off her cheek. Hassan had wanted to do it for her, but instinct was warning him not to. 'Tonight Zafina asked me outright if I had any idea of the life I was condemning you to if I held onto a marriage destined to have no children.'

His eyes flashed with raw anger, his lips pressing together on an urge to spit out words that would make neither of them feel any better. But he made a mental note that from tomorrow Leona went nowhere without himself or Rafiq within hearing.

'And I saw your face, Hassan,' she went on unsteadily. 'I heard what Abdul said to you and I know why he said it. So why are you being so stubborn about something we both know is—'

He shut her up in the most effective way he knew. Mouth to mouth, tongue to tongue, words lost in the heat of a much more productive form of communication. She fought him for a few brief seconds, then lost the battle when her flailing fingers made contact with his naked flesh.

He had no clothes on, she had too many, but flesh-warmed silk against naked skin achieved a sensual quality he found very pleasurable as he lifted her up and settled her legs around his hips.

'You are such an ostrich,' she threw into his face as he carried her back to bed. 'How long do you think you can go on ignoring what—!'

He used the same method to shut her up again. By then he was standing by the bed with her fingernails digging into his shoulders, her hair surrounding him and her long legs clinging to his waist with no indication that they were going to let go. If he tried for a horizontal position he would risk hurting her while she held him like this.

So—who needed a bed? he thought with a shrug as his fingers found the elastic waistband to her pyjama bottoms and pushed the silk far enough down her thighs to gain him access to what he wanted the most. She groaned as he eased himself into her, and the kiss deepened into something else.

Fevered was what it was. Fevered and hot and a challenge to how long he could maintain his balance as he stood there with his hands spanning her slender buttocks, squeezing to increase the frictional pleasure, and no way—no way— would he have believed three nights without doing this could leave him so hungry. Twelve months without doing this had not affected him as badly.

'You're shaking.'

She'd noticed. He wasn't surprised. He wasn't just shaking, he was out of control, and he could no longer maintain this position without losing his dignity as well as his mind. So he lowered her to the bed with as much care as he could muster, pushed her hair from her face and stared blackly into her eyes.

'You tell me how I deny myself this above all things?' he demanded. 'You, only you, can do this to me. It is only you I want to do it with.'

The words were spoken between fierce kisses, between possessive thrusts from his hips. Leona touched his face, touched his mouth, touched his eyes with her eyes. 'I'm so very sorry,' she whispered tragically.

It was enough to drive an already driven man insane. He withdrew, got up, swung away and strode into the bathroom, slammed shut the door then turned to slam the flat of his palm against the nearest wall. Empty silences after the loving he had learned to deal with, but tragic apologies in the middle were one large step too far!

Why had she said it? She hadn't meant to say it! It was just one of those painful little things that had slipped out because she had seen he was hurting, and the look had reminded her of the look he had tried to hide from her when she had been cuddling Hashim.

Oh, what were they doing to each other? Leona asked

herself wretchedly. And scrambled to her feet as the sickness she had been struggling with for days now came back with a vengeance, leaving her with no choice but to make a run for the bathroom with the hope that he hadn't locked the door.

With one hand over her mouth and the other trying to recover her slipping pyjama bottoms, she reached the door just as it flew open to reveal a completely different Hassan than the one who had stormed in there only seconds ago.

'You may have your wish,' he informed her coldly. 'As soon as it is safe for me to do so, I will arrange a divorce. Now I want nothing more to do with you.'

With that he walked away, having no idea that her only response was to finish what she had been intending to do and make it to the toilet bowl before she was sick.

CHAPTER EIGHT

LEONA was asleep when Hassan let himself back into the room the next morning. She was still asleep when, showered and dressed, he left the room again half an hour later, and in a way he was glad.

He had spent the night stretched out on a lounger on the shade deck, alternating between feeling angry enough to stand by every word he had spoken and wanting to go back and retract what he had left hanging in the air.

And even now, hours later, he was not ready to choose which way he was going to go. He'd had enough of people tugging on his heartstrings; he'd had enough of playing these stupid power games.

He met Rafiq on his way up to the sun deck. 'Set up a meeting,' he said. 'Ten o'clock in my private office. We are going for broke.'

Rafiq sent him one of his steady looks, went to say something, changed his mind, and merely nodded his head.

Samir was already at the breakfast table, packing food away at a pace that made Hassan feel slightly sick—a combination of no sleep and one too many arguments, he told himself grimly.

Leona still hadn't put in an appearance by the time everyone else had joined them and finished their breakfast. Motioning the steward over, he instructed him to ring the suite.

'I'll go,' Evie offered, and got up, leaving her children to Raschid's capable care.

And he was capable. In fact it irritated Hassan how capable his friend was at taking care of his two children. How did he run a Gulf state the size of Behran and find time to learn how to deal with babies?

The sun was hot, the sky was blue and here he was, he acknowledged, sitting here feeling like a grey day in London.

'Hassan…'

'Hmm?' Glancing up, he realised that Sheikh Imran had been talking to him and he hadn't heard a single word that he had said.

'Rafiq tells us you have called a meeting for ten o'clock'

'Yes.' He glanced at his watch, frowned and stood up. 'If you will excuse me, this is the time I call my father.'

To reach his office required him to pass by his suite door. It was closed. He hesitated, wondering whether or not to go in and at least try to make his peace. But Evie was in there, he remembered, and walked on, grimly glad of the excuse not to have to face that particular problem just now. For he had bigger fish to fry this morning.

Faysal was already in the office. 'Get my father on the phone for me, Faysal,' he instructed. 'Then set the other room up ready for a meeting.'

'It is to be today, sir?' Faysal questioned in surprise.

'Yes, today. In half an hour. My father, Faysal,' he prompted before the other man could say any more. He glanced at his watch again as Faysal picked up the telephone. Had Leona stayed in their suite because she didn't want to come face to face with him?

But Leona had not stayed in their suite because she was sulking, as Hassan so liked to call it. She was ill, and didn't want anyone to know.

'Don't you dare tell anyone,' she warned Evie. 'I'll be all right in a bit. It just keeps happening, and then it goes away again.'

'How long?' Evie looked worried.

'A few days.' Leona shrugged. 'I don't think I've got anything your children might catch, Evie,' she then anxiously assured her. 'I'm just—stressed out, that's all.'

'Stressed out.' Evie was looking at her oddly.

'It's playing havoc with my stomach.' Leona nodded and took another sip of the bottled water Evie had opened for her. 'Who would not be feeling sick if they were stuck on this boat with a load of people they liked as little as those people liked them? You and your family excluded, of course,' she then added belatedly.

'Oh, of course.' Evie nodded and sat down on the edge of the bed, a bed with one half that had not been slept in. Hassan had not come back last night, and Leona was glad that he hadn't.

'I hate men,' she announced huskily.

'You mean you hate one man in particular.'

'I'll be glad when this is over and he just lets me go.'

'Do you really think that is likely?' Evie mocked. 'Hassan is an Arab and they give up on nothing. Arrogant, possessive, stubborn, selfish and sweet,' she listed ruefully. 'It is the moments of sweetness that are their saving grace, I find.'

'You're lucky, you've got a nice one.'

'He wasn't nice at all on the day I sent him packing,' Evie recalled. 'In fact it was the worst moment of my life when he turned to leave with absolutely no protest. I knew it was the end. I'd seen it carved into his face like words set in stone…'

'I know,' Leona whispered miserably. 'I've seen the look myself…'

Evie had seen the same look on Hassan's face at the breakfast table. 'Oh, Leona.' She sighed. 'The two of you have got to stop beating each other up like this. You love each other. Can't that be enough?'

Raschid was not in agreement with Hassan's timing. 'Think about this,' he urged. 'We have too much time before we reach dry land. Time for them to fester on their disappointment.'

'I need this settled,' Hassan grimly insisted. 'Leona is a mess. The longer I let the situation ride the more hesitant I appear. Both Abdul and Zafina Al-Yasin are becoming so over-confident that they think they may say what they please. My father agrees. It shall be done with today. *Inshallah*,' he concluded.

'*Inshallah*, indeed,' Raschid murmured ruefully, and went away to prepare what he had been brought here specifically to say.

An hour later Evie was with her children, Medina and Zafina were seated quietly in one of the salons sipping coffee while they awaited the outcome of the meeting taking place on the deck below, and Leona and Samir were kitting up to go jet-skiing when Sheikh Raschid Al-Kadah decided it was time for him to speak.

'I have listened to your arguments with great interest and some growing concern,' he smoothly began. 'Some of you seem to be suggesting that Hassan should make a choice between his country and his western wife. I find this a most disturbing concept—not only because I have a western wife myself, but because forward-thinking Arabs might be setting such outmoded boundaries upon their leaders for the sake of what?'

'The blood line,' Abdul said instantly.

Some of the others shifted uncomfortably. Raschid looked into the face of each and every one of them and challenged them to agree with Sheikh Abdul. It would be an insult to himself, his wife and children if they did so. None did.

'The blood line was at risk six years ago, Abdul.' He smoothly directed his answer at the man who had dared to offer such a dangerous reason. 'When Hassan married, his wife was accepted by you all. What has changed?'

'You misunderstand, Raschid,' Jibril Al-Mahmud quickly inserted, eager to soothe the ruffled feathers of the other man. 'My apologies, Hassan, for feeling pressed to say this.' He bowed. 'But it is well known throughout Rahman that your most respected wife cannot bear a child.'

'This is untrue, but please continue with your hypothesis,' Hassan invited calmly.

Flustered, Jibril looked back at Raschid. 'Even in your

country a man is allowed, if not expected, to take a second wife if the first is—struggling to give him sons,' he pointed out. 'We beg Hassan only take a second wife to secure the *family* line.' Wisely, he omitted the word 'blood'.

'Hassan?' Raschid looked to him for an answer.

Hassan shook his head. 'I have the only wife I need,' he declared.

'And if Allah decides to deny you sons, what then?'

'Then control passes on to my successor. I do not see the problem.'

'The problem is that your stance makes a mockery of everything we stand for as Arabs,' Abdul said impatiently. 'You have a duty to secure the continuance of the Al-Qadim name. Your father agrees. The old ones agree. I find it insupportable that you continue to insist on giving back nothing for the honour of being your father's son!'

'I give back my right to succession,' Hassan countered. 'I am prepared to step down and let one or other of you here take my place. There,' he concluded with a flick of the hand, 'it is done. You may now move on to discuss my father's successor without me...'

'One moment, Hassan...' It was Raschid who stopped him from rising. Worked in and timed to reach this point in proceedings, he said, 'I have some objections to put forward against your decision.'

Hassan returned to his seat. Raschid nodded his gratitude for this, then addressed the table as a whole. 'Rahman's land borders my land. Your oil pipeline runs beneath Behran soil and mixes with my oil in our co-owned holding tanks when it reaches the Gulf. And the old ones criss-cross our borders from oasis to oasis with a freedom laid down in a treaty drawn up and signed by Al-Kadah and Al-Qadim thirty years ago. So tell me,' he begged, 'with whom am I expected to renegotiate this treaty when an Al-Qadim is no longer in a position to honour his side of our bargain?'

It was an attack on all fronts. For Rahman was landlocked. It needed Behran to get its oil to the tankers that moored up at its vast terminals. The treaty was old and the tariffs laid down in it had not been changed in those thirty years Raschid had mentioned. Borders were mere lines on maps the old ones were free to ignore as they roamed the desert with their camel trains.

'There is no question of altering the balance of power here in Rahman,' It was Sheikh Jibril Al-Mahmud who declaimed the suggestion. He looked worried. Crown Prince Raschid Al-Kadah was not known as a bluffing man. 'Hassan has our complete loyalty, respect and support.'

'Ah,' Raschid said. 'Then I am mistaken in what I have been hearing here. My apologies.' He bowed. 'I believed I was hearing Hassan about to step down as his father's natural successor.'

'Indeed no such thing ever crossed our minds.' You could almost see Sheikh Jibril shifting his position into the other camp as he spoke. 'We are merely concerned about future successors and question whether it is not time for Hassan to consider taking steps to—'

'As the old ones would say,' Raschid smoothly cut in, 'time is but a grain of sand that shifts in accordance with the wind and the will of Allah.'

'*Inshallah*,' Sheikh Jibril agreed, bringing Sheikh Abdul's house of cards tumbling down.

'Thank you,' Hassan murmured to Raschid a few minutes later, when the others had left them. 'I am in your debt.'

'There is no debt,' Raschid denied. 'I have no wish to see the spawn of Sheikh Abdul Al-Yasin develop in to the man who will then deal with my son. But, as a matter of interest only, who is your successor?'

'Rafiq,' Hassan replied.

'But he does not want the job.'

'He will nonetheless acquire it,' Hassan said grimly.

'Does he know?'

'Yes. We have already discussed it.'

Raschid nodded thoughtfully, then offered a grim smile.

'Now all you have to do, my friend, is try to appear happy that you have achieved your goal.'

It was Hassan's cue to begin smiling, but instead he released a heavy sigh and went to stand by the window. Outside, skimming across the glass-smooth water, he could see two jet-skis teasing each other. Leona's hair streamed out behind her like a glorious banner as she stood, half bent at the knees, turning the machine into a neat one-hundred-and-eighty-degree-spin in an effort to chase after the reckless Samir.

'The victory could be an empty one in the end,' he murmured eventually. 'For I do not think she will stay.'

Raschid's silence brought Hassan's head round. What he saw etched into the other man's face said it all for him. 'You don't think she will, either, do you?' he stated huskily.

'Evie and I discussed this,' Raschid confessed. 'We swapped places with you and Leona, if you like. And quite honestly, Hassan, her answer made my blood run cold.'

Hassan was not surprised by that. East meets west, he mused as he turned back to the window. Pride against pride. The love of a good, courageous woman against the—

'In the name of Allah,' he suddenly rasped out as he watched Leona's jet-ski stop so suddenly that she was thrown right over the front of it.

'What?' Raschid got to his feet.

'She hit something,' he bit out, remaining still for a moment, waiting for her to come up. It didn't happen. His heart began to pound, ringing loudly in his ears as he turned and began to run. With Raschid close on his heels he took the stairs two at a time, then flung himself down the next set, heading for the rear of the boat where the back let down to form a platform into the water. Rafiq was already there, urgently lowering another jet ski into the water. His taut face said it all; Leona still had not reappeared. Samir had not even noticed; he was too busy making a wide, arching turn way out.

Without hesitation he wrenched the jet-ski from Rafiq and

was speeding off towards his wife before his brother had realised what he had done. Teeth set, eyes sharp, he made an arrow-straight track towards her deadly still jet-ski as behind him the yacht began sounding its horn in a warning call to Samir. The sound brought everyone to the boatside, to see what was going on.

By the time Hassan came up on Leona's jet-ski, Rafiq was racing after him on another one and Samir was heading towards them at speed. No one else moved or spoke or even breathed as they watched Hassan take a leaping dive off his moving machine and disappear into the deep blue water. Three minutes had past, maybe four, and Hassan could not understand why her buoyancy aid had not brought her to the surface.

He found out why the moment he broke his dive down and twisted full circle in the water. A huge piece of wood, like the beam from an old fishing boat, floated just below the surface—tangled with fishing net. It was the net she was caught in, a slender ankle, a slender wrist, and she was frantically trying to free herself.

As he swam towards her, he saw the panic in her eyes, the belief that she was going to die. With his own lungs already wanting to burst, he reached down to free her foot first, then began hauling her towards the surface even as he wrenched free her wrist.

White, he was white with panic, overwhelmed by shock and gasping greedily for breath. She burst out crying, coughing, spluttering, trying desperately to fill her lungs through racking sobs that tore him to bits. Neither had even noticed the two other jet-skis warily circling them or that Raschid and a crewman were heading towards them in the yacht's emergency inflatable.

'Why is it you have to *do* this to me?' he shouted at her furiously.

'Hassan,' someone said gruffly. He looked up, saw his brother's face, saw Samir looking like a ghost, saw the inflatable almost upon them, then saw—really saw—the woman he held crushed in his arms. After that the world took on a blur as Rafiq and Samir joined them in the water and helped to lift Leona into the boat. Hassan followed, then asked Raschid and the crewman to bring in the other two men on the jet-skis. As soon as the jet-skis left the inflatable he turned it round and, instead of making for the yacht, he headed out in the Red Sea.

Leona didn't notice, she was lying in a huddle still sobbing her heart out on top of a mound of towels someone had had the foresight to toss into the boat, and he was shaking from teeth to fingertips. His mind was shot, his eyes blinded by an emotion he had never experienced before in his life.

When he eventually stopped the boat in the middle of nowhere, he just sat there and tried hard to calm whatever it was that was raging inside of him while Leona tried to calm her frightened tears.

'You know,' he muttered after a while, 'for the first time since I was a boy, I think I am going to weep. You have no idea what you do to me, no idea at all. Sometimes I wonder if you even care.'

'It was an accident,' she whispered hoarsely

'So was the trip on the gangway! So was the headlong fall down the stairs! What difference does it make if it was an accident? You still have no idea what you do to me!'

Sitting up, she plucked up one the towels and wrapped it around her shivering frame.

'Are you listening to me?' he grated.

'No,' she replied. 'Where are we?'

'In the middle of nowhere where I can shout if I want to, cry if I want to, and tell the rest of the world to get out of my life!' he raged. 'I am sick of other people meddling in it. I am sick of playing stupid, political games. And I am sick and tired of watching you do stupid madcap things just because you are angry with me!'

'Hassan—'

'What?' he lashed back furiously, black eyes burning

body so taut it looked ready to snap in two. He was soaking wet and he was trembling—not shivering like herself.

'I'm all right,' she told him gently.

He fell on her like a ravaging wolf, setting the tiny boat rocking and not seeming to care if they both ended up in the water again. 'Four minutes you were under the water—I timed it!' he bit out between tense kisses.

'I'm accident prone; you know I am,' she reminded him. 'The first time we met I tripped over someone's foot and landed on your lap.'

'No.' He denied it. 'I helped you there with a guiding hand.'

She frowned. He grimaced. He had never admitted that before. 'I had been watching you all evening, wondering how I could get to meet you without making myself appear over-eager. So it was an opportunity sent from Allah when you tripped just in front of me.'

Leona let loose a small, tear-choked chuckle. 'I tripped in front of you on purpose,' she confessed. 'Someone said you were an Arabian sheikh, rich as sin, so I thought to myself. That will do for me!'

'Liar,' he murmured.

'Maybe.' She smiled.

Then the teasing vanished from both of them. Eyes darkened, drew closer, then dived into each other's to dip into a place so very special it actually hurt to make contact with so much feeling at once.

'Don't leave me—ever.' He begged her promise.

Leona sighed as she ran her fingers through his wet hair. Her throat felt tight and her heart felt heavy. 'I'm frightened that one day you will change your mind about me and want more from your life. Then what will I be left with?'

'Ethan Hayes is in love with you,' he said.

'What has that got to do with this?' She frowned. 'And, no, he is not.'

'You are frightened I will leave you. Well, I am frightened

that you will one day see a normal man like Ethan and decide he has more to offer you than I ever can.'

'You are joking,' she drawled.

'No, I am not.' He sat up, long fingers reaching out to pluck absently at the ropework around the sides of the boat. 'What do I offer you beside a lot of personal restrictions, political games that can get nasty enough to put your well-being at risk, and a social circle of friends you would not pass the day with if you did not feel obliged to do so for my sake.'

'I liked most of our friends in Rahman,' she protested, sitting up to drape one of the towels around her head because the sun was too hot. 'Those I didn't like, you don't partic-ularly like, and we only used to see them at formal func-tions.'

'Or when we became stuck on a boat with them with no means of escape.'

'Why are we having this conversation in this small boat in the middle of the Red Sea?' she questioned wearily.

'Where else?' He shrugged. 'In our stateroom where there is a convenient bed to divert us away from what needs to be said?'

'It's another abduction,' she murmured ruefully.

'You belong to me. A man cannot abduct what is already his.'

'And you're arrogant.' She sighed.

'Loving you is arrogant of me?' he challenged.

Leona just shook her head and used the corner of the towel to dry her wet face. Her fingers were trembling, and she was still having a struggle to calm her breathing. 'Last night you promised me a divorce.'

'Today I am taking that promise back.'

'Here…' she held her arm out towards him. '…can you do something about this?'

Part of the netting she had been tangled in was still cling-ing to her wrist. The delicate skin beneath it was red and chafed. 'I'm sorry I said what I did last night,' he murmured.

'I'm sorry I said what I did,' Leona returned. 'I didn't even mean it the way it came out. It's just that sometimes you look so very...'

'Children are a precious gift from Allah,' Hassan interrupted, dark head sombrely bent over his task. 'But so is love. Very few people are fortunate enough to have both, and most only get the children. If I had to choose then I would choose, to have love.'

'But you are an Arabian sheikh with a duty to produce the next successor to follow on from you, and the choice no longer belongs to you.'

'If we find we want children then we will get some,' he said complacently, lifting up her wrist to break the stubborn cord with the sharp snap of his teeth. 'IVF, adoption... But only if we want them.' He made that fine but important point. 'Otherwise let Rafiq do his bit for his country,' he concluded with an indifferent shrug.

'He would give you one of his stares if he heard you saying that.' Leona smiled.

'He is an Al-Qadim, though he chooses to believe he is not.'

'He's half-French.'

'I am one quarter Spanish, and one quarter Al-Kadah,' he informed her. 'You, I believe, are one half rampaging Celt. I do not see us ringing bells about it.'

'All right, I will stay,' she murmured.

Dark eyes shrouded by a troubled frown lifted to look at her. 'You mean stay as in for ever, no more argument?' He demanded clarification.

Reaching up, she stroked her fingers through his hair again. 'As in you've got me for good, my lord Sheikh,' she said soberly. 'Just make sure you don't make me regret it.'

'Huh.' The short laugh was full of bewildered incredulity. 'What suddenly brought on this change of heart?'

'The heart has always wanted to stay, it was the mind that was causing me problems. But...look at us, Hassan.' She sighed 'sitting out in the middle of the sea in a stupid little

boat beneath the heat of a noon-day sun because we woul
rather be here, together like this, than anywhere else.' Sh
gave him her eyes again, and what always happened to them
happened when he looked deep inside. 'If you believe love
can sustain us through whatever is waiting for us back there
then I am going to let myself believe it too.'

'Courage,' he murmured, reaching out to gently cup he
cheek. 'I never doubted your courage.'

'No,' she protested when he went to kiss her. 'Not here
when I can feel about twenty pairs of eyes trained on u
from the yacht.'

'Let them watch,' he decreed, and kissed her anyway
'Now I want the privacy of our stateroom, with its very larg
bed,' he said as he drew away again.

'Then, let's go and find it.'

They were halfway back to the yacht before she remem
bered Samir telling her about the planned meeting. 'Wha
happened?' she asked anxiously.

Hassan smiled a brief, not particularly pleased smile. '
won the support I was looking for. The fight is over. No
we can begin to relax a little.'

As a statement of triumph, it didn't have much satisfactio
running through it. Leona wanted to question him about i
but they were nearing the yacht, so she decided to wait unti
later because she could now clearly see the sea of face
watching their approach—some anxious, some curious, som
wearing expressions that set her shivering all over again. No
everyone was relieved that Hassan had plucked her out o
the ocean, she realised ruefully.

Rafiq and a crewman were waiting on the platform to hel
them back on board the yacht. 'I'll walk,' she insisted whe
Hassan went to lift her into his arms. 'I think I have looke
foolish enough for one day.'

So they walked side by side through the boat, wrapped i
towels over their wet clothing. Neither spoke, neithe
touched, and no one accosted them on their journey to thei
stateroom. The door shut them in. Hassan broke away fror

er side and strode into the bathroom. Leona followed, found
he jets in the shower already running. She dropped the tow-
ls, Hassan silently helped her out of the buoyancy aid that
ad not been buoyant enough and tossed it in disgust to the
led floor. Next came her tee shirt, her shorts, the blue one-
iece swimsuit she was wearing beneath.

It was another of those calms before the storm, Leona
ecognised as she watched him drag his shirt off over his
ead and step out of the rest of his clothes. His face was
omposed, his manner almost aloof, and there wasn't a single
ell in her body that wasn't charged, ready to accept what
ad to come.

Tall and dark, lean and sleek. 'In,' he commanded, holding
pen the shower-cubicle door so that she could step inside.
He followed, closed the door. And as the white-tiled space
ngulfed them in steam he was reaching for her and engulf-
ag her in another way.

Think of asking questions about how much he had con-
eded to win his support from the other sheikhs? Why think
bout anything when this was warm and soft and slow and
o intense that the yacht could sink and they would not have
oticed. This was love, a renewal of love; touching, tasting,
ving, breathing, feeling love. From the shower they took it
ith them to the bed, from there they took it with them into
slumber which filtered the rest of the day away.

Questions? Who needed questions when they had this
epth of communication? No more empty silences between
he loving. No more fights with each other or with them-
elves about the wiseness of being together like this. When
he received him inside her she did so with her eyes wide
pen and brimming with love and his name sounding softly
n her lips.

eyond the room, in another part of the yacht, Raschid
ooked at Rafiq. 'Do you think he has realised yet that to-
ay's victory has only put Leona at greater risk from her
nemies?' he questioned.

'Sheikh Abdul would be a fool to show his hand now, when he must know that Hassan has chosen to pretend he had no concept of his plot to take her.'

'I was not thinking of Abdul, but his ambitious wife,' Raschid murmured grimly. 'The woman wants to see her daughter in Leona's place. One only had to glimpse her expression when Hassan brought them back to the yacht to know that she has not yet had the sense to give up the fight...'

CHAPTER NINE

LEONA was thinking much the same thing when she found herself faced by Zafina later that evening.

Before the confrontation the evening had been surprisingly pleasant. Leona made light of her spill into the sea, and the others made light of the meeting that had taken place as if the battle, now decided, had given everyone the excuse to relax their guard.

It was only when the women left the men at the table after dinner that things took a nasty turn for the worse. Evie had gone to check on her children and Leona used the moment to pop back to the stateroom to freshen up. The last person she expected to see as she stepped out of the bathroom was Zafina Al-Yasin, standing there waiting for her.

Dressed in a traditional jewel-blue *dara'a* and matching *thobe* heavily embroidered with silver studs, Zafina was here to cause trouble. It did not take more than a glance into her black opal eyes to see that.

'You surprise me with your jollity this evening.' The older woman began her attack. 'On a day when your husband won all and you lost everything I believed you stood so proudly for, I would have expected to find you more subdued. It was only as I watched you laugh with our men that it occurred to me that maybe, with your unfortunate accident and Sheikh Hassan's natural concern for you, he has not made you fully aware of what it was he has agreed to today?'

Not at all sure where she was going to be led with this, Leona demanded cautiously, 'Are you implying that my husband has lied to me?'

'I would not presume to suggest such a thing,' Zafina denied with a slight bow of respect meant in honour of Hassan, not Leona herself. 'But he may have been a little...eco-

135

nomical with some of the details in an effort to save you from further distress.'

'Something you are not prepared to be,' Leona assumed.

'I believe in telling the truth, no matter the pain it may course.'

Ah, Leona thought, the truth. Now there was an interesting concept.

'In the interest of fair play, I do feel that you should be fully informed so that you may make your judgements on your future with the full facts at hand.'

'Why don't you just get to the point of this conversation, Zafina?' Leona said impatiently.

'The point is…this…' Zafina replied, producing from inside the sleeve of her *dara'a* a piece of paper, which she then spread out on the bed.

Leona did not want to, but she made herself walk towards it, made herself look down. The paper bore the Al-Qadim seal of office. It bore the name of Sheikh Khalifa.

'What is it?' she asked, oddly unwilling to read the closely lined and detailed Arabian script that came beneath.

'A contract drawn up by Sheikh Khalifa himself, giving his blessing to the marriage between his son Sheikh Hassan and my daughter Nadira. This is my husband's copy. Sheikh Khalifa and Sheikh Hassan have copies of their own.'

'It isn't signed,' Leona pointed out.

'It will be,' Zafina stated certainly, 'as was agreed this morning at the meeting of the family heads. Sheikh Khalifa is dying. His loving son will deny him nothing. When we reach Rahman the signing will take place and the announcement will be made at Sheikh Khalifa's celebration banquet.'

He will deny him nothing… Of everything Zafina had said, those words were the only ones that held the poison. Still, Leona strove to reject them.

'You lie,' she said. 'No matter what this piece of paper says, and no matter what you imply. I know Hassan. I know my father-in-law, Sheikh Khalifa. Neither would even think of deceiving me this way.'

'You think not?' She sounded so sure, so confident. 'In the eyes of his country, Sheikh Hassan must prove his loyalty to them is stronger than his desire to pander to your western principles.'

More certain on having said it, Leona turned ice-cold eyes on the other woman. 'I will tell Hassan about this conversation. You do realise that?' she warned.

Zafina bowed her head in calm acquiescence. 'Face him,' she invited. 'Tell him what you know. He may continue to keep the truth from you for his father's sake. He may decide to confess all then fall on your mercy, hoping that you will still go to Rahman as his loyal first wife to help save his face. But mark my words, Sheikha,' she warned, 'my daughter will be Sheikh Hassan's wife before this month is out, and she will bear him the son that will make his life complete.'

Stepping forward, she retrieved her precious contract. 'I have no wish to see you humiliated,' she concluded as she turned towards the door. 'Indeed I give you this chance to save your face. Return to England. Divorce Hassan,' she advised. 'For, whether you do or not, he will marry my daughter, at which point I think we both know that your usefulness will be at an end.'

Leona let her go without giving her the satisfaction of a response, but as the door closed behind Zafina she began to shake. No, she told herself sternly, you will not let that woman's poison eat away at you. She's lying. Hassan would not be so deceitful or so manipulative. He loves you, for goodness' sake! Haven't you both just spent a whole afternoon re-avowing that love?

I will deny him nothing... Hassan's own words, exactly as spoken only days ago. Her stomach turned, sending her reeling for the bathroom. Yet she stopped herself, took a couple of deep controlling breaths and forced herself to think, to trust in her own instincts, to believe in Hassan!

He would not do it. Hands clenched into tense fists at her

sides, she repeated that. *He would not do it!* The woman is evil. She is ambitious. She cannot accept failure.

She used your own inadequacies against you. How dare you so much as consider anything she said as worthy of all of this anguish?

You promised to believe in him. How dare you let that promise falter because some awful woman wants you out of his life and her daughter in it?

A contract. What was the contract but a piece of paper with words written upon it? Anyone could draw up a contract; it was getting those involved to sign it that was the real test!

She would tell Hassan, let him deny it once and for all, then she could put all of this behind her and—

No she wouldn't. She changed her mind. She would not give that woman the satisfaction of causing more trouble between the families, which was what was sure to happen if Hassan did find out what Zafina had said.

Trust was the word. Trust she *would* give to him.

The door opened. She spun around to find Hassan standing there. Tall and dark, smooth and sleek, and so heart-achingly, heart-breakingly, precious to her.

'What is wrong?' He frowned. 'You look as pale as the carpet.'

'N-nothing,' she said. Then, because it was such an obvious lie, she admitted, 'H-headache, upset stomach…' Two tight fists unclenched, one hand going to cover her stomach the other her clammy forehead. 'Too much food tonight. T-too much water from my dip in the sea, maybe. I…'

He was striding towards her. Her man. Her beautiful, grim-faced man. He touched her cheek. 'You feel like ice.' He picked up her chafed wrist between gentle finger and thumb. 'Your pulse is racing like mad! You need the medic.' He spun towards the telephone. 'Get undressed. You are going to bed…'

'Oh…no, Hassan!' she cried out in protest. 'I will be okay in a couple of minutes! Please…' she pleaded as he picked up the telephone. 'Look!' she declared, as he glared at her from beneath frowning black brows. 'I'm feeling better already. I—took something a few minutes ago.' With a mammoth gathering together of self-control, she even managed to walk over to him without stumbling and took the receiver from his hand.

'No,' she repeated. 'I will not spoil everyone's enjoyment tonight. I've caused enough fuss today as it is.' And she would not give Zafina a moment's smug satisfaction. 'Walk me back along the deck.' Firmly she took his hand. 'All I need is some fresh air.'

He wasn't sure. But Leona ignored his expression and pulled him towards the door. Actually the walk did her more good than she had expected it to do. Just being with him, feeling his presence, was enough to help reaffirm her belief that he would never, ever, do anything so cruel as to lie about a second wife.

He's done it before, a small voice inside her head reminded her.

Oh, shut up! she told it. I don't want to listen. And she pasted a bright smile on her face, ready to show it to their waiting guests—and Zafina Al-Yasin—as she and Hassan stepped back into the salon.

Zafina wasn't there, which in a way was a relief and in another was a disappointment, because she so wanted to outface the evil witch. She had to make do with shining like a brilliant star for those left to witness it, and she wondered once or twice if she was going to burn out. And she was never more relieved when it became time to retire without causing suspicion that this was all just a dreadful front.

Raschid and Imran had collared Hassan. So she was free to droop the moment she hit the bedroom. Within ten minutes she was curled up in bed. Within another ten she was up again and giving in to what had been threatening to happen since Zafina's visit. Fortunately Hassan was not there to witness it. By the time he came to bed she had found escape in sleep at last, and he made no move to waken her, so morning arrived all too soon, and with it returned the nauseous sensation.

She got through the day by the skin of her teeth, and was pleasant to Zafina, who was not sure how to take that. She spent most of her morning with Evie and her children, taking comfort from the sheer normality of their simple needs and amusements. It was while she was playing with Hashim that the little boy inadvertently brushed against her breasts and she winced at their unexpectedly painful response.

Evie noticed the wince. 'You okay?' she enquired.

Her shrug was rueful. 'Actually, I feel a bit grotty,' she confessed. 'I ache in strange places after my fight with the fishing net yesterday, and I think the water I swallowed had bugs.'

'The same bugs that got you the day before that?' Evie quizzed.

'Okay,' she conceded. 'So I'm still stressed out.'

'Or something,' Evie murmured.

Leona's chin came up, 'What's that supposed to mean?' she demanded.

It was Evie's turn to offer a rueful shrug, then Raschid walked into the room and the conversation had to be shelved when he reminded them that lunch was being served.

After lunch came siesta time. Or, for those like Hassan and Raschid, time to hit the phones and deal with matters of state. Leona had never been so glad of the excuse to shut herself away in her room because she was really beginning to feel ill by then. Her head ached, her bones ached, her stomach was objecting to the small amount of food she had eaten for lunch.

Maybe it was a bug, she mused frowningly as she drew the curtains across the windows in an effort to diffuse the light that was hurting her eyes. Stripping off her top clothes, she then crawled into the bed.

Maybe she should have steered well clear of Evie's children just in case she had picked up something catching, she then added, and made herself a promise to mention it to Evie later just before she slipped into a heavy sleep.

She came awake only as a scarlet sunset seeped into the room. The last sunset before they reached Jeddah, she recalled with relief. And found the reminder gave her a fresh burst of energy that she took with her into the bathroom where she indulged in a long leisurely shower then took her time getting ready for dinner. She chose to wear a calf-length tunic made of spearmint-blue silk with a matching pair of slender-cut trousers.

Hassan arrived in the room with a frown and his mind clearly preoccupied.

'Hello stranger,' she said.

He smiled. It was an amazing smile, full of warmth, full of love—full of lazy suggestions as he began to run his eyes over her in that dark possessive way that said, Mine, most definitely mine. It was the Arab-male way. What the man did not bother to say with words he could make up for with expressive glances.

'No,' Leona said to this particular look. 'I am all dressed up and ready to play hostess, so keep your lecherous hands to yourself.'

'Of course, you do know that I could easily change your mind?' he posed confidently.

Jokes. Light jokes. Warm smiles and tender communication. Would this man she knew and loved so well look at her like this yet still hold such terrible secrets from her?

No, of course he would not, so stop thinking about it! 'Save it until later,' she advised, making a play of sliding the silk scarf over her hair.

His eyes darkened measurably. It was strange how she only now noticed how much he liked seeing her dressed Arabian style. Was it in his blood that he liked to see his woman modestly covered? Was it more than that? Did he actually prefer—?

No. She stopped herself again. Stop allowing that woman's poison to get to you.

'Wait for me,' he requested when she took a step towards the door. 'I need only five minutes to change, for I showered ten minutes ago, after allowing that over-energetic Samir talk me into a game of softball on the sun deck.'

'Who won?' she asked, changing direction to go and sit on the arm of one of the chairs to wait as requested.

'I did—by cheating,' he confessed.

'Did he know you cheated?'

'Of course,' Hassan replied. 'But he believes he is in my debt so he allowed me to get away with it.'

'You mean you played on his guilty conscience over my accident,' she accused.

He turned another slashing grin on her. It had the same force as an electric charge aimed directly at her chest. Heat flashed across her flesh in a blanket wave of sensual static. Followed by another wave of the same as she watched him strip off western shirt and shorts to reveal sleek brown flesh just made for fingers to stroke. By the time he had replaced the clothes with a white tunic he had earned himself a similar possessive glance to the one he had given her.

See, she told herself, you can't resist him in Arab dress. It has nothing to do with what runs in the blood. She even decided to tease him about it. 'If there is one thing I have learned to understand since knowing you, it is why men prefer women in dresses.'

'This is not a dress,' he objected.

Getting up, she went to stand in front of him and placed her palms flat against the wall of his chest to feel warm skin, tight and smooth, and irresistible to seeking hands that wanted to stroke a sensual pathway over muscled contours to his lean waist.

'I know what it is, my darling,' she murmured seductively. 'It is a sinful temptation, and therefore no wonder that you don't encourage physical contact between the sexes.'

His answering laugh was low and deep, very much the sound of a man who was aware of his own power to attract. 'Remind Samir of that, if you will,' he countered dryly. 'He is very lucky I have not beaten him to a pulp by now for the liberties he takes with my wife.'

But Samir, Leona discovered as soon as they entered the main salon, was more interested in extolling the liberties Hassan had taken with him. 'He cheats. He has no honour. He went to Eton, for goodness' sake, where they turn desert savages into gentlemen!'

'Oh…' Leona lifted her head to mock her husband. 'So that's what it is I love most about you.'

'The gentleman?'

'The savage,' she softly corrected.

He replied with a gentle cuff to her chin. Everyone laughed. Everyone was happy. Zafina tried very hard to hide her malicious glare.

They ate dinner beneath the stars that night. Leona was surprised to see a bed of ice holding several bottles of champagne waiting on a side table. Some of her guests drank alcohol; some of them did not. Wine was the favoured choice for those who did imbibe. But even when there had been cause to celebrate yesterday evening champagne had not been served.

'What's going on?' she asked Hassan as he saw her seated.

'Wait and see,' he replied frustratingly, and walked away to take his own seat at the other end of the table.

Ah, the last supper, she thought then, with a pinch of acid wit. And, believing she had her answer, she turned her attention to her meal, while Rafiq continued his opinions of men in high positions who could lower themselves to cheat.

The first spoonful of what was actually a delicious Arabian soup set Leona's stomach objecting. 'Never mind,' she said to soothe Samir's dramatically ruffled feathers as she quietly laid aside her spoon. 'Tomorrow you and I will race on the jet-skis and I promise that I, as an English gentlewoman, will not cheat.'

'Not on this trip, I am afraid,' Hassan himself inserted smoothly. 'All water sports are now stopped until we can replace the buoyancy aids with something more effective.'

Leona stared down the table at him. 'Just like that?' she protested. 'I have an unfortunate and one-in-a-million-chance accident and you put a stop on everyone else's fun?'

'You almost drowned. The life jacket did not do what it is designed to do. A million-to-one chance of it happening again makes the odds too great.'

'That is the voice of the master,' Samir noted.

'You heard it too, hmm?' Leona replied.

'Most indubitably,' Hassan agreed.

After that the conversation moved on to other things. Soup dishes were removed and replaced with a fish dish she didn't even attempt to taste. A richly sauced Arab dish followed, with a side bowl each of soft and fluffy steamed white rice.

The rice she thought she could just about manage to eat, Leona decided, listening intently to the story Imran Al-Mukhtar was telling her as she transferred a couple of spoonfuls of rice onto her plate then added a spoonful of sauce just for show.

One spoonful of soup, two forkfuls of rice. No fish. No attempt to even accept a sample of the thick honey pudding to conclude. Hassan watched it all, took grim note, glanced to one side to catch Evie's eye. She sent him a look that said that she had noticed too.

'The Sheikha Leona seems a little...pale,' Zafina Al-Yasin, sitting to one side of him, quietly put in. 'Is she not feeling quite herself?'

'You think so?' he returned with mild surprise. 'I think she looks exquisite. But then, I am smitten,' he allowed. 'It makes a difference as to how you perceive someone, don't you think?'

A steward came to stand at his side then, thankfully relieving him from continuing such a discussion.

With a nod of understanding he sent the steward hurrying over to the side table where he and his assistants began deftly uncorking the bottles of champagne. Picking up a spoon, he gave a couple of taps against a wine glass to capture everyone's attention.

'My apologies for interrupting your dinner,' he said, 'but in a few minutes our captain will sound the yacht's siren. As you can see, the stewards are in the process of setting a glass of champagne before each of you. It is not compulsory that you actually drink it,' he assured with a grin for those who never imbibed no matter what the occasion, 'but as a courtesy, in the time-honoured tradition of any sailing vessel. I would be most honoured if you would stand and join me by raising your glass in a toast. For we are about to cross the Tropic of Cancer...'

With the perfect timing of a man who was adept at such things, the siren gave three short sharp hoots at the same moment that Hassan rose to his feet. On a ripple of surprise everyone rose up also. Some drank, some didn't, but all raised their glasses. Then there was a mass exodus to the yacht's rail, where everyone stood gazing out into the inky dark Red Sea as if they expected to see some physical phenomenon like a thick painted line to mark this special place.

Of course there was none. It did not seem to matter. Moving to place his hands on the rail either side of his wife, Hassan bent to place his lips to her petal-smooth cheek.

'See anything?' he questioned teasingly.

'Oh, yes,' she replied. 'A signpost sticking out of the water. Did you miss it?'

His soft laugh was deep and soft and seductive. As she tilted back to look at him the back of her head met with his shoulder. She was smiling with her eyes. He wanted to drown in them. Kiss me, they were saying. An Arab did not kiss in front of guests, so a raised eyebrow ruefully refused the invitation. It was the witch in her that punished him for that refusal when one of her hands slid backwards and made a sensual sweep of one of his thighs.

Sensation spat hot pricks of awareness like needles deep into his flesh. She was right about the *dishdasha*, he conceded, it had to be one of the ancient reasons why his culture frowned upon close physical contact with the opposite sex whilst in the company of others.

'I will pay you back for that later,' he warned darkly.

'I am most seriously worried, my lord Sheikh,' she replied provokingly.

Then, in the way these things shifted, the private moment was broken when someone spoke to him. He straightened to answer Jibril Al-Mahmud who, since the meeting had spent every minute he could possibly snatch trying to squeeze himself back into Hassan's good graces. Leona took a sip at her champagne. That dreadful intruder, Samir, claimed the rest of her attention. He was, Hassan recognised, just a little infatuated with Leona, which offered another good reason why he would be happy when their cruise ended tomorrow.

Jibril's timid little wife came to join them. She smiled nervously at him and, because he felt rather sorry for her, Hassan sent her a pleasant smile back, then politely asked about her family. Raschid joined in. Evie and Imran went to join Leona and Samir. Abdul and Zafina were the last to join his own group but at least they did it, he acknowledged.

Tonight there was no splitting of the sexes. No lingering at the table for the men. They simply mingled, talked and lingered together. And, had it not been for one small but important detail, Hassan would have declared the evening—if not the whole cruise—a more than satisfactory success.

That small but important detail was Leona. Relaxed though she might appear, content though she might appear, he could see that the strain of the whole ordeal in general had begun to paint soft bruises around her eyes. He didn't like to see them there, did not like to notice that every so often the palm of her hand would go to rest against the flat of her stomach, as if to soothe away an inner distress.

Nor had he forgotten that she had barely eaten a morsel of food all day. He frowned down at his champagne glass, still brimming with its contents. Tomorrow they reached Jeddah. Tomorrow he would take her to visit a doctor, he decided grimly. If there was one rule you were taught never to ignore when you lived in a hot country, it was the rule about heeding any signs of illness. Maybe it was nothing.

Maybe it was all just down to stress. But maybe she had picked up something in the water when she fell in. Whatever—tomorrow he would make sure that they found out for definite.

It was a decision he found himself firmly repeating when they eventually retired to their stateroom and the first thing that Leona did was wilt.

'You are ill,' he said grimly.

'Just tired,' she insisted.

'Don't take me for a fool, Leona,' he ground back. 'You do not eat. You are clearly in some sort of discomfort. And you *look* ill.'

'All right.' She caved in. 'So I think I have developed a stomach bug. If we have time when we reach Jeddah tomorrow I will get something for it.'

'We will make time.'

'Fine.' She sighed.

He sighed. 'Here, let me help you...' She even looked too weary to undress herself.

So he did it for her—silently, soberly, a concentrated frown darkening his face. She smiled and kissed him. It really was too irresistible to hold the gesture in check. 'Don't turn into a minx just because I am indulging you,' he scolded, and parted the tunic, then let it slide to her feet.

'But I like it when you indulge me,' she told him, her eyes lowered to watch him reach for the front clasp holding the two smooth satin cups of her cream bra together. As the back of his knuckles brushed against the tips of her breasts she drew back with a sharp gasp.

'What?' he demanded.

'Sensitive.' She frowned. He frowned. They both glanced down to see the tight distension of her nipples standing pink and proud and wilfully erect. A small smug smile twitched at the corner of his mouth. Leona actually blushed.

'I'll finish the rest for myself,' she decided dryly.

'I think that would be wise,' Hassan grinned, and pulled

the *dishdasha* off over his head to show her why he had said that.

'I don't know.' She was almost embarrassed by how fiercely one responded to the closeness of the other. 'I'm supposed to be ill and tired and in need of much pampering.'

A set of warm brown fingers gently stroked the flush blooming in her cheek. 'I know of many ways to pamper,' he murmured sensually. 'Slow and gentle. Soft and sweet…'

His eyes glowed darkly with all of those promises; hers grew darker on the willingness to accept. The gap between them closed, warm flesh touched warm flesh, mouths came together on a kiss. Then he showed her. Deep into the night he showed her a hundred ways to pamper a woman until she eventually fell asleep in his arms and remained there until morning came to wake them up.

At breakfast she actually ate a half-slice of toast with marmalade and drank a full cup of very weak tea—hopefully without giving away the fact that it was a struggle not to give it all back up.

Little Hashim came to beg to be allowed to sit on her lap. Leona placed him there and together they enjoyed sharing the other half of her slice of toast, while Hassan looked on with a glaze across his eyes and Evie posed a sombre question at her husband, Raschid, with expressive eyes.

He got up and stepped around the table to lay a hand on Hassan's shoulder. The muscles beneath it were fraught with tension. 'I need a private word with you, Hassan,' he requested. 'If you have finished here?'

The same muscle flexed as Hassan pulled his mind back from where it had gone off to. 'Of course,' he said, and stood up. A moment later both men were walking away from the breakfast table towards the stairs which would take them down to the deck below and Hassan's private suite of offices.

Most watched them go. Many wondered why Sheikh Raschid felt it necessary to take Sheikh Hassan to one side. But none, friend nor foe—except for Evie, who kept her attention firmly fixed on the small baby girl in her arms—came even close to guessing what was about to be discussed.

By the time Raschid came to search his wife out she was back in their suite. She glanced anxiously up at him. Raschid lifted a rueful shoulder, 'Well, it is done,' he said. Though neither of them looked as if the statement pleased them in any way.

Well, it is done. That more or less said it. *Well it is done,* now held Hassan locked in a severe state of shock. He couldn't believe it. He wanted to believe it, but did not dare let himself because it changed everything: the view of his life; the view of his marriage.

He had to sit down. The edge of his desk was conveniently placed to receive his weight, and his eyes received the cover of a trembling hand. Beyond the closed door to his office his guests and the tail end of the cruise carried on regardless, but here in this room everything he knew and felt had come to a complete standstill.

He couldn't move. Now his legs had been relieved of his weight, they had lost the ability to take it back again. Inside he was shaking. Inside he did not know what to feel or what to think. For he had been here in this same situation before—many times—and had learned through experience that it was a place best avoided at all costs.

Hope—then dashed hopes. Pleasure—then pain. But this was different. This had been forced upon him by a source he had good reason to trust and not to doubt.

Doubt. Dear heaven, he was very intimate with the word doubt. Now, as he removed the hand from his eyes and stared out at the glistening waters he could see through the window, he found doubt being replaced by the kind of dancing visions he had never—ever—allowed himself to see before.

A knock sounded at the door, then it opened before he had a chance to hide his expression. Rafiq walked in, took one look at him and went rock solid still.

'What is it?' he demanded. 'Father?'

Hassan quickly shook his head. 'Come in and close the door,' he urged, then made an effort to pull himself together—just in case someone else decided to take him by surprise.

Leona.

Something inside him was suddenly threatening to explode. He didn't know what, but it scared the hell out of him. He wished Raschid had said nothing. He wished he could go back and replay the last half hour again, change it, lose it—

'Hassan...?' Rafiq prompted an explanation as to why he was witnessing his brother quietly falling apart.

He looked up, found himself staring into mirrors of his own dark eyes, and decided to test the ground—test those eyes to find out what Leona would see in his eyes if she walked in here right now.

'Evie—Raschid,' he forced out across a sand-dry throat. 'They think Leona might be pregnant. Evie recognises the signs...'

CHAPTER TEN

SILENCE fell. It was, Hassan recognised, a very deathly silence, for Rafiq was already showing a scepticism he dared not voice.

Understanding the feeling, Hassan released a hard sigh, then grimly pulled himself together. 'Get hold of our father,' he instructed. 'I need absolute assurance from him that I will not be bringing Leona back to a palace rife with rumour attached to her return.' From being hollowed by shock he was now as tight as a bowstring. 'If he has any doubts about this, I will place her in Raschid's safekeeping, for she must be protected at all cost from any more anguish or stress.'

'I don't think Leona will—'

'It is not and never has been anyone else's place to *think* anything about my wife!' The mere fact that he was lashing out at Rafiq showed how badly he was taking this. 'Other people's thinking has made our life miserable enough! Which is why I want you to speak to our father and not me,' he explained. 'I will have this conversation with no one else. Leona must be protected from ever hearing from anyone else that I am so much as suspecting this. If I am wrong then only I will grieve over what never was. If I am correct, then she has the right to learn of her condition for herself. I will not take this away from her!'

'So I am not even to tell our father,' Rafiq assumed from all of that.

'He and Leona communicate daily by e-mail,' Hasssan explained. 'The old man may be too puffed up with excitement to hold back from saying something to her.'

'In the state you are in, all of this planning may well be a waste of time,' Rafiq remarked with a pointed glance at

151

his watch. 'In one hour we arrive in Jeddah. If you do not
pull yourself together Leona will need only to look at your
face to know that something catastrophic has taken place.'

Hassan knew it. Without warning he sank his face into his
hands. 'This is crazy,' he muttered thickly.

'It is certainly most unexpected,' his brother agreed. 'And
a little too soon for anyone, including the Al-Kadahs, to be
making such confident judgements?' he posed cautiously.

Behind his hands Hassan's brain went still. Behind the
hands it suddenly rushed ahead again, filling him with the
kind of thoughts that made his blood run cold. For Rafiq was
right: three weeks was not long enough—not to achieve what
he was suggesting. As any man knew, it took only a moment
to conceive a child. But which man—whose child?

On several hard curses he dragged his hand down. On
several more he climbed to his feet then strode across the
room to pull open the door that connected him with his aide.

'Faysal!' The man almost jumped out of his skin. 'Track
down my father-in-law, wherever he is. I need to speak with
him urgently.'

Slam. The door shut again. 'May Allah save me from the
evil minds of others,' he grated.

'I do not follow you.' Rafiq frowned.

'Three weeks!' Hassan muttered. 'Three weeks ago Leona
was sleeping in the same house as Ethan Hayes! It was one
of the problems which forced me into bringing her to this
yacht, if you recall...'

Leona didn't see Hassan until a few minutes before they were
due to arrive in Jeddah. By then most of their guests were
assembled on the shade deck taking refreshment while
watching the yacht make the delicate manoeuvres required
to bring such a large vessel safely into its reserved berth in
the harbour.

In respect of Saudi Arabian custom everyone was wearing
traditional Arab daywear, including little Hashim, who
looked rather cute in his tiny white tunic and *gutrah*.

Hassan arrived dressed the same way; Rafiq was less than a step behind him. 'Hello, strangers.' Leona smiled at both of them. 'Where have you two been hiding yourselves all morning?'

'Working.' Rafiq smiled, but Hassan didn't even seem to hear her, and his gaze barely glanced across her face before he was turning to speak to Samir's father, Imran.

She frowned. He looked different—not pale, exactly, but under some kind of grim restraint. Then little Hashim demanded, 'Come and see,' and her attention was diverted. After that she had no time to think of anything but the formalities involved in bidding farewell to everyone.

A fleet of limousines stood in line along the concrete jetty waiting to speed everyone off to their various destinations. Accepting thanks and saying goodbye took over an hour. One by one the cars pulled up and took people away in a steady rota. Sheikh Abdul and Zafina first—relieved, Leona suspected, to be getting away from a trip that had not been a pleasant one for them, though their farewells were polite enough.

Sheikh Imran and Samir were the next to leave. Then she turned to smile at Sheikh Jibril and his wife, Medina, who made very anxious weight of their farewell, reminding Hassan several times that he had complete loyalty. In Jibril's case money talked much louder than power. He had no desire to scrape his deep pockets to pay Sheikh Raschid for the privilege of sending his oil across his land.

Raschid and his family were the last ones to leave. As with everyone else it would be a brief parting, because they would come together again next week, when they attended Sheikh Kalifa's anniversary celebration. Only this time the children would be staying at home with their nurse. So Leona's goodbyes to them were tinged with a genuine regret, especially for Hashim, who had become her little friend during their cruise. So, while she was promising to come and visit with him soon, she missed the rather sober exchanges between the others.

Eventually they left. Their car sped away. Rafiq excused himself to go and seek out Faysal, and Hassan said he had yet to thank his captain and walked away leaving her standing there, alone by the rail, feeling just a little bit rejected by the brevity with which he had treated her.

Something was wrong, she was sure, though she had no idea exactly what it could be. And, knowing him as well as she did, she didn't expect to find out until he felt ready to tell her. So with a shrug and a sigh she went off to follow Hassan's lead and thank the rest of the staff for taking care of everyone so well. By the time they came together again there was only time left to make the dash to the airport if they wanted to reach Rahman before nightfall.

Rafiq and Faysal travelled with them, which gave Hassan the excuse—and Leona was sure it *was* an excuse—to keep conversation light and neutral. A Lear jet bearing the gold Al-Qadim insignia waited on the runway to fly them over Saudi Arabia and into Rahman. The Al-Qadim oasis had its own private runway. A four-wheel drive waited to transport them to the palace whose ancient sandstone walls burned red against a dying sun.

Home, Leona thought, and felt a lump form in her throat because this was home to her. London...England—both had stopped being that a long time ago.

They swept through the gates and up to the front entrance. Hassan helped her to alight. As she walked inside she found herself flanked by two proud males again and wanted to lift her head and say something teasing about *abayas*, but the mood didn't allow for it somehow.

'My father wishes to see us straight away.' Hassan unwittingly explained the sombre mood. 'Please try not to show your shock at how much he has deteriorated since you were last here.'

'Of course,' she replied, oddly hurt that he felt he needed to say that. Then she took the hurt back when she saw the old sheikh reclining against a mound of pillows on his favourite divan.

His sons strode forward; she held back a little to allow them the space to greet him as they always did, with the old sheikh holding out both hands and both hands being taken, one by each son. In all the years she had known Sheikh Kalifa she had never seen him treat his two sons less than equal. They greeted each other; they talked in low-toned Arabic. They touched, they loved. It was an honour and a privilege to be allowed to witness it. When the old sheikh decided to acknowledge her presence he did so with a spice that told her that the old spirit was still very much alive inside his wasted frame.

'So, what do you think of my two warriors, huh?' he asked. 'They snatch you back with style and panache. A worthy woman cannot but be impressed.'

'Impressed by their arrogance, their cheek, and their disregard for my safety,' Leona responded, coming forward now that he had in effect given her permission to do so. 'I almost drowned—twice—and was tossed down a set of stairs. And you dare to be proud of them.'

No one bothered to accuse her of gross exaggeration, because he laughed, loving it, wishing he could have been there to join in. Reclaiming his hands, he waved his sons away and offered those long bony fingers to Leona.

'Come and greet me properly,' he commanded her. 'And you two can leave us. My daughter-in-law and I have things to discuss.'

There was a pause, a distinct hesitation in which Hassan looked ready to argue the point. The old man looked up at him and his son looked down; a battle of the eyes commenced that made Leona frown as a strange kind of tension began to sizzle in the air. Then Hassan conceded by offering a brief, grim nod and left, with Rafiq making the situation feel even stranger when, as he left with him, he placed a hand on Hassan's shoulder as if to reassure him that it would be okay.

'What was all that about?' she enquired as she reached down to brush a kiss on her father-in-law's hollowed cheek.

'He worries about you,' the old sheikh answered.

'Or he worries about you,' she returned.

He knew what she was referring to and flicked it away with a sigh and a wave of a hand. 'I am dying,' he stated bluntly. 'Hassan knows this—they both do. Neither likes knowing they can do nothing to stop it from happening.'

'But you are resigned?' Leona said gently.

'Yes. Come—sit down here, in your chair.' Discussion over, he indicated the low cushion-stuffed chair she had pulled up beside his divan years ago; it had remained there ever since. 'Now, tell me,' he said as soon as she was settled, 'have you come back here because Hassan bullied you into doing so, or because you still love him?'

'Can it be both?' she quizzed him.

'He needs you.'

'Rahman doesn't.'

'Ah,' he scathed, 'that stupid man, Abdul, thought he could force our hand and soon learned that he could not.'

'So it was Sheikh Abdul who plotted to take me,' Leona murmured ruefully.

Eyes that were once a rich dark brown but were now only pale shadows sharpened. 'He did not tell you,' he surmised on an impatient sigh. 'I am a fool for thinking he would.'

'Maybe that is why he didn't want to leave me alone with you,' Leona smilingly replied. 'Actually, I had already guessed it,' she then admitted, adding quietly, 'I know all about Nadira, you see.'

The name had a disturbing effect on Sheikh Khalifa: he shifted uncomfortably, pulled himself up and reached out to touch her cheek. 'Rahman needs my son and my son needs you. Whatever has to happen in the future I need to know that you will always be here supporting him when I can no longer do so.'

Strange words, fierce, dark, compelling words that sealed her inside a coating of ice. What was he saying? What did he mean? Was he telling her that Nadira was still Hassan's only real option if he wanted to continue in his father's foot-steps?

But before she could ask him to elaborate, as after most brief bursts of energy, Sheikh Khalifa suddenly lay back exhausted against the cushions and, without really thinking about it, Leona slipped back into her old routine. She picked up the book lying face down on the table beside him and began reading out loud to him.

But her mind was elsewhere. Her mind was filling up with contracts and Hassan's method of feeding her information on a need-to-know only basis. She saw him as he had been that same morning, relaxed, at peace with both her and himself. Then Raschid had begged a private word. When he'd eventually reappeared later it had been as if he had changed into a different man—a tense, preoccupied and distant man.

A man who avoided eye contact, as if he had something to hide...

The old sheikh was asleep. Leona put down the book.

Doubts; she hated to feel the doubts return. It was no use, she told herself, she was going to have to tackle Hassan about what Zafina had said to her. Once he had denied everything she could put the whole stupid thing away, never to be dredged up again.

And if he didn't deny it? she asked herself as she left the old sheikh's room to go in search of the younger one. The coating of ice turned itself into a heavy cloak that weighed down her footsteps as she walked in between pale blue walls on a cool, polished sandstone flooring.

She didn't want to do this, she accepted as she trod the wide winding staircase onto the landing where pale blue walls changed to pale beige and the floor became a pale blue marble.

She didn't want to reveal that she could doubt his word, she thought dully as she passed between doors made of thick cedar fitted tightly into wide Arabian archways, the very last one of which led through to Hassan's private suite of offices.

Her head began to ache; her throat suddenly felt strange:

hot and tight. She was about five yards away when the door suddenly opened and Hassan himself stepped out. Slender white tunic, flowing blue *thobe*, no covering on his raven-dark head. He saw her and stopped, almost instantly his expression altered from the frowningly preoccupied to... nothing.

It was like having a door slammed in her face. Her doubts surged upwards along with her blood pressure; she could feel her pulse throbbing in her ears. A prickly kind of heat engulfed her whole body—and the next thing that she knew, she was lying on the pale blue marble floor and Hassan was kneeling beside her.

'What happened?' he rasped as her eyes fluttered open.

She couldn't answer, didn't want to answer. She closed her eyes again. His curse wafted across her cheeks. One of his hands came to cover her clammy forehead, the other took a light grasp of her wrist then he was grimly sliding his arms beneath her shoulders and knees and coming to his feet.

'Ouch,' she said as her breasts brushed his breastbone.

Hassan froze. She didn't notice because from absolutely nowhere she burst into tears! What was the matter with her? she wondered wretchedly. She felt sick, she felt dizzy, she hurt in places she had never hurt before! From another place she had never known existed inside her, one of her clenched fists aimed an accusing blow at his shoulder.

Expecting him to demand what he had done to deserve it, she was thrown into further confusion when all he did was release a strained groan from deep in his throat, then began striding back the way from which she had come. A door opened and closed behind them. Lifting her head from his shoulder, she recognised their old suite of rooms.

Laying her on the bed, he came to lean over her. 'What did my father say to you?' he demanded. 'I knew I should not have left you both alone! Did he say you should not have come back, is that it?'

Her eyes flew open, tear-drenched and sparkling. 'Is that what he thinks?'

'Yes—no!' His sigh was driven by demons. But what demons—? The demons of lies? 'In case you did not notice, he does not think so clearly any more,' he said tightly.

'Sheikh Abdul was behind the plot to abduct me; there is nothing unclear about that, as far as I can see.'

'I knew it was a mistake.' Hassan sighed, and sat down beside her.

He looked tired and fed up and she wanted to hit him again. 'You lied to me again,' she accused him.

'By omission,' he agreed. 'And Abdul's involvement cannot be proved,' he added. 'Only by hearsay which is not enough to risk a war between families.'

'And you've always got the ready-typed contract involving Nadira if things really do get out of hand...'

This time she saw the freeze overtake him. This time she got the answer she had been desperately trying to avoid. Sitting up, Leona ignored the way her head spun dizzily. Drawing up her knees, she reached down to ease the straps of her sandals off the backs of her heels, then tossed them to the floor.

'He told you about that also?' Hassan asked hoarsely.

She shook her head. 'Zafina did.'

'When?'

'Does it really matter when?' she derided. 'It exists. I saw it. You felt fit not to warn me about it. What do you think that tells me about what is really going on around here?'

'It means nothing,' he claimed. 'It is just a meaningless piece of paper containing words with no power unless several people place their signatures against it.'

'But you have a copy.'

He didn't answer.

'You had it in your possession even before you came to Spain to get me,' she stated, because she knew it was the truth even though no one had actually told her so. 'What was it—firm back-up in case Raschid failed to bail you out of trouble? Or does it still carry a lot of weight around with it?'

'You could try trusting me,' he answered.

'And you, my lord sheikh, should have tried trusting me, then maybe it would not be the big problem it is.' With that, she climbed off the bed and began walking away.

'Where are you going?' He sighed out heavily. 'Come back here. We need to—'

The cold way she turned to look at him stopped the words; the way she had one hand held to her forehead and the other to her stomach paled his face. 'I am going to the bathroom to be sick,' she informed him. 'Then I am going to crawl into that bed and go to sleep. I would appreciate it if you were not still here when I get to do that.'

And that, Hassan supposed, had told him. He watched the bathroom door close behind her retreating figure.

He got up and strode over to the window beyond which an ink dark evening obliterated everything beyond the subtle lighting of the palace walls.

So where do we go from here? he asked himself. When Zafina Al-Yasin had picked her weapon, she'd picked it well. For Hassan could think of nothing more likely to shatter Leona's belief in his sincerity than a document already drawn up and ready to be brought into use should it become necessary. She would not now believe that he had agreed to the drawing up of such a document merely to buy him time. Why should she when he had refrained from telling her so openly and honestly before she'd found out by other means?

Sighing, he turned to leave the room. It was simpler to leave her alone for now. He could say nothing that was going to change anything, because he had another problem looming, he realised, One bigger and more potentially damaging than all that had tried to damage his marriage before.

He had a contract bearing his agreement to take a second wife. He had a wife whom he suspected might be carrying his first child. Leona was never going to believe that the former was not an insurance policy to protect him against the failure of the latter.

'Faysal,' he said as he stepped into his aide's office, which guarded the entrance to his own, 'get Rafiq for me, if you please...'

'You look pale like a ghost,' the old sheikh remarked.

'I'm fine,' Leona assured him.

'They tell me you fainted the other day.'

'I still had my sea legs on,' Leona explained. 'And how did you find out about it?' she challenged, because as far as she knew no one but herself and Hassan had been there at the time!

'My palace walls are equipped with a thousand eyes.' He smiled. 'So I also know that when he is not with me my son walks around wearing the face of a man whose father is already dead.'

'He is a busy man doing busy, important things,' Leona said with a bite that really should have been resisted.

'He also has a wife who sleeps in one place while he sleeps in another.'

Getting in practice, Leona thought nastily. 'Do you want to finish this chapter or not?' she asked.

'I would prefer you to confide in me,' the old sheikh murmured gently. 'You used to do so all the time, before I became too sick to be of any use to anyone...'

A blatant plucking of her heartstrings though it was, Leona could see the concern in his eyes. On a sigh, she laid the book aside, got up to go and sit down beside him and picked up one of his cool, dry, skeletal hands to press a gentle kiss to it.

'Don't fret so, old man,' she pleaded gently. 'You know I will look after your two sons for you. I have promised, haven't I?'

'But you are unhappy. Do you think this does not fret me?'

'I—struggle with the reasons why I am here,' she explained, because she wasn't going to lie. It wasn't fair to lie to him. 'You know the problems. They are not going to go away just because Hassan wants them to.'

'My son wants you above all things, daughter of Victor Frayne,' he said, using the Arab way of referring to her, because by their laws a woman kept her father's name after marriage. 'Don't make him choose to prove this to you...'

CHAPTER ELEVEN

DON'T make him choose... The next day, those words played inside Leona's head like a mantra, because she had just begun to realise that Hassan might not be forced to choose anything.

Sickness in the morning, sickness in the evening, a certain tenderness in her breasts and other changes in her body that she could no longer ignore were trying to tell her something she was not sure she wanted to know.

Pregnant. She could be pregnant. She *might* be pregnant. She absolutely refused to say that she was *most definitely* pregnant. How could she be sure, when her periods had never been anything but sporadic at best? Plus it had to be too soon to tell. It had to be. She was just wishing on rainbows—wasn't she?

A month. She had been back in Hassan's life for a tiny month—and not even a full month! Women just didn't know that quickly if they had conceived, did they? She didn't know. At this precise moment she didn't know anything. Her brain was blank, her emotions shot and she was fighting an ever-growing battle with excitement that was threatening to turn her into a puff of smoke!

It was this morning that had really set her suspicions soaring, when she'd climbed out of bed feeling sick and dizzy before her feet had managed to touch the floor. Then, in the shower, she'd seen the changes in her breasts, a new fullness, darkening circles forming round their tips. She'd *felt* different too—inside, where it was impossible to say how she felt different, only that she did.

Instinct. What did she know about the female instinct in such situations?

Doubt. She had to doubt her own conclusions because the specialists had given her so little hope of it ever happening for them.

But even her skin felt different, her hair, the strange, secret glint she kept on catching in her own eyes whenever she looked in a mirror. She'd stopped looking in the mirror. It was easier not to look than look and then see, then dare—*dare* to hope.

I want Hassan, she thought on a sudden rocketing rise of anxiety.

I don't want Hassan! she then changed her mind. Because if he saw her like this he would know something really drastic was worrying her and she couldn't tell him—didn't dare tell him, raise his hopes, until she was absolutely sure for herself.

She needed one of those testing kits, she realised. But, if such a thing was obtainable, where could she get one from without alerting half of Rahman? There was not a chemist's in the country she could walk into and buy such an obvious thing without setting the jungle drums banging from oasis to oasis and back again.

But I need one. I *need* one! she thought agitatedly.

Ring Hassan, that tiny voice inside her head persisted. Tell him your suspicions, get him to bring a pregnancy testing kit home with him.

Oh, yes, she mocked that idea. I can just see Sheikh Hassan Al-Qadim walking into a chemist's and buying one of those!

Rafiq, then. No, *not* Rafiq! she all but shouted at herself. Oh, why could there not be some more women in this wretched house of Al-Qadim? Why do I have to be surrounded by men?

Maids. There were dozens of maids she could call upon—all of whom would be just as proficient at belting out the message across the whole state.

As if she'd conjured her up a knock sounded on the door and one of the maids walked into the room. She was carrying a dress that Leona had ordered to be delivered from one of her favourite couturier's in the city.

'It is very beautiful, my lady,' the maid said shyly.

And very red, Leona thought frowningly. What in heaven's name had made her choose to buy red? Made by a local designer to a traditional Arabian design, the dress was silk, had matching trousers and *thobe*, and shimmered with beautifully embroidered golden threads. And she never, ever wore red!

'The sheikha will shine above all things tomorrow night,' the maid approved.

Tomorrow night, Leona repeated with a sinking heart as the maid carried the dress into her dressing room. For tomorrow night was *the* night of Sheikh Kalifa's anniversary celebration, which meant she had a hundred guests to play hostess to when really all she wanted to do was—

Oh, she thought suddenly, where is my head? And she turned to walk quickly across the room towards the telephone which sat beside the bed.

Pregnant.

Her feet pulled to a stop. Her stomach twisted itself into a knot then sprang free again, catching at her breath. It was a desperate sensation. Desperate with hope and with fear and a thousand other things that—

The maid appeared again, looked at her oddly because she was standing here in the middle of the room, emulating a statue. 'Thank you, Leila,' she managed to say.

As soon as the door closed behind the maid she finished her journey to the telephone, picked up her address book, flicked through its pages with trembling fingers, then stabbed in a set of numbers that would connect her with Evie Al-Kadah in Behran.

Hassan was fed up. He was five hours away from home, on his way back from Sheikh Abdul's summer palace, having just enjoyed a very uncomfortable meeting in which a few home truths had been aired. He should be feeling happy, for

the meeting had gone very much his way, and in his possession he now had the sheikh's copy of one ill-judged contract and the satisfaction of knowing the man and his wife
now understood the error of their ways.

But it had required a five-hour drive out to mountains of
Rahman to win this sense of grim satisfaction, which meant
they now had to make the same journey back again. And
Rafiq might feel *he* needed the physical exercise of negoti-
ating the tough and challenging terrain but, quite frankly, so
did he. He felt tense and restless, impatient to get back to
Leona now that he could face her with an easy conscience.

So the flat tire they suffered a few minutes later was most
unwelcome. By the time they had battled in soft sand on a
rocky incline to jack the car up and secure it so they could
change the wheel time was getting on, and the sun was beginning to set. Then, only a half-mile further into their journey, they became stuck in deep soft sand. And he couldn't
even blame Rafiq for this second inconvenience because he
had taken over the driving for himself. Proficient though they
were at getting themselves out of such difficulties, time was
lost, then more time when they were hit by a sandstorm that
forced them to stop and wait until it had blown past.

Consequently, it was very late when they drove through
the gates of the palace. By the time he had washed the sand
from his body before letting himself quietly into the bedroom
he found Leona fast asleep.

Did he wake her or did he go away? he pondered as he
stood looking down on her, lying there on her side, with her
glorious hair spilling out behind her and a hand resting on
the pillow where his head should be.

She murmured something, maybe because she sensed he
was there, and the temptation to just throw caution to the
wind, slide into the bed and awaken her so he could confide
his suspicions then discover whether she felt he was making
any sense almost got the better of him.

Then reality returned, for this was not the time for such
an emotive discussion. It could backfire on him and deeply

hurt her. And tomorrow was a day packed with strife enough
for both of them, without him adding to it with what could
be merely a foolish dream.

Anyway, he had some damage limitation to perform, preferably before this new development came into the open—
just in case.

So, instead of waking her, he turned away, unaware that
behind him her eyes had opened to watch him leave. The
urge to call him back tugged at her vocal cords. The need to
scramble out of the bed and go after him to confide her
suspicions stretched nerve ends in every muscle she possessed.

But, no, it would not be fair to offer him hope where there
might be none. Better to wait one more day until she knew
for sure one way or another, she convinced herself.

So the door between their two rooms closed him away
from her—just as it had closed him away before, when he
had decided it was better to sleep elsewhere than risk another
argument with her.

Maybe he was right. Maybe the common sense thing to
do was stay out of each other's way, because they certainly
didn't function well together unless they were in bed!

They had a battleground, not a marriage, she decided, and
on that profound thought she turned her back on that
wretched closed door and refused to look back at it.

The next day continued in much the same fashion. He
avoided her. She avoided him. They circulated the palace in
opposing directions like a pair of satellites designed never to
cross paths. By six o'clock Leona was in her room preparing
for the evening ahead. By seven she was as ready as she
supposed she ever would be, having changed her mind about
what to wear a hundred times before finally deciding to wear
the red outfit.

When Hassan stepped into the room a few minutes later
he took her breath away. Tall, lean and not yet having covered his silky dark hair, he was wearing a midnight blue long
tunic with a standing collar braided in gold. At his waist a

wide sash of gold silk gave his body shape and stature, and the jewel encrusted shaft belonging to the ceremonial scabbard he had tucked into his waistband said it all.

Arrogance personified. A prince among men. First among equals did not come into it for her because for her he was it—the one—her only one. As if to confirm that thought her belly gave a skittering flutter as if to say, And me, don't forget me.

Too soon for that, too silly to think it, she scolded herself as she watched him pause to look at her. As always those dark eyes made their possessive pass over her. As always they liked what they saw.

'Beautiful,' he murmured.

Tell me about it, she wanted to say, but she couldn't, didn't dare say anything in case the wrong thing popped anxiously out.

So the twist his mouth gave said he had misread her silence. 'Forgiveness, my darling, is merely one sweet smile away,' he drawled as he walked towards her.

'But you have nothing to forgive me for!' she protested, glad now to use her voice.

'Throwing me out of your bed does not require forgiveness?' An eyebrow arched, the outfit, the coming occasion, turning the human being into a pretentious monster that made her toes curl inside her strappy gold shoes. With life, that was what they curled with. Life.

I love this man to absolute pieces. 'You left voluntarily,' she told him. 'In what I think you would describe as a sulk.'

'Men do not sulk.'

But you are not just any man, she wanted to say, but the comment would puff up his ego, so she settled for, 'What do they do, then?'

'Withdraw from a fight they have no hope of winning.' He smiled. Then on a complete change of subject, he said, 'Here, a peace offering.' And he held out a flat package wrapped in black silk and tied up with narrow red ribbon.

Expecting the peace offering to be jewellery, the moment

she took possession of the package she knew it was too light. So...what? she asked herself, then felt her heart suddenly drop to her slender ankles as a terrible suspicion slid snake-like into her head.

No, she denied it. Evie just would not break such a precious confidence. 'What is it?' she asked warily.

'Open it and see.'

Trembling fingers did as he bade her, fumbling with the ribbon and then with the square of black silk. Inside it was a flat gold box, the kind that could be bought at any gift shop, nothing at all like she had let herself wonder, and nothing particularly threatening about it, but still she felt her breath snag in her chest as she lifted the lid and looked inside.

After that came the frown while she tried to work out why Hassan was giving her a box full of torn scraps of white paper. Then she turned the top one over, recognised the insignia embossed upon it and finally realised what it was.

'You know what they are?' he asked her quietly.

'Yes.' She swallowed.

'All three copies of the contract are now in your possession,' he went on to explain anyway. 'All evidence that they were ever composed wiped clean from Faysal's computer hard disk. There, it is done. Now we can be friends again.' Without giving her a chance to think he took the gift and its packaging back from her and tossed it onto the bed.

'But it doesn't wipe clean the fact that it was written in the first place,' she pointed out. 'And nor does it mean it can't be typed up again in five short minutes if it was required to be done.'

'You have said it for yourself,' Hassan answered. 'I must require it. I do not require it. I give you these copies for ceremonial purposes, only to *show* you that I do not require it. Subject over, Leona,' he grimly concluded, 'for I will waste no more of my time on something that had only ever been meant as a diversion tactic to buy me time while I decided what to do about Sheikh Abdul and his ambitious plans.'

'You expect me to believe all of that, don't you?'

'Yes.' It was a coldly unequivocal yes.

She lifted her chin. For the first time in days they actually made eye contact. And it was only as it happened that she finally began to realise after all of these years *why* they avoided doing it when there was dissension between them. Eye contact wiped out everything but the truth. The *love* truth. The *need* truth. The absolute and utter *total* truth. I love him; he loves me. Who or what else could ever really come between that?

'I think I'm pregnant,' she whispered.

It almost dropped him like a piece of crumbling stone at her feet. She saw the shock; she saw the following pallor. She watched his eyes close and feared for a moment that *he* was actually going to faint.

For days he had been waiting for this moment, Hassan was thinking. He had yearned for it, had begged and had prayed for it. Yet, when it came, not only had he not been ready, the frightened little remark had virtually knocked him off his feet!

'I could kill you for this,' he ground out hoarsely. 'Why here? Why now, when in ten short minutes we are expected downstairs to greet a hundred guests?'

His response was clearly not the one she had been expecting. Her eyes began to glaze, her mouth to tremble. 'You don't like it,' she quavered.

'Give me strength.' He groaned. 'You stupid, unpredictable, aggravating female. Of course I like it! But look at me! I am now a white-faced trembling mess!'

'You just gave me something I really needed. I wanted to give you something back that you needed,' she explained.

'Ten minutes before I face the upper echelons of Arabian society?'

'Well, thanks for being concerned about how I am feeling!' she flashed back at him.

She was right. 'You've just knocked me for six,' he breathed unsteadily.

'And I might be wrong, so don't start going off the deep end about it!' she snapped, and went to turn away.

Oh, Allah, help him, what was he doing here? With shaking hands he took hold of her by her silk-swathed shoulders and pulled her against him. She was trembling too. And she *felt* different, slender and frail and oh, so precious.

He kissed her— What else did a man do when he was so blown away by everything about her?

'I should not have dropped it on you like this,' she murmured repentantly a few seconds later.

'Yes, you should,' he argued. 'How else?'

'It might come to nothing.' Anxiety was playing havoc with her beautiful eyes.

'We will deal with the something or the nothing together.'

'I am afraid of the nothing,' she confessed to him. 'I am afraid I might never get the chance to feel like this again.'

'I love you,' he said huskily. 'Can that not be enough?'

'For you?' She threw the question back at him, clinging to his eyes like a vulnerable child.

'We know how I feel, Leona,' he said ruefully. 'In fact, the whole of Rahman knows how I feel about you. But we hardly ever discuss how you feel about the situation I place you in here.'

'I just don't want you to have to keep defending my place in your life,' she told him. 'I hate it.'

Hassan thought about the damage-control exercise he had already set into motion, and wished he knew how to answer that. 'I like defending you.' His words seemed to say it all for him.

'You won't tell anyone tonight, will you?' she flashed up at him suddenly. 'You will keep this our secret until we know for sure.'

'Do you really think I am that manipulative?' He was shocked, then uncomfortable, because he realised that she knew him better than he knew himself. 'Tomorrow we will bring in a doctor,' he decided, looking for an escape from his own manipulative thoughts.

But Leona shook her head. 'It would be all over Rahman in five minutes if we did that. Look what happened when I went to see him to find out why I couldn't conceive?'

'But we have to know—'

'Evie is bringing me a pregnancy testing kit with her,' she told him, too busy trying to smooth some semblance of calmness into herself to notice how still he had gone. 'I rang her and explained. At least I can trust her not to say anything to anyone.'

'What did she say?' Hassan enquired carefully.

'She said I should make sure I tell you. Which I've done.' She turned a wry smile on him. 'Now I wish that I hadn't because, looking at you, I have a horrible feeling you are going to give the game away the moment anyone looks at you.'

Confess all, he told himself. Tell her before the Al-Kadahs tell her that you already suspected all of this, days ago. A knock at the door was a thankful diversion. Going to open it, he found Rafiq standing there dressed very much like himself—only he was wearing his *gutrah*.

'Our guests are arriving,' he informed him. 'You and Leona should be downstairs.'

Guests. Dear heaven. His life was in crisis and he must go downstairs and be polite to people. 'We will be five minutes only.'

'You are all right?' Rafiq frowned at him.

No, I am slowly sinking beneath my own plots and counter-plots. 'Five minutes,' he repeated, and closed the door again.

Leona was standing by a mirror, about to fix her lipstick with a set of very unsteady fingers. The urge to go over there and stop her so that he could kiss her almost got the better of him. But one kiss would most definitely lead to another and another. In fact he wanted to be very primitive and drag her off by her beautiful hair to his lair and smother her in

kisses. So instead he stepped back into the other room and
came back a moment later wearing white silk on his head,
held by triple gold thongs, to find that Leona had also covered her hair with a gold-spangled scarf of red silk.

The red should have clashed with her hair but it didn't. It
merely toned with the sensual colour on her lips. She lifted
her eyes to look at him. He looked back at her. A different
man, a different woman. It was amazing what a piece of silk
laid to the head could do for both of them, because neither
was now showing signs of what was really going on inside
them.

His smile, therefore, was rueful. 'Showtime,' he said.

And showtime it was. As on the yacht, but on a grander
scale, they welcomed heads of state from all over Arabia,
diplomats from further afield. Some brought their wives, sons
and even their daughters, and some came alone. Some
women were veiled; all were dressed in the exotic jewelled
colours favoured by Arabian women.

Everyone was polite, gracious, and concerned about
Sheikh Khalifa's well-being. He had not yet put in an appearance, though he had every intention of doing so eventually. This was his night. He had in fact planned it as much
as he could from his sick bed. Today his doctor had insisted
he be sedated for most of the day to conserve his energy.
But he had looked bright-eyed and excited when Leona had
popped in to see him just before she had gone to get ready.

'Rafiq should be doing this with us,' Leona said to Hassan
when she realised that his brother was nowhere to be seen.

'He has other duties,' he replied, then turned his attention
to the next person to arrive at the doors to the great hall. A
great hall that was slowly filling with people.

Sheikh Abdul arrived without his wife, Zafina, which
seemed a significant omission to Leona. He was subdued but
polite to her, which was all she could really expect from him,
she supposed. They greeted Sheikh Jibril and his wife,
Medina, Sheikh Imran, and of course Samir.

When Sheikh Raschid Al-Kadah and his wife, Evie, arrived, there were some knowing glances exchanged that made Leona want to blush. But the real blushing happened every time Hassan glanced at her and his eyes held the burning darkness of their secret.

'Don't,' she whispered, looking quickly away from him.

'I cannot help it,' he replied.

'Well, try.' A sudden disturbance by the door gave her someone new to divert her attention, only to have her heart stop in complete surprise.

Two men dressed in black western dinner suits, white shirts and bow ties. She flicked her eyes from one smiling male face to the other, then on a small shriek of delight launched herself into the arms of her father.

Tall, lean and in very good shape for his fifty-five years, Victor Frayne caught his daughter to him and accepted her ecstatic kisses to his face. 'What are you doing here? Why didn't you tell me? Ethan—' One of her hands reached out to catch one of his. 'I can't believe this! I only spoke to you this morning. I thought you were in San Estéban!'

'No, the Marriott, here.' Her father grinned at her. 'Thank your husband for the surprise.'

Hassan. She turned, a hand each clinging to her two surprises. 'I love you,' she said impulsively.

'She desires to make me blush,' Hassan remarked, and stepped forward, took his wife by her waist, then offered his hand to his father-in-law and to Ethan Hayes. 'Glad you could make it,' he said.

'Happy to be here,' Ethan replied with only a touch of dryness to his tone to imply that there was more to this invitation than met the eye.

Leona was just too excited to notice. Too wrapped up in her surprise to notice the ripple of awareness that went through those people who had dared to believe rumours about her relationship with her father's business partner. Then, with the attention to fine detail which was Hassan's forte, another diversion suddenly appeared.

People stopped talking, silence reigned as Rafiq arrived,

pushing a wheelchair bearing Sheikh Khalifa ben Jusef Al-Qadim.

He looked thin and frail against the height and breadth of his youngest son. A wasted shadow of his former self. But his eyes were bright, his mouth smiling, and in the frozen stasis that followed his arrival, brought on by everyone's shock at how ill he actually looked, he was prepared and responded. 'Welcome...welcome everyone,' he greeted. 'Please, do not continue to look as if you are attending my funeral, for I assure you I am here to enjoy myself.'

After that everyone made themselves relax again. Some who knew him well even grinned. As Rafiq wheeled him towards the other end of the room the old sheikh missed no one in reach of his acknowledgement. Not even Leona's father, whom he had only met once or twice. 'Victor,' he greeted him. 'I have stolen your daughter. She is now my most precious daughter. I apologise to you, but I am not sorry, you understand?'

'I think we can share her,' Victor Frayne allowed graciously.

'And...ah...' he turned his attention to Ethan '...Mr Hayes, it is my great pleasure to meet Leona's very good friend.' He had the floor, as it should be. So no one could miss the messages being broadcast here. Even Leona began to notice that something was going on beneath the surface here. 'Victor...Mr Hayes...come and see me tomorrow. I have a project I believe will be of great interest to you... Ah, Rafiq, take me forward, for I can see Sheikh Raschid...'

He progressed down the hall like that. As Leona watched, she gently slipped her arm around Hassan's waist. She could feel the emotion pulsing inside him. For this was probably going to be the old Sheikhs final formal duty.

But nothing, nothing prepared her for the power of feeling that swept over everyone as Rafiq and his father reached the other end of the hall where Sheikh Khalifa's favourite divan had been placed upon a raised dais, ready for him to enjoy the party in reasonable comfort.

Rafiq bent and lifted his father into his arms and carried the frail old man up the steps then gently lowered his father down again. As he went to straighten, the sheikh lifted a pale bony hand to his youngest son's face and murmured something to him which sent Rafiq to his knees beside the divan and sent his covered head down.

The strong and the weak. It was a painful image that held everyone in its thrall because in those few seconds it was impossible to tell which man held the strength and which one was weaker.

'Hassan, go to him,' Leona said huskily. 'Rafiq needs you.'

But Hassan shook his head. 'He will not thank me,' he replied. And he was right; Leona knew that.

Instead Hassan turned his attention to causing yet another diversion by snapping his fingers to pull a small army of servants into use.

They came bearing trays of delicately made sweets and Arabian coffee and *bukhoor* burners, which filled the air with the smell of incense. The mood shifted, took on the characteristics of a traditional *majlis*, and the next time Leona looked the dais was surrounded by the old sheikhs from the desert tribes sitting around on the provided cushions while Sheikh Khalifa reclined on his divan enjoying their company.

Hassan took her father and Ethan with him and circulated the room, introducing them to their fellow guests. The timid Medina Al-Mahmud attached herself to Leona's side like a rather wary limpit and, taking pity on her, Leona found herself taking the older woman with her as they moved from group to group.

It was a success. The evening was really looking as if it was going to be a real success. And then from somewhere behind her she heard Sheikh Abdul say, 'A clever ploy. I am impressed by his strategy. For how many men here would now suspect Mr Hayes as his lovely wife's lover?'

She pretended not to hear, smiled her bright smile and just kept on talking. But the damage was done. The evening was ruined for her. For it had not once occurred to her that her father and Ethan were here for any other purpose than because Hassan wanted to please her.

Evie appeared at her side to save her life. 'Show me where I can freshen up,' she requested.

As Leona excused herself from those she was standing with, a hand suddenly gripped her sleeve. 'You heard; I saw your face. But you must not listen,' Medina advised earnestly. 'For he has the bad mouth and his wife is in purdah after Sheikh Hassan's visit yesterday.'

Sheikh Hassan's visit? Curiouser and curiouser, Leona thought grimly as she took a moment to reassure Medina before moving away with Evie Al-Kadah.

'What was that all about?' Evie quizzed.

'Nothing.' Leona dismissed the little incident.

But from across the room Hassan saw the green glint hit her eyes and wondered what had caused it. Had Evie let the proverbial cat out of the bag, or was it the timid Medina who had dared to stick in the knife?

He supposed he would soon find out, he mused heavily, and redirected his attention to whoever it was speaking to him, hoping he had not missed anything important.

The evening moved on; the old sheikh grew tired. His two sons appeared by the side of his divan. He did not demur when Hassan gently suggested he bid goodnight to everyone. Once again Rafiq lifted him into his wheelchair with the same gentleness that would be offered a fragile child. His departure was achieved quietly through a side door, as the old Sheikh himself had arranged.

Leona was standing with her father and Ethan as this quiet departure took place. 'How long?' Victor asked her gravely.

'Not very long,' she answered, then chided herself because Sheikh Khalifa wished his thirtieth celebration to be an occasion remembered for its hospitality, not as his obituary.

It was very late by the time people began leaving. Even later before Leona felt she could dare to allow herself a sigh of relief at how relatively pain-free the whole evening had turned out to be.

Which suddenly reminded her of something she still had to do that might not be as pain free. Her heart began thudding as Hassan came to take her hand and walk her towards the stairs. She could feel his tension, knew that his mind had switched onto the same wavelength as her own. Hand in hand they trod the wide staircase to the floor above. The door to the private apartments closed behind them.

'Did Evie bring—'

'Yes,' she interrupted, and moved right away from him. Now the moment of truth had arrived Leona found she was absolutely terrified. 'I don't want to know,' she admitted.

'Then leave it for now,' Hassan answered simply.

She turned to look anxiously at him. 'But that's just being silly.'

'Yes,' he agreed. 'But tomorrow the answer will still be the same, and the next day and the next.'

Maybe it was a good thing that the telephone began to ring. Hassan moved away from her to go and answer it. Thirty seconds later he was sending her a rueful smile. 'My father is restless,' he explained. 'Over-excited and in need of talk. Will you mind if I go to him, or shall I get Rafiq to—?'

'No,' she said quickly. 'You go.' She really was a pathetic coward.

'You won't...do anything without me with you?' he murmured huskily.

She shook her head. 'Tomorrow,' she promised. 'W-when I am feeling less tired and able to cope with...' *The wrong answer*, were the words she couldn't say.

Coming back to her, Hassan gave her a kiss of understanding. 'Go to bed,' he advised, 'Try to sleep. I will come back just as soon as I can.'

He was striding towards the door when she remembered. 'Hassan... My father and Ethan were invited here for a specific purpose, weren't they?'

He paused at the door, sighed and turned to look at her. 'Damage limitation,' he confirmed. 'We may not like it. We may object to finding such a demeaning act necessary. But the problem was there, and had to be addressed. *Inshallah.*' He shrugged, turned and left.

CHAPTER TWELVE

INSHALLAH—as Allah wills. It was, she thought, the perfect throwaway answer to an uncomfortable subject. On a dissatisfied sigh she moved across the room to begin to prepare for bed.

Already tucked out of sight in the drawer of her bedside cabinet lay the offerings Evie had brought with her from Behran. Just glancing at the drawer was enough to make her shudder a little, because the pregnancy testing kit had too much power for her comfort. So she turned away to pull on her pyjamas, slid into bed and switched off the light without glancing at the cabinet again. Sleep came surprisingly quickly, but then it had been a long day.

When she woke up, perhaps an hour later, she thought for a few moments that Hassan must have come back and disturbed her when he'd got into the bed. But there was no warm body lying beside her. No sign of life in evidence through the half-open bathroom door.

Then she knew. She didn't know how she knew, but suddenly she was up and pulling on a robe, frantically trying the belt as she hurried for the door. It was as if every light in the palace was burning. Her heart dropped to her stomach as she began racing down the stairs.

It was the sheikh. Instinct, premonition, call it what you wanted; she just knew there was something badly wrong.

On bare feet she ran down the corridor and arrived at his door to find it open. She stepped inside, saw nothing untoward except that neither the sheikh nor Hassan was there. Then she heard a noise coming from the room beyond, and with a sickening thud her heart hit her stomach as she made her way across the room to that other door.

On the other side was a fully equipped hospital room that had been constructed for use in the event of emergencies like the one Leona found herself faced with now.

She could not see the old sheikh because the doctors and nurses were gathered around him. But she could see Hassan and Rafiq standing like two statues at the end of the bed. They were gripping the rail in front of them with a power to crush metal, and their faces were as white as the *gutrahs* that still covered their heads.

Anguish lurked in every corner, the wretched sound of the heart monitor pulsing out its frighteningly erratic story like a cold, ruthless taunt. It was dreadful, like viewing a scene from a horror movie. Someone held up a hypodermic needle, clear liquid sprayed into the air. The lights were bright and the room bare of everything but clinical-white efficiency.

No, she thought, no, they cannot do this to him. He needs his room, with his books and his divan and his favourite pile of cushions. He needed to be surrounded by love, his sons, gentle music, not that terrible beep that felt to her as if it was draining the very life out of him.

'Switch it off,' she said thickly, walking forward on legs that did not seem to belong to her. 'Switch if off!' she repeated. 'He doesn't want to hear that.'

'Leona...' Hassan spoke her name in a hoarse whisper.

She looked at him. He looked at her. Agony screamed in the space between them. 'Tell them to switch it off,' she pleaded with him.

His face caved in on a moment's loss of composure. Rafiq didn't even seem to know that she was there. 'Don't...' he said huskily.

He wanted her to accept it. Her throat became a ball of tears as she took those final few steps then looked, really looked down at the ghost-like figure lying so still in the bed.

No, she thought again, no, they can't do this to him. Not here, not now. Her hand reached out to catch hold of one of his, almost knocking the nurse who was trying to treat him.

He felt so cold he might have been dead already. The tears moved to her mouth and spilled over her trembling lips. 'Sheikh,' she sobbed out, 'you just can't do this!'

'Leona…'

The thin, frail fingers she held in her hand tried to move. Oh, dear God, she thought painfully. He knows what is happening to him! 'Switch that noise off—switch it off!'

The fingers tried their very best to move yet again. Panic erupted. Fear took charge of her mind. 'Don't you dare bail on us now, old man!' she told him forcefully.

'Leona!' Hassan warning voice came stronger this time. He was shocked. They were all shocked. She didn't care.

'Listen to me,' she urged, lifting that frighteningly cold hand up to her cheek. The fingers moved again. He was listening. He could hear her. She moved closer, pushing her way past the doctor—a nurse—someone. She leaned over the bed, taking that precious hand with her. Her hair streamed over the white pillows as she came as close to him as she could. 'Listen,' she repeated, 'I am going to have a baby, Sheikh. Your very first grandchild. Tell me that you understand!'

The fingers moved. She laughed, then sobbed and kissed those fingers. Hassan came to grasp her shoulder. 'What do you think you are doing?' he rasped.

He was furious. She couldn't speak, couldn't answer, because she didn't *know* what she was doing. It had all just come out as if it was meant to. *Inshallah*, she thought.

'He can hear.' She found her voice. 'He knows what I am telling him.' Tremulously she offered Hassan his father's hand. 'Talk to him,' she pleaded. 'Tell him about our baby.' Tears were running down her cheeks and Hassan had never looked so angry. 'Tell him. He needs to hear it from you. Tell him, Hassan, please…'

That was the point when the monitor suddenly went haywire. Medics lunged at the sheikh, Hassan dropped his father's hand so he could grab hold of Leona and forcibly drag her aside. As the medical team went down in a huddle

Hassan was no longer just white, he was a colour that had never been given a name. 'You had better be telling him the truth or I will never forgive you for doing this,' he sliced at her.

Leona looked at the monitor, listened to its wild, palpitating sound. She looked at Rafiq, at what felt like a wall of horrified and disbelieving faces, and on a choked sob she broke free from Hassan and ran from the room.

Back down the corridor, up the stairs, barely aware that she was passing by lines of waiting, anxious servants. Gaining entrance to their apartments, she sped across the floor to the bedside cabinet. Snatching up Evie's testing kit, trembling and shaking, she dropped the packet twice in her attempt to remove the Cellophane wrapping to get the packet inside. She was sobbing by the time she had reached the contents. Then she unfolded the instruction leaflet and tried to read through a bank of hot tears, what it was she was supposed to do.

She was right; she was sure she was right. Nothing—nothing in her whole life had ever felt as right as this! Five minutes later she was racing downstairs again, running down the corridor in between the two lines of anxious faces, through doors and into the sheikh's room and over to her husband.

'See!' she said. 'See!' There were tears and triumph and sheer, shrill agony in her voice as she held out the narrow bit of plastic towards Hassan. 'Now tell him! *Please...!*' she begged him.

'Leona...' Hassan murmured very gently.

Then she heard it. The silence. The dreadful, agonising, empty silence. She spun around to look at the monitor. The screen was blank.

The screen was blank. 'No,' she breathed shakily. 'No.' Then she sank in a deep faint to the ground.

Hassan could not believe that any of this was really happening. He looked blankly at his father, then at his wife, then at the sea of frozen faces, and for a moment he actually thought he was going to join Leona and sink into a faint.

'Look after my son's wife.' A frail voice woke everyone up from their surprise. 'I think she has earned some attention.'

Before Hassan could move a team of experts had gone down over Leona and he was left standing there staring down at the bit of white plastic she had placed in his hand.

She was pregnant. She had just told him that this red mark in the window meant that she was pregnant. In the bed a mere step away his father was no longer fading away before his eyes.

Leona had done it. She'd brought him back from the brink, had put herself through the trauma of facing the answer on this small contraption, and she'd done both without his support.

'Courage,' he murmured. He had always known she possessed courage. 'And where was I when she needed my courage?'

'Here,' a level voice said. 'Sit down.' It was Rafiq, offering him a chair to sit upon. The room was beginning to look like a war zone.

He declined the chair. Leave me with some semblance of dignity, he thought. 'Excuse me,' he said, and stepped through the kneeling shapes round Leona, and bent and picked her up in his arms. 'But, sir, we should check she is...'

'Leave him be,' the old sheikh instructed. 'He is all she needs and he knows it.'

He did not take her far, only to his father's divan, where he laid her down, then sat beside her. She looked pale and delicate, and just too lovely for him to think straight. So he did what she had done with his father and took hold of her hand, then told her, 'Don't you dare bail out on us now, you little tyrant, even if you believe we deserve it.'

'We?' she mumbled.

'Okay, me,' he conceded. 'My father is alive and well, by

the way. I thought it best to tell you this before you begin
to recall exactly why you fainted.'

'He's all right?' Her gold-tipped lashes flickered upwards,
revealing eyes the colour of a sleepy lagoon.

I feel very poetic, Hassan thought whimsically. 'Whether
due to the drugs or your bullying, no one is entirely certain.
But he opened his eyes and asked me what you were talking
about just a second after you flew out of the room.'

'He's all right.' Relief shivered through her, sending her
eyes closed again. Feeling the shiver, Hassan reached out to
draw one of his father's rugs over her reclining frame.

'Where am I?' she asked after a moment.

'You are lying on my father's divan, ' he informed her.
'With me, in all but effect, at your feet.'

She opened her eyes again, looked directly at him, and
sent those major parts that kept him functioning into a steep
decline.

'What made you do it?'

She frowned at the question, but only for a short moment,
then she sighed, tried to sit up but was still too dizzy and
had to relax back again. 'I didn't want him to go,' she explained simply. 'Or, if he had to go, I wanted him to do it
knowing that he was leaving everything as he always wanted
to leave it.'

'So you lied.'

It was a truth she merely grimaced at.

'If he had survived this latest attack, and you had been
wrong about what you told him, would that have been a fair
way to tug a man back from his destiny?'

'I'm pregnant,' she announced. 'Don't upset me with lec-
tures.'

He laughed. What else was he supposed to do? 'I apologise for shouting at you,' he said soberly.

She was playing with his fingers where they pleated firmly
with hers. 'You were in trauma enough without having a
demented woman throwing a fit of hysterics.'

'You were right, though. He did hear you.'

She nodded. 'I know.'

'Here…' He offered her the stick of white plastic. Taking it back, she stared at it for a long time without saying a single word.

'It doesn't seem so important now,' she murmured eventually.

'The proof or the baby?'

She shrugged then pouted. 'Both, I suppose.'

In other words the delight she should be experiencing had been robbed from the moment. On a sigh, he scooped her up in his arms again and stood up.

'Where are you taking me now?' she questioned.

'Bed,' he answered bluntly. 'Preferably naked, so that I can hold you and our child so close to me you will never, ever manage to prise yourself free.'

'But your father—'

'Has Rafiq,' he inserted. 'And you have me.'

With that he pushed open the door to the main corridor, then stopped dead when he saw the sea of anxious faces waiting for news.

'My father has recovered,' he announced. 'And my wife is pregnant.'

There, he thought as he watched every single one fall to their knees and give thanks to Allah, that has killed two birds with one single stone. Now the phones could start buzzing and the news would go out to all corners of the state. By the time they arose in the morning there would not be a person who did not know what had taken place here tonight.

'You could have given me a chance to break the news to my own father.' Leona showed that her own thoughts were as usual not far from his own.

'He knows—or suspects. For I told him when I asked him to come here tonight. That was while we were still sailing the Red Sea, by the way,' he added as he walked them through the two lines of kneeling bodies. 'Raschid alerted me at Evie's instigation. And I am telling you all of this because I wish to get all my guilty machinations out of the way before we hit the bed.'

'You mean that Evie knew you suspected when I called her up yesterday and she didn't drop a hint of it to me?'

'They are sneaky, those Al-Kadahs,' he confided as he trod the stairs. 'Where do you think I get it from?'

'And your arrogance?'

'Al-Qadim through and through,' he answered. 'Our child will have it too, I must warn you. Plenty of it, since you have your own kind of arrogance too.'

'Maybe that's why I love you.'

He stopped halfway up the stairs to slash her a wide, white rakish grin. 'And maybe,' he said lazily, 'that is why I love you.'

She smiled, lifted herself up to touch his mouth with her own. He continued on his way while they were still kissing— with an audience of fifty watching them from the floor below.

Why not let them look? Sheikh Hassan thought. This was his woman, his wife, the mother of his coming child. He would kiss her wherever and whenever. It was his right. *Inshallah.*

TAMING THE SHEIKH

Carol Grace

Carol Grace has always been interested in travel and living abroad. She spent her junior year of college in France and toured the world working on the hospital ship HOPE. She and her husband spent the first year and a half of their marriage in Iran, where they both taught English. She has studied Arabic and Persian languages. Then, with their toddler daughter, they lived in Algeria for two years. Carol says that writing is another way of making her life exciting. Her office is her mountain-top home, which overlooks the Pacific Ocean and which she shares with her inventor husband, their daughter, who just graduated from college, and their teenage son.

Don't miss Carol Grace's latest novel,
Her Sheikh Boss, **out in May 2008**
from Mills & Boon® Romance!

Chapter One

It was the most beautiful wedding of the year. The sun shone through the stained-glass windows of the church atop Nob Hill in San Francisco. The scent of roses filled the air. Bridal consultant Carolyn Evans walked down the aisle to marry Sheik Tarik Oman to the strains of the wedding march played on the magnificent pipe organ. It was an occasion no one would ever forget. Especially bridesmaid Anne Sheridan.

As the groom lifted the bride's veil and kissed her, there wasn't a dry eye in the front row where the family sat. Anne's eyes filled with tears, too. So many they threatened to spill down her cheeks. But it was not because she was overcome with emotion or because her pink silk shoes pinched her toes. It was an allergic reaction. While many people were allergic to grasses and trees, she knew from being tested last year she was allergic to flowers. She was allergic to the peonies and lilies in her bouquet, to the stephanotis at the end of each aisle, and even to the arrangements of roses at the altar.

To prepare for the wedding and guard against sneezing in the middle of the ceremony, she'd asked her doctor for extra-strength antihistamines which she'd taken an hour ago. Even so, her throat was raw and her eyes watered. I was clear she'd need another pill before the flower-filled garden reception to be held at the groom's mansion. Unable to reach for a tissue, she blinked back the tears and bit her lip. She was grateful all eyes were on the bride so no one would notice her red-rimmed eyes and obvious discomfort.

But someone did notice. One of the groomsmen at the altar was staring at her and not the bride. It was one of Sheik Tarik's twin cousins she'd met the night before at the rehearsal dinner. He was good-looking in an exotic way but she couldn't tell the difference between the twin brothers. They'd both flirted with every woman there except for her. She wasn't the type men flirted with. She was a sane and sensible private-school teacher who stayed in the background and watched the festivities.

Whichever twin he was, he wasn't flirting now, he was just looking at her intently as if he couldn't believe she was getting carried away and crying at her best friend's wedding. He raised one eyebrow, and she knew he must think she was an emotional basket case. As if she cared. After today she'd never see him again. He and his brother were just two of the out-of-town guests here for the wedding and would be leaving soon afterward.

She tore her gaze from his admittedly handsome face and focused on her friend Carolyn, thinking how happy she was for her. Marrying a rich and gorgeous sheik. After years of planning weddings for others, Carolyn was finally able to plan one for herself. And what a wedding it was. Somehow Anne got through the rest of the ceremony without coughing or sneezing and made it down the aisle and out in front of the church where she took a deep breath of fresh air.

"Are you all right?" A deep voice, a hand on her bare shoulder made a shiver go up her spine. Somehow she knew before she turned around. It was him.

"Of course, I'm fine," she said breathlessly, trying to ignore the warmth of his hand on her bare skin. Telling herself the goosebumps that had popped out on her arms were due to the cool air and not his warm touch.

"Look, it's just a wedding. Nothing to cry about," he said. "If anyone's crying it should be Tarik. Losing his freedom. Yes, it's enough to make every man in the place weep." He gave her a good-natured grin and removed his hand from her shoulder.

Immediately she missed the warmth of his touch. Ridiculous. A strange man took his hand away and she felt a chill. She tried to shrug off his remarks, which were obviously those of a confirmed cynic. He was just a typical, macho male with a commitment phobia. "You don't understand," she said. "I wasn't crying...."

"Not crying?" There was amused surprise in his tone. Surprised that she'd try to deny it. Surprised that she'd dared disagree with him. He leaned forward until his face was only inches from hers and studied her carefully. His eyes held her gaze for a long moment. She tried to look away but couldn't. She was trapped in the depths of those deep-brown eyes. Could that be sympathy she saw there or curiosity or something else? All she knew was she felt he was looking deep into her soul and she didn't want him to. After all, she didn't even know him.

He brushed a thumb against her cheekbone to wipe away a tear. A surprisingly gentle touch from a sophisticated man who looked like he came straight out of *GQ*. She felt a quiver run up her spine. Her legs felt like jelly. What was wrong with her, anyway? It must be the wedding, the tears, the joy and the music that were having an effect on her.

Not to mention those allergy pills. No man had ever made her feel like this. No man had ever brushed away her tears either.

"Those were tears there," he continued, cocking his head to one side. "You're not a very good liar, sweetheart. I know what I saw."

Anne took a deep breath and looked around. She had to get away from this man. Just in case it wasn't the music, the tears and the flowers, just in case her condition had something to do with this man, with the way he looked at her, the way his thumb left an imprint on her cheek and the way his hand felt on her shoulder. She had to escape, right now. Before this cousin of the groom jumped to the conclusion that his unwanted attention was affecting her one way or another. That it was because of him she felt cold on the outside and hot on the inside. Or that she was afraid to look into his eyes again, which she absolutely was not.

She didn't know where to go. Looking around, it seemed everyone was with someone. The photographer was snapping candid pictures, people were throwing rice and laughing and talking. No one was looking at her except him. She wished he wouldn't. She wished he'd go join one of those other groups. But he didn't. He just stood there looking at her. As if she were some rare bird like the ones she tracked on their migratory routes.

Thank heavens no one heard him call her "sweetheart" or noticed him touching her. Thank heavens no one knew what an effect that touch had on her. She felt it even now, the brush of his thumb on her skin. What an innocent she was. Any other woman would have shrugged it off, because it didn't mean anything after all. Not to him.

"All right," she said, "you saw tears, but not because...not for the reason you thought."

"Cheer up," he said with a smile that showed a flash of white teeth against his bronzed skin. "Think of it this way, you're not losing a friend, you're gaining a sheik."

"Is that a good thing?" she asked, trying to strike a light-hearted, bantering tone, as if she dealt with handsome sheiks every day of the week. If she did she'd know how to deal with this man who undoubtedly needed a dose of humility. Not that she was the one to teach him. She taught six-year-olds to count and spell and read. She'd never met a sheik until Carolyn introduced her to Tarik, her fiancé, a kind and charming man who was obviously totally different from his cousin.

"A *very* good thing," he said, his dark eyes dancing with fun.

Flirting. That's what he was doing, she realized with a start. He was flirting with her, but she didn't know how to flirt back. So she just stood there staring at him, wondering why he bothered with her. Why not hit on one of the other bridesmaids who'd know what to do, know what to say to a good-looking bachelor on the prowl. Anyone else would know how to put him in his place with a lighthearted riposte.

She was saved from responding to this bit of braggadocio by a request from the photographer for a picture of the entire wedding party inside the church.

"I guess that means me," she said, grateful for the distraction.

"It means *us*," he said, offering his arm.

She smiled weakly. As much as she wanted to, she knew it would be rude to ignore him, to stalk on ahead as if he hadn't spoken, as if he hadn't held out his arm. So she gingerly took his arm, so gingerly that he paused.

"I won't bite, you know," he said, slanting a teasing glance in her direction. Again his eyes danced with fun. At

her expense. She didn't know what to say, so she didn'
say anything. And they walked back up the aisle of th
church. Thank heavens she wasn't a bride, because sh
stumbled on the red carpet halfway to the altar, whic
caused the sheik to tighten his grip on her arm. He finall
had to let her go so she could take her place with the brides
maids and so he could take his place next to the groom.

But before the flashbulbs starting popping, she was com
pelled to cast a glance in his direction and found him look
ing at her. When he caught her eye he winked flirtatiousl
at her, and she quickly looked away.

Luckily she had to help the bride with her train on th
way back down the aisle, and she lost sight of the sheik
Otherwise who knew what would have happened? Sh
might have ridden with him back to the reception. Sh
might have been wedged into one of the limos next to hin
all the way through town. The thought of his thigh presse
against hers, his shoulder next to hers caused the heat t
rise to her head. She paused to take another allergy pil
while she gave herself a stern warning about handsome me
on the prowl.

Instead of riding with the sheik, luckily she caught a rid
to the reception with Carolyn's mother and aunt, durin
which they oohed and ahhed about what a lovely weddin
it was and how beautiful Carolyn looked. Anne agreed en
thusiastically, but when they started talking about the twi
brothers, Rafik and Rahman, she closed her eyes and leane
back against the leather seat. She didn't want to hear abou
them and she didn't want to talk about them. She had noth
ing to say. She didn't even know which one was which
This second dose of allergy medicine made her feel increas
ingly tired and groggy. If she could just make an appear
ance at the reception, she'd sneak out early and take a tax
home.

But she couldn't ignore the conversation floating around her in the car. She couldn't help feeling as if she were listening to a dialog from a movie.

"Aren't those twins the handsomest men you've ever seen? You know, they arrived for the wedding a few weeks ago, but I heard they like it so much in San Francisco, they're opening a branch of the family business here," Carolyn's mother said. "They're going to be quite an addition to the social scene. With their looks and their money and their status."

"So handsome," Carolyn's aunt murmured.

"Absolutely adorable, if I were thirty years younger...."

The two women burst into girlish laughter and even Anne had to smile. What was it about weddings that brought out the frivolous in everyone? Everyone but her.

"Anne, dear, how are you?" Carolyn's mother asked anxiously observing her daughter's best friend. "Weddings can be so exhausting. I know I'm going to spend the next week recovering. But you'll feel better once we get to the reception. They've booked the most wonderful band and the caterer is the best in town."

Anne nodded. She was sure everything about the reception would be perfection, if she knew Carolyn. They'd been friends since high school, spending hours together daydreaming about the future. Carolyn sketching bridal gowns, clipping articles on weddings from the society pages, destined for bridal bliss herself. Anne studying hard, determined to be a teacher, picturing herself surrounded by children as she read the stories to them that she'd loved as a child.

When Anne was diagnosed with scoliosis in her sophomore year Carolyn stood by her. She took notes for her friend when she had to miss school for doctor's appointments. Cheered her up when she had to wear a back brace right up to graduation. Tried to lure her out to parties and dances. But Anne was shy and unsure of herself around boys. Who in their right mind would be interested in a girl in a brace? No one, that's who.

Anne was never jealous of Carolyn. Even now with a lifetime of happiness ahead of her, Anne only wished her the best. Carolyn deserved it. After spending years planning weddings for other people, she'd finally planned her own to a man she was madly in love with.

Anne was determined to try to enjoy the reception for as long as she could. The good news was she'd been able to avoid the groom's cousin completely so far. The bad news was she was so terribly tired. All she wanted to do right now was to lie down and take a nap. It was a side effect of the medicine, she knew. At least her tears had dried up and she wouldn't be accused of getting emotional over a wedding.

The house on the bluff above the ocean was beautiful. The view from the garden was spectacular. Guests were handed a glass of champagne or sparkling fruit juice as they arrived at the entrance to the patio. Anne sipped her champagne gratefully. Her mouth was as dry as cotton. She found a chair half hidden behind a native fern and drained her glass. She heard voices, saw shapes and forms but hoped that no one, especially no one from the wedding party, could see her or they'd ask her what was wrong, insist she join the party, meet someone and say something. Never a social butterfly, she had never felt less social than today.

Suddenly the murmur of voices got louder. Voices she recognized.

"Say, Carolyn," a familiar male voice said, "have I told you how beautiful you look? Too bad Tarik saw you first. He has all the luck."

"I'm the one who's lucky, Rafik. And so happy. One of these days we'll be dancing at your wedding."

"Have you been talking to my father? That's his idea of happiness, not mine. Why get married when there are so many wonderful willing women around. By the way, who's your bridesmaid?"

"Which one?"

"In the pink dress."

"They're all in pink dresses."

"Reddish hair, blue eyes."

"You mean Anne. My best friend from high school. Stay away from her, Rafik. She's a wonderful woman, but she's not willing. And she's too good for a player like you," Carolyn said in a teasing voice.

"Why don't we let her decide?" he asked. "Besides, everything's about to change. I'm going to be in charge of the new office here in San Francisco. I'm afraid my party days are over and my playboy ways are going to be sharply curtailed. Not that I'll ever settle down, but I can't stay out all night partying anymore if I'm going to be in the office at nine every morning. Woe is me."

"You're too much, Rafik. Let me introduce you to Lila. She's a lot of fun."

"I met her. She's fine but not my type. Have you seen Anne around?"

"Rafik, I warned you…" Carolyn sighed. "No, I haven't seen her since the church."

Just as Anne was congratulating herself on her apparent invisibility, the pollen from the flowers that bordered the ferns she was hiding behind overcame her antihistamines and she sneezed.

Carolyn peeked around the plants. "There you are," she said. She and Rafik circled around the ferns and stood look-

ing down at her. "Come on and join the party. You've me
Tarik's cousin Rafik, haven't you?"

"Yes, of course, I mean, that is I...I...." she stammered
"Not formally."

Rafik held out his hand and he pulled her to her feet. I
it weren't for him she might have fallen over. Her knee:
wobbled and she felt dizzy. She hoped they wouldn't no
tice. Carolyn didn't, but then her head was in the clouds
Rafik gave Anne a searching second glance.

"Happy to meet you, Anne," he said, trapping her hand
between both of his. She tugged, but he had no intentior
of letting her go. Maybe it was just as well. Without his
support she might have toppled over.

"If you two will excuse me," Carolyn said. "I must say
hello to some people. Rafik, remember what I said," she
added pointedly.

Anne wanted to go with her. Surely there were people
she had to say hello to, too. But she couldn't move. So she
stood there, her hand still being held tightly by the sheik
who showed no sign of remembering anything Carolyn had
said. Why? she asked herself. Why didn't he go off and
dance with Lila, why stay with her?

"You look like you could use something to drink," he
said, studying her with narrowed eyes.

She nodded. "I'm really thirsty."

"Let's get some champagne and a few of those deliciou:
hors d'oeuvres." He tucked her hand securely under his
arm for the second time that day and they strolled over to
a table laden with all kinds of delectable canapés. With his
support, she felt stronger, more in control.

"Champagne?" she asked. "I didn't know you were per
mitted to drink."

"My brother and I were sent to boarding school in the
U.S. as kids. Then we stayed in this country for university

on the east coast since the family business is multinational. I'm afraid we're pretty much Americanized by now. For better or worse." Again that disarming grin. The one that charmed all those willing women who were no doubt in his life. "You notice Tarik is serving fruit juice, too, for those like my parents who observe the religious rules of our country."

Anne felt much better after she'd eaten two stuffed mushrooms and drunk another glass of champagne. "I'm fine now," she said to the sheik. "Thank you." *You can go now. Don't feel obliged to take care of me.*

"Sure you're all right? Not going to cry anymore?"

"For the last time, I wasn't crying." *Goodbye.*

"Right. You notice I didn't mention it to your friend Carolyn."

"I appreciate that," Anne said. "If you'll excuse me I'm going to uh…I see some friends over there. Nice meeting you." If that wasn't a decided exit, she didn't know what was, she thought as she walked slowly across the lawn, her high heels scraping the ground. She didn't turn to see if he'd hurt his feelings. She was sure she wasn't capable of any such thing. He was most likely on his way to find another woman, chat up another bridesmaid, hoping she'd be more receptive to his so-called charm.

Rafik stood watching the woman wobble across the lawn, Carolyn's words ringing in his ears. *A wonderful woman. Stay away from her. Too good for you.*

She was right. Anne was just the type he was not interested in. Shy. Quiet. Emotional. Heaven save him from the weepy kind of women who cry at weddings. Oh, it was okay if you were the mother of the bride or groom. So what was wrong with him, hitting on a woman who was most definitely not his type? There was something about her, the way she tried to hold back the tears that brought

out the protector in him. She made him feel admirable. Th
way she looked at him through damp lashes, cheek
flushed, her face framed in that gorgeous red-gold hair.

He reminded himself he was not interested in being ad
mirable. He was not looking to protect someone. He wa
looking for a smooth, sexy, smart and sassy woman wh
could protect herself. Anne Sheridan was none of th
above. Besides she was a friend of Carolyn's, his nev
cousin-in-law whom he respected. Half-reluctantly, h
turned and looked over the bevy of lovely women, enoug
women gathered here to please a whole family of sheiks
For some reason he couldn't seem to focus on any one o
them.

"Hey," his brother threw an arm around his shoulders
"Having fun? Who was the lady in pink I saw you with?"

"Just one of the bridesmaids."

"I *know* it was one of the bridesmaids," Rahman said
"What's her name?"

"Anne Sheridan. A friend of Carolyn's. Why?"

"I don't know. Don't remember her from the rehearsa
dinner. Thought I'd met every pretty woman there. I migh
introduce myself. Unless you…?"

"No, absolutely not," Rafik said. "Wouldn't touch he
with a ten-foot pole. Not my type. Not yours either."

"Okay. Just asking. What a party, huh?"

It *was* quite a party, and Rafik would have been a foo
to miss a moment of it. He threw himself into enjoying th
music, the dancing, and oh, yes, chatting up the women
So much so, he almost forgot about the auburn-haire
bridesmaid in the pink dress. Out of sight, out of mind
That's the way it always was with him. But in one smal
corner of his mind during the fun, he wondered what ha
happened to her. He hoped his brother had followed hi
advice and ignored her. Not that he really cared. Not tha

he was his responsibility. It was just that she seemed so
ragile and so vulnerable. It was obvious somebody ought
o be responsible for her. Just so it wasn't him or anyone
e knew.

Yes, he'd all but forgotten about her, until at the end of
he afternoon, as dusk was falling over the manicured
rounds, after the eating, drinking and dancing, he was
alled upon to make a toast. He stood on the dance platform
n front of the musicians who were packing up and told
ome anecdotes about Tarik that made everyone laugh. Just
s he lifted his glass of champagne to toast his cousin and
is bride, he saw Anne at the edge of the crowd. She lifted
er glass and caught his eye. She definitely looked like
he'd had a few too many glasses of champagne. Funny.
Ie wouldn't have picked her for a lush.

Maybe he ought to bring her a piece of wedding cake
nd see how she was doing. But when he went looking for
er, cake in hand, she was gone. It was just as well.

"Rafik." Carolyn got up from the small table where she
vas sitting with a group of older people and caught his
rm. "Do me a favor, will you? Anne isn't feeling well.
:ould you give her a ride home?"

"Sure. Where is she?"

"At the front door. She wanted to call a taxi, but I'm a
ttle worried. I want to be sure she gets home all right."

"Okay," he said.

He pulled his car up in front of the house and left the
notor running while he bounded up the front steps. He
ound her standing in the doorway of the house, looking
onfused.

"Oh," Anne said, startled to see Rafik at the door.

"Come on," he said, putting his arm around her waist.

"I'm waiting for a taxi. Thanks anyway," she said, try-
ng unsuccessfully to disengage his arm.

"I'm the taxi," he said. "I'm taking you home. Orders from Carolyn."

"That's not necessary," she said. Of all people. She did not want to be indebted to this man, who thought he was God's gift to womankind. Who'd already seen her at her worst. She'd managed to avoid him for the past few hours and now here he was again.

"Really. I'm fine. I just need…." She just needed to lie down and close her eyes. Her head was pounding, the room was spinning, and Rafik's face was going in and out of focus. When he picked her up as easily as if she weighed no more than a rag doll and carried her down the steps to his waiting car, her head bobbed against his shoulder. She pounded him on his back in an attempt to make him let her go, but it had no effect on him at all.

He very carefully installed her in the passenger seat, taking her small clutch bag from her hand and removing her shoes before he tucked her feet in. She sighed. Despite her protests, she had to admit it felt so good to be taken care of. So good to have those tight shoes off. Again she was surprised that a big, broad-shouldered, dashing man-about-town would have such a gentle touch. As he fastened her seat belt, his hand grazed the bodice of her silk dress and she gasped. Her eyes flew open and met his amused gaze.

"Just following the seat-belt law," he said innocently. "Wouldn't want to be stopped for any kind of violation."

"Right," she said.

Did he know, could he tell she was unaccustomed to being touched there? Unused to being touched at all by a man? That just a brush of his hand had left her shaky and breathless? Or was that, too, the effect of the champagne and the medicine? What did it matter? He'd been instructed to take her home and he was doing it. She ought to be grateful.

"Where do you live?" he asked.

"In the Sunset," she said. "Out by the....you know...."

he hoped he knew because the names of the streets of San Francisco were going round and round in her brain. Such nice names. Which one was hers? "Octavia. Laguna. Chestnut. Larkin. Pine and Bush," she murmured.

"What?" he said. "I'm new in town. You'll have to give me better directions than that."

"Take Geary," she said. "No, no better take California."

"I know California Street," he said confidently. "No problem. You just relax till we get there."

Relax? She was so relaxed she might never move again. "Nice car," she said, though all she knew was that it smelled like leather and the seat was so comfortable she wanted to stay there forever.

"It's new," he said. "I didn't need a car when we lived in New York, but I do here," he said. "My life is about to change. Drastically."

"No more playboy, hmm?"

"Where'd you hear that?" he asked sharply.

"Heard you talking."

"I thought maybe you'd been talking to my father."

She shook her head. Just to utter another word would require too much effort.

"He thinks it's time I grew up. Took over the business and got married. I'm the elder son, you know."

"I thought...twins," she murmured.

"Yes, we're twins, but I was born first. By thirty minutes. So Rahman's allowed some slack while I'm the heir apparent. I'm the one who gets the corner office. I'm the one who gets the responsibility of running it. I'm the one who's supposed to find a wife and settle down. Don't tell anyone I said that. I'm trying to talk him out of that one.''

As if she could tell anyone anything. Her lips were numb, her eyes refused to open. He was still talking. She could hear the words but they made no sense. None at all.

When Rafik got to California Street he turned to ask Anne which way to turn, but her eyes were closed and she was breathing softly and steadily. She'd fallen asleep.

''Hey, wake up,'' he said. ''Which way on California?'' He shook her gently by the shoulder. Nothing. ''Anne. Where do you live? Come on, sweetheart, speak to me.'' But she didn't. She slid down even farther in the seat. Too much to drink, obviously. Well, it wasn't the first time he'd been stuck with an inebriated date. Though he usually knew where they lived. He could go back to the wedding or call Carolyn, but the truth was, he was tired himself. It had been a week of nonstop pre-wedding parties along with setting up a new office and frankly he was beat. He, the man who loved a good time, who'd never met a party he didn't like, was slowing down. What was the matter with him?

Another thing. He didn't relish telling Carolyn her friend had passed out before he even got her home. It might put a damper on the remainder of the party for her. And it would make her best friend look bad. The only thing to do was take her back to his hotel with him. It was a comfortable suite with great room service and a giant king-size bed. When she came to, he'd sober her up with coffee, find out where she lived and drive her home.

Unfortunately Anne was still out of it when they arrived at the hotel. How was he going to get her up to his room without causing a scene? He pulled up to the front entrance and tried once more to wake her up. ''We're here,'' he said loudly. ''Come on. Do me a favor and wake up.'' She didn't stir.

The doorman opened the passenger door and waited.

Rafik jumped out of the car and lifted Anne up in his arms.

''Fell asleep in the car,'' Rafik explained to the blue-uniformed doorman. ''She'll be fine. Have the valet park it, will you?''

''Certainly, sir,'' he said, as if comatose guests arrived every day and had to be carried into the hotel.

The lobby was crowded with well-dressed guests. There was a party going on in one of the ballrooms. Not all of the people turned to stare at the man in the tuxedo carrying a redheaded woman in a strapless pink silk dress to the elevator. But most of them did. The decibel level fell about twenty points as a kind of hush fell over the crowd. The hush was replaced with murmurs.

''*Who* is *that?*''

''One of those sheiks. He shut down the bar the other night. Isn't he too much?''

''No, I mean her. Who's she? I've never seen her before.''

''It couldn't be...no, if I didn't know better I'd think it was Emma's teacher, Miss Sheridan.''

''Anne Sheridan, the first-grade teacher at Pinehurst?''

''It isn't, of course, but the hair...such a gorgeous color. There aren't many people... No, what am I thinking? It couldn't be her. What would she be doing in the arms of a playboy going up to his hotel room or hers? She's not the type. All of the teachers at Pinehurst are screened carefully. Models of decorum. At least in public. No, it can't be her.''

Rafik, who'd done just about every outrageous thing in the last few years in New York, felt his ears turn red. *Not the type. Not his type.* He knew that. But he'd brought her here anyway. What was wrong with him? He knew what was wrong with him. He didn't want to let her go. Didn't want to leave her anywhere. Not until he knew she was all right. On the other hand, she was a big girl. She could take care of herself. But not tonight. Tonight he was taking care of her whether she wanted him to or not. It made no sense. It made no sense at all. But there it was.

At least he should have covered Anne with something. It was one thing, as part of a colorful and wealthy international family, to be talked about in hotel lobbies. It wasn't the first time that had happened to him. But to expose Anne to gossip was not fair. He shouldn't have brought her here. He should have driven back to the reception, found out where she lived and taken her home. But hindsight is always 20/20. It was a little late to change his game plan.

He stared straight ahead, his teeth clenched in his jaw, praying for an early arrival of the elevator. After an eternity it arrived and gratefully he entered, Anne's face pressed against his chest. He awkwardly hit the button for the twentieth floor and heaved a sigh of relief. But he wasn't home free.

The elevator wasn't empty.

"Big night?" a man in a dark suit asked with a smirk.

Rafik managed a tight smile. There was no way to explain that wouldn't exacerbate the situation.

"Oh, my," said an elegant woman in a beige suit, eyeing Anne's inert body with surprise. "Is she all right?"

"Fine. She's just fine. Just tired."

"Beautiful red hair. Say, aren't you one of those sheiks?" she asked.

He'd removed his headdress this morning, but somehow the woman knew. Maybe because the family had taken over the entire twentieth floor.

"Yes," he said. "I am."

Damn. He could have lied. Could have said he was the hotel manager escorting a guest to her room or a doctor with a case of Lyme disease on his hands. How many more people was he going to run into before he got her to his floor, to his suite? He could only be glad he wasn't going to meet any family members, presumably all still at the reception. He especially wanted to avoid his father who'd had a talk with him that very morning about his new image, about public relations and the family business. This kind of situation was exactly what his father was talking about. Only it wasn't really. It just looked like it. Unfortunately his father was into appearances. In a big way.

He finally arrived in the cool, calm, quiet, high-ceilinged suite. He strode into the bedroom and laid her down on the bed on her back. Her face was pale. He sat on the edge of the bed and pressed his ear against her chest. She was breathing slowly and regularly. Thank God. Rafik knew from experience she just needed to sleep it off.

It would be just a matter of time before she came to. When she did, he'd offer her coffee and if that didn't work, he'd mix her up a concoction that worked for him—tomato juice with Worcestershire and a touch of lemon and pepper. He'd spirit her out of the hotel, down the back stairs, if there were any, and take her home. And that would be that. Carolyn would never know. She'd be on her honeymoon. All she wanted was for him to take the woman home. Which he'd tried to do. Which he would do. Eventually.

He sat on the edge of the bed observing her, his forehead furrowed. The woman in the elevator was right. She had beautiful hair. A delicious strawberry color that curled in wisps around her face. A smattering of freckles across her nose. She looked so young and innocent. She couldn't be that young. She was Carolyn's age. So she couldn't be innocent either, could she? He sighed. He knew many beautiful women with beautiful hair. Blondes, brunettes and red-heads. He'd met several today at the wedding.

But he'd never met anyone quite like this woman here on his bed. Damned if he could say what it was about her that intrigued him the way she did. Maybe it was just that she *wasn't* his type. Yes, that must be it. Opposites attract. Combine that with Carolyn's warning and it had made her damned near irresistible. He loosened his tie and looked down at her. He had an uncontrollable desire to run his fingers over her bare shoulder and down her arm to her hand that was curled up. He knew what her skin would feel like. Satin smooth. Just the way it had when he touched her this afternoon after the wedding. He fought off a shaft of desire that threatened to overtake him.

He sighed loudly, wishing she'd wake up. Wishing he could get out of this monkey suit. He imagined Anne would be more comfortable without the fancy dress she'd been wearing all day, too. After a long moment of contemplation, he rolled her gently on her side and tugged clumsily at the zipper on the back of her dress.

Carefully he pulled the dress down over her hips and tossed it on a chair. Underneath the dress she was wearing lace bikini panties and a strapless bra. He sat there staring as if he'd never seen a woman in that state before. Truth was, he'd seen many female bodies in his time. Dressed and undressed. But there was something special about this one. Something that made his heart pound. Made him short of breath. It might have been the scattering of freckles across her chest, the swell of her breasts, or the curve of her hips. She was defenseless and therefore untouchable. And oh, yes, not the most beautiful woman he'd ever seen, and definitely not his type, but very appealing, and very desirable.

This was a situation where other men might have taken

advantage of her. But there was a code of conduct he adhered to which was based on a respect for women and an obligation to help those in his care.

An obligation to make them comfortable. To protect them. He tore off his shirt, the buttons flying and covered her with it. Then he very carefully put one of her arms in the sleeve, then awkwardly the other arm. He was breathing hard from exertion. Very slowly he reached under the shirt for the strapless bra she was wearing. From experience he knew how those bras worked. Unhook the front and slip it off. But should he? What if she woke up? If she did, he'd just explain. And if she did, well, wasn't that what he wanted after all?

Under the shirt, unable to see what he was doing, he reached for the snap, but his fingers, usually so deft, felt like stubs. Finally he slid the bra off, pulled the blankets back and covered her up. She was now wearing his shirt and her panties. He'd done the best he could do.

He stood at the edge of the bed looking down at her. The red-gold hair against the white pillow. The pale face and the curve of her cheek. So sweet, so lovely. And so wrong for him. He knew that. Of course he did. As soon as he could he'd get her out of here. But when would that be? How long before she woke up? Did he dare doze off himself? All he wanted was to get her out of his bed, out of his room and out of his mind. But he couldn't. Not now. Not yet while she was still sleeping it off.

He closed the bedroom door behind him and paced back and forth in the living room, staring out the window at the lights of the city below. As tired as he was, he just couldn't go to bed. His mind was spinning. Images of the wedding filled his mind. The bride, the groom. The bridesmaid. Some time later there was a knock on the door.

"What happened to you?" his brother asked when he

opened the door. "Couldn't believe you left so early. You missed the throwing of the garter. I caught it."

"Good, that means you'll be the next to be married. And not me."

"You first," Rahman said. "You're the eldest."

"Forget it. I've heard enough of that from father. You know what happened the last time he tried to arrange a marriage for me."

"Don't blame father for that. It was nobody's fault," his brother said. "You can't give up on marriage because of one woman."

"I can't? Why not? If you feel that way, then why don't you lead the way and set an example for me," Rafik said, knowing it was a safe suggestion. Rahman was an even bigger playboy than Rafik had ever been.

"I'll give it a thought," Rahman said amiably. "Hey, aren't you going to invite me in? We can order up some coffee and rehash the wedding."

"Uh...I don't think so." Good Lord, what if the woman woke up and stumbled into the room? Not that Rahman would be shocked. Rafik just...he just didn't want his brother to think she was that kind of woman. Of course he himself didn't know what kind of woman she really was, but he could guess. She was the type to drink to cover her shyness, to make it easier to socialize.

"All right. But you still haven't explained why you left so early. I thought you and I would be rolling up the sidewalk." Leaning against the door frame, Rahman looked at his brother curiously.

"I've got to be in the office at nine tomorrow. They're installing the computer system. That's why I left early. Yeah, that's it. I can't carouse the way I used to, you know." Brilliant. That ought to satisfy his brother who knew about the increased duties his father had put on him.

Rahman observed him closely. No one knew him as well as his brother. If he could fool him, he was home free.

A soft muffled sound came from the bedroom. A sound like a sneeze.

"What was that?" Rahman asked, raising an eyebrow.

"Nothing." Damn. She hadn't made a peep since they'd arrived and she chose that moment to sneeze. Next thing he knew she'd be opening that bedroom door and...

Rahman grinned. "You've got somebody in there, haven't you? You're holding out on me. Who is it? Is it that bridesmaid I saw you with? Yeah, it's her, isn't it?"

"No, it isn't. Goodnight, Rah. Get some sleep. You need it. See you tomorrow." Very firmly and very forcefully Rafik closed the door on his brother and locked it. Then he strode across the room and flung the bedroom door open.

Chapter Two

Rafik held his breath. She was still there. Still asleep. Curled up on her side, one bare arm on the spread, her copper-colored hair still spread over the pillow, a vibrant splash of color in the soft lamplight. His heart stopped beating for a full moment, maybe longer. Good Lord, whether she was his type or not, she really was beautiful. Damn. He'd been hoping that sneeze meant she'd be up and dressed and ready to leave. Not yet.

What to do? He couldn't think straight. He was exhausted. He went into the bathroom and stripped down to his boxers. When he came out, he stood at the end of the bed debating about what to do. Watching her sleep make him feel tired and envious. Why should she get a chance to sleep in that big, comfortable bed and not him? He'd had just as hard a day as she had. Was just as tired. On the opposite side of the bed, he slid beneath the sheets and closed his eyes. Just for a few minutes.

The next thing he knew the phone was ringing. It was

his wake-up call. He jumped out of bed and did a double take. She was still there.

"Anne," he said, "wake up. It's morning."

She sighed softly. It wasn't possible for anyone to sleep through a wake-up call. She'd wake up any minute now. But he couldn't wait around until she did. He hurried into the bathroom to take a shower, then came out and dressed carefully but quickly. He couldn't be late today. From the closet he chose a London-tailored suit with a pin-striped shirt and dark tie. Then went to the living room and briskly wrote a note on his new business stationery.

"Dear Anne," he began. No, too formal. He crumpled the paper and tossed it in the wastebasket.

"Anne," he wrote. No, too brusque. Another toss in the basket.

"Hi." Yes, just the right casual tone.

Thanks for a great evening. We'll do it again some time when you're in better shape. Sorry I couldn't take you home last night but it didn't work out that way for obvious reasons. I've got things to do this morning or I'd stick around and see some more of you. I'll give you a call. Here's some taxi money.

Sheik Rafik Harun.

Anne turned over when she heard a door close somewhere in the distance. She tried to open her eyes, but the sunlight that shone through the window was blinding. She pulled the sheet over her head and wondered what time it was. Though she was enjoying a summer off from teaching, she was usually up early, out in her backyard, filling her bird feeders and the birdbath. Funny. She couldn't hear the chirp of a single robin or the screech of a blue jay reminding her of her obligation to feed them and give them water.

She threw back the covers, sat up in bed and gasped. She was in a huge king-sized bed. The opposite side from hers was rumpled, covers thrown back and an indentation in the pillow. She picked it up and pressed it against her face. There was a distinct manly smell that clung to the soft cotton. What on earth? Where was she? How did she get here? Who had slept with her and, just as important, what was she wearing? It appeared to be a large man's shirt with several buttons missing. She always slept in a long flannel nightgown, suitable for the cool San Francisco summer nights. But for some inexplicable reason she had slept in someone else's shirt. And she hadn't slept alone.

She swallowed hard. Her pulse was racing. "Hello?" she called weakly. No answer. She tried again, this time louder. Silence.

Across the room her pink dress was spread across a chair. It all came back to her in a rush. The wedding. The champagne. The allergy medicine. The flirtatious sheik. But where was she? She'd obviously never made it home.

Wherever she was, she was alone. And she had a splitting headache. She was scared she couldn't remember what had happened. Even more scared she might remember.

She jumped out of bed, pressed one hand against her aching head and went to the window. She muffled a shriek. She was high above the sidewalk, looking out at the city and the San Francisco Bay. Fortunately no one could look in the window at that height, to see her in a man's white dress shirt with missing buttons, but she ought to get dressed. She found her strapless bra on the bureau and stared at it. How, where, why…and who?

She took off the shirt and buried her face in it for a brief moment. The smell was pure exotic masculinity the likes of which she'd never smelled before, and it caused her knees to tremble. The smell of the shirt reminded her of someone or something but she couldn't remember who it was. It made her head hurt more to try to remember. There were no answers to her questions. No one to ask. It was time to get dressed and get out of there. Before someone came back. The someone who'd slept next to her. The someone who belonged to the shirt.

Once she was dressed in her own clothes, she walked into the large living room, picked up the phone and pressed O for Operator.

"Front Desk."

"Yes," Anne said. "Where am I?"

"You're in room 2004 at the Stanford Arms," said a bored, uninterested voice.

"Oh, of course. Thank you." The Stanford Arms. She couldn't afford to stay at the Stanford Arms, a luxurious landmark hotel on Nob Hill. She especially couldn't afford to stay in a top-of-the-line suite there. That was when she saw the note on the table and read, the words ringing through her head:

A great evening…better shape…see more of you…taxi money…Sheik Rafik Harun.

Who on earth was that? What on earth had happened? She sat on the edge of a large overstuffed chair with her head in her hands and told herself to think. To remember. But it was so hard with her head feeling as if it were caught in a vise. Slowly, slowly it came to her. The handsome groomsman. The flirtatious sheik, driving her home. Why hadn't he? Could it be that he'd never intended to take her home? That he'd wanted to seduce her, not because she was so gorgeous or desirable, which she wasn't, but just to add another notch to his belt?

But had he? How would she know? She was a virgin. She had no idea how you felt after a night of lovemaking. She only knew that her head hurt and her whole body felt as if she'd been wrung through a wringer. Someone had removed her bra. Someone had put his shirt on her. Someone had slept next to her. That someone was a sheik. What else had he done? What had she done? The jumble of thoughts, the myriad of possibilities made her face flame. Oh, Lord, what was she going to do now? She was going to get out of there. Then she was going to find the sheik and find out what had happened last night.

She stumbled into the bathroom to wash her face. The mirror was still steamed up. The smell of soap and aftershave still in the air. She'd just missed him. Why hadn't he woken her up? Because that's the way it was. After a night of seduction, after the man got what he wanted, he left you a note saying he'd call you, left taxi money and then disappeared. Out of your life forever. Though she'd had no experience of spending the night with strange men, or any men for that matter, she knew that's how it was.

In this case he'd left his address and phone number on the stationery, as if she'd want to call him! She didn't want him to call her either. She never wanted to see him again. But she had to. She had to find out what had happened. If she could only find her shoes. And more important, her little clutch purse with her money and her house keys. They weren't under the bed and they weren't in the closet. The closet contained only men's clothes. Very expensive men's clothes. Not only suits and shirts and ties, but slacks and designer jeans and polo shirts.

She took a deep breath, picked up the phone and dialed the office number on his stationery. Her palms were damp. What would she say exactly?

How dare you take advantage of me?

Where are my shoes and my purse?

What happened anyway?

I never want to see you again!

What would he say? Would he pretend nothing happened? That he didn't know what she was talking about? She didn't get a chance to say anything because she got his voice mail and she froze. The things she thought she would say, the questions she wanted to ask, could not be spoken into a machine. They had to be spoken to a person. Sheik Rafik to be exact. She hung up.

There was only one thing to do. She'd call the house where the wedding reception had been. Perhaps the housekeeper had found her purse there.

"There was no purse here," the housekeeper said when Anne got her on the phone. "I believe you had it with you when the gentleman drove you home."

The gentleman! If only he was a gentleman. Maybe she'd left her purse and shoes in his car. She thanked the housekeeper, grabbed the money from the table and walked out the door, barefoot. She would have loved to have left the money there, but under the circumstances, she couldn't afford to. She got quite a few stares in the elevator, and even more in the lobby as she sauntered through, head held high, trying to act as if spending the night with a rich, eligible bachelor and sneaking out the next morning in the same dress happened to her every day. Why couldn't she remember coming in last night?

If only she could sneak out. But it was hard to sneak when you were barefoot, and wearing a pink bridesmaid's dress. You were bound to get a few curious glances in your direction. She got more than a few.

What a relief to get into a taxi. The driver barely gave her a second glance as she gave him Rafik's office address. Thank heavens for blasé cabdrivers. The only expression on his face was a frown when she handed him the hundred-dollar bill. He emptied his pockets and gave her change which she clutched in her hand after giving him a generous tip.

Then she stood in front of the office building on Montgomery Street in the heart of San Francisco's financial district. The pavement was cold beneath her bare feet as she stood staring up at the high-rise. Bike messengers whizzed by, horns honked, but she scarcely noticed. She wondered which office was his, wondered if she'd have the nerve to actually go up and confront him.

She had to. She had no choice. She squared her shoulders, walked through the revolving doors and strode across the marble lobby as if she belonged there. She looked straight ahead, pretending she had blinders on, ignoring whatever curious looks were directed her way, and they must have been numerous.

The office of United Venture Capitalists was on the fourteenth floor and smelled of fresh paint and new carpets. A well-groomed receptionist behind a cherrywood desk first greeted her with a smile then her mouth fell open in surprise as she took in Anne's unusual and unbusiness-like appearance.

"My name is Anne Sheridan. I'm here to see Sheik Rafik Harun," Anne said, summoning all the dignity she had.

"Uh…yes. Do you have an appointment?" the receptionist asked. As if a barefoot woman in a formal dress *would* have an appointment with a sheik.

"No, but I have to see him."

"I'll see if he's in," she said coolly. "Won't you sit down?"

Anne was too nervous to sit down. Instead she stood looking at the pictures on the wall of the ventures the company had funded. She examined a portrait of the grandfather who'd founded the company, a distinguished-looking sheik in traditional Arab dress. When she heard male voices approaching, she whirled around. It was not Rafik. It was an older man who looked very much like the sheik in the picture on the wall with an American who was wearing jeans and a T-shirt.

"May I help you, my dear?" the older man asked with a slight bow.

She swallowed hard. "I'm here to see Rafik."

His gaze flicked over her dress. He pressed his lips together in a tight line. He seemed to understand without asking, just what had happened. Though he couldn't possibly know when she didn't even know herself. Unless it was a common occurrence for women to appear in evening gowns unannounced, asking for his son. She wouldn't be surprised.

"I see," he said. "Where is my elder son?" he asked the receptionist.

Her gaze fluttered from her desk to her telephone to the elder sheik. "I...I believe he's in his office."

"Then show the young lady in," he ordered.

"Yes, sir, right away." She jumped up from her desk and while the two men watched she led Anne down the hall to the large office on the corner. She knocked on the door and when Rafik yelled for her to come in, the woman opened the door, ushered Anne in and then disappeared.

Rafik was seated behind an enormous desk talking on the phone with his back to the door and to Anne. She had an excellent view of the back of his handsome head and his broad shoulders in his well-tailored suit jacket. Her heart was hammering in her chest like a tom-tom. This was a terrible idea. She should just turn around and walk out while she still could. He'd never know. But his father would tell him. And she still didn't have her purse.

"Yes, of course I'll be there," he said. "The whole family will be there and very pleased to be hosting the benefit

this year.... It gives us a chance to meet the community....
No, not yet. I'm new in town, you know. Haven't had a
chance to meet many women...." That was the only reason
he'd spent the night with her, Anne thought. He didn't
know any other women. He chuckled, and Anne shivered.
If only she had a jacket, a coat, a sweater. Anything. But
no sweater would prevent the chill that his words sent
through her. If she left now, he'd never know she was ever
there. But she couldn't. Even if she'd wanted to. Her feet
were made of lead. She couldn't move a muscle.

"A woman in my hotel room?" Rafik asked, sounding
shocked at the very idea. Anne wished she could sink into
the Oriental carpet and disappear. "You must have me confused with someone else," he said genially. "I know how
important the social column is," he continued, "but I'm
afraid I can't help you there. I can't imagine who the
woman was, but I know she wasn't with me. I realize I've
had an image as a swinging bachelor, but all that's in the
past. From now on I'll have no more time for partying.
Well," he said, "it's been a pleasure to talk to you. I can't
emphasize enough that the whole family is very serious
about being a part of this beautiful city. Both the business
community and the social scene and the local charities. We
want to do our part." He hung up and spun his chair around
to face her.

Anne swallowed hard. She'd forgotten how handsome
he was. So handsome in his dark suit and bronzed skin
against his striped shirt that she almost fainted. Of course,
that feeling could also come from hunger or shame. She
wrapped her arms across her waist.

"Oh," he said, standing and stuffing his hands in his
pockets. If he was surprised to see her, he didn't show it.
Neither did he show pleasure or dismay at her appearance.
Of course, sheiks were probably trained to handle situations

like this. Smoothly, suavely, with savoir faire. "It's good to see you again...Anne."

He remembered her name. That was a good start.

"What happened last night?" she blurted.

"Happened? As in between you and me?"

"Yes, exactly."

"Well, you passed out," he said matter-of-factly. "A little too much champagne. It can happen to anyone. It's happened to me. Nothing to worry about."

"Nothing to worry about? I was in your car. You were taking me home. Why didn't you?"

"I tried, believe me, I tried. But I didn't know where you lived, and you were in no condition to tell me."

"So you took me to your hotel," she said.

"Right," he said. "I had no choice. Then you fell asleep in my bed. End of story."

"That's it? That's all?" How desperately she wanted to believe that. "Wait a minute. How did I get my dress off and your shirt on?"

He raised his right hand. "Guilty as charged. Only because you looked so uncomfortable. I thought you'd sleep better in my shirt." He walked around his desk and gave her a long, lingering look, trying but not succeeding to conceal the smile on his face. "Yes, you looked much more...how shall I say, comfortable, in my shirt. You'll be glad to know I averted my eyes at all the appropriate moments. As any gentleman would."

"Any gentleman would have woken me up."

He shook his head. "I tried, darling, believe me, I tried. You were out cold. Don't tell me it's never happened to you before?"

"No, it hasn't. But I imagine it's happened to you. Taking a woman back to your hotel and then...and then..."

"Yes, it has. A time or two. But last night was different."

"Really." What did that mean?

He smiled. "Definitely."

"Maybe you think this is funny," she fumed, running out of patience. "To be stuck in a hotel without your shoes or your purse." *Not to know if you'd made love to a total stranger.* "But I don't."

"No, of course not," he said. "Here's what happened. I took your shoes off in my car. And I saw your bare feet. You can't object too strongly since everyone else you've run into today probably enjoyed the same pleasure."

"I'm not worried about people seeing my feet. It's my...it's the rest of my...you know."

"I can assure you no one saw but me. No one knows but me. No one will know for sure what really happened. Some may have doubts, like my father and my brother who are both suspicious types. But I won't tell if you don't tell."

"How can I tell when I don't know?"

"You'll just have to trust me."

Trust him? Trust a Middle Eastern sheik whom she didn't even know? Not likely.

"I need my shoes and my purse," she said.

"They must be in my car. I forgot completely. I'll send someone to get them right away." He picked up the phone and gave the order. Then he turned back to her. "Why don't you sit down and make yourself comfortable? It will only take a few minutes. In the meantime, take my jacket. You look..." he shot her a swift appraising look "...cold." He went to a closet and removed a soft, cashmere suit jacket and put it around her shoulders. His fingertips grazed her bare shoulders. It all came back to her. The wedding, her tears, his touch. Her face grew hot. She thrust her arms stiffly into the sleeves of the jacket.

"I'll stand," she said. Though she didn't know how long her legs would hold her up, she had her pride. He shrugged. There was a long silence. He leaned against his desk and his gaze locked with hers. Those eyes, those deep, dark eyes a woman could get lost in. A woman could forget why she was there, forget the questions she'd come to ask. Especially a woman with no experience in matters like this.

In a few minutes someone would appear with her shoes and her keys and she'd leave, never to see him again. If she didn't ask now, she'd never know.

She took a deep breath and gathered her wits about her. "What really did happen in your hotel room?"

He didn't answer for a long moment. She could almost sense the indecision that hovered in his mind. Something flickered in his dark eyes. Then he spoke. "You and I had the most incredible night of our lives. At least I did. I can't speak for you."

Before her knees collapsed under her, Anne sank into the leather chair next to his desk, the one she'd spurned a few minutes ago, and buried her head in her hands. "I don't believe it," she said in a muffled tone.

"Why not? Am I that unattractive? Do I repulse you?" he asked.

She peeked at him between her fingers. No, he didn't repulse her. In fact, he was the most attractive man she'd ever met. The thought of him making love to her raised the temperature of her whole body about ten degrees. Surely he knew how handsome he was. He was teasing her.

"Of course not," she said. "If it was the most incredible night of my life, I wish I could remember it."

"All I can say is we'll have to do it again," he said, a smile playing at the corner of his mouth. "When you're in better shape."

"Wait a minute. You think I was drunk, don't you? I

wasn't. I'd taken a strong antihistamine for my allergies and that combined with two glasses of champagne did me in. Not that it matters. I just didn't want you to think I was the kind of person who drinks too much and passes out in some stranger's bed.''

''You're not?'' he asked, a spark of laughter in his eyes. ''That's too bad.''

Anne opened her mouth to retort, but no sound came out. She had no practice in bantering with sexy men. He was an expert in lighthearted repartee. She wasn't. He wasn't serious. But what if he was? What if she'd made love to a perfect stranger? She knew for sure they'd shared a bed. Anything could have happened. But did it? Would she ever get a straight answer from him?

Fortunately, Rafik's phone rang and he began another conversation, as if she weren't there at all, sparing her the effort of trying to pin him down and him the effort of continuing to evade her questions. She crossed and uncrossed her legs. She squirmed and wiggled. It was a comfortable chair but she was far from comfortable. It was that awful dress. At one time she'd thought it beautiful. She'd helped Carolyn pick them out and agreed that they were not only becoming, but could be worn again, to the kind of party Anne never went to. But never mind about that.

The dress made her skin itch and squeezed her waist. But the jacket was wonderfully warm and smelled like him. Like leather and exotic soap. How did she know what he smelled like? That was a good question. But not *the* question. Had they been intimate?

When was the person coming with her purse and shoes so she could get out of there? Rafik didn't want her there, and she didn't want to be there. There was a knock on the door. Rafik hung up. She got to her feet. At last. But it was not her shoes and purse. It was his father.

"May I present my father, Sheik Massoud Harun."

Anne murmured something polite.

"Who, may I ask, son, is this lovely lady? She looks familiar, but I can't quite place her. You must forgive an old man, my dear, but my memory is not what it used to be."

"This is Anne...Anne Sheridan," Rafik said. "You met her at the wedding yesterday, Father. She was one of the bridesmaids."

"Ah, yes, of course. How nice to see you again."

Anne murmured something polite. It was too bad Rafik didn't have half the charm his father did. Maybe some day, years from now, he'd acquire it. But she wouldn't be around to see it. If the old man thought her apparel strange or wondered why she was there, dressed as she was in a dress and his son's jacket, he gave no indication at all. Or else he was past wondering at his son's exploits.

"Well, I won't interrupt you two young people any longer," Rafik's father said. "I imagine you have a lot to talk about. Don't forget to invite her to our gala benefit this month, Rafik. Since we're new in town, we want to expand our circle of acquaintances. Beautiful female acquaintances especially."

Rafik stared at his father with surprise. Not a happy surprise. He recovered quickly. "Consider it done," he said swiftly. "Ms. Sheridan is on our guest list. It will be delightful to see her again."

His father left the room wearing a satisfied smile, his mission obviously accomplished.

"Don't worry," Anne said as soon as the door closed behind him. "I have no wish to go to any gala benefit. I've had enough fancy parties this month to last me a lifetime."

"I understand completely," Rafik said, feeling a giant surge of relief. "I'll convey your regrets to my father."

Anne Sheridan would have been totally out of place at this party. Ostensibly a benefit for a charity, it was really a thinly veiled device for his father to find a bride for him. Not Rahman, just him. It wasn't fair. Thirty minutes seniority and his father's focus was on him. While Rahman played the field, played golf whenever he wanted to, and came to work whenever he felt like it, Rafik was expected to take over the investments of a huge family corporation.

He agreed it was time to get to work, he welcomed the chance to put his stamp on the family investments, but he didn't agree it was time to get married. His plan was to reject all the women as unsuitable no matter what his father said or how impeccable their credentials. He didn't know if it would work, but he'd give it a try because there was no way in hell he was going to get married. He'd tried that. He'd gone so far as to get engaged. It hadn't worked. His father knew it, but he hadn't given up. Not yet.

A few minutes later, the messenger knocked on the door, handed Anne her purse and shoes then closed the door behind him.

"My driver will take you home," Rafik said. "He'll be waiting at the front entrance." He took her by the hand and leaned over to give her a perfunctory kiss on the cheek. But she turned her face at the last moment and their lips met. Just a brush of her lips, and he felt as if he was falling down a slippery slope. He couldn't stop himself. Operating on pure instinct, he put one hand on her shoulder, the other cradled the back of her head and he deepened the kiss. He felt her gasp of surprise, felt her try to back off, then sigh and give in. She didn't kiss him back, but neither did she pull away. She could have. He wasn't holding her that tightly. Frankly he was shocked at his reaction. An ordinary kiss had caused a surge of desire to course through his veins. What the hell was wrong with him?

When he came to his senses and dropped his hands he saw she had turned several shades of pink brighter than her dress. "How dare you," she said.

"How dare I? After what we've been through together? That was nothing." It *was* nothing. Just a kiss. But what a kiss. Didn't she feel it, too?

"Nothing?" She spun on her bare heels and headed for the door. But before she left, she raised her arm and threw a handful of dollar bills across the room. "There. That's the change from your hundred dollars. I'll send you a check for what I owe you for the cab fare."

"Come on, Anne, I don't want your money."

"And I don't want yours. I never want to see you again."

"Wait a minute." He couldn't let her leave like this, thinking he'd seduced her. It was a matter of pride. "Nothing happened last night. I mean it. I was teasing you."

"Nothing?" she said again.

Solemnly, he shook his head.

She gave him a long look, then she shook her head, walked out the door and slammed it behind her. Rafik collapsed into the same chair she'd been sitting in. Which was where his brother found him ten minutes later.

Rahman sat on the edge of Rafik's desk and observed his brother with a mixture of humor and complacence. "So you got caught, did you?"

"I don't know," Rafik said. "Did I?"

"Father thinks so. Of course I told him nothing of what I knew."

"That's because you know nothing."

"So you say," Rahman said. "I know she was with you last night and I know she was here today. The woman in pink. Still wearing the same dress as yesterday. How can you deny something happened between you?"

Rafik sighed loudly. "Why should I bother? No one believes me. In any case, she's history."

"That's not what I heard. Father says she's coming to the party," Rahman said.

"He invited her but she won't come. Not her kind of thing. She's really not the party animal you think."

"It doesn't matter what I think. What do you think?" Rahman asked.

"I don't think. I just did what I had to do. Can we forget the woman for a moment? I told you she's history. She doesn't want to see me again and I don't want to see her."

"A one-night stand."

"Yes. Whatever." Rafik didn't want to see Anne, think about her, talk about her or examine his unexpected reaction to that strange kiss. "I have bigger problems. The biggest being this damned scheme of Father's to find me a bride. What am I going to do? How am I going to put him off?"

"What you need is a decoy. How do they call it? A beard."

"What's that?" Rafik asked. Sometimes his brother was amazing. Often when he'd discounted him as a hopeless hedonist, he'd come up with a brilliant idea. He hoped this was one of those times.

"You find a woman who will pretend to be your girlfriend, fiancée, whatever it takes to pacify Father, then he'll stop looking," Rahman said.

"But I don't know anyone like that. I'm new in town as are you. We don't know any women we can ask such a favor of."

"We don't?" Rahman asked. "Are you sure?"

"Sure. Absolutely sure."

"What about that woman you spent the night with last night. What's wrong with her?"

"Wrong with her? Everything. No, absolutely not. Didn't you hear me tell you she didn't ever want to see me again?"

"When has that ever stopped you from pursuing a woman? Usually you like a challenge."

"Anne Sheridan is more than a challenge. She's a stone wall." But kissing her was not like kissing a stone wall. It was more like kissing flower petals. The memory caused a wave of sensual awareness to rocket through his body.

"We'll buy her off. Even a stone wall has a price. We'll offer her money to play the part. She can't refuse," Rahman suggested.

"Hah. You see this money all over the floor? She threw it there. Does that sound like a woman who can be bought? No, your plan won't work. Besides…"

"Besides what? You're afraid to get entangled with her, aren't you? You have feelings for her. I knew it last night. You can't fool me. Don't even try. I'm your twin. I know what you're thinking."

"Not this time," Rafik said, glaring at his brother. It was true. The twins didn't often have secrets from each other. But this was one secret Rafik was determined to keep. He didn't want his brother interfering with him and this woman. Though there was really nothing to interfere with. It was over. He wasn't going to see her again.

"Then prove it. Offer her something in return. Something she wants. Everybody wants something. So she threw your money at you. Maybe she was angry," Rahman suggested.

"Maybe? You know what they say about redheads. You should have seen her. There were sparks coming from her eyes. She was breathing fire."

Rahman chuckled. "Sounds like your type. She's quite a woman. Looks good in your jacket, too. I saw her on her

way out. Okay, you say you're not interested? No feelings?
Then you won't mind if I give her a call?''

Rafik jumped up from his chair and grabbed his brother
by the collar of his shirt. ''Don't even think about it.''

''I'll think about it. Unless you do something. Go see
her. Ask her. I dare you.''

When had Rafik ever refused a dare? Especially from his
brother? It was like showing a red cape to a bull.

Chapter Three

A few days later Anne was still trying desperately to forget the unpleasant and disturbing encounter she had had with the sheik in his office. First there was the humiliating journey from the hotel to downtown. And then their face-to-face meeting. It was not like her to lose her temper and throw things like money or to slam doors. But he'd asked for it. Teasing her about what had happened the night before. Which story was she supposed to believe? She wanted to think that nothing had happened. So she resolved to accept that story. Fine. But what really bothered her was the kiss. No, not the kiss. That was to be expected from a playboy sheik.

It was her reaction to the kiss that shocked her. She was ashamed to admit how much she'd liked it. She was disturbed at what an effect it had on her. All the way home in his chauffeured car she'd felt her lips tingle and her heart pound. As usual, she took refuge in the backyard of the small house her parents had helped her buy on a quiet street in the Sunset district of San Francisco.

She'd spent the last few days planting and replanting shrubs and bushes and pruning her raspberry plants, part of a grand plan to turn a small plot of earth into a minor bird sanctuary of her own. She had a whole summer ahead of her, but she'd set a timetable for herself. Her friends teased her about being overly organized, but she liked to know what she was doing and when. She had goals and deadlines, even in the summer. When she had it finished she was going to host a meeting of bird-watchers. She looked forward to sharing the fruits of her work with those who would truly appreciate it. Not only the birds, but her fellow bird lovers.

She was planting a small oak sapling when she heard someone call her name from the side of her house. She wiped her dirty hands on her overalls, went to the wooden gate and peered over it.

It was him. She rocked back on her heels, speechless with surprise. How had he found out where she lived? He looked just the same as the last time she'd seen him. Except he was lacking his suit jacket in keeping with the informality of her informal abode. Otherwise he was perfectly groomed in a tailored shirt that looked as though it had been made for him, carefully creased slacks, a subdued tie and polished wing-tip shoes. Every dark hair was combed in place except for a strand that fell across his forehead. Then it came to her; she realized why he was there.

"I'm terribly sorry," she said.

"I thought you would be," he said from the other side of the fence. "When you'd had a chance to think it over."

"What?"

"I knew you were going to apologize for throwing my money at me. Can I come in?" he asked.

She wanted to say no. She wanted him to disappear. If that wasn't possible she wished she could disappear. She also wished she'd just hidden and pretended no one was at home. But unfortunately it was too late to do anything of the sort. Instead, she reached up and unlatched the gate. And suddenly he was in her garden. He had intruded on her own personal haven. She sighed loudly. It was her own fault.

"Stay right here," she said. "I'll get it."

"Get what?" he asked.

"Your jacket. Isn't that why you're here?"

"No." He stood there a moment, between her lavender plants in all their purple glory and her birdbath and her small raised vegetable garden. His gaze traveled from her unruly hair brushing her shoulders to her dirt-stained overalls and the skimpy white T-shirt underneath. His eyes also took in her flip-flops and her dusty toes. "What are you doing?" he asked, his forehead furrowed.

"I'm planting a tanbark oak sapling. The redheaded woodpeckers will love the acorns. Of course that stage is a long way off, but in the meantime the junipers and the cedars I put in give shelter and nesting sites and..." She stopped before she got carried away. He looked interested, his gaze didn't waver, but after all, what did he care about her provisions for migratory and local birds? "I might ask you the same thing," she said. "What are *you* doing? If you didn't come for your jacket, why did you come?"

"Yes, good question. Can we sit down somewhere?" he asked, looking around the garden. She had to admit he didn't look quite as sure of himself, quite as arrogant as he did in his office. She almost smiled to see him look just a little anxious, perhaps a trifle unsure of himself after their last meeting. Now they were on her turf. Whatever he wanted with her, he wasn't sure he was going to get it. Unless it was just his jacket.

She motioned grandly to a wrought-iron bench which he

sat on. She pulled up a small wooden stool she used to reach the top branches of her crabapple tree and sat down to face him.

"I apologize for not calling first. Actually I did call first," he explained, "but no one answered. Carolyn's mother was kind enough to give me your address. I hope you don't mind."

"Actually it will save me a trip to the post office. I was going to send your jacket back. Why don't I run upstairs and get it?" She stood up. He got up and put his hand on her arm.

"First I need to ask you something."

She shrugged and sat down again.

He sat down and looked around. "I thought you had allergies. How do you manage to have a garden?"

She was sure that wasn't the question he'd come all this way to ask, but she answered it anyway. "I'm only allergic to flowers. I didn't find out until I had skin tests done last year and when I got the results I had to replant. As you can see I don't have any flowers in the garden now and I'm fine."

"I see. It's very beautiful. Who takes care of it for you?" he asked.

"I do," she said. "As you see. Does that surprise you?"

"A little. Where I come from women don't like to get their hands dirty. So they hire a gardener."

"I can't afford a gardener, and even if I could, I think I'd do it myself. I have gloves, but I confess I like the feel of the dirt between my fingers. It's very therapeutic, getting your hands dirty." She looked down at her feet. "And your toes, too."

"Therapeutic, you say. Is there some reason you need therapy?" The question seemed innocent enough, but there was a gleam in his eyes that indicated he was teasing her again.

She felt her cheeks flush. It hadn't taken long for him to assume his former personality. The one that liked to tease and annoy her so much. The one that liked to pry into her personal life just to see how far he could push her. She got up off her wooden stool and stood looking at him.

"Everyone needs therapy some time. This is the kind that doesn't cost a penny and doesn't require any professional help. I assume you are the exception to the rule. A person who needs nothing. So if you didn't come for your jacket and you don't need anything, why are you here?"

"Ah, yes. That. I am here to ask you to reconsider your decision not to attend our gala ball."

"You drove all the way out here from your office to ask me that?"

"I told you I tried to call."

"The answer is still no."

"There's more," he said as if he hadn't heard her turn him down.

She opened her mouth to say she didn't want to hear any more, but he continued before she could speak.

"I need a fiancée."

She was astonished at his brashness. What did that have to do with her? Why should she care if he needed a fiancée or even a white elephant, for that matter? "Good luck," she said.

He gave her a rueful smile. "You think I'll have trouble finding one."

"In a word, yes."

"Some women find me charming," he said.

"Then ask one of them. Now I'll get your jacket."

"Wait. Please. I don't mean a real fiancée. Though that's what my father, Massoud, whom you met the other day, wants for me. I'm thirty-one and he thinks I should get married and settle down. For many reasons too numerous to go into right now, I am against this plan.''

''Why get married when there are so many willing women around?'' she asked.

His eyes narrowed for a moment and then he smiled. ''Exactly. Then you heard. What I'm looking for is not a real fiancée but someone who's willing to pose as one for a short time. A very short time. Maybe just one evening.''

''So what's the problem? Ask one of those willing women to pose for you. How could they say no to a charming man like you?'' Anne was proud of herself for coming up with a suitable reply. Charming? He was just too full of himself, this handsome sheik.

Rafik gave her a quick, admiring glance and held one finger in the air. ''Touché,'' he said. ''I deserve that. Actually I haven't asked anyone yet. Since I'm new in town I don't know many women. And so…''

His gaze drifted around the garden, lingering on the bird house hanging from the eaves of her house. She tried to wait patiently, but she was running out of patience. She had weeds to pull and shrubs to plant. His presence made her uneasy. Maybe it was the memory of their last meeting. That kiss she had tried so hard to forget. She plucked a few dead leaves off the low branches of her apple tree.

''I thought perhaps you…'' he continued.

''Me?'' Her eyes widened in surprise. ''You thought I would pose as your fiancée? Why would I do that?''

''Obviously not on account of my charm,'' he said ruefully.

''Obviously,'' she said.

''Perhaps there's something you need, something you want. A gardener… No, you don't want a gardener. You prefer to feel the dirt between your fingers, isn't that right?''

"That's right. I have everything I need.'' So he thought he could buy her the way he bought everything else he wanted. Of course, she didn't have everything she needed or wanted. A small pond, a recycling water supply and sprinklers for the garden were things she would love to have eventually. Also her bird-watching club was raising money to buy the marshland south of the city for a preserve, but that had nothing to do with him.

"All right,'' he said. "I hope you don't think I was trying to bribe you.''

"Not at all,'' she said calmly. "Before you go, let me get your…''

"There is just one thing,'' he said getting to his feet.

She paused.

"I thought after reflecting on that night we spent together, the hours we shared…you might feel differently about me,'' he said. "You might want to help me out.''

She stared at him. "That night we spent together, according to you, nothing happened. That's what you said. Nothing happened.''

"I didn't want to upset you.''

"Well you have upset me. I want to know the truth.''

"Ah, the truth. What is the truth after all? All I can say is that it was…''

"The most incredible night of your life. I know. You said that before. Before you said nothing happened. I will not come to your gala and I will most definitely not pretend to be your fiancée. Now, if you'll excuse me, I have a lot of work to do.''

He nodded. But he didn't look as chastened or discouraged as she'd hoped. He broke off a sprig of lavender and stuck it in his shirt pocket. Then he gave her a brief smile

and left the same way he came. Anne stood in the middle
of the garden staring at the gate. Remembering that she'd
forgotten to give him his jacket. Pleased and proud of herself for standing her ground. For not giving in. For not
admitting even to herself that the man had entirely too
much charm for his own good. Good luck to him in finding
a woman to pose as his fiancée. She sat down with a thud
on the bench just vacated by him and let out a large breath
of air she didn't know she was holding.

Somehow she knew this garden would never feel the
same to her. Though he was gone, it was almost as if he
was still there. She felt his presence as if he were still
sitting on this bench. His golden-brown skin contrasting
with his white shirt and his teeth. His dark eyes always
laughing at her. Always teasing her. *The night we spent
together, the hours we shared....* He almost had her believing that something did happen that night. That was his
intent. To make her worry and make her wonder. Well, it
wasn't going to work. She broke off a sprig of lavender a
he'd done and the perfume filled the air. She was afraid
she'd always think of him when she smelled lavender in
the air. Damn, damn, damn.

Rafik stopped in front of her house for a brief moment
before he went to his car. It was a small, modest house
with similar two-story stucco houses on either side. He
imagined that hers was the only one with an amazing garden that she apparently had planted herself. No flowers
which he remembered she was allergic to, just aromatic
bushes and trees and a vegetable plot arranged in a way
that made a pleasing impression and would have practical
benefits. The whole thing mirrored his impression of Anne.
A practical girl, but decorative as well. Yes, very decorative.

Like Anne, there was more to the garden than met the
eye at first glance. The longer he sat there on her bench,
the more aware he was of the garden's hidden charms, like
the purple cabbage planted in a concentric circle around
artichoke plants. As for Anne's hidden charms…he had
become more aware of her high spirits, her pride in her
garden and of course of her physical attributes hinted at by
her overalls and skimpy T-shirt.

He removed the lavender sprig from his pocket and
crushed it between his fingers, releasing the most wonderful
fragrance. As spicy and piquant as Anne was herself. Shy
on the outside, she had a spirit that was far from shy. When
aroused, she was downright fiery. He could only imagine
what kind of a lover she'd be. Not that he would ever find
out. She'd made it quite clear how she felt about him. She
couldn't stop him from dreaming, however. Or stop him
from thinking about her soft skin with the smattering of
freckles across her chest. Or wondering how it would feel
if he tangled his fingers in her red-gold hair.

Seeing her in those dungarees and T-shirt had surprised
him. She looked even more desirable than in her pink dress.
Another surprise. She didn't seem fazed by having a guest
see her like that. He didn't know any women who wouldn't
have run inside to change their clothes at the sight of a
caller at the door. Or who liked feeling the dirt between
their fingers.

How different she was from his former fiancée, the one
his family had chosen for him. She had appeared to be the
perfect choice. *Perfect* was the word for her. Perfect ease
in social situations, perfect clothes and hair, perfect manners. Until he discovered she was only interested in his
money and position. The breakup led him to his decision
never to marry. Never to trust another woman. His parents,
on the other hand, had not lost faith. They had become even

more determined to find him another bride. This one would be better, they assured him. This one would be the right one. They'd been trying to find her ever since. Determined to see him settled down, in the job and in his personal life as well. Fortunately, as for a wife, they hadn't yet had any luck.

As he drove back to his office Rafik was only slightly discouraged. Maybe he should be more so. Anne certainly hadn't given him any encouragement. In fact, she'd been just as spirited in her refusal as she'd been when she refused to accept any money from him and had thrown it across the floor. He smiled at the memory. Her flushed cheeks, her flashing eyes, her disheveled hair. And at the memory of that kiss they'd shared. He wondered if she remembered it. He didn't know what he'd do next. He only knew he wasn't giving up. He was determined to see her again. To persuade her at least to come to the gala if not to pose as his fiancée.

Pinehurst School was a wonderful place to teach and to learn. The classes were small, the students were all above average and the campus was beautiful. Teachers were dedicated and respected. The school was located on the grounds of a mansion once owned by a San Francisco millionaire. For fifty years it had been a private school for the children of the well-to-do in Pacific Heights, a neighborhood that enjoyed spectacular views of the Bay and the Golden Gate Bridge.

It was now summer vacation for the children, though some took advantage of the summer enrichment program. The headmistress was in her office when she telephoned Anne that week and asked her to stop by for a moment when she had time.

As Anne walked through the leafy campus, hearing the

houts of the small soccer players as they ran up and down
he field, she wasn't worried. But she was curious. She'd
urned in her student evaluations the week before, taken
lown the posters on the walls so her classroom could be
ainted over the vacation and in general had left things
retty shipshape. At least she thought so.

"Come in and sit down," Leona Feathergill said to
Anne. "I hope you're having a pleasant summer?"

"Yes, lovely," Anne said, feeling a small tremor of anx-
ety somewhere between her shoulder blades. Now she
new what it must be like for her students when summoned
the headmistress's office. Leona could be stern, but she
vas usually fair also. What on earth was this all about?
iurely she hadn't been called into the office to talk about
er summer vacation. "I've been doing quite a bit of work
n my garden and bird-watching," she added.

"Is that all?" Leona asked.

Anne gave a little shrug which she hoped could mean
lmost anything. She wanted to ask what she should be
oing? She had no idea what the woman was getting at.

Leona nodded absently and shuffled some papers on her
esk. She almost seemed more nervous than Anne. She
leared her throat.

"You've always been one of our most outstanding teach-
rs," Leona said. "I hear nothing but praise from both the
tudents and their parents for you."

"Thank you," Anne said. Now she was getting worried.
his sounded like the top of the sandwich from one of those
ooks on how to succeed, how to manage a staff and get
long with your colleagues and underlings. The strategy
vas to use first the praise on top, then the criticism in the
niddle and then finish off the bottom layer with some more
raise. How she wished the woman would get on with it.

"I had a call from one of the parents the other day
Actually from more than one."

"Oh?"

"It seems they saw you in a compromising position in
a hotel downtown. I hardly knew what to say."

Anne's heart sank. How long would the memory of that
infamous night continue to haunt her? "I think I know what
you're referring to," she said quickly. But she didn't. Were
they referring to the morning when she tiptoed through the
lobby or the evening, which was a blank in her memory.
Her mind was spinning. What to say. How to explain.

"I never pry into any of my teachers' private lives,"
Leona continued. "And yet when it affects their reputation
and that of the school, I feel I should give them a chance
to respond."

"Yes, of course." Anne was stalling for time.

"It involved a man. Of course I know you aren't married
and you have a perfect right to have dates
er...relationships, whatever. It's just that the parents who
saw you reported that this was in a very public place and
that you were in a very compromising position."

Anne knew only one thing. If it involved a man, they
must be referring to the evening. She wondered just what
they'd seen. Since she'd been unconscious at the time, she
wasn't sure. What did a *compromising position* mean exactly? She realized she couldn't ask that. Leona was waiting. She had to say something.

"I think I can explain," she said, pressing her palms
together.

"Good. I assume the man was someone you are well
acquainted with," Leona said. "Since he carried you across
the lobby and up to his room."

"Oh, yes," she said. "Of course." *Across the lobby and
up to his room? How many people saw her?* "You see, I'

been to a wedding reception where I was the bridesmaid. I was feeling ill so my...my fiancé brought me back to the hotel where the wedding party was staying.''

''You included.''

''That's right,'' Anne said gratefully. ''We were all staying there.''

Then why were you still wearing your pink bridesmaid dress the next morning? she imagined Leona asking. But thankfully, she didn't. Maybe no one she knew saw her in the morning. She could only hope.

Leona appeared to relax. She even smiled. ''I didn't know you were engaged, Anne. Congratulations.''

''Thank you.'' She didn't know it herself, she thought. It had just popped into her mind. She knew why. It was all that talk about a faux fiancée. If he could get one, so could she. She'd had no idea if a fiancé would make a difference until she saw the relief on Leona's face. Then she knew she'd said the right thing and her impulse had been correct. ''I know it must have looked scandalous,'' Anne continued. ''But it was all quite innocent.'' But was it? Would she ever find out the truth? Only one person knew what had happened that night, and he was not to be believed. For her own peace of mind she decided to accept his version of what happened. And that was that nothing happened.

''And quite romantic,'' Leona said.

In lieu of a response, Anne forced a smile. She'd run out of lies and excuses. She just wanted to get out of the office and back to her real life. A life out of the spotlight. A life without sheiks and their problems. Without fancy clothes and chauffeur-driven cars. A life without tension. Without lies. Assuming the interview was over, Anne stood up.

''I'd like to meet him,'' Leona said. ''And so would the rest of the staff. After all, it isn't every day one of our teachers gets engaged to a sheik.''

Anne's heart skipped a beat. She licked her lips. She tried to say something but no words came out. If she could have spoken she would have said, *Who said he was a sheik? What makes you think I am engaged to a sheik?*

As if she'd heard Anne's silent questions, Leona casually mentioned that the parents who'd seen her in the hotel were aware of the buzz in the lobby. The questions, the gossip, the interest in finding out who was the woman the sheik was with.

"It would be my pleasure to have a little get-together as we did for Marcia last spring when she got engaged," Leona said as she reached for her calendar. "After all, we like to think we're one big happy family here at Pinehurst."

Anne stood still as a statue. Inside a voice was shouting *no no no. No get-together. No engagement. No sheik.* But there was silence in the room as Leona perused her calendar. "What about a week from Saturday in the Hall?" she asked.

"I...I...I'll have to..." Anne stammered.

"Of course you'll have to check with your fiancé, the sheik." She smiled. "My sources reported that he's quite handsome."

And rich, Anne wanted to add. *And arrogant.* Haven't your sources reported that yet?

Somehow she managed to leave the office and walk through the campus to the parking lot without running into any students or other teachers. She tried to replay the conversation to figure out how on earth she'd gotten herself into this fix. She tried to think of how she could have avoided it, and lastly she tried to think of a way to get out of it. But her brain refused to cooperate. Once in her car, she rested her head against the steering wheel. She tried to blink back the tears of frustration, but they fell against the leather.

All afternoon she told herself to get it over with. She had to call him. Tell him she'd go to the gala. That's all. Take the first step. See how it went. If she couldn't abide his manners, his authoritarian way, his so-called charm, she'd go back to the school, tell Leona it was all a mis-understanding. She wasn't engaged. That wasn't even her in that compromising position. It must have been someone else. The way she had it worked out in her mind, it all made sense. Then why did she dread making that call? She wasn't afraid of him. Especially when he wasn't occupying the same space as she was.

In the back of her mind it occurred to her that maybe he wasn't so bad. Maybe she'd gone overboard in thinking badly of him. Maybe she could tolerate him for an evening at his gala in return for his pretending to be her fiancé for a short reception. Then when school began in the fall her colleagues might have forgotten about her so-called en-gagement.

Forget about an engagement to a sheik? Probably not. But she'd worry about that later. There were months left to summer vacation, months left to come up with an expla-nation. All she needed to do was to call him. That shouldn't be so hard.

She could deal with a disembodied voice on the phone. She had a harder time when he was right there in her garden or in his office. Where she was only too aware of the way he looked at her, as if he was going to eat her up. Aware too of the tension in the air, the force of his personality that caused her to come up with answers, to match him word for word. She could feel herself changing when she was around him. Becoming more sure of herself, more con-fident and yes…more feminine, more desirable. That part wasn't bad. The part that scared her was that she didn't know what he'd do next. He didn't seem to get the message that she was not interested in having anything more to do with him. Now that she knew nothing had happened that night, he could forget about her and she could forget about him. Then why did she keep thinking about him? Why did she wonder what he was going to do next?

Rafik was about to go into a meeting with his father and his brother. Before he went into Massoud's office, he paused at the secretary's desk. ''If I get a call from an Anne Sheridan, please let me know. It's important.''

When he looked up he saw his brother leaning against the door and listening to every word he'd said. Rahman raised an eyebrow. Together they walked into their father's office to wait for the old sheik.

''What happened?'' Rahman asked.

''Nothing,'' Rafik said. He hated to admit defeat.

''Did you ask her?''

''I asked her. She said no,'' Rafik said.

''But you expect her to call you and change her mind, according to what I just heard you say to Ruth. After all, how many women have turned you down? I'd say zero, just offhand.''

''This is different. I've never asked anybody to pretend to be my fiancée before,'' he said with a quick glance around as if his father might be hiding somewhere behind a bookcase.

''But why? Why wouldn't she go for it?'' Rahman asked.

''I guess I didn't make a very good case for it. Don't worry. I haven't given up.''

''That's my brother. Never give up. Never surrender.''

''I won't. Especially when I think of the alternative to choosing my own fiancée. My own *temporary* fiancée,'' he added quickly. "There's no way I'd want a real one. Father's idea of someone suitable is miles away from my idea. She has to agree, she *has* to." But what he'd do if she didn't, he didn't know. There was a stubborn look about Anne Sheridan, as sweet and innocent as she was, that worried him. Something about the set of her slender shoulders, the tilt of her chin that concerned him. If she'd really made up her mind, he didn't know how he'd change it. She seemed impervious to whatever charm he had.

During the meeting Rafik couldn't keep his eyes off the door to the outer office. But no one came in. No one knocked and said, "You have a call, Rafik, it's from a Ms. Sheridan." No matter how much he willed it to happen, it didn't. Instead his father gave him a steely look from time to time, no doubt to see if he was paying attention. When the meeting finally broke up and Rafik walked out, Massoud's secretary stopped him and handed him a slip of paper.

"I got a call?" he said to Ruth. "I thought I said..."

"Yes, I know," she said. "I told her to hold on and I'd get you, but she insisted on leaving a message."

"Yes, what was the message?" he asked, staring at the paper which only said "Anne called" and the time of her call.

"She said to tell you she can come to the gala after all."

"That's it? That's all she said?" Had she changed her mind about posing as his fiancée also?

"That's it. I'm sorry," Ruth said.

"*You're* sorry," he muttered as he walked down the hall to his office. If only he'd been able to speak to Anne, he could have judged her mood, found out why she'd changed her mind, and if she'd changed her mind about the fiancée part, too. Once in his office with the door closed, he dialed her number, but there was no answer. He left a message on her machine.

"Anne, I got your message and I'm very happy you can make it to the gala. I'll pick you up that night at your house. I'm sorry I didn't get a chance to talk to you. Give me a call at the office so we can firm up our plans. Did I say that I am very glad you can come?" Yes, of course he'd said that. He was repeating himself, and making a fool of himself, no doubt. He had so much to say to her, and it was frustrating not to be able to say it in person. He hung up and stared out the window for a long time before he could get back to work.

Chapter Four

It was a cool, damp morning on the marshes some thirty miles south of San Francisco along the San Mateo County coast. At least twenty bird-watchers were out holding binoculars to their eyes watching herons swoop into the reeds looking for food.

"Some people would think we were crazy to get up at six to watch birds," Anne remarked to her friend Sally. "But I wouldn't miss it for the world. Who knows, I might even add a new bird to my list today."

"That's the fun of it," Sally agreed. "You never know what you're going to see."

"And it's so peaceful, so quiet. The world is new and fresh." Anne sighed. "It makes me feel a lot better when I'm out here."

Sally put her binoculars down and gave Anne a sideways glance. "School's out. You're on vacation. Anything wrong?" she asked

"No, of course not," Anne said. "It's just...well I am a little worried. I'm going to a gala ball on Saturday night."

"How exciting. What's to be worried about?"

"Oh...uh..." How to explain that the problem was one overbearing sheik who'd caused her no end of troubles since she'd first met him at the wedding. Him and his search for a fiancée. Him and his teasing about what happened that night in the hotel. Then there was her headmistress's assumptions and Anne's need to protect her own reputation. She couldn't bring herself to mention any one of these things, so she brought up the one problem she could mention.

"I don't know what to wear to a gala."

"You don't have anything?"

"Nothing but a pink bridesmaid dress I wore to my friend's wedding. I'm sure that won't do, and besides, I really don't want to wear it again." She said this with a little more vehemence than absolutely necessary. The dress brought back memories of traipsing through the lobby of the hotel, standing in the middle of Montgomery Street looking up at the sheik's office building and entering his office without her shoes on. She had stuffed the dress to the back of her closet and didn't ever want to see it again.

"I'd be happy to go shopping with you," Sally offered. "If you're thinking of buying something new."

"That's exactly what I was thinking. Would you really?"

"Really. I'm even free this afternoon."

"I would love that. I can't tell you how much that means to me. First, I have no idea what's appropriate and second I...I need support. I don't go to galas very often. In fact I've never been to one."

"Neither have I," Sally said. "But I've seen the pictures in the society section of the newspaper of the charity balls so I kind of know what the women wear. And I know the tickets cost upwards of a thousand dollars."

"A piece?" Anne was shocked. Though she shouldn't have been.

"I assume your date can afford it," Sally said.

"Yes, I...I assume he can."

"This is so exciting to have an excuse to buy a special dress. Lucky you."

"Lucky?" Anne murmured. "I'm not sure about that."

After a stop at home to change out of her knee-high boots and fleece jacket, Anne met her friend for lunch in the food court of the mall before they went to the fancy dress section of one of the large department stores. Sally wasn't the only one who thought it was exciting to be invited to a gala ball and have the chance to buy a new dress for it. The sales clerk also got into the spirit and threw herself into the task, bringing in dress after dress. Some were long and sequined. Some were short and strapless. Another was bright red and form-fitting.

"Stunning with her hair," the clerk declared, standing back for a long look.

"I feel too conspicuous," Anne said. "I never wear red."

"Hmm," Sally said. "With your skin I think something in black might work better."

The clerk nodded and went back out on the floor to look for more dresses.

"I assume your date will be in black tie," Sally said.

"My date? Oh, yes, my date," Anne said, taking a seat on the dressing room bench while she waited for the saleswoman. "Actually he's just a friend, no, more of an acquaintance. He only asked me because he's new in town and doesn't know many women. I really don't know what he's wearing. I haven't talked to him since he asked me. We've been playing phone tag."

This was a lie. Anne was letting her answering machine

take her messages so she wouldn't have to talk to Rafik. She had nothing to say to him on the phone. She knew she'd have to broach the subject of the pretend engagement sooner or later, but she preferred that it be later. As late as possible.

"Whatever he wears," Anne continued, "it will be appropriate, I know that for sure."

The dress they all agreed on, Sally, Anne and the clerk, was a floor-length black chiffon dress that was bare on one shoulder and had a wispy scarf that they showed her how to toss over the other shoulder. The fabric clung very snugly to her curves then flared out before it hit the floor. While Anne stood in front of the mirror, the other two women voiced their approval.

"Stunning."

"Sensational."

"Makes her skin look like porcelain."

"Elegant."

"Sexy in a subdued way."

Anne blushed. But she did like the dress. She felt like everything they said she looked. Even sexy. She also felt a tingle of excitement at the thought of the ball, almost overriding her dread at seeing Rafik again.

Next was the shoe salon where Sally kept the salesman busy bringing out pair after pair of strappy sandals until they found some that were under four inches high so she wouldn't throw her back out in the first half hour.

"As for a pedicure," Sally said, "I'd go with some gorgeous shade of Jungle Red."

A pedicure? She'd never had one in her life.

"I'll give you the name of my nail salon," Sally offered as if she'd read Anne's thoughts.

"Thank you."

Before the two friends parted in the parking lot of the

mall, Sally told Anne she'd help her get ready that night, if she wanted her to. "I'm no good at nails, but I could blow-dry your hair if you don't want to sit in a beauty salon all day."

"I'd love some help. I'm going to be a nervous wreck," Anne confessed.

"I'll bring my makeup kit, too," Sally said. "Not that you need any. Just a hint of blush, maybe and some eye shadow."

Anne thought she'd hate subjecting herself to a pedicure, but she loved it. Especially the foot massage that came with it. It put her into a state of relaxed nirvana that lasted for hours. But as time passed that day, she gradually lost her composure. She was glad to see Sally arrive to distract her from her thoughts and worries and also because applying mascara when one's hand is shaking is a recipe for disaster. Sally, on the other hand, was cool and calm and collected and her hands were steady. Of course she wasn't going to a ball with a sheik who some people thought she was already engaged to.

"Tell me more about your date," Sally said as she zipped up Anne's dress.

"He's not really..."

"I know he's not really your date. But he is calling for you, isn't he? That sounds like a date to me."

"I think it's more like he's afraid I won't go to the ball if he doesn't come and get me," Anne explained. "As I said, he doesn't know many women in town and that's why I got invited."

"Well, I'll just slip away before he comes then so I won't be in the way," Sally said.

"No," Anne said. "Don't leave. I might do something rash. Like run away." She laughed nervously, but that's exactly what she wanted to do. Run as far as she could so she didn't have to face the man. Because she was going to have to swallow her pride and explain why she needed a fiancé as much as he did.

Sally laughed too at the ridiculousness of the idea of her running away in her new black dress from a gala ball. But then she didn't know the whole story. Anne was afraid that she herself didn't know the whole story either. And neither did Rafik for that matter. He didn't know about her headmistress and the pressure on her and though he'd told her his side of the story, she didn't know what really happened that night. She sighed and the doorbell rang. Her heart stopped beating for one moment, then she took a deep breath and went to the door.

Instantly all of the air in her lungs seemed to rush out, leaving her totally out of breath. He was that handsome. She'd seen him in a tuxedo before, but somehow she hadn't appreciated his dark good looks before. Maybe it was the porch light shining on his coal-black hair. Maybe it was the gasp she heard Sally make when she saw him. Maybe it was that he was simply the most attractive man she'd ever met. Physically, that is.

Anne stepped back, and Rafik walked through the open door. He too seemed to have lost his ability to speak. He just stood staring at her. Of course, she looked a little different from the last time he'd been there when she was in dungarees and a T-shirt.

Finally she caught her breath and remembered her manners. "I...Rafik this is my friend Sally. She came by to...uh..."

"To say hello," Sally said. "Happy to meet you, Rafik. I'll be off now. You two have a wonderful time."

At the door, Rafik engaged Sally in conversation before she left while Anne went to get her wool coat. She could tell by the look on Sally's face she thought he was charming. He didn't even know how charming he was being, she thought. It was so much a part of him. But Sally knew. Before she left, she gave Anne a knowing wink and a thumbs-up. Then they were on their own. In the car they talked about the weather and about the newlyweds who were back from their honeymoon. They talked about anything but the matters at hand. Anne was grateful that he was a good conversationalist.

She dreaded silence between them. Silence would give her time to think and worry. It would give her time to think about him and what she had to ask him. She was only too aware of the way he surrounded her with soft music from his sound system, the smell of leather and the heated seats. It was luxury pure and simple. Of course she'd been in this car before, but she hadn't been alert enough to appreciate the quiet purr of the engine and the skill of the driver. He kept up an effortless stream of conversation without any mention of an engagement, false or otherwise.

When they arrived at the historic hotel on Market Street, Rafik helped Anne from the car.

"May I be the first to say before we go inside, that you look very beautiful tonight?" he said in his deep quiet voice.

"Thank you," she said. She was afraid he said that to all his dates. Maybe flattery was just one of the tools he used to get what he wanted. But he sounded sincere. He looked sincere, too. His dark eyes were fixed on hers and of course she wanted to believe him. She also wanted to tell him how very gorgeous he looked, but she thought he probably already knew that and she was way too shy to say anything so personal anyway.

They walked into the high-ceilinged ballroom together, arm in arm. The scent of expensive perfume was in the air.

The candles in gold sconces along the wall gave off a warm
light. The tight knot of nervousness in the pit of Anne's
stomach relaxed somewhat. Rafik put his hand on the small
of her back, a gesture which might have been annoying
coming from someone else, but tonight in that atmosphere,
it felt protective and reassuring.

Rafik introduced her to many people, whose names she
instantly forgot. She met his mother, who was a small and
graceful older woman with silver hair swept back from her
unlined face. She told Anne how much she had been looking forward to meeting her.

"My sons and my husband have told me so much about
you," Nura Harun said in lightly accented English. "Rafik," she chided her son. "You didn't tell me she was so
beautiful."

He smiled. "I wanted to surprise you, Mother. In any
case, Anne's looks are secondary to her good nature."

"I'm delighted to meet you at last," the older woman
said. "I didn't have a chance at the wedding." Then she
asked Anne how she knew Carolyn and posed some questions about her teaching job. Apparently satisfied by what
she had learned, she shooed them toward the dance floor.
"Now don't let me keep you from enjoying the party," she
said.

Rafik led Anne to the dance floor. Out of the corner of
his eye he saw his parents in earnest discussion while their
glances followed him and Anne. He could just imagine
what they were saying. How happy they must be, thinking
what a good choice Anne would be for him. She would be
too if he wanted to get married. But he didn't. At least not
for quite some time. After he'd had his fill of playing the
field. When he'd learned how to judge women better.

As for Anne, he didn't know if she was interested in
marriage, but if she was, he was quite certain it wouldn't

be to him. She'd made it clear he was not her type. But that didn't mean she couldn't do him a small favor and pretend to be his fiancée.

He was just going to ask her about that little favor, but once he put his arms around her, and her hair brushed his cheek and the fragrance of her skin filled his senses, he couldn't do it. He didn't want to spoil the mood. She fitted perfectly in his arms, as if she'd been made for him. Which was probably what his parents were thinking as they watched them dance.

He probably ought to move away, just put a little distance between them to avoid any gossip, if possible. But she felt so good, so right in his arms. He pressed her close and heard her sigh softly. He didn't know what it meant. But if she'd wanted to pull away, she could have. After a few songs, he thought of taking a break and getting a glass of champagne for each of them, but he didn't want to break the spell. The music, the soft lights and a beautiful woman in his arms. What more could a man want?

She didn't speak and neither did he. What was there to say? He wished the music would never end. When it did end, and the orchestra took a break, they stayed where they were, hand in hand, their gazes locked on each other. What did he see in her eyes? He saw something he'd never seen before. Something he hadn't seen in any other women he'd romanced. And there had been quite a few. They were usually beautiful, always sexy and self-assured. They played the same games he did. They knew the rules. Nobody gets involved and nobody gets hurt. They were fun and exciting. You could talk to these women, laugh with them and love them. For a while.

Anne was not one of these women. She was different. In her eyes he saw honesty and trust. He saw a woman without pretense, without guile. A woman who didn't know the rules. And that scared him. It scared him so much he wanted to run away. But even more he wanted to stay. Stay with her in his arms there on the dance floor forever.

He thought he knew a lot about women. But he didn't know how to handle Anne. The music started again, and she went into his arms without a word, as if it was meant to be. So much for his running away. He knew there were other couples around, he knew that the lights went up again and then dimmed, he knew that time was passing, but all he really knew was that he wanted the night to go on forever.

He wondered if Anne felt the same. He couldn't get over how stunning she looked tonight. Her one bare shoulder tantalized him. He wanted to bare the other one, too. He wanted to press his lips against her skin. He wanted to inhale her scent and never let her go. She was by far the most beautiful woman in the room. The sexiest and the most desirable. And she was his. His for tonight, anyway.

She was his until his brother tapped him on the shoulder and cut in. Before he could tell him to buzz off and leave them alone, Rahman introduced himself to Anne.

"Hello," Rahman said to Anne. "I don't believe we've met, but I've heard so much about you. I'm Rahman, the younger, good-looking twin. I'm sure you don't mind leaving my brother for a dance or two. You two have been at it forever as my parents have noted. It's time you stopped monopolizing this lovely lady, Rafik," he said to his brother.

"Get lost," Rafik said, glaring at his brother. "Go find somebody else to dance with. Anne is taken."

"Really? That sounds serious. By the way, Rafik, the parents want a word with you. They're getting ideas."

"Ideas. What does that mean? Oh, all right." Rafik recognized the determined look on his brother's face and he didn't want to make a scene on the dance floor, so he clamped his lips together and walked away just as he heard his brother saying to Anne, "May I say that you look sensational tonight?"

Rafik almost turned around and cut back in, but he didn't want to overreact. His brother was a born flirt. He used words like that all the time. Most women didn't take him seriously. But Anne was different. She might think he was serious. He looked serious, Rafik thought with a quick glance over his shoulder. It was a mistake to look backward, he realized, as he ran right into his parents. He found that they were positively beaming at him.

His father put his arm around his shoulder. "We're very pleased with your choice of partner, Rafik," Massoud said. "She's a lovely girl."

"Partner? You mean dance partner, of course. Yes she is very lovely, Father, but don't get the wrong idea."

"I couldn't possibly get the wrong idea about such a woman," Massoud said. "Nor could your mother. We all agree you couldn't have made a better choice."

Choice? Choice of partner? Did his father mean choice of dance partner or life partner? He was just about to warn his father not to jump to conclusions, but at that moment a business acquaintance interrupted them with some news of an investment prospect for his father. Rafik leaned against the wall by himself moodily watching his brother dance with his date. Not only dance, but talk animatedly, as if they were old friends. Anne didn't seem shy at all. He regarded them with narrowed eyes, hoping Rahman would feel his animosity from there and give her back to him. How soon would it be proper to cut in on them, he wondered. And why didn't his brother find his own woman to dance with?

He couldn't stand it another moment. He went out to the

dance floor and as politely as possible told his brother it
was his turn now. Rahman shrugged and retreated.

"I'm sorry you got stuck with my brother," Rafik said,
taking Anne into his arms again.

"I wasn't stuck," she said. "I enjoyed talking to him."

"More than you enjoy talking to me?" he asked.

She blushed but didn't answer. Maybe because the answer was yes.

"You've made quite an impression on my family," Rafik said.

"They seem very nice, but I hardly know them," she
protested.

"They like what they see," he said. "I'm afraid that's
your fault. You look beautiful and you're charming, too.
I'm afraid they're going to be disappointed when they find
out you're not going to be my fiancée. That is if you
haven't reconsidered my proposition."

Anne knew what she had to say. She just couldn't say
it. Now that she needed him to pretend as much as he
needed her, she was tongue-tied. When she was in his arms,
swaying to the music, her head against his chest, she felt
as if she was made of molten lava. The way he looked at
her made her feel very desirable. His arms around her made
her feel soft and fragile and protected.

But then that was his way. He was born to seduce
women. Pretending anything with him could be very dangerous. Like playing with fire. She reminded herself that
he was a handsome, rich man who only wanted a fiancée
to please his parents. As he'd told her, he had no intention
of getting engaged or married for real. But she was not a
player the way he was. She was a vulnerable young woman
who'd never had a serious boyfriend. Any more romancing,
dancing and flattery and she might succumb and start believing…that fantasy was reality. She'd allowed herself to

come under the spell of the night and the music and the man. Now was the time to shake off these romantic delusions and face the facts.

She knew what she had to do. She must tell him now that she couldn't possibly reconsider any scheme to fool his parents. Not for her sake or theirs. Yes, it might cause her a problem at the school, but she'd have to deal with that. It would be better than tricking his family, whom she was beginning to like. His brother was amusing and fun and his parents seemed very kind and not at all overbearing. If he was going to disappoint them, that was his problem. They had no business fooling such nice people as that.

The music stopped and she pulled away out of Rafik's arms and immediately felt the loss. She realized she could spend hours in his arms, with his breath fanning her cheek, the scent of his skin and his clothes surrounding her, seducing her. Making her want more. Yes, it was time to put an end to this charade. He was not interested in her except as a novelty, and she was not interested in him. She didn't belong in this society any more than a robin belongs in an aviary. She dropped one hand from his shoulder but he didn't let go of the other.

"Rafik," she said. "I have no intention..."

A hush fell over the room as his father stepped onto the bandstand. The drummer executed a drumroll. Anne had a feeling of foreboding. She wished she'd spoken to Rafik earlier.

"What does this mean?" she whispered.

"I don't know," he said, his forehead drawn in a frown.

"Ladies and gentlemen," Sheik Massoud Harun began. "We have invited you here tonight to get to know you. And for you to get to know us. We are strangers here in San Francisco, but you have made us feel welcome. My

wife and I have the honor to announce the engagement of
our elder son, Rafik.''

Anne felt the blood drain from her face. ''What on
earth…'' she murmured.

''What did you tell him?''

''I told him not to get the wrong idea,'' he muttered.
''But apparently he did. He told me he was pleased with
my choice of a partner. I thought he meant dance partner.
I should have known. Don't worry. It's just a misunderstanding. I'll straighten him out.''

''He seems to be beckoning to us,'' Anne said. She felt
her face flame. She wished she could find a hole and hide.
Instead she felt all eyes on her as she and Rafik walked
hand in hand to the bandstand. How would he tell his father
that it was a mistake when everyone in the whole room was
clapping, the orchestra was playing something romantic and
the lights had been turned up so everyone could see them?

In fact, telling his father at this moment would be next
to impossible. She knew and Rafik must also know that his
family would be humiliated. So they stood next to his parents on the bandstand for what seemed to be an eternity.
She smiled until she felt her face would crack while Rafik
whispered in her ear that she was not to worry, that he'd
fix everything.

When they'd received congratulations from dozens,
maybe hundreds of strangers, they finally filed into the dining room where white tables were set up for a sumptuous
buffet. Seeing the pride on Rafik's parents' faces, she knew
he couldn't tell them now. With her plate full of lobster
thermidor and slices of rare roast beef, tiny new potatoes
and green beans amandine, she was seated between Rafik
and his mother. Rafik seemed subdued. She couldn't blame
him. He had an enormous task ahead of him, telling his
parents it was all a mistake. Anne supposed she too ought

to be subdued, knowing she had an unpleasant task ahead of her, trying to explain to her headmistress that she was no longer engaged.

Fortunately there was no more dancing after the dinner. Rafik promised they'd leave as soon as possible, but so many people wanted to talk to him and congratulate him, it took at least another hour to get away. It was an hour of agony for Anne. She could hardly bear to look at his parents and listen to them telling everyone how happy they were for the young couple. She could tell that both his mother and father were genuinely pleased. That this was something they had wanted for a long time. She seriously wondered how Rafik would be able to burst their bubble and tell them it wasn't true.

Rafik's mother took her aside and told her how happy she was. "We will have to get to know each other better," Nura said.

Anne didn't know what to say. All she could manage was a nervous smile.

"We don't have a house yet for entertaining, but I would like to invite you to tea at the hotel. They tell me they do it rather nicely. Nothing like the Dorchester in London, of course, but if you are free one day…?"

Again, Anne could only smile, which seemed enough encouragement for Rafik's mother.

"Shall we say Tuesday then? Since you are a school-teacher—such a suitable occupation for a young unmarried woman—then I hope you will be free to join. Meet me in the lobby of the St. Francis at two, if that is convenient."

Anne nodded. How could she say no? How could she say anything at all with her throat clogged? Nura was so kind and would be so disappointed when she learned the truth. Anne hoped she wouldn't have to face her after that happened. As soon as Rafik explained that the engagement was not for real, the invitation would probably be recalled.

In the car on the way back to her house Rafik promised her that he would tell them.

"Just do me a favor and give me a little time," he said as he pulled up in front of her house.

If this wasn't the time for Anne to ask Rafik a favor, then the time was never, she thought. "Actually," she said. "I have a favor to ask of you, too."

"Anything," he said, turning to face her from the driver's seat. In the light from the streetlight, she could see his dark eyes glowing and his jaw jutting forward. His features were strong, just like his personality. She had the feeling she could ask him anything and he'd do it for her. She thought that if he gave his word he wouldn't let her down.

"I'm in a bit of trouble at my school," she began.

"No," he said, anxiously. "What is it? What can I do to help?"

"It seems that some of the parents saw me that night at the hotel when I was...uh...when you were carrying me up to your room. I don't know how it happened, but they got the wrong idea."

A small smile briefly played on the sheik's lips, then he was serious. "I'm sorry about that," he said. "I would have done anything possible to spare you the embarrassment, but I was caught in a situation that wasn't entirely of my own making." He didn't say whose making it was, but they both understood that she had to take part of the blame for her condition.

"I understand," she said, "but they didn't understand. Though the headmistress can't dictate what the teachers do in their free time, naturally she and the board of directors want us all to be above suspicion."

"Of course. So what can I do? Speak to your headmistress and to the board? Explain…"

"Explain what? That I wasn't really inebriated? After all, I did have two glasses of champagne. Or that I really didn't spend the night with you in your bed? You can't deny that, can you?" Anne squeezed her hands into tight fists, realizing that now was the time to ask him what really happened that night. "You say that nothing happened between us. And I believe you. I just want to know why. Was I so unattractive? Was I that unappealing? You're a sheik. A playboy by your own admission. A man who doesn't want to get engaged or married. A man who's looking for women to seduce. Can you tell me what made you leave me and my virtue untouched?" she blurted. By the time she'd finished saying the things that had bothered her since that night, her voice had risen and tears had sprung to her eyes.

"Anne," he said, taking her hands in his and stroking her ice-cold fingers until they were warm and supple. "Believe me, you were very appealing. So appealing, so seductive and so attractive that it took all my willpower to leave you on your side of the bed. To undress you and not touch your body. I know what you must think of me. You're right, people say I'm a playboy, and I've earned that reputation. But even playboys have scruples. Sheiks have rules. One of them is that the woman must be awake and willing. I have never forced myself on a woman. I've never needed to and I never will."

Anne let go of a breath she was holding. Her whole body was flooded with relief.

"If the day or night comes along when you are willing, then I would make love to you most tenderly, most exquisitely. I would take your clothes off, not the way I did that night but…"

Anne felt her face burning and her limbs trembling at the thought of being seduced by the sheik. "Please," she said.

"Please what?" he said lightly. "You'll have to be more specific. Please stop, Rafik, or please start?"

"Stop," she gasped. "I'm not used to men like you. I don't have affairs with sheiks, or anybody for that matter."

"You mean you've never...?"

"Never. I'm a...virgin." It was hard to say the word, but necessary. He needed to know who she was and what she was before they went any further in this strange relationship.

There was a long silence. Anne couldn't look him in the eye. She didn't want to see his shock and surprise at finding himself in the company of a twenty-eight-year-old virgin.

"I see," he said gravely. "And this is because of moral scruples or...?"

"It's for all sorts of reasons," she said. "I don't believe in indiscriminate sex and it's also for lack of opportunity."

"I don't believe that," he said.

She told him then about the disease she'd suffered in high school when she had to wear a brace. She told him how unattractive she'd felt. How she'd missed out on a normal adolescence. He listened gravely, and when she'd finished he told her how touched he was that she'd confided in him.

"I will treasure your confidence," he said, tracing his finger around the curve of her cheek. "And endeavor to deserve your trust in me. Now what was the favor you were going to ask me?"

The mere touch of his finger made it almost impossible to think. But with an effort, Anne remembered what it was she needed to ask him. "Oh, yes, it was about my school and the headmistress. In an effort to explain my behavior I told her that you were my fiancé.''

Rafik smiled.

''I know what you're thinking. That I'm impulsive and dishonest. I can't explain what came over me. What I said didn't make sense, but she'd caught me off guard. I wanted her to know that I was not in the company of a stranger, someone I'd just met at a wedding, for example. So I said the first thing that came into my head. After all that talk about a fiancée, the word just popped out. Yes, I know I was borrowing a page from your book. For some reason I thought it might explain why I was in the hotel that night with you in a very compromising situation.''

''Did it work?'' he asked.

''I guess it did, because the next thing I knew the head-mistress had forgotten how disturbed she was and she was arranging an engagement party for you to meet the staff. It's a kind of tradition, an effort to instill the feeling that our staff is one big happy family.''

''So I'm to be a part of your family just as you are of mine,'' he said.

''Only temporarily,'' she assured him.

''Of course,'' he said. ''I'd be delighted.''

''Would you really? I'm afraid it might be awkward for you.''

''I think I can handle it.''

''Yes, I suppose you can,'' she said. Why did she doubt that Rafik would be completely at ease in any social situation and charm every single faculty member without any effort?

''Then it's settled,'' he said. ''We have an agreement. I suggest we seal it with a kiss.''

Once again she was caught off guard. Not that she hadn't thought about his kissing her. While they were dancing with his body pressed against hers, it was hard not to think about kissing him. She'd imagined it happening more than once. But when it happened it was not the kind of kiss she expected. It was not the kind of kiss between two parties merely sealing an agreement. It was the kind of kiss that an engaged couple would exchange if they were madly in love. It was the kind of kiss that lovers who have been holding back for one reason or another would exchange. It was full of passion and pent-up frustration finally let loose.

Not at first. The first kiss was a mere whisper of his lips against hers. A promise of things to come. Then he pulled back for a moment and framed her face with his hands. He looked deep into her eyes as if searching for something, a sign or a wish, and then, when he appeared to be satisfied with what he saw, his lips met hers once again. This time for real.

She wrapped her arms around his neck and angled her mouth to meet his. She had never been kissed like this. So deeply, so profoundly and so passionately. She'd never kissed anyone like that either, with all her heart and soul. Somewhere deep inside her she knew she shouldn't. She knew it was all pretend, and it would come back to haunt her some day. But she couldn't stop herself. And she certainly didn't want to stop him.

His kisses made her feel like she was on a fast train. It was a thrilling ride and where it would end she didn't know or care. The ride was all that mattered. She slid into his arms from across the leather seat of his car. His lips moved to the hollow of her throat, then to her bare shoulder. She shivered.

"Are you cold?" he murmured.

"No, I'm on fire," she murmured. She really felt like she might burn up. She was radiating heat, she knew her skin must be hot to the touch, every nerve ending was tingling, and she thought she might burst into flames if anyone held a match up to her.

She felt his lips curve in a smile against her bare skin. She tangled her fingers in his dark hair. He smelled so good. Like leather and exotic spice and fine soap. She could hear his heart pounding in time to her own. How had this happened? She, an innocent schoolteacher, was locked in the arms of a rich and experienced man she barely knew. Or did she know him better than she thought?

Then she stopped thinking and gave in to the sensations that spiraled through her. Rafik pulled her across his legs until she was in his lap. He cradled her in his arms and, as tight as it was in his front seat, she settled there as if she could stay forever. He was kissing her lips again, teasing her by slowly nibbling at them, and then his mouth was open and he was using his tongue to turn up the heat even further. Shyly she opened her mouth to him and met his tongue with hers. It was incredible. She'd never felt such intimacy with anyone. She never dreamed that something so daring could feel so right.

"I can feel your heart pounding, Anne," he said breathlessly. "I don't want to stop, but I must. I'm afraid I'm going to have to take you in now." She pulled back and looked down, afraid to meet his gaze. Once again he'd called a halt to what might have been. She was confused. Wasn't the woman supposed to be the one to say no? What was wrong with her? Did she really have no morals? Didn't she know when to say no? Was her abstinence only because of lack of opportunity as she'd said? Her face was hot with shame. She untangled herself from him and reached for the door handle. Before he could come around and open it for her, she was out of the car and on the sidewalk.

"Wait a minute," he said catching her by the hand.

"I can see myself in," she said, pulling away. "Thank you very much."

"I've offended you," he said. "What have I said to hurt you?"

"Nothing. Nothing at all. Good night."

He stood on the sidewalk and watched her unlock her front door. She could feel his bafflement at her behavior, but she couldn't stop herself. She couldn't explain herself either. It was too humiliating. She stood inside the darkened living room, leaning against the closed front door and listened for the sound of his car engine. When she finally heard it she sagged against the door. Her lips were swollen, her face was flushed and her whole body ached as though she'd been pounded with a mallet. All she could think was that it was a good thing they weren't really engaged. She was relieved knowing that he wasn't really her fiancé. If pretending had left her in this state of semi-consciousness, what would a real engagement do to her? She shuddered at the thought.

Chapter Five

The handball courts at the Pacific Heights Health Club were crowded. By the time the brothers started playing, it was almost six o'clock in the evening. Rafik was full of nervous energy. He'd had a terrible day during which he had accepted numerous congratulations on his engagement, tried to get in touch with Anne to no avail, attended some tedious meetings, and put up with his brother's remarks. He was looking forward to beating Rahman at handball and perhaps shutting him up for a while.

After a half hour they were both tired and sweat poured off their faces. They'd each won a set and neither wanted to give up without being the victor.

"You used to beat me," Rahman said. "Your mind wasn't on the game tonight."

"If you know so much, what was it on then?" Rafik asked, wiping his face on a towel in the locker room.

"Your fiancée perhaps? I still don't know how you pulled it off."

"I didn't pull it off. Father made the announcement and

I still don't know what got into him. I never said Anne had agreed to the engagement.''

"Don't blame Father. He saw what everyone else saw. You two were oblivious to the world for hours out there on the dance floor. He assumed you were serious about each other. So did I.''

"Wait a minute. Did you have anything to do with this?''

"Who, me?''

Rafik shot a glance at his brother. His innocent expression didn't fool him for a minute. "What did you do? What did you say?'' he demanded.

"I really don't remember. In any case you got what you wanted. You can't deny you needed a fiancée. Now you've got one. I can see I'll get no thanks for helping you out. Besides I didn't notice Ms. Anne Sheridan protesting.''

"What did you expect, that she'd stand up there in front of all those people and say it was all a mistake? She's too polite for that. She went along with it. But I can't say she's happy about it. Neither am I.''

"Of course you are. It's what you wanted. A stand-in fiancée which pleases the parents and gets you off the hook. Remember it's just for a short time. From the looks of you two on the dance floor I can't believe it's much of a hardship on either of you.''

"You don't think so? I don't know. I can't figure her out. Anne is the strangest girl. First she's cool then she's hot. She comes to the gala but she won't answer my calls.''

"Maybe she's busy. Maybe she's not sitting at the phone waiting for you to call her. That would be a blow to your ego, wouldn't it?''

"No, it wouldn't. I don't want a woman who has nothing to do but wait for me to call. She's got a life and I like that about her.''

"What else do you like about her? Her red hair? Her gorgeous body?"

Rafik snapped a towel at his brother. "Enough. She's a nice girl. But she's not my type. She's way too serious." But even as he said the words, he conjured up her face, he remembered how she felt in his arms and how she responded to his kisses. She *was* too serious for him or was he too much of a lightweight for her?

"Have you bought her a ring yet? I'm only asking because Father asked me."

"A ring? No, do I have to do that? I suppose I do. Aren't you supposed to take your fiancée with you to pick it out?"

"How should I know? I've never been engaged. I'll let you lead the way as always. What happens to the ring when you break your engagement?"

Rafik shrugged. "I'll let her have it. I'll owe her for being such a sport about it."

"Then go for it," his brother said.

Before Rafik could change his mind, he punched in her phone number on his cell phone. Maybe this time he'd get lucky and actually get to talk to her.

"Anne? Thank God I got you. We have to talk."

She sounded so subdued. And she declined his offer to come by her house. She finally agreed to meet him at a bar near the health club. "But only for a short time," she said.

"Why is that?" he asked. "You don't have another date, do you? Remember you're engaged to me."

"Not really."

"No, but…maybe we need to talk about that." He couldn't have her dating other men when it was imperative she appear to be engaged to him. Of course, the same applied to him, but he realized that he had no desire to date anyone else. He didn't know many other women in town anyway, but one seemed to be all he could handle at this time.

"Wouldn't it be easier if I dropped by your house?" he said.

"No." Anne didn't want him invading her privacy. His last visit to her garden had left an indelible impression. Every time she went out there she pictured him sitting on her bench. Every time she smelled the lavender, she remembered him crushing it between his fingers. "I'll meet you at the bar you mentioned."

He told her the address on Laguna. She said she'd be there in an hour. How could she say no again? But she was not accustomed to meeting men in bars on weeknights, or any nights for that matter.

So she went. Feeling totally out of her element, she sidled her way through the crowd of yuppies, hearing snatches of their conversations.

"Didn't I see you at Tahoe last weekend?"

"You remind me of someone I know."

"I heard you quit your job. How's it going?"

"I got laid off."

"That's nothing. My stock options just evaporated."

"Did you hear about Brian? He just got made partner."

She felt totally out of place in this world. Was this the kind of place and the kind of people Rafik frequented? If it was, it was a good thing this was a fake engagement, because if this was his scene, then they were even more different than she'd thought. Where was he? If he didn't show up in two more minutes she was going home. It had taken her a half hour to find a place to park in the neighborhood. Now she couldn't find him. Her nerves were frazzled. What did he want to talk about, anyway, that couldn't be discussed on the phone?

Just when she was about to give up, she saw him in the

corner at a table by himself, a glass of beer in front of him and a frown on his face. When he saw her, the frown faded. He got to his feet and beckoned her to the table.

"I was worried that you'd never come," he said.

"I had a hard time finding a parking place," she said, taking a seat opposite him. He was wearing a leather jacket and he looked like many of the other men in the place except more attractive than any one of them. It was the bronzed color of his skin and his coal-black hair and eyes. She didn't know if she'd ever get used to the way he looked at her. Even now. Even before they'd had their discussion, whatever it was. He looked at her with so much intensity she felt trapped by the look in his eyes. Did he do that to everyone? Was it all part of his allure that he turned off or on to women?

She studied his face. He didn't look unhappy. He just looked a little anxious with his eyebrows knitted together. She hoped he'd forgotten how she'd stormed out of the car after the ball the other night. She realized now how immature she must have seemed. Even worse, it might have seemed that she was upset because he hadn't seduced her the night of the wedding. Now *there* was a ridiculous thought.

"This was your idea to meet here," he said. "I would have been happy to come to your house. Now what would you like to drink? Some champagne?"

She stiffened. "Please don't remind me. I'll have coffee. What do you want to talk about?"

He hesitated while he ran his hand around his beer glass. "I can't tell my parents the engagement isn't for real," he said.

"But you said..."

"I know I did and I tried, but they're so happy about it, so pleased that I found someone like you...I just couldn't do it. All I can say is I'll have to wait a little while until things have cooled down a little. You have your reception at your school this week anyway, don't you?''

''Yes, if you're still willing to do it. I guess it won't hurt to continue a little longer.''

''Of course I'm willing. After what you put up with at the ball, it's the least I can do.''

''I promise you it won't last as long as the ball did.''

The corners of his mouth turned down. ''I had a good time. I thought you did, too. I hope you weren't bored,'' he said stiffly.

She blushed. ''No, that's not what I meant. I just wanted to assure you it would be a simple affair. It will be held in the old mansion of the school with just a few of the teachers there. Nothing special. But you will have to play the role of fiancé. By the way, your mother invited me to tea at the hotel next week.''

''I know. She told me. She always wanted a daughter. I think she thinks she's got one.''

''Oh, dear. I don't want to hurt her or your father. What should I do?''

''Go. Go have tea with her. It will make her happy.''

''And when she finds out…?''

He shook his head. ''They asked for it. They asked me for a fiancée and I've given them one. Who can say that any engagement will last? Of course we all hope for a happy ending. In their case a happy ending means my marriage. In my case…''

''Yes?'' she asked. She knew only too well that marriage was not his idea of a happy ending. She wanted to hear him say it, because it was something she had to engrave in her memory in case she started getting fooled into thinking this was all for real. Naturally, marrying a sheik was about as far from reality as she could get. She knew that.

"In my case, marriage is not one of my goals. Maybe one day when I'm older I will do my duty and marry, but not now."

"Of course. I understand."

"What about you, Anne, what would your parents say?"

"If they thought I was engaged? They'd be happy, I'm sure. But they live in Arizona and they're not likely to hear about it, not from me, anyway. So there will be no tears when it's over."

She imagined her mother hearing she was engaged to a sheik.

A sheik? You mean one of those Arab sheiks who come riding across the desert and carry you off to their tent, or is it their castle? Does he have a harem and oil wells?

"Who has the red hair in your family, is it your mother?" He reached across the table and twisted an auburn curl around his finger. She licked her lips. Why did he do these things? Why had he kissed her in the car? Why did he look at her that way? There was no one in the bar to impress or to fool into thinking they were really engaged. Then why...why...why...did he lean forward across the table and drink her in as if he was a thirsty man in the desert?

"My hair?" She was having a hard time coming up with an answer. It wasn't the question, it was him. He rattled her, he disturbed her and he knew it. "No, uh, it's my grandmother who had red hair. They say I look like her."

"She must have been beautiful," he said softly.

"I guess that's a compliment," she said.

"If I were to guess, I'd say you haven't had many."

"No. When I was small, the kids teased me and called me carrot-top. Then in high school...but I told you about high school. When I had scoliosis, I withdrew from social activities. No one noticed me or my hair. It was kind of a relief.''

"I can't believe no one noticed you," he said. "They must have been blind."

"Rafik, you don't need to compliment me," she said. "I've already agreed to this arrangement. It suits me as well as it suits you. I take responsibility for my part in the debacle at the wedding. I'm grateful to you for respecting my virtue that night and…and…so…" She didn't know how to make it any clearer.

"I don't understand," he said, leisurely unwrapping her hair from around his finger and leaning back against the bench. "Do you think what I say to you is calculated to win you over? It's not. I know what you think. That sheiks are all playboys. But we're not all bad. Give me credit for some sincerity."

"Of course. I didn't mean…" Now she was really confused. She'd hurt his feelings without meaning to.

"Surely someone before me has told you how beautiful you are."

She wanted to say yes. She wanted to brush off his compliments with a laugh or a shrug of her shoulders the way other women did, but she couldn't. The truth was that she'd never thought of herself as beautiful. She didn't know if anyone else did either, except some of her young students, none of whom was over six years old. Apparently her silence spoke volumes.

Rafik nodded. "I see," he said. She was afraid he did see. He saw too much.

"I must be going," she said, getting to her feet.

He put some money on the table and followed her out of the bar, with his hand resting possessively on her shoulder. She held her head high. She had to admit he made her feel attractive, appreciated and yes…even beautiful. Was hat because he was skilled in the arts of flattery and pleasing women? Probably. Or was it, as he claimed, sincerity? How much she wanted to believe it was the latter.

He walked her to her car and paused. "Thank you for coming out tonight," he said. "You've made an awkward situation much better for me. I can't tell you how much I appreciate it."

She nodded, told him the time and place of the reception at her school. He told her he'd pick her up, and then he kissed her on the cheek before he opened her door for her.

She told herself there was no reason for her cheeks to burn up on the drive home. It was only a kiss on the cheek. But she was so inexperienced, she had so little defenses against the charm of a sheik. How was she to know what to do, what to say? She didn't know.

A few days later Carolyn, her newlywed friend, called her. Before Anne could ask about her honeymoon, Carolyn demanded to know if the rumor she had heard about Anne and Rafik was true.

"Sort of, I mean what did you hear exactly?" Anne asked cautiously. This was awful. She couldn't lie to her good friend. And yet if she told her the truth....

"Tarik said he heard you were engaged to his cousin. I told him it couldn't possibly be true. You just met him at the wedding, right?"

"Yes, of course, but it's not what you think," Anne said.

"Good, because he's not your type," Carolyn said.

"I know that, I definitely know that," Anne said.

"So how did the family get this crazy idea?" Carolyn asked.

"I can explain...I think. You see...Carolyn this is strictly between you and me. You can't breathe a word of this to anyone, especially anyone in the family."

"Even Tarik? I don't know if I can keep a secret from him."

"But can you trust him?"

"With my life," Carolyn said.

Anne sighed. How wonderful to be in love with someone you could trust that way. She took a deep breath. "All right, then. Here's what happened. Rafik needed a fiancée…"

"What for? He distinctly told me he wasn't interested in getting married."

"Yes, yes, exactly. That's why he needs a fiancée, not a real fiancée but just someone to act like one. That's what I'm doing."

"But why? Why would you do such a thing?"

"I…I don't know exactly except that he's a very persuasive person and the whole thing happened at the gala ball which you missed. It was a giant misunderstanding between him and his parents. They're set on his getting married, but, as you know, he has no intention of getting engaged or married. So for some reason when they saw us together at the ball, they assumed I was his fiancée and announced it to everybody."

"Oh, no."

"Oh, yes. I didn't know what to do. I couldn't get up there and say it wasn't true. Not when everyone was so happy, congratulating him and me. I was in a state of shock."

"And Rafik, what state was he in?" Carolyn asked.

"He was shocked, too. He says he'll explain it to them. Just not right now. Because he actually wants a fiancée, not a real one of course. A false one, someone who will pretend to be a fiancée, to get them off his case, so to speak."

"So everybody got what they wanted. Or at least they think they did. His parents got a future daughter-in-law whom they approve of, I would suppose. Who wouldn't approve of you?''

''As a matter of fact, they do. His mother invited me to tea and they both have been truly nice to me.''

''So the parents get you, Rafik gets off the hook, but what about you, what do you get out of it? I won't stand for Rafik taking advantage of you.''

''No, no, he isn't. He's been very good about the whole thing. And he's doing me a favor, too....'' Anne stopped. She didn't want to go into the false engagement she'd gotten herself into with her headmistress, so she didn't finish her sentence, hoping Carolyn wouldn't notice.

''I hope he's doing you lots of favors,'' Carolyn said. ''Because I don't see what you're getting out of it. What do you want out of it?''

Anne didn't know what to say. She didn't want to say *I want what you have. A husband who loves you and whom you can trust.* She didn't want to sound envious.

''Never mind,'' Carolyn said. ''You don't have to tell me. I know you too well. You only want what's best for everyone else. But what's going to happen when everyone finds out?''

''That's what I'm worried about. But Rafik doesn't seem to be worried. He thinks he can just explain that the engagement was broken off. After all, it happens. It's happened to him once already, I understand. But I don't like it. I really don't. Especially if I have to get to know his parents. I feel like such a fraud.''

''That's got to be tough,'' Carolyn said sympathetically. ''Oh, my. I'm overwhelmed. But believe me I won't tell anybody but Tarik, and I'll swear him to secrecy. But please, Anne, don't let yourself be taken advantage of. Because I won't sit by and let that happen. I know, Rafik is now a part of my family, but you are my friend and I'm responsible for introducing you to him.''

''I won't, believe me. I can take care of myself,'' she assured her friend. After she'd hung up, she paced around her living room, getting more worried by the minute. Wondering if she should have told Carolyn. But it felt so good to confide in someone. And the secret had begun to burn a hole in her psyche. On the other hand, the more people that knew about this charade, the more dangerous it became that the wrong people would find out. She sat down at her desk and looked at her calendar, checking off the obstacles ahead of her. First was tea with his mother. Then the reception at the school which she'd confirmed with the headmistress who had promised to gather together all the teachers and staff who were around during the summer.

After that she could relax and attend a seminar on new methods in teaching reading put on by the state teachers' association. It was to be held at a rustic lodge on the ocean near Monterey, and there would be no sheiks in attendance, just teaching colleagues from around the state. There would be stimulating, late-night sessions around the fireplace where they would exchange techniques for teaching children from the brightest to the most disadvantaged. There she could relax and be herself, a competent first-grade teacher who enjoyed her work and her life the way it was. No need to pretend anything in front of her fellow teachers. They knew who she was, and best of all, she knew who she was.

Rafik was trying to avoid his parents, afraid of having to enter into an awkward conversation about his ''love life,'' but since he worked with Massoud in the office, it was difficult not to see him. The good thing was that they had plenty of business affairs to discuss, so avoiding the topic of Anne and his engagement hadn't been as hard to do as he'd imagined. It was his mother who caught him off guard one day in his office.

He jumped to his feet and kissed her on the cheek. "What a surprise," he said. "I thought you were busy furnishing your new apartment."

"I always have time for my sons," Nura said.

"I'll get Rahman," Rafik offered, reaching for his phone. "So we can all get together for a few minutes. Then I'm afraid I have to take off to see one of our clients." Rahman would be a good distraction. His mother couldn't possibly bear down on him with him in the room, too.

His mother shook her head. "I've just seen your brother. I know you're busy so I won't take a moment."

"Sit down," he said politely. He didn't like the determined look on her face. If it had anything to do with his future it could mean trouble.

She took a seat across from his desk and gave him a look that made him uneasy.

"I'm having tea with Anne today," she said.

"Ah, yes, she mentioned it to me. I'm sure she's looking forward to it."

"As am I," she said. "I just want to know if there is anything I shouldn't mention, such as your former fiancée."

"I would appreciate your discretion, Mother. There's no need to bring that up. It's past history."

"What about the time you fell off your polo pony and lost the match for your team?" she asked.

"Perhaps you should let me tell that story. We haven't known each other long enough to delve into each other's childhoods yet." But he realized that though they hadn't known each other very long at all, he already knew about Anne's scoliosis and the humiliation she had felt wearing

a brace. It had helped him understand her shyness, and he
unawareness of her charm and looks.

"Another thing, about the engagement...."

Rafik braced himself for the worst. And it came.

"I wondered if you'd set a wedding date yet?"

"Uh...no. Not yet. We both believe in long engage
ments. Especially considering what happened the las
time."

"I hope your unhappy memories from the past won'
prevent you from seeing the difference between Anne an
your previous fiancée. They are as different as night an
day, from what I can see."

"You couldn't be more right about that. Still we're i
no hurry."

"You're over thirty," she reminded him.

"What about Rahman?" he asked. "He's over thirty
too."

She smiled. "I've spoken to Rahman."

"That's good. He needs to be spoken to."

Nura opened her mouth to say something else, but for
tunately the telephone rang and when he hung up, hi
mother had left. He breathed a huge sigh of relief.

After his mother left, Rafik picked up the phone an
called Anne's number but no one answered. He wanted t
warn her to tell the same story to his mother, that she als
believed in long engagements. He thought he could cour
on her. She most certainly wouldn't agree to a date n
matter what his mother said to her. All the same, he woul
have liked to speak to her before she walked into tea wit
his mother. For a shy person like Anne, it could be likene
to walking into a lion's den.

He knew that his mother, who seemed to be as tradition
as a wife could be and the type to let her husband mak
all the decisions, was really quite a power behind the scene

of her marriage and her family. She knew what she wanted and she almost always got it. It had been Nura's decision to open an office in San Francisco in the hope that the family could all be together there, instead of the boys in New York and she and their father in the Gulf. She had chosen the new apartment, and now she wanted to choose Rafik's wife for him. That was what concerned Rafik. She wanted to see him married. Not just married, but to Anne. But he too had a strong will, perhaps inherited from his mother, and he had no intention of letting her win the battle of the marriage. It was his life, after all. He just wished he could be a fly on the wall of the tearoom.

There were no flies on any wall of the St. Francis Hotel's tearoom. Everything was sumptuous and luxurious from the thick Oriental carpets to the embossed wall-coverings to the white-jacketed waiters to the woman in the long skirt who played the harp.

Anne was glad she'd worn her one and only suit, and her gloves when the doorman held the door for her and she saw the elegant setting on the first floor. It was a suit she saved for presentations made in front of the teachers' association or on parents' night at school. She noticed that Rafik's mother was wearing an elegant blue silk dress and a hat that set off her silver hair.

She tried to calm the butterflies in her stomach. She knew this was not an ordinary tea. She was going to be asked questions, and she might say the wrong thing or be caught contradicting herself or Rafik. So far she liked the woman very much and she understood that the family as a whole liked her. So what was the real problem? That they liked her *too* much.

Mrs. Harun smiled at her across the room and motioned to her to join her at her small round table.

"What a lovely custom, tea in the afternoon," Nura Ha run said. "How kind of you to join me."

Anne murmured that it was her pleasure. Rafik's mothe ordered jasmine and Earl Grey tea and sandwiches an cakes. Then she settled back in her chair and surveyed th woman who she surely hoped would be her future daughter in-law.

"I hope your parents are as happy about your engage ment as we are," she said.

Anne murmured something she hoped sounded positive Mrs. Harun seemed satisfied.

"I hope you'll forgive me for asking some questions," his mother said.

Anne nodded calmly. But inside, her heart was doin flip-flops. What kind of questions? she wanted to ask. Bu she didn't. She'd find out soon enough.

"Rafik tells me you haven't set a date for the wedding.

"No, no date." That was an easy question and an eas answer. But the woman obviously wasn't finished. seemed she was just getting started.

"What kind of a wedding do you have in mind?" sh asked.

"Well, I'm afraid we haven't discussed it yet," Ann said.

"I see. I'm afraid men are very bad at planning wed dings. So if you need any help I would love to step in Provided your family wouldn't be offended, of course. Yo see, I have no daughters, only sons. So I have no chanc to plan a wedding unless it's for one of the boys."

"I understand."

Fortunately, the small white pots of tea arrived at tha moment along with trays of sandwiches: walnut and cu cumber, and cream cheese and smoked salmon and chicke salad. The arrival of the food and tea gave Anne an excus to exclaim over the beautiful presentation. Mrs. Harun poured them each a cup of tea and while they nibbled at the sandwiches any further serious conversation was postponed. Anne would have been happy if it had been canceled completely. But after the sandwiches and before the tarts and cakes, the older woman got down to the subject at hand.

"I thought your friend Carolyn had a lovely church wedding."

"Yes, lovely."

"Would you too be interested in that kind of wedding?" Nura asked very casually.

Anne tried to see herself coming down the aisle at Grace Cathedral as Carolyn had done, preceded by a host of bridesmaids, her husband-to-be and a line of groomsmen at the altar but she knew her wedding—should she marry—would never be as spectacular.

"I think it would be too grand for me," she explained. "I would prefer something at home. I have a garden I'm working on that would be perfect for a wedding. Provided the weather was good and that I'd finished my plantings by then." As soon as she'd said them, she wished she could take back the words. What on earth possessed her to say those things? She'd never consciously thought of her garden as a wedding site before. Never.

Not only that, she was not going to get married any time in the near future. She had no business imagining a wedding anywhere, any time. Still she truthfully couldn't think of a nicer venue than her own backyard. It could be so personal, so private, so intimate, and so romantic. But not at all suitable for a rich sheik. She couldn't share that bit of information with his mother, of course.

"I see," his mother said, setting her teacup in the saucer. "Something small and intimate. It sounds lovely. I wonder...I don't want to impose, but I have a gown that I wore at my wedding. It was designed for me. Of course it wouldn't fit me now, but when I was married I was about your size.'' Her gaze traveled over Anne's slender figure. ''What I mean is that I would be honored if you would wear it. But it is completely up to you. Perhaps you have something in mind already?''

''No, no, nothing,'' Anne said.

His mother smiled. ''It's been in storage, but I could bring it to show you one day. Believe me, I won't be one bit offended if you don't like it or if it doesn't fit you. It's just.... I always wanted to pass it down to someone.'' There was a wistful tone in her voice Anne couldn't help but notice. It made her feel worse than ever about not marrying her son.

''Thank you,'' Anne said, touched by the generous offer. ''That's very kind of you. I'd love to see it.'' But she wouldn't be wearing it, she thought. His mother would just have to keep it in storage for a while longer, until one of her sons really decided to get married. That could be years from now or never, she thought. But that was none of her business. The dear woman had no idea how opposed to the idea of marriage her son was and Anne was not going to be the one to tell her.

Apparently satisfied by the way things were progressing in regard to her son's wedding, Nura then changed the subject. Anne was so relieved she was able to relax and happily converse for another hour. Nura Harun was really a very nice person. Because of her background in a foreign country she had many stories to tell, which Anne found fascinating. If Anne ever had a mother-in-law in the future someone like Rafik's mother would be a good choice. Not that anyone gets to choose her mother-in-law.

After they'd devoured every last crumb of the orange

nd currant scones and tiny iced cakes, Anne thanked Mrs.
Karun. In front of the hotel his mother kissed her on the
heek and promised they'd get together very soon, and reminded her of the wedding dress.

"Don't feel obligated in any way to wear it," she said.
"After all, it may not be your style at all."

Anne assured her she'd love to see it. Before they parted,
Jura took Anne's left hand in hers. Looking at her ring
nger, she frowned.

"But you have no engagement ring."

"Oh, uh, no, no, not yet." Just when Anne was con-
ratulating herself on escaping from the tea with no con-
equences, she was caught. She didn't know what to say.
They'd never discussed a ring. She always assumed they'd
e unengaged before the question came up. But here the
uestion was, rearing its ugly head and leaving her tongue-
ed and fumbling for a suitable answer.

"No engagement ring," his mother repeated. She looked
noughtful as she said goodbye and they parted. Anne
valked down the street, conscious of her bare ring finger.
'or the first time in her life, Anne imagined herself wearing
diamond engagement ring and a wedding dress, standing
n a leafy arbor like the one in her backyard. She wished
ne man in her imagination waiting for her at the end of
ne flagstone path under a trellis didn't have a face and a
ame. But he did.

Chapter Six

When Rafik picked up Anne to go to her school reception the first question he asked was about the tea with his mother.

"I had a very nice time," she said, once again enjoying the luxury of the heated seats and the smell of leather in the interior of his sleek foreign sports car.

"So did Mother," Rafik said. "Now she's talking of nothing but the wedding. Did you have to be so agreeable?"

Her mouth fell open in surprise as she turned to look at him. Was he seriously upset? "What did you expect, that I'd be rude and unpleasant?"

"No, of course not," he assured her. "It's not in your nature to be the least bit unpleasant. I don't know what you could have done. I just know that instead of less, there's more pressure than ever on me to get married."

She studied his profile. His forehead was lined with worry, his jaw was clenched. Fortunately he didn't say anything about a ring. Maybe his mother had forgotten a about it. She could only hope so. "Maybe this was a bad idea," she suggested.

"I certainly couldn't have imagined it backfiring," he said dourly.

"If you'd prefer to call it off now, we can turn around and skip this reception."

"Wouldn't that make you look bad?" he asked with a glance in her direction.

"Yes, I suppose it would, but…"

"Then we're going. For all intents and purposes, as far as the rest of the world knows, I'm your fiancé. As for my family, I'll handle them. Now, at your school, is there anything special I'm supposed to tell them?"

"Just act like a responsible and serious man, not like someone who'd carry a female across a hotel lobby on the way to seduce her in his room."

He smothered a smile. "In other words I'm to dispel all notions that I'm some kind of playboy."

"Exactly."

"That shouldn't be a problem."

"Why, because you're such a good actor?" she asked.

"No, because I'm not a playboy anymore." He raised his eyebrows. "Haven't you noticed?"

"Well…"

"I don't hang out in bars anymore, except to meet you. I don't ogle women or attempt to pick them up. I don't even stay up late, not when I have to be in the office by nine. I'm a different person, whether you've noticed or not." He sounded slightly offended that she hadn't noticed, so she tried to reassure him.

"I'm sure you are. But since I didn't really know you before your transformation, you can't blame me for not noticing." She reached over to touch his shoulder as a reassuring gesture and he smiled at her. She smiled back and their eyes met. Her pulse raced. He might not be a playboy anymore, but he hadn't lost his ability to turn women on especially women like her who hadn't had time to build up a set of defenses against men like him. She withdrew her hand and turned to look out the window to escape the aura around him.

She told herself it was all an act. She warned herself not to get caught up in the act. Because pretending to be Rafik's fiancée, while often stressful, was sometimes enjoyable. If she could call tremors and sudden waves of heat coursing through the body enjoyable sensations. If she didn't mind the dreams involving her and him that interrupted her sleep. She'd been dreaming of her wedding, something she'd never done in her life.

Many girls, such as her friend Carolyn, had been planning their weddings for years, but not Anne. What worried her was that she not only had dreamed of the wedding, but of the honeymoon, too. The honeymoon which took place in a small hotel in some European city with a view over the rooftops and churches and other vaguely famous landmarks. In the dream, they'd close the shutters and tumble back onto the bed where they would make passionate love for hours. She couldn't believe she could even imagine such details. Of how Rafik taught her the secrets of love making. Of how quickly she learned.

She'd wake up in the morning after one of these dreams feeling aware of her body in a way she'd never been before. Her skin was warm and tingly. She had to stand under the shower for many minutes to dispel the notion that she'd actually made love with her husband under a down comforter then eaten croissants and drunk café au lait in bed. She told herself it was just a dream. Where these dreams came from, she couldn't say. She didn't read travel magazines or bride magazines. And she certainly never read those articles with such titles as, "Fifty Ways To Please Your Mate," that she'd seen on the racks in the supermarket.

Since she'd never been to Europe, she wasn't sure which city it was in her dreams. Perhaps it was Paris. She'd taken French in college, and she'd always thought Paris must be the most romantic place in the world. Maybe it was. She would probably never know unless she went along as a chaperone for the older students at her school.

Rafik interrupted these thoughts by asking for directions to the school and Anne started guiltily. The smile on his face made her wonder if he had a way of reading her thoughts. But that was impossible. How could he? Fortunately she didn't worry about him letting her down in front of the faculty and staff of her school. She knew him well enough to know he'd come through for her. What she didn't know was that he had reserves of charm he hadn't even tapped yet, at least not in front of her.

Once inside the ballroom of the sprawling old mansion that made up the centerpiece of the beautiful campus, he made a favorable impression on everyone. He seemed to know just what to say and how long to say it. He asked thoughtful questions, and he answered questions about his background and his business, spending just the right amount of time talking to each person or group of people. He never monopolized the conversation. She didn't think he'd learned that anywhere. It had to be inborn. If she lived to be one hundred, she'd never have his ease in social situations. Together with his looks, it was an unbeatable combination.

Considering it was summer vacation, there was a large crowd gathered, everyone sipping punch, eating cookies and eagerly awaiting a chance to say hello to a genuine, bona fide sheik. Anne knew how surprised they must be to

find their quiet, serious first-grade teacher suddenly en
gaged to an exotic sheik. She could just imagine how many
questions they wanted to ask her, such as how had she met
him? How long had she known him? How rich was he?
Where would they live? and Would she continue to teach?

They did ask some of these questions, excluding the one
about how rich he was, of course. She was able to be vague
about future plans, but she soon realized how hard it was
to skirt around the truth with people she knew so well. She
also realized it wasn't going to be quite as easy as she'd
thought to explain a broken engagement later. Not when
everyone was so happy for her, so delighted with her choice
of a man. These thoughts spun around in her mind, and her
face hurt from smiling so much.

At one point she was listening to a group of colleagues
talk about their fall schedules and Rafik was talking to one
of the school's trustees. Listening to his conversation with
one ear, she strained to hear what he was saying. She was
surprised to hear him talking about his country. About the
changes in the last decade, the plans for modernization, the
difference between his life and his grandfather's, the old
gentleman whose picture she'd seen on the wall of his of
fice. She'd never heard him speak seriously before, and she
was impressed with his knowledge and his reverence for
the past as well as his enthusiasm for the future. She was
so caught up in listening to him, she completely tuned out
what her fellow teachers were talking about.

When they asked her a question, she looked blank. They
laughed and accused her of being in love. She blushed, and
of course she couldn't deny it. She was supposed to be
engaged, after all. She tried to explain, but they wouldn't
accept her half-hearted explanation. All in all, everyone
seemed so happy for her, she didn't argue. Any protest she

might make would just make matters worse, so she just let them carry on.

As soon as she could, she excused herself to go to the punch bowl by herself, looking for a few moments to give her mouth a rest from the constant smiling, to cool her overheated skin, gather her thoughts and to try to shake the beginnings of a tension headache. Rafik seemed to be able to carry on forever, but she couldn't. She would never be the social animal he was. Especially when she was pretending to be engaged to a sheik.

At the refreshment table, she ran into Jean Stuart, a teacher who had team-taught a class with her the year before. They'd gotten along so well, Anne was sorry she hadn't kept her promise to keep in touch during the summer.

"Now I know why I haven't heard from you," Jean said with a smile. "You've had other things on your mind."

"But we must get together," Anne said, trying to ignore the mention of "other things."

"In any case, you're still going to the conference this weekend in Monterey, aren't you?" Jean said.

"Of course. And we're rooming together. I'm looking forward to it. Shall we carpool?" Anne asked.

"Good idea. I'll drive," Jean offered. "If you can get along without your fiancé for that long. I'd love to bring Art along, but we couldn't get a baby-sitter. I'm telling you, take advantage of these times while you're young and single and still unencumbered. You look great, you know. Falling in love must agree with you."

Anne didn't know whether to laugh or cry. She had a wild desire to tell her friend the truth. She wondered how she'd endure a whole weekend without spilling the truth. With any luck they'd be talking nonstop about reading techniques and would have no time to discuss personal mat-

ters. She also wondered how she could look great when sh
was living a lie and was worried sick she'd be caugh
Fortunately Jean didn't wait for an answer.

"I can see why. Your fiancé is absolutely adorable."

At least she didn't say charming, Anne thought with re
lief. She was so tired of hearing him described that way.
was even more annoying because he most definitely we
charming.

"You make a great couple," Jean continued. Just the
Rafik glanced over at Anne and winked at her, causing he
to blush. Of course, Jean noticed. "What's it like," sh
asked, "to be in love with a sheik?"

"Oh, well...." Anne said. "It's uh...it's not any diffe
ent from being in love with anyone else." As if she knev
She'd never been in love with anyone, let alone with Rafi
and he wasn't in love with her. She wondered how the
could fool so many people. Everyone here today probab
believed them, just as Rafik's family believed them.

"The way you can tell two people are in love," Jea
said, as if she'd read Anne's thoughts, "is that their eye
keep meeting. Oh, yes, even though I'm an old marrie
lady, I remember. The thrills, the excitement. No matt
where you are, I notice your fiancé always knows where t
find you," Jean said. "And you're the same."

Of course she was the same. She had to keep Rafik i
her sight in case he needed rescuing from some verbo.
staff member. As if Rafik needed help in any situation. F
moved fluidly from group to group until he ended up at th
punch bowl with Jean and Anne. In a moment the hea
mistress joined them also. So much for Anne's trying t
shake her headache. Instead it got worse. She stole a loo
at her watch and wondered how long they had to stay t
be polite.

"I'm so impressed with the faculty and the staff here

Pinehurst," Rafik told the headmistress. "These are very lucky children who attend this school."

"If you have children, we would hope to have them enroll here," Leona said. "We have a strong language program for our many international students who go on to study here or abroad."

Rafik reached for Anne's hand. "I can't think of a better place for our children, can you?" he asked her.

Though her hands were cold, her face was flaming. She tried to convey to Rafik with a nudge of her arm and a swift glance that there was no need to carry on about nonexistent children. As skillful in the art of conversation as Rafik was, he could have changed the subject. But he didn't. In fact he pulled Anne close to his side and squeezed her hand, then asked more questions about the preschool program. She wanted to sink through the floor.

"Anne," the headmistress said, "I've unlocked your classroom if you'd like to show it to your fiancé. The painters have finished in there, and I must say it looks quite nice."

Anne glanced at Rafik. She was sure seeing a first-grade classroom would bore him, though he nodded enthusiastically. But it took what seemed an eternity to get out of the reception. They had to make the rounds once again, thanking everyone for coming and for putting on such a nice party. Anne didn't know what to say when people asked about the wedding. Especially when she was separated from Rafik at the moment. She had no idea what he had been saying about it to everyone. They should have gotten their stories straight before they got here. A small wedding in the far-distant future seemed the safest. That way no one would be expecting their invitations in the mail any time soon, or any time at all.

Finally she and Rafik were alone together outside the

mansion on the front steps. "We don't have to look at the classroom, you know," she said.

"I'd be honored if you'd show it to me," he said. "That way I can picture you at work. After all, you've seen me in my office. Although you perhaps don't have exactly a happy memory of that occasion."

She couldn't deny it. The very thought made her shiver. "I can't imagine what everyone in your office thought of me that day," she said. "Or what conclusions they had drawn. There was your father, your brother, your receptionist... And there I was in my bridesmaid gown and bare feet. Everyone must have been shocked."

"No one, not even Father, ever mentioned it again, and he's pleased about the engagement to say the least, so I guess it didn't hurt your reputation at all. As for mine... I don't think it could have been worse than it was. This engagement has done a lot for it and I have you to thank."

"I thought you were proud of being a playboy."

"Did you?" he asked. They walked in silence down the winding sidewalk from the reception center to the class rooms. "I suppose I was," he said thoughtfully.

The classroom did look good with its freshly painted walls and new carpet. Her desk was back in place along with the little chairs and tables for the students. But the walls were bare and it lacked the warmth and color that only a roomful of six-year-olds and their books and their equipment and her own personal touches could provide.

"Of course it will be more cheerful with posters on the walls and the pictures my students draw."

"I can picture you sitting at your desk with the children sitting quietly, looking at you from their seats, awaiting your instruction," he said.

Anne smiled at the false picture he had of American classrooms. "Actually, they very seldom sit in their seat for very long," she explained. "Sometimes we all sit on the rug and I read a story or we sing a song. They're very lively and restless at this age so I try to keep them busy with a choice of various learning activities. Reading, writing, counting. Last year I set up a play storefront over there in the corner with pretend products and play money. Some children were customers and others clerks. They had a good time and didn't even realize they were doing math."

"That doesn't sound like the kind of elementary school I went to in my country," Rafik said. "We had individual desks and never got up or spoke without the teacher's permission. Math was learned from a book."

"Things have changed," Anne said, leaning against her desk.

"For the better," he said. "I think it would be an enjoyable experience to be in your class." His lips curved in a smile that could only be described as sexy. He must not be aware of the effect it had on her. Of how fast her heart was beating and how the sparks traveled through her body right down to her toes.

"Thank you," she said briskly. "Well, now that you've seen it...." She couldn't imagine anyone being that interested in a classroom unless they were a student or teacher, but Rafik didn't seem to want to leave. He kept looking around the room and back at her, until finally he was only looking at her. She tried to look away, but she couldn't. The room seemed so small with him in it. He was so big and so out-of-place. He was so far away from her. She felt alone and small. Almost like one of her students. It must be the lack of furnishings or the new paint and the carpet. He kept looking at her. She didn't know what that look in his eyes meant. She just knew she couldn't look away. She also knew she was trembling inside. Before she started trembling on the outside, too, she ran her damp palm against her skirt and started for the door.

"I'd like to come again, when you have your posters up and the art work on the walls...if I may," he said.

"Of course," she said, pushing the door open. "There' an open house in September." By September their false engagement would surely be over and he would have no reason to visit her classroom. For one thing he was probably not sincere, merely expressing his good manners. She didn't know exactly how long this engagement would last and she didn't want to ask. One of these days it would become clear. It would be over as fast as it had begun. With as little warning. So she'd better be prepared.

When they got to the car, Anne reclined her seat, leaned back and closed her eyes. She was mentally exhausted. But Rafik seemed to be energized.

"You're fortunate to have a nice group of people to work with," he said.

"I know, but it's the children who make it all worthwhile."

"I can see you enjoy your job very much."

She nodded, too tired to speak.

"If we had a wedding, would you be obliged to invite the entire staff?"

She sat up straight and stared straight ahead. "We aren' having a wedding. We aren't even engaged. Remember?"

"Of course I remember," he said.

"I wish you hadn't mentioned our children going to school there." Just saying the words made the heat rush to Anne's cheeks once again.

"What do you mean? Wouldn't you want our children to attend your school?"

"Of course, but we aren't having any children. We aren'

engaged and we aren't getting married." She emphasized each word in turn, as much for him as for herself.

"Obviously you feel quite strongly about it," he said stiffly.

"Don't you?" she asked.

He gave her a long thoughtful look, then opened his mouth to say something, but didn't.

Surely he must know how she felt. How embarrassing it was for her to think of having children with a man who wasn't interested in marriage, either to her or anyone else. A man who could have any woman he wanted. If he wanted to get married, it would certainly be to someone rich and beautiful and socially acceptable. Why not?

"I have to thank you for the wonderful job in there, by the way. But did you have to be so agreeable?" she asked, deliberately mimicking his earlier words.

"Did you expect me to be arrogant and egotistical?"

"No, of course not. It's just that now that they know you, and they obviously like you, everyone will be asking about you and the wedding and you know…"

"Indeed I do know," he said. "It seems that we've unleashed a genie from out of a bottle. We're both in the same situation. For better or for worse."

For better or for worse. The words from the wedding ceremony hung in the air. She didn't know if he knew the significance of them, but she did. She wished she could forget about weddings, especially her own imaginary wedding, but everything and everyone seemed to remind her.

"Anyway it's over," she said. "I won't see any of them until fall, except for Jean who will be at the same conference at Asilomar next weekend."

"You'll be gone all weekend?" he asked, driving down the steep hill on California Street.

"Yes, at a conference center on the beach in Monterey.

It's a secluded spot not many people know about with views of sand dunes and the sound of crashing waves and fireplaces in every room. I'm looking forward to it.''

"Is it only for teachers?" he asked.

"The conference is, but if they're not fully booked the rooms are available to visitors who appreciate the solitude and rustic atmosphere."

"It sounds romantic," Rafik remarked.

"You would think of that," Anne said. She would never admit that she'd thought of it, too. Too many romantic thoughts were in her mind these days. Not to mention those romantic dreams. "But no one will be thinking of romance." Especially not her. Not if she could help it. "We'll be too busy discussing teaching reading to children,"

"Do you need a ride down there?" he asked.

"My friend Jean is driving."

"I'll miss you."

"You don't need to say things like that," she said with a frown. "There's no one around to hear."

"I meant it."

She didn't know what to say. He sounded sincere. But why would he miss her? It didn't make sense. He took her home and walked her to the door. He looked as if he was reluctant to leave. He kept making small talk until she took out her key and opened her front door.

"I haven't seen much of the inside of your house," he said. She'd run out to meet him when she heard his car pull up in front of her house earlier that day. The night of the gala, he'd come in to the living room only.

"Yes, I know. If I didn't have a headache, I'd invite you in, but…"

"I didn't mean to force myself on you," he said. "If

you have plans, I understand. You don't have to make up a story about a headache. You can be honest with me.''

"Thank you," she said stiffly. "I do have a headache and I am being honest with you. I've told so many lies in the past few days, I couldn't possibly manage another one. Maybe that's why my head hurts. Thanks again." She let herself in and closed the door behind her.

Rafik drove away reluctantly. He had more things to say to Anne. Many more. He had questions to ask her. He felt he scarcely knew her at all. When he'd seen her in her classroom, she seemed to be a different person. Her eyes sparkled and her face glowed when she described her job. He'd always thought her attractive, but she was more than that. The more he got to know her, the more appealing she was. Today she was so beautiful he could hardly take his eyes from her.

He could picture her on the rug with her students gathered around her, their eyes on her as she read to them. How lucky they were to have such a fine teacher as she must be. Just as the headmistress had told him. He wondered how many sides to her personality there were. It seemed he'd have to know her for a long time before he found out. He was envious of Anne's weekend plans. For some reason he felt as if he really *was* engaged and his fiancée was going out of town without him. He knew it didn't make sense, but he felt left out. Now that he was supposed to be engaged he could hardly call other women. Not that he wanted to.

That week he had to endure his mother rhapsodizing about what a wonderful girl Anne was, about the kind of small, garden wedding she wanted and how she was going to try on his mother's wedding dress until he didn't know how much more he could take. Anne had never told him she wanted a garden wedding. Though now that she mentioned it and he'd seen her garden, he had no trouble imagining it. He didn't know why she hadn't told him herself, instead of having to hear it from his mother.

That wasn't all his mother said. She told him that a fiancée needed an engagement ring. She insisted on giving him a ring that had belonged to his grandmother that she thought would be appropriate.

"Although if you want to choose your own…"

"I don't know, Mother. I'll check with Anne."

She pressed the small jeweler's box into his hand. "Just see if she likes it. Your grandmother would be so happy if she knew."

"Yes. All right. Fine," he said, putting the box into his pocket.

At least he could let down his pretenses with his brother, the only one who knew the truth about his engagement.

"How's it going?" Rahman asked on Friday afternoon. "Got a big weekend planned with your *fiancée?*" He grinned at his brother.

Rafik crumpled a sheet of paper and threw it at his brother. "My *fiancée* is going out of town."

"Without you?"

"Yes, without me. She's going to a teacher's conference in Monterey."

"I hear it's a beautiful place," Rahman said. "Sand dunes, crashing surf, sea lions. Why don't you go along?"

"It's for teachers. They'll be doing whatever teachers do. Besides she didn't invite me."

"Since when do you need an invitation to go to Monterey, to book a room at the same place she's staying? Maybe she was too shy to invite you. Maybe she's dying for you to join her there so she can escape all those boring teacher-types. Anyway, she can't be doing her teacher thing every minute, can she?''

''I don't know. What are you doing?''

''Golf tomorrow. Strictly business. A group of investors. Of course if you're not busy, you can join us.''

Rafik had used to like playing golf. But playing with a group of investors sounded dull compared to walking on the sand dunes in Monterey. He knew it wouldn't be very exciting walking there alone. But if he was walking hand in hand with Anne, that was a different story. It shouldn't be impossible if they were both staying at the same place.

He pictured her hair curling in damp tendrils in the ocean spray, her cheeks pink from the breeze off the sea. His brother was right. He didn't need an invitation to visit Monterey. If he ran into Anne while he was there, it would be a coincidence. He'd soon get the hint if she didn't want him around, in which case he would tactfully disappear back to his room with his own fireplace where he would read various prospectuses from his briefcase which were piling up on his desk.

He couldn't get the image of the wood-burning fireplace in the rustic cabin out of his mind. If he really had a fiancée it would be only normal for them to spend a weekend together on the ocean, making love in the cabin in front of the flickering flames. But with Anne, who was not only *not* his fiancée, but a virgin to boot…there was no chance. Maybe it was time he found a real fiancée. On the other hand, the last time he had had a real fiancée, it had been a disaster. His parents had been thrilled, just as they were now, for a while. He'd been happy, too—at least he'd thought he was. Until it ended.

But he hadn't known the woman. He'd just thought he had. When she'd walked out, taking his ring and his joie de vivre and his trust with her, he'd sworn he'd never do it again. Never fall in love, never get engaged and never, never get married. He still felt the same. But that had nothing to do with his urge to see Anne this weekend in a different setting. He couldn't get the image out of his mind: the wind in her hair, her cheeks glowing from the walk on the beach...

"I don't know, Rahman. I'm in a tough spot. I'm not really engaged, but I have to act as if I am. I can't play the field, but I don't have the benefits of a real fiancée either." He ran his hand through his hair.

"Well, you have the parents off your back."

"Hah. Now they're pressuring me to get married. And it's all your fault. This was your idea, remember? Why don't you get engaged? That would distract them."

"Sure, if I could find someone like Anne, I might think about it. But I suspect she's one in a million. Sweet, high-spirited..."

"Kind, beautiful, smart, sexy..." Rafik murmured.

"What was that?" Rahman asked.

Rafik got out of his swivel chair. "Nothing. Enough of this. I've got some phone calls to make. See you later."

"Wait a minute. How much later? Are you going to take my advice? Where are you going?"

"Nowhere." He put one hand on his brother's shoulder and ushered him to the door and closed it behind him. Outside he could hear Rahman protesting.

"You can't get rid of me so easily," Rahman complained from the other side of the door. "Answer my questions. I'm your brother."

Rafik laughed quietly and picked up the phone.

Chapter Seven

Instead of having his secretary do it, Rafik made the reservation at the conference center himself. They asked if he was a part of the teachers' group, he said no. He was afraid they'd say they were booked up, but they found an ocean-view cottage for him, only steps from the beach. He wanted to ask how far that was from Anne's lodgings, but he didn't. At the hotel in the city where he was staying along with Rahman until they found an apartment, he packed his bag. Tossing casual slacks and sweaters into a duffel bag, he felt more excited than he had any right to be. He told himself she might not be happy to see him. She might not have time to see him. He told himself it didn't matter. He was seeing a part of the state he hadn't seen before. But what he wanted was to see a part of Anne he hadn't seen before.

Of course, he'd seen quite a bit, considering she was a virgin and she wasn't engaged to him at all. But he wanted more. He wanted to break down her reserves. He wanted to know how she really felt about him. But what if she

asked the same thing of him? What would he say? He
didn't know. He only knew his feelings were changing by
the day, by the minute. Every meeting with her revealed a
new layer of her personality. It was like peeling an onion.
He'd only just begun, and he didn't want to stop.

What else did he want? He couldn't deny he wanted to
make love to her. There was a chemistry between them;
there had been since he'd first set eyes on her at his cousin's
wedding. She wasn't his type, he'd known that from the
beginning also. That didn't stop him from pursuing her. She
must feel the attraction, too, no matter how hard she tried
to put him off. He couldn't be the only one. But he didn't
know if she'd continue to resist him. Or how far he would
go, knowing she was a virgin.

He left on Friday afternoon, choosing to drive on Highway One, taking the scenic route south from San Francisco.
He thought about calling Anne before he left, but he was
afraid if he told her his plans, she'd express surprise and
no pleasure. He didn't know what he'd do then. He could
go anyway or stay home. This way if she didn't want him
there, it would be too late. She'd have to deal with his
presence, unless she just ignored him. He didn't like that
idea and he had no contingency plan, unless it was to walk
the dunes by himself, a lonely figure tramping about in the
mist, which might encourage her to feel somewhat sympathetic toward him. But he couldn't count on that.

He didn't know what route Anne and her friend had
taken, but he wished she was with him to share the ride,
to share the view of the sun glittering on the vast blue
ocean. He'd point out how the ocean seemed to stretch
forever to the horizon. He loved seeing her face light up
with pleasure at something simple, like the joys of her garden.

One of the reasons he was on his way to Monterey was

to watch the changing expressions on her face. He'd seen the delight at her garden, despair at her predicament with her school, disgust at his teasing, and mixed emotions as sexual awareness crept up on her and threatened to overwhelm her at the gala ball. He was aware that her face might not light up at the sight of him arriving to interfere with her plans for the weekend. He could only hope if she wasn't exactly happy to see him, she'd at least be polite. Of course she would be. That was Anne.

When he arrived at the sprawling, low, brown-shingled conference buildings, he parked his car and was shown to his cottage through the trees. It was everything he'd imagined, and completely different from any other weekend retreat he'd been to. The cabin was outfitted with a king-sized bed covered with a down comforter. There were native blankets hung on the walls and handwoven rugs on the floor. The fire was laid in the fireplace and the view of the dunes and the ocean from his window was spectacular. This was California, a different California than he'd seen. Now, if only he had someone to share it with. Someone special. Like his fiancée.

Anne was walking through the fir trees from her cabin to the main lobby where the welcome reception was being held before dinner. Passing the parking lot she noticed a low-slung black sports car, and she stopped in her tracks and stared at it. Her heart thudded wildly, though she tried to dismiss the reason. There were many sports cars in California. She just hadn't noticed this one when they'd arrived an hour ago. She didn't know much about sports cars. She couldn't tell the difference between a Porsche and a BMW unless she looked at the logo, but this car looked familiar. It couldn't be his, of course, because Rafik was in San Francisco.

She took a deep breath and continued walking. Inside the lounge, she pinned a name tag on her sweater and refastened the clip in her hair that the wind had loosened, then proceeded to make the rounds of the room, greeting old friends from previous conferences and introducing herself to people she didn't know. It was the kind of gathering where, though she didn't know everyone, she was at ease. These were her colleagues from around the greater Bay Area. She would have been even more at ease if she didn't have the nagging feeling that it was just remotely possible that Rafik was here somewhere.

Because of this feeling, she found herself losing her train of thought in the middle of a conversation. She found herself looking out the large picture windows at the dunes in the dusk, as if he might be sauntering by, his collar up against the cold air, his black hair blown back in the wind. But of course he wasn't. He was back in San Francisco. She had no idea what he was doing. She hadn't asked him. She'd just figured it was none of her business. Of course if he were her fiancé, it would be her business. If he were her fiancé, he might be there with her, waiting in the cottage, a fire burning, a bottle of wine chilling.... She dismissed these ridiculous thoughts from her mind.

The next event was a family-style dinner followed by a short welcoming speech from the president of the teachers' association, who handed out a packet of materials and a schedule of the weekend's activities. Anne gathered her materials and put them into her book-bag. Though she had no reason to think so, she had a funny feeling she was being watched.

She glanced out the huge windows into the darkness and saw nothing. There was nothing to see in the dark. She put her jacket on, then made her way back to her cottage by the lighted pathways. She sniffed the air, redolent with pine and fir, and resolved not even to glance toward the parking lot. Sports cars all looked the same, no matter who owned them, especially in the dark.

"Hello, Anne."

Her heart pounded erratically at the sound of his voice. She stopped walking, frozen in place. The voice came from the darkness a few feet ahead of her, and in a moment he appeared, his hair wind-tossed and his face half in shadows.

"Rafik, what are you doing here?"

"I wanted to get some fresh air," he said, "and a change of scenery. Besides, the city was dull and boring without you."

She almost laughed at this flimsy excuse. "I can't imagine you bored in the city just because I wasn't there. How did you get along for thirty-some years without me?"

"I don't know," he said solemnly. "But it's beautiful here, just as you said. And I'm glad I came."

"Are you staying here?" She looked around, staring at the dark shapes of the trees, still in shock at the idea of Rafik here in Monterey. If she'd thought she couldn't picture him in a rustic setting like this because he was always so perfectly groomed and so citified, she was wrong. Because now that he was here, in a thick, Irish fisherman's sweater that appeared to have been knitted especially for him, he seemed to fit in as much as anyone. So far she'd seen him at a formal wedding reception, in his office, at a gala ball, a school function, in her garden and now this. In each setting, he seemed as at ease as if he'd been born to it. Probably, like a chameleon, he would be equally at ease in a tent in the desert or in the palace of a sheik.

"Despite the fact that you teachers are taking up much of the grounds, they luckily had an empty cottage for me," he said in answer to her question. He took her book-bag out of her hand as if it were way too heavy for a fragile

thing like her and it was the most natural thing in the world
that he should carry her belongings. He tucked her arm in
his as if she belonged to him.

She stifled the urge to pull her arm away and say she
could manage by herself. But she restrained herself. After
all, he'd come all this way to…to do what? Breathe some
fresh air? Escape from boredom? See her? Not likely. She
didn't know what to think.

"You shouldn't be out here by yourself in the dark," he
said. "Where's your friend?"

"Jean? She left the meeting early tonight. Her husband
is with her. He decided at the last minute to come and enjoy
the surroundings." Left unsaid was that he'd decided to
enjoy his wife in these bucolic surroundings—the romantic
fireplace, the giant bed and the freedom from his work
schedule and from their kids. Anne had seen the sparkle in
her friend's eyes when she'd told her about the change in
plans.

"I hope you don't mind, Anne," Jean had said. "We
don't get away from the kids together very often. Art found
a baby-sitter so he could come along. I figure I won't be
busy every minute and…well, we'll have some quality time
together, just the two of us." She could have sworn Jean
blushed at the word *quality*. Knowing Jean had been married for some years and had two children, Anne was impressed to find romance was on her friend's mind. And on
her husband's.

"Wasn't she to be your roommate?" Rafik asked.

"That's right. But her husband also booked a cabin. She
gained a husband for the weekend, but I lost a roommate."

"Too bad," he said. But he didn't sound like he thought
it was too bad. "Then I'll see you back to your cabin."

"Thank you, but…" But what? She couldn't think of
any excuse why he shouldn't walk her back to her cabin.

This time she wouldn't be as rude as she'd been when he'd walked her to her front door and she'd refused to let him come in. That time he would have invaded her private space. Her room here wasn't really hers. It couldn't hurt for him to come in for a moment for a cup of coffee made from the little complimentary packets and small coffee-maker provided by the management.

He didn't hesitate when she issued the invitation. Perhaps he remembered what had happened last time, when she'd almost closed the door in his face. She was surprised to find a bottle of wine propped up against her door with a note from Jean which she read out loud.

"Sorry to wimp out on you, Anne. Here's a bottle of wine for company. It's not as old as I am, but enjoy! See you at the morning session."

"How thoughtful of your friend," Rafik said. He quickly made himself at home in her cabin, lighting the fire in the fireplace while she poured the water into the coffeemaker.

"Shall I open the wine?" he asked. "Or are you taking your antihistamines?"

She blushed at the memory of the last time she'd combined alcohol with allergy medicine. "Go ahead," she said. "I should be able to handle a glass of wine tonight."

"If you pass out, at least you'll be close to your bed," Rafik said, with a pointed glance at the large bed that seemed to dominate the room.

"I won't pass out, I promise you," Anne said, determined to look anywhere but at the bed. "I learned my lesson. Pills or alcohol, but not both at the same time. I'll never forget—"

"—sleeping with me?" he asked with a gleam in his eye as he poured some wine into a water glass for her.

"I don't remember that part," she said stiffly. There he went, teasing her again. She didn't know if she'd ever get over having spent the night in bed with a stranger. Or if she'd ever be able to handle his teasing. "I suppose most of the women who sleep with you never forget it," she countered.

"I don't know about that," he said. "I can only say it was an unusual beginning for a relationship."

"A relationship?" she asked. "Is that what we have?"

He handed her a glass of wine. "What do you call it?" he asked. "Sometimes I feel like we're really engaged, other times like I'm just getting to know you."

She didn't know what to say to that. She was just getting used to the idea of him being there, in her room, when he lifted his glass to hers.

"Here's to getting to know you better," he said in a low voice that was so full of suggestions it sent a chill through her body, though her skin was burning. "Come here by the fire," he said, as if he felt she needed to warm up. They sat next to each other on the soft carpet, legs stretched out toward the fire, shoulders touching. It was all so natural, so comfortable, and yet there was an electric current of excitement in the air. She didn't know what was going to happen next. She kicked off her loafers and curled her toes in anticipation of what she didn't know. She noticed Rafik had left his shoes at the door, perhaps an Arabian custom.

"I didn't come here for the scenery or the fresh air," he said solemnly, setting his wineglass on the hearth. "I came because of you."

She tried to say something, but her throat was clogged with emotion. She wanted to believe him. She didn't know why he'd lie about something like that, but she was afraid to believe him, too.

"I've never felt this way before," he said, taking her hand in his and massaging her palm with his thumb. "I've been thinking about you all the time. When I'm not with

you, I miss you. I want to know where you are and what
you're doing. You're different from every woman I've ever
known. You have me wrapped around your finger.'' He
brought her hand to his lips and kissed her index finger.
''This one.''

His touch sent her pulse hammering. She turned to meet
his gaze in the flickering firelight. His voice reached deep
down into her and touched her as she'd never been touched
before. Something inside her melted and flowed and threatened to overwhelm her. If she could have found her voice,
she would have told him she'd never wrapped anyone
around her finger. If he didn't look so serious, so sincere
and so genuine, she would have doubted him.

He leaned toward her and framed her face with his strong
fingers. She knew he was going to kiss her. She wanted it
more than anything she'd ever wanted before. She wanted
him to kiss her and never stop. She wanted him to brand
her with his kiss. She wanted him to claim her for his own,
though rationally she knew it would never happen. She was
not thinking rationally. This time it was not the wine. She'd
barely had time for one sip. She was under his spell. Under
the spell of his voice and his dark eyes and his overwhelm-
ing presence. She didn't know what he was waiting for.
She was ready. She was beyond ready. She was desperate.
If he didn't kiss her soon, she'd have to—

When his lips finally met hers she sighed in the back of
her throat and gave in to the sensations that rushed through
her body. The heat that suffused her limbs spread and invaded her core. Frightened by her own reaction, she pulled
back and reached awkwardly for her wineglass. ''This
might be better if I had a little more to drink,'' she said.

He shook his head. ''This time I want you to know exactly what's happening,'' he said. ''Because last time...''
He didn't finish his sentence. Instead, he pressed his lips

against her neck, under her ear where her pulse beat rapidly.

"Don't remind me," she breathed.

"That was then," he whispered in her ear. "This is
now."

He kissed her again. This time his mouth was hot and
heavy and demanding. This time she didn't even think
about pulling back. She was no longer afraid of her own
reaction. She was only afraid he'd stop too soon. She met
his kiss with one of her own, just as hot and just as intense
as his. He moaned low in his throat and pulled her to him
so her breasts were pressed against his hard chest. He tangled his hand in her hair and removed the clip that fell onto
the carpet.

The heat from the fire and the heat that built inside her
set her body on fire. She struggled to remove her sweater,
knowing she was wearing a turtleneck shirt underneath. But
somehow Rafik was helping her out of both garments, tossing them aside and then gazing at her in rapt admiration.
Her breasts ached and her nipples budded under his gaze.
She'd never been so aware of her body before. Never knew
it could feel this way.

"You are so beautiful," he said reverently, lifting one
lacy bra strap to kiss her shoulder, trailing kisses to the
valley between her breasts. Her body responded as if she'd
been touched by a live wire. She felt as if the blood in her
veins had turned to molten lava. She shuddered from the
sheer ecstasy of his mouth on her tender skin.

"Your skin is like delicate porcelain," he murmured. "I
want to kiss every inch from your head to your toes. I want
you, Anne. I want you so much it hurts. I think I have since
the first moment I saw you. If I had the chance I'd make
love to you in a way you'd never forget. Sweetly, tenderly,

passionately. Tell me if you feel the same. If you want what I want.''

She gazed into his eyes, her skin burning, her whole body throbbing with desire. She could imagine what a gentle considerate lover he would be. How he could awaken in her such passion as she had only heard about. ''Yes,'' she breathed. ''Oh, yes, but…'' But she knew she couldn't do this. She knew that no matter how she felt about Rafik he was the same playboy he had been the first moment she'd seen him. He didn't want a fiancée then and he didn't want one now. Not really.

He didn't want to get married. He might never get married. And if he did, it wouldn't be to her. It would be to one of those sophisticated women she'd seen at the gala ball. The only reason one of them wasn't playing the role of his fiancée was that he hadn't asked them. The thought of Rafik with another woman made her so sad a tiny tear sprang to her eye and trickled down her cheek.

''What is it?'' he asked anxiously. ''What have I said to make you cry?''

She reached for her shirt and pulled it on over her head. She took her sweater and put it on over her shirt. ''Nothing. It's nothing you said. It's what you are.''

''What I am? What am I?'' he asked, his eyebrows drawn together in a puzzled frown.

With her shirt on and her sweater in her hand, she inched away from him on the carpet though she wanted to stay in his arms more than anything she'd ever wanted before. She wanted him to make love to her all night long. She wanted to learn the sensual secrets only he knew. She wanted him to awaken her to every physical pleasure in the world. But that was not going to happen, even though every iota of her being was demanding to know why she was stopping what could be the most incredible, most unforgettable night of her life.

Somewhere a voice inside her was telling her she might never have another chance like this. She was in romantic surroundings with a man she could fall in love with if she had half a chance. A man she was in very great danger of falling in love with in spite of everything she knew about him.

It was not going to happen because, despite these feelings, Anne had learned long ago to protect herself from being hurt. Her instincts told her that this man could hurt her more than she'd ever been hurt before, if she let him. If she let him, he'd make mad, passionate love to her and be gone in the morning. Or if he wasn't gone in the morning, he would be gone sometime in the future.

Some day very soon he'd be gone from her life, despite the fact that his family approved of her, that his mother wanted her to wear her wedding dress and despite the fact that there was a physical attraction between them. An attraction that heightened her awareness of him and of herself every time she was in his presence. When he looked at her she felt faint. When he touched her she thought she might burn up. She reminded herself that Rafik was not going to marry her. She had to keep that simple fact in mind at all times. Because if she forgot, she was in terrible danger. His question hung in the air.

What am I?

She got to her feet and stumbled to the edge of the bed, where she sat looking down at him. She owed him an answer. She owed him an explanation for misleading him into thinking she'd make love to him tonight or ever.

"You're a sheik, for one thing," she said, elbows on her knees, resting her chin in her hands.

He smiled. "Surely you don't hold that against me."

"You're a sheik," she repeated, "you're rich and you have everything you want. I'm a schoolteacher. I work for a living. Everything I want I must earn."

"You make me sound like a spoiled brat," he said. "I, too, work for a living," he insisted.

"Of course, I didn't mean... What I meant was that I'm not in your league."

"No one cares about that," he said.

"I care," she said. "I told you I was a virgin. You asked me why and I told you it was partly for lack of opportunity. Now I know that isn't the whole story. I know now that even given the opportunity to lose my virtue, I will remain a virgin until I marry. I want to marry someone who respects me, who loves me and who appreciates me."

"But, Anne, I respect you and I appreciate you, more than you know."

She nodded sadly. She noticed he hadn't said he loved her because he didn't. At least he was honest. He hadn't said he'd marry her either, but that was not a surprise.

"I know you do," she said. "And I also know I don't know if I'll ever find anyone who will offer me what you have tonight. But I know I'm not going to make love with anyone until I find that person, the person I'm going to spend the rest of my life with."

Rafik's face was a display of disappointment. His eyes were dark pools of sadness. "And if you don't?" he asked.

"If I don't, it won't be the end of the world," she said. "I have a life. I never went around looking for a man to marry and I never will. I never felt unfulfilled. I never yearned for a man to complete my life either. If it happens, it happens." She was proud of how level her voice was, how calm she sounded when inside she was a mass of contradictions.

Her body was still on fire, she ached for Rafik to make

love to her. She knew deep down she might never have another chance, and this saddened her more than she'd ever let him know. She also knew she was right. And this certainty gave her the courage to call a halt to his lovemaking and tell him how she felt.

He got slowly to his feet. For the first time since they'd met she thought he looked uncertain as to what to do next. Whether to stay or whether to go. He looked as if he wanted to say something, to try to persuade her to change her mind. He looked as though he wanted to stay but knew he must leave. After a long, searching look at her face, he seemed to make his decision.

"I'll say good-night then," he said, his voice slightly uneven. "I hope I haven't spoiled your weekend. It's the last thing I wanted to do."

He didn't say what the first thing he'd wanted to do was, but she thought she knew. He'd come to make love to her. She was flattered, disturbed, excited, let-down and sad all at the same time. She didn't get up to see him to the door. She didn't trust her legs to support her. She buried her face in her hands and didn't look up until she heard the door close softly. Then he was gone.

She didn't sleep well that night. She wondered if he did. She tossed and turned, as erotic images of what might have been played across her mind like an X-rated movie. She knew she'd made the right decision, but she couldn't banish the doubts. Couldn't deny the voice in her mind that told her she might never have another chance. That she might go to her grave a virginal spinster schoolteacher. She'd told Rafik she'd never gone around looking for someone to marry. Never yearned for a man in her life or felt unfulfilled. But that was then. This was now. She was not the same person who'd met a sheik at a wedding some weeks ago.

She now knew what she was missing. She knew that Rafik had opened up a whole new world to her. A world of feelings and emotions she'd never experienced before. Or if she'd felt them, she'd kept them under wraps. She had no idea that her body could respond the way it had, so strongly that she almost gave in to temptation. That didn't change anything. It didn't change the fact that he wasn't in love with her and even if he had been, he had no intention of marrying her.

The next morning, she was full of resolve not to let Rafik spoil her weekend. She hoped he'd gone home, but if he hadn't, that was up to him. It had nothing to do with her. She was determined to get as much out of the conference as possible. She walked briskly along the winding path to the main center for the continental breakfast.

Her friend Jean caught up with her on the path. "How was it?" she asked.

Anne stared at her for a long moment. Did she know? Had she seen Rafik leaving her cabin? "Fine. Oh, the wine. It was great. Thank you so much."

"I hated to leave you in the lurch like that."

Anne was determined not to say a word about Rafik, the less said about his visit the better. Especially now that she realized Jean didn't know he was there. Or had been there. She could only hope he'd gone back to San Francisco. But he hadn't. He came up behind them, announcing himself with a cheerful good morning. Anne caught her toe and stumbled on the pavement. Her heart leaped almost to her throat.

"How are you ladies this morning?" he asked.

Jean turned and her mouth fell open in surprise. All three of them stopped to exchange greetings. Anne knew it was the only thing to do, though every instinct told her to run.

She even had enough composure to ask Jean if she remembered Rafik and reintroduce him.

"Remember him? How could I forget?" Jean asked. Then she turned to Rafik. "What are you doing here?" she asked. Then she chuckled. "As if I didn't know. Anne, you devil, you never said a word."

Fortunately Rafik knew what to say, because Anne was tongue-tied. "It was a surprise," Rafik said. "She didn't know I was coming. Neither did I until the last minute."

"You should have told me," Jean chided them both. "Do you play golf? Because Art is going to Pebble Beach this morning and he's looking for a partner."

Rafik assured her he did play golf and would be delighted to join her husband at one of the famed Pebble Beach golf courses. He turned around and went off to connect with Jean's husband so they could make plans.

"What a surprise," Jean said with a sideways glance at Anne after Rafik had left. "No wonder you look like you haven't slept a wink."

Anne gulped. How could she answer that? She couldn't. All she could do was to smile enigmatically. Fortunately some other teachers joined them and that was the end of any more talk about Rafik. But not the end of Anne's thoughts about him. If only he'd left early that morning. Or better yet, last night. Now he was playing golf today and heaven only knew when he'd leave for good. She couldn't go through another evening like last evening. She thought Rafik was sensitive enough not to want to either.

The day dragged by. Though the sessions were interesting, Anne couldn't concentrate. She couldn't stop thinking of Rafik, wondering what his plans were and how he felt about last night. She hoped she hadn't hurt his feelings. She hoped when he thought it over, he'd realize why she'd said no. Why she was saving herself for marriage. She hoped he didn't think she'd led him on, then changed her mind.

After the last workshop, Anne avoided Jean. She didn't want to have to explain anything to her. Didn't want to answer any questions about their plans for the evening in case she suggested the four of them get together. She hoped Rafik would go home, then she could explain that he had business to attend to and couldn't stay any longer.

Anne made a quick trip to her cabin to grab her jacket, determined to enjoy a walk on the beach by herself while she had the chance. Fortunately there was neither a note pinned to the door nor a bottle of wine on the porch. She hoped she'd be alone tonight. She'd build her own fire and sit there watching the flames by herself. She might be lonely, but lonely was better than losing her virtue to a man who had seduction and not marriage on his mind. She hoped Rafik would be far away by then. But would he be far from her thoughts? She had to make an effort to banish him to the periphery of her consciousness where he belonged. Some day he'd be gone altogether from her life, but not quite yet.

She headed out onto a rickety boardwalk through the ice plant toward the dunes. The wind blew; the sun shone its last rays on the shimmering water. She needed the cold air to blow away her problems and soothe her anguished psyche. There were a few other people on the beach, some walking their dogs, a few couples arm in arm as they trudged through the sand.

But as dusk fell, she kept her head down and didn't see anyone. Her thoughts were filled with ways of getting out of this awkward arrangement with Rafik. She wondered when and how they could break off the engagement. It couldn't happen any too soon for her. Surely, after last night Rafik must be feeling the same.

She was so wrapped up in her worries, she didn't realize how far she'd walked or how late it was until she looked at her watch. Only then did she turn around and start back. Instead of walking, she jogged. The cold air filled her lungs, and she was glad she'd come out this evening. The exercise took her mind off her problems. It might be hard going, plodding through the sand, but she ought to do this more often. She needed to get out and run. It was good for the body and good for the soul, too. If you pushed yourself to the limits, you couldn't worry about a little thing like a false engagement.

She continued to congratulate herself on her newfound love of exercise until she stumbled over a large piece of driftwood and twisted her ankle. She gasped in pain and fell forward, bracing herself with her hands, as she landed on the sand. She lay there panting. When she caught her breath she touched her ankle and jumped as the pain shot through the bone. She sat with her legs stretched out in front of her staring at her feet. With an effort, she got to her knees and told herself to get up and walk. But she couldn't. She fell back onto her rear, realizing her ankle was not going to support her. After only a few minutes it had swollen to the size of a tennis ball.

Tears of frustration filled her eyes. She felt foolish and stupid. She'd come too far. She hadn't told anyone where she was going. She hadn't paid attention to the time or the distance. She'd been thinking of Rafik. It was all his fault. Gingerly she touched her ankle again, thinking she'd been a wimp. It might not be so bad. It might even be getting better. She ran her fingers over the lump, hoping the swelling had gone down, but it hadn't. The tears ran down her cheeks. She sobbed.

She told herself crying would not help. She couldn't just lie there crying like a baby. She had to do something. Like call for help. She swallowed hard, then she called for help over and over. But no one heard. No one came. She yelled until her voice was hoarse. She crawled across the sand, dragging her sore ankle behind her until she finally stopped to rest. She wouldn't give up. Even though at this rate it would take all night to get back to the conference center. It didn't matter. She had to do it. She forced herself to move. Sand blew into her ears, sifted into her mouth and grated her skin.

She took a deep breath and tried again. "Help, help! Anybody. Please help me. Rafik. Rafik. Where are you?"

She was cold. She'd never been so cold. The wind went right through her windbreaker and the sweater she wore. She had visions of hot chocolate, of a warm fire. But the vision she couldn't dismiss was Rafik. Rafik trudging across the dunes to rescue her. That's when she knew she must be hallucinating.

Chapter Eight

Rafik spent a pleasant day on the golf course with Jean's husband. He had learned to play as a boy in his country a a club where the course was made of rough greenery an watered with recycled water. As usual, he and his brothe had kept up a friendly rivalry in golf, digging holes in th sand for a makeshift putting green at the family compound They competed in golf as they did in all sports, from touc football to sailing races in the Gulf waters, and as they di in life in general. Rafik managed to keep up a friendl conversation with Jean's husband while his mind was o Anne and the events of last night.

He'd certainly misjudged Anne. Even worse, he'd mis judged himself. He'd thought he could seduce her. He' thought he could seduce anyone he wanted. He always ha in the past. Also he felt sure she wanted him as much a he wanted her. The strange part was, she probably did, bu her scruples prevented her from doing anything about i He'd never run into anyone like her before.

He respected her for that. She was saving herself fo

marriage. He wondered what kind of a man she'd marry when she did marry. He had no doubt she'd marry. She was everything a man wanted. A man who wanted to get married, that is. She was sweet and beautiful and sexy and smart, too. Even Rahman had noticed.

She wouldn't marry a sheik. She'd made that quite clear. That decision didn't hurt his feelings. Not at all. She was entitled to her opinion that sheiks were rich and spoiled. He had to admit that comparatively speaking, he was rich. Maybe he was spoiled, too. He had everything he wanted. Except for Anne. She wasn't available except for marriage. It was frustrating, but he thought he'd better get used to the idea, because if ever he saw determination in anyone's eyes or heard it in their voice, it was last night in her room when she'd told him in no uncertain terms that she wasn't interested in an affair with him.

As soon as he saw her he'd tell her he understood, and he wished her the best. Then he'd call off the engagement. He'd make up some story for his family and let her get on with her life. There was no reason for her to waste any more time on him. Before he walked out of her life, he wished for two things. The first was impossible—that he could make love to her—and the second was faintly possible; he wanted to show her he wasn't the selfish spoiled rich brat she took him for.

He was so engrossed in his plans for the future, he let Jean's husband win the game, something he never would have permitted, not without a battle, in his past matches. Losing would have bothered the old, competitive Rafik. Now he just didn't seem to care all that much. Jean's husband bought him a beer in the clubhouse after the game, and it was almost dark as they drove back.

In the car, as they passed the manicured greens on one side of the highway and the dark blue bay on the other, Art

told him how much he was looking forward to spending
the evening with his wife. His eyes brightened when he
talked about his two children, and he remarked on what a
rarity it was to get his wife alone for the weekend, at least
part of the weekend. When they parted in the parking lot
Rafik felt almost envious. Those cabins with their big fireplaces and huge beds covered with down quilts were made
for making love. But not for him. Not tonight. And not
ever with Anne.

He was practicing his speech as he walked to Anne's
cabin, about how much he respected her and understood
her position. But when he got there he could see it was
dark inside, and there was no response when he knocked.
He went to Jean and Art's cabin to ask about her, but she
wasn't there. Jean said she hadn't seen her since that afternoon. He strode briskly to the main building, a slight
feeling of apprehension nagging him.

Maybe the sessions had gone on late, or maybe she was
lingering over coffee, talking to friends. But the session was
over and there were only a few teachers gathered in informal discussions. He asked them if they knew where she
was, but they didn't even know her. One suggested that he
check the beach. She'd seen someone in a jacket pass by
the window an hour or so ago heading up the beach.

Rafik frowned. It was dark out there. The moon was
nowhere to be seen. If she'd gone for a walk, she'd be back
by now. Unless something had happened. A wave washing
her out to sea. An encounter with a rabid animal. He
shrugged off such preposterous ideas, but he couldn't get
rid of the worry that nagged him. He pushed open the heavy
door to the deck and stood there listening to the pounding
surf for a moment. The wind howled in the cypress trees
and whistled across the sand. He had a choice. He could
go back to his cabin and pace up and down and wait for

her to call him. After all, she might have found a ride and gone back to the city. No matter how she felt about him, he didn't really think she'd go without telling him. So he had no choice really. He had to try to find her.

His mind was full of images. Anne on a cliff, washed out to sea by a huge wave. Anne tossed about by an angry sea. Anne surrounded by sharks. Or Anne being torn to shreds by mad dogs on the beach. He walked faster and faster until he was running. He thought he was running, but the wind pushed him back, the sand pulled at his feet and dragged him back. He wondered if he was making any progress at all.

"Anne. Anne." When he called her name, the wind tore the words from his mouth and swallowed them up. It was so dark he could only see a few feet ahead of him. He stopped and stood on the wet sand staring out to sea. He could see nothing, hear nothing but the roar of the ocean.

He plowed into the wind again, calling her name until he was hoarse. He had no idea how far he'd come, but he imagined he could hear her voice. He wanted to hear it so badly he thought he did hear it. He crisscrossed the beach and then he saw her, sprawled out on the sand. His heart thudded. She had to be all right, she had to. If anything had happened to her...

He bent down and lifted her up in his arms. She clung to him like a limpet clinging to a rock. He could feel her heart beating steadily through her jacket. A rush of relief filled his body.

"Rafik," she mumbled. "You came. I knew you would."

"Of course I would," he said, pressing her close to him. "What happened?"

"My ankle. I fell. I can't walk."

"It's okay. I'll carry you." He shifted her in his arms.

She wrapped her arms around his neck, and he plowed forward. It wasn't easy to make his way through the drifting sand, but at least he had the wind at his back this time. She buried her face in his sweater and didn't say a word.

"Are you all right?" he asked.

"Cold," she said. He held her even tighter. She wasn't heavy, it was his legs that felt too heavy to lift them up and take step after step. His heart was pounding from the effort. He wanted to sit down and rest, but he was afraid she might be suffering from hypothermia, and he had to get her back.

After an eternity, when his legs felt like lead and he thought he couldn't make them move forward another step, and his arms were numb, he saw the lights from the cottages of the conference center.

"We're back. We made it," he told her.

She murmured something incoherent.

He turned up the path and headed for his cabin. Still holding her with one arm, he extracted his key from his pocket and shoved the door open. He set her on the bed and collapsed next to her. Suddenly he remembered that night at the hotel. He remembered trying to wake her up, undressing her, sleeping next to her. He was enormously relieved when she sat up on the bed and sighed loudly.

"You had me worried," he said, staring at her with disbelief. It all seemed like a bad dream—her being lost and hurt. His worst fears were almost realized. "I thought you might have been swept out to sea or...or attacked. Thank God I found you. What happened?"

"I went for a walk on the beach. I wasn't thinking about where I was going and suddenly it was dark. I decided to run back and I tripped over something. I think it was driftwood. I tried to walk, but I couldn't. My ankle just wouldn't work. I dragged myself for a while then I gave

. It's this ankle," she said, stretching her leg out in front
 her. "I think I sprained it."

"Let me see." Very gently he removed her shoe and
ck and held her foot in his hand. "That doesn't look
od," he said, observing the huge reddened lump on her
kle. He took off her other sock and shoe to compare her
kles.

"Look," he said. "It's huge. You need to see a doctor.
st to make sure nothing's broken."

"Not now," she said. "I don't want to go anywhere."
e leaned back against the pillows and closed her eyes.

"Of course you won't go anywhere," he said. "We'll
t someone to come here."

"I'm sure I'll be fine in the morning," she assured him.
Anyway, doctors don't make house calls anymore."

"You let me worry about that. In the meantime we fol-
w the first aid instructions—Rest, Ice, Compression and
evation." First he turned the thermostat up to high. Then
 found two extra pillows from the closet and put them
der her ankle. Scooping some ice from the ice bucket on
 table, he wrapped it in a towel from the bathroom and
essed it gently but firmly against her ankle.

"How's that?" he asked watching her anxiously from
r bedside.

Anne nodded gratefully. Her ankle was cold, but the rest
 her was gradually warming up. She couldn't believe he'd
scued her just as she'd dreamed he would. Just when she
as about to give up. She didn't think she was going to
e. She just thought she'd be there all night, half-buried
 sand until someone stumbled across her the next day.
at she was here, with Rafik, being cared for so expertly,
emed like a miracle.

"How did you know where I was?" she asked.

"I didn't. I just knew you weren't in your cabin or any-

where else I looked. One person said they'd seen someon
on the beach. I thought it might be you. I had no othe
choice but to look there. Which reminds me that I shoul
call your friends. I went to their cabin looking for you.''

''You could have gone to dinner or just…just forgotte
about me.'' Her voice trembled as she said the last fev
words. If he had, she'd still be there, lost, alone, hur
frightened… ''I can't believe you came out looking fe
me.''

''What did you think I'd do? There's no way I coul
forget about you.''

She managed a weak smile. She didn't know how t
thank him so she didn't even try. When she felt better, sh
would. But now she had another question.

''How do you know how to do…'' She waved her han
in the direction of the pillows, the ice and her ankl
''…this.''

''Just common sense,'' he said modestly. But he wasn
through yet. Another trip to the bathroom and he came bac
with a glass of water and two aspirins. ''For the pain ar
the swelling.''

She swallowed the pills and finished the glass of wate

''You must be hungry,'' he said. ''I'll order us son
food and something hot to drink.''

''The kitchen might be closed by now.'' She had no ide
what time it was, and it seemed almost too much of
effort to even look at her watch.

''Don't worry.''

Her eyes drifted shut for a few moments. She heard Raf
speaking quietly into his cell phone, but her tired bra
made no sense of what he was saying. All she knew w
that she had the sense that he had everything under contr
She'd never felt so cared for, so safe as she did with hi
Of course ordering dinner or finding a doctor who'd mal

house calls were easier when you had plenty of money. But
money had nothing to do with him rescuing her on the
beach. That took fortitude and strength and caring enough
to make the effort.

She didn't know anyone else who would have come out
in the dark looking for her on the off chance she might be
out there. She told herself it wasn't just for her. She thought
he was the kind of man who'd do it for anyone who needed
rescuing. She was ashamed to think of how she'd wished
he'd go home today. If he had, where would she be right
now? She feared she'd still be out there on the sand.

She watched him behind heavy-lidded eyes as he pulled
a chair next to the bed. Watched him shut the curtains,
heard him running water in the bathroom. She doubted he'd
find a doctor at any price, but he did. The physician was
young and capable and looked nothing like any doctor
she'd ever seen. Instead of a white coat he was in jeans
and a jacket. He said he'd been on a friend's boat in the
harbor when he'd been paged. He was new to the practice
and got the worst call schedule—Saturday nights and Sundays. He seemed to be relieved to see she only suffered
from a sprained ankle. He said Saturday-night emergencies
were often gunshot wounds or motorcycle accidents.

"Your wife is going to have to stay off her ankle for a
week or so," he told Rafik. Anne felt herself blushing furiously. Fortunately, no one was looking at her face. No
one corrected him. She opened her mouth to tell them they
weren't married, but it didn't seem to be worth the trouble.
Both the doctor and Rafik were focused on her ankle.

"Tomorrow it will look even worse than it does today,"
the doctor continued. "But that's part of the healing process." He talked about getting a tensor bandage, about ice
and elevation. He told her she could hobble to the bathroom
but otherwise to stay right there in bed. She tried to tell

him this was not her room, that she couldn't stay there i
Rafik's bed, she'd already been there and done that—t
disastrous results, but somehow the words just wouldn
come. Before he left, Rafik told the doctor to send him th
bill. This time she was able to speak up and tell him sh
had health insurance, but he was already at the door an
didn't appear to hear her.

After he'd gone, she told Rafik the doctor didn't under
stand the situation... "For some reason he thought we wer
married."

"I can't really blame him, can you?" Rafik asked. "Her
we are in the same cabin."

"Yes, here we are."

"I notice you didn't correct him," Rafik said.

"Neither did you," she said. "In any case, I certainl
intend to go back to my cabin."

"And disobey the doctor's orders?" he asked incredu
lously. "I'm afraid I can't permit that."

"I think he was being overly cautious," she said. '
can't spend the night here. I have to go back."

"You can't walk, that's for certain and I'm afraid I can
carry you there tonight. I think I might have strained m
back out there on the beach."

"Oh, no. This is my fault. You should have told th
doctor."

"I'll be fine in the morning," he assured her. "Now ju
relax. The food will be along any minute." He shoved th
small table next to the bed and sure enough, the food a
rived, carried by a uniformed delivery man. He brought
covered dishes and stacked them on the table. He broug
plates and silverware and glasses.

While Anne watched dumbfounded, he uncovered th
dishes, served soup in wide bowls, then wished them "B

appetit!'' and left promising to return the next morning for the dishes.

"It smells wonderful," Anne said. Until that moment she hadn't realized how hungry she was. "Where did he come from? How did you arrange this?"

"Very simple. I just made a few calls. Many restaurants deliver, you know."

"No, I didn't know," she said. The idea of ordering food to be delivered from a restaurant was totally unknown to her. Not only must it be prohibitively expensive, under normal circumstances, there was no need. She told herself these were not normal circumstances. Dining with a sheik in his bed. Having him wrap her ankle, call a doctor, order food, prop the pillows on her lap and set her soup there, all that was most abnormal. And very luxurious. Almost worth spraining an ankle for. But not quite. Sipping a delicious broth made her almost forget about her ankle. Or the consequences.

"This is wonderful," she said. She would worry about her ankle later.

"Not bad," he agreed. He sat down next to the bed so he could eat next to her and serve her food. "How are you feeling?"

"Much better," she said. "I'd almost forgotten about my ankle. The pills must be kicking in. That and the hot food." And you, she wanted to say. She felt surrounded by the warmth of his presence, by his soothing voice and his calm capability. He gave her the sense that things would be all right. That all her problems could be solved. Rafik had a way of making her feel she was in good hands. She'd never felt so cared for. Was it only last night she'd been thinking how rich and spoiled he was? He might be rich, of course he *was* rich, but he was also the most thoughtful man she'd ever known.

Who else would have gone looking for her and when he found her hurt his own back by carrying her what seemed like miles across the beach? No one. And now he was doing everything for her as if she meant something to him. Maybe he felt he owed her a debt for pretending to be his fiancée. But he didn't. It had served them both equally. But now it was time for the charade to be over. She must tell him that. Not yet. Not while he was spooning some sauce onto her dinner plate around the lamb chops and rice pilaf and creamed spinach.

She ate slowly, savoring every bite.

"I'm proud of you," he said when she finally set her fork down. "You cleaned your plate, so you can have dessert."

"Dessert?" she asked, lying back against the pillow and closing her eyes. "All this and heaven, too."

"You're easy to please," he said.

She opened her eyes and met his gaze. "I've never had dinner in bed before."

"I understand there are many other things you've never done in bed before," he said. Then he caught himself. "I'm sorry. I shouldn't have brought it up again. You made your position quite clear last night."

"Rafik…"

"I understand," he said, "and I respect your morals. Now let's see what they've brought for dessert."

The dessert was a combination of many small things. A tiny chocolate mousse, an apple dumpling with caramel sauce, one perfect slice of tiramisu. She couldn't imagine what such a dinner must have cost him. She had a bite of each along with coffee. He smiled proudly at her as if she'd done something wonderful by eating so much, then he removed the dishes and put the table back next to the window. She knew she should insist on returning to her cabin.

ut she sensed he'd resist, and that he'd win. She wanted
 ask him where he'd sleep, but she was afraid to hear
im say he'd sleep in the chair.

Next he ran a hot bath for her, helped her hobble into
ie bathroom, supplied her with one of his clean shirts and
ft her alone in the bathroom. She could hear the muted
ounds of the television set in the background as she
ropped her ankle on the rim of the tub and felt the hot
ater seep into her body.

Getting in and out of the tub without bumping her ankle
as a difficult process and seemed to take ages. She knew
ien she couldn't go any farther than his bed tonight no
atter how wrong it was. No matter how many people
new about it. Wrapping his well-pressed cotton shirt
round her was almost like being enveloped in his arms
ith his masculine scent surrounding her.

Rafik turned when he heard the bathroom door open.
nne came out in a cloud of steam, her red-gold hair in a
amp tangle. Wearing his shirt, which grazed her knees,
ie was delectable. He took a deep breath to try to rid
imself of the lecherous thoughts that rushed at him like
ie tides out there on the beach.

He had arranged the blankets so she could lie under them
nd still have her foot elevated.

"What about you?" she asked, drawing the sheet up to
er chin.

"Don't worry about me," he assured her. "I'm not tired.
ll be fine in the chair."

"The chair?" she said. "Not with your back. The mus-
les will tighten up and you'll get worse."

His back. He'd forgotten he'd made up that story. There
vas nothing wrong with his back, but he certainly didn't
rant to sit up all night. Still…

"There's plenty of room in the bed for both of us," sh
said.

He'd imagined her saying those very words, so when sh
actually did, he wasn't sure he'd heard her right until sh
patted the area next to her pillow. He had to admit the king
sized bed looked big enough for two people even if the
weren't engaged, married or in love. Since neither of them
fell into any of those categories there was nothing to worr
about, was there? Of course he had to admit he lusted afte
Anne's body, and he thought she felt an attraction to him
But given her moral standards, he wasn't going to do any
thing about his lust problem except try to ignore it.

Being in bed with her might not be the best way to ignor
it. But right now he was too tired to protest. So he shrugge
casually, though he felt anything but casual, and went t
take a shower. By the time he got out, she was asleep. Th
memories of that first night came flooding back. At the tim
he'd thought she looked beautiful with her hair spread o
on the pillow. Now she was even lovelier. But then, he'
thought that before. Once at the gala ball, then in her ga
den. Come to think of it, each time he saw her he wa
convinced she was more beautiful than the last time.

Very carefully, so as not to wake her, he crawled int
his side of the bed. Instead of looking at her, he deliberatel
faced the wall. He didn't dare even glance her way. It wa
bad enough to smell the soap she'd used, the sweet sme
of her skin and her hair. Bad enough to imagine touchin
her soft skin, holding her in his arms all night. He force
his eyes closed, but the images continued. He saw her o
the beach, a crumpled form and he shuddered to think wha
would have happened if he hadn't found her. But he had
She was safe and sound in his bed. What would it be lik
if she were there every night? If he could make love to he
every night?

He shifted his body and told himself to stop dreaming. There was no way Anne would ever be in his bed again, and most certainly she would never make love with him unless he married her. Married her. That's what his parents thought was going to happen. They thought he'd actually found the woman of his dreams. Maybe he had. But there was no way he was getting married. Of course Anne was special. But so was his last fiancée. Or so he'd thought. His parents had been just as crazy about her as they were about Anne. Just as certain he'd made the right choice. Of course it wasn't his choice at all, it was theirs.

It was only by luck he'd discovered the true nature of his fiancée before they got married. Marriage was forever. If and when he ever got married, he intended to stay married. It was better not to take a chance and ruin his life. Tomorrow he and Anne would decide how best to end this engagement. He was sure she'd be more than happy to see it end. It hadn't been easy for her to live a lie any more than it had for him. With this decision made, he finally fell asleep.

When Anne awoke Rafik was already up and dressed. She thought he'd slept next to her in bed, but she couldn't tell. Not by any indentation in the pillow or by the expression on his face. He'd already been out to get some flaky croissants and coffee for them when she woke up. "You're going to spoil me," she said as he spread a towel across a pillow and put it in her lap so she could eat in bed.

"I'm trying," he said, "but I don't think it's possible."

"The doctor was right," Anne said after she'd finished her coffee and examined her ankle. "It looks even worse today." It was swollen and discolored. She sat there looking at it in dismay.

When her friend Jean came to see how she was, she threw a blanket over her leg.

"It's nothing," Anne said. "Just a sprain. But it looks awful."

"What a shame," Jean said, sitting on the edge of the bed. "You'll miss the brunch this morning and the closing remarks. I suppose you'll be heading back to town soon?"

Anne looked at Rafik and he nodded. He asked Anne for the key to her cabin and went to pick up her belongings.

"When Rafik called us last night to say he'd found you I was so relieved. And so was he. He was so worried about you. I'd say frantic, but that wasn't it. He was just determined to find you."

"I...I can't believe he did find me. I was lying there in the sand thinking I'd be spending the night there...feeling stupid for going off like that by myself."

"It's been quite a weekend for you," Jean said.

Anne couldn't have agreed more. If Jean only knew the half of it. This weekend, she'd almost been seduced. She'd turned down an offer from a man she was wildly attracted to. She'd faced hypothermia and an injury last night on the beach. She'd been rescued and now she had a new perspective on Rafik. He was not the arrogant, spoiled, rich man she once thought. Instead he was kind and caring. He was extremely confident, but he had a right to be. He was the kind of man a woman would be lucky to have for a fiancé. But he wasn't hers. He never would be, no matter how much his parents wanted it. No matter how much she wanted it.

Chapter Nine

On the ride home Anne was as comfortable as Rafik could make her. He'd moved the passenger seat back so she could recline and elevate her foot. They talked about everything and nothing as he drove along the two-lane scenic highway. No mention was made of their so-called engagement, though it was on Anne's mind, and she was sure it wasn't far from Rafik's either. Somehow, sometime, something was going to have to happen.

That something was the cancellation of their engagement. She couldn't bring herself to mention it. It was so nice just to sit there and watch the green fields on one side and the ocean on the other and not think about the problems on the horizon. She enjoyed Rafik's conversation. She'd never realized he knew so much about so many things. About the tides and the weather and the crops that grew in the farms alongside of the road.

She was almost disappointed when the ride ended, and he brought her home to her house. Never had three hours passed so quickly. He insisted on carrying her inside, though she told him she could easily hobble in by herself. She sat on the couch with her leg stretched out in front of her while he brought her suitcases in.

She thanked him profusely and told him she'd be fine. She promised to stay off her foot as much as possible. She assured him she had a freezer full of food and that her bedroom was on the first floor so there was no danger of her climbing stairs or being on her feet for any length of time.

There was an awkward silence when she'd finished answering all his questions, while he stood in the middle of her living room looking around. He didn't seem to know whether to go or stay. He didn't seem to know what to say either or what to do. Which wasn't like him at all. As long as she'd known him, he was completely at ease in any social situation.

"All right," he said at last. "Call me if you need anything." He put her phone on the end table next to the couch, then he stood there for a long moment looking down at her as if he'd forgotten something. At that moment she almost told him not to go, but of course she didn't. There was no reason he should stay, none at all. No reason for her to tell him she didn't want him to leave, that she needed him, wanted him, didn't want to live without him. She could only imagine the look of panic on his face if she did. She had a sprained ankle but that didn't mean she needed a full-time nurse. She could take care of herself. She knew it and he knew it, too.

After a moment, he left. He hadn't touched her after he'd put her on the couch. It seemed to her that he'd stayed as far away as he could, as if she had some communicable disease instead of a sprained ankle. He didn't kiss her good-bye either. Not that she'd expected him to. It was just…it

as just that it was so lonely, so unexpectedly lonely there
ithout him.

She missed his voice, she missed his touch, the way he
arried her with his arms wrapped around her. She missed
aving him in the same room with her. Missed knowing he
as there for her. All that was over, she told herself. She
y on the couch listening to the sound of his car pulling
way. She looked around her living room and a tear trickled
own her cheek.

The silence was unbearable. Since she'd lived alone for
ears and had never been bothered by silence before, or by
oneliness, she had to wonder what was wrong with her.
he cleared her throat, and the sound echoed through the
mpty rooms. The house was empty and so was she. It was
e kind of emptiness that no food can fill. She knew be-
ause they'd stopped for lunch at a drive-in. She thought,
is is what it must be like to lose one's best friend. The
ars and the emptiness, the utter bleakness of the future.

future without Rafik. She repeated to herself what she'd
ld Rafik. She had a life. She'd never looked for a man.
ever felt unfulfilled, never yearned for a man in her life.
o, she never had. Not until now.

He'd said he didn't think it was possible to spoil her, but
e had. She was spoiled. In two days she'd been spoiled
id she feared it might be a permanent condition. He'd
scued her, he'd taken care of her, he'd kissed her and
e'd fed her. Yes, he tried to seduce her, but when she'd
ld him how she felt, he'd respected her. Night fell and
e buried her face in the cushion on the couch and fell
leep.

Rafik went to the office the next day, determined not to
ink about Anne quite as much as he had. She'd assured
m she'd be fine, that she'd call if she needed anything,

but it had been many hours since he'd dropped her off, and
he hadn't heard from her. When he saw his brother he told
him what had happened over the weekend, excluding the
part about Anne being a virgin and saving herself for marriage.

"So you did it, you took my advice," Rahman said with
a self-satisfied smile. "You spent the weekend romancing
her."

"Yes, you could say that, and now what am I supposed
to do?" Rafik asked.

"That's obvious. You've got to take care of her. She's
hurt, she's wounded. She needs you," Rahman said. "It's
a perfect opportunity to make yourself indispensable."

"You think so? I'm not so sure. She's got an indepen-
dent streak. I'm afraid of stepping over the boundaries she's
set up. You should have heard what she said to me. She's
not looking for a man in her life. She's not unfulfilled and
she doesn't need anyone, and that means me."

"That's perfect," Rahman enthused, refusing to accept
defeat. "She sounds like you. You're made for each other.
You can continue this affair without strings until you get
tired of each other."

Rafik winced at the word *affair*. "You're forgetting
about the parents and the pressure they're putting on me to
set a wedding date," he said. "Mother even gave me a
family ring to give to Anne."

Rahman whistled between his teeth.

"So you see it's not as easy as you think. In fact, I think
I'm at a dead end. I'm going to have to bite the bullet and
break off the engagement which never was an engagement
anyway. It will hurt Mother and Father, but they'll get over
it." He pictured their faces the night of the gala ball, how
they'd watched Anne and him from across the dance floor,
how they'd beamed at him. He thought of his mother en-

rusting the ring to him, thinking he'd finally found the
woman of his heart.

Maybe he had, but how did one know? He'd been fooled
before. He was not going to take a chance again.

"They'll get over it," Rahman said. "But will you?"

"Me? I never wanted to get engaged and I certainly
don't want to get married. You of all people should appreciate that."

"Never? You mean you'll *never* get married?" Rahman
asked.

"Who can say never?" Rafik said. "I only know how I
feel now." But even as he said the words he realized he
didn't know how he felt about marriage. All he knew was
that right now he felt terrible. After only one weekend together, he missed her. He wanted to take care of her.
Whether she wanted to be taken care of was the question.
All he knew was that he had to see her.

"Hold down the fort," he said to his surprised brother.
"I've got matters to attend to."

"Go for it," his brother murmured as Rafik walked out
of the office.

When Anne didn't answer her front door, Rafik went
round to the side and let himself in through the gate. When
he saw her in her garden he was worried she'd disobeyed
the doctor's orders and had resumed gardening. Then he
saw she was sitting on the bench surrounded by flats of
plants in plastic containers with her leg propped up. She
was wearing a pair of faded blue jeans and a sweatshirt.
Her hair was pulled back and fastened with a band. But
small tendrils had escaped and brushed against her temples.
He couldn't tell by the look on her face if she was glad to
see him or not.

"How's your ankle?" he asked. He knelt down next to

her so he could look at it up close. It seemed more swollen
and very discolored.

"It looks worse than it feels," she said.

"You haven't been walking on it, have you?"

"Not any farther than to this spot right here. But look."
She waved her hand at the plants stacked up around the
garden. "These native plants were delivered while I was
gone. I'd actually forgotten how many I'd ordered. I should
be planting them right now, but..."

"No, absolutely not," he said.

"I know, I know. It's so frustrating. I need to get them
in the ground." She sighed. "I have so much work to do
here. The summer is half over, my bird-watchers' group is
meeting here in two weeks. I've told them about my garden
and they're coming to see what you can do to attract birds
to a garden in the city without using flowers which I'm
allergic to. I thought I'd have a lot done by then, but
now...."

"I'm sure they'll understand," he said.

"The bird-watchers will but the plants won't," she said.
"They need to get established."

"Can I help?" he asked.

She looked him up and down, taking in his tailored suit
and immaculate shirt and matching tie. "I don't think so."

"I have other clothes," he said.

"I'm sure you have none suitable for getting down on
your knees in the dirt."

"Don't be too sure," he said. But she was right. He had
nothing like that. But he could get some.

"Moreover, you don't have the time. Shouldn't you be
at work?"

"Rahman can handle the work. It's good for him to have
some responsibility. I'll just go get the proper clothes."

She put her hand on his arm. "Rafik, I can't impose on ou this way. The plants can wait."

"You just said they need to get established." But Rafik /as thinking more about himself than the plants. Compared ɔ his office, this place offered solace and peace. More im- ɔrtantly, it offered a chance to spend more time with Anne 1 her garden. Also the smell of the lavender and of the amp earth satisfied something inside him he didn't know xisted. Something very basic. He was beginning to realize /hy Anne was attracted to the soil. Maybe he'd even come ɔ understand why she liked getting her hands dirty.

"Of course you'll have to tell me what to do," he said. 'I've never done any gardening."

Before she could protest again, he left the garden. In the ar he called Rahman and told him what needed to be done t the office.

"Wait a minute," Rahman said. "I'm on my way to ɪnch."

"This was your idea," Rafik reminded him. "I'm count- ɪg on you to fill in for me."

"For how long?" he asked.

"As long as it takes," Rafik said.

Rahman agreed reluctantly and Rafik went to a neigh- orhood thrift shop. He had never been to one before. The ɪstomers gave him more than one curious look as he sifted ɪrough the racks of jeans and shirts. He didn't want Anne ɔ think he'd gone out and bought gardening clothes. He /anted her to think he'd simply gone home to change lothes. And that he was a regular guy and not a spoiled ɪch man.

He changed clothes in the small dressing room and gave imself a critical look in the mirror. He was pleased with ɪe way the faded jeans fit him and the gray sweatshirt. He /as pleased with everything except for the shoes. He

needed some kind of sandals if he was to get the full effec
and feel the dirt between his toes as Anne did. His nex
stop was a shoe store where he bought the kind of sturdy
sandals he thought would be appropriate. He couldn't help
the fact that they were new and not used.

On his way back to Anne's he picked up sandwiches and
salads from a take-out shop. He'd been thoughtless not ask
ing what food she needed. He was gratified by the look on
Anne's face when he returned. She didn't say anything, she
just looked him up and down, taking in the change in his
appearance. She must have been surprised by his transfor
mation, because obviously she'd never stopped thinking o
him as a spoiled, rich sheik. But the clothes were only hal
the battle. Now that he looked the part, he had to be able
to act the part as well, show her he could do what, in his
country, only servants did.

After lunch in the garden, he began the job of digging
planting and watering, according to Anne's instructions
She was uncomfortable giving orders, at least at first. He
had to admit he was a little uncomfortable getting them
too. He made mistakes. He uprooted some miners' lettuce
which he'd never heard of, thinking it was a weed. He
trampled on a fern. But they settled into a routine. She'd
point to a new plant and decide where to put it. He'd dig
a hole and plant it. Then he'd surround it with fertilize
and mulch and water it.

At the end of the afternoon he wiped his brow and sa
down next to her on the bench. He was tired, but it was a
good feeling. Almost as good as the feeling he had after a
few sets of handball.

"My mother told me you want to get married in you
garden," he said.

"Oh, well, I was just, you know, talking off the top o
my head. I have no intention..." She turned her head s

he couldn't see her face, but not before he noticed her cheeks had turned pink.

"Why not?" He looked around. "The trellis would serve as the altar."

"I suppose it could, but I'm not getting married. I only said that because she asked me. I had to come up with something. I certainly couldn't picture getting married in the cathedral like Carolyn." She cleared her throat. "I can't thank you enough, Rafik. You've been so much help," Anne said.

He got the distinct impression she was trying to dismiss him. But he wasn't ready to be dismissed. "It looks like there's a lot more to do," he said.

"It can wait," she said.

"Why should it?" he asked. "I can come back tomorrow. That is if you want me to."

"Well of course, but..."

"Now let's see what's in that freezer of yours for dinner. All that work has made me hungry."

Before she could protest, he swooped her up in his arms and carried her into the house. He paused in the doorway and looked into her eyes. "I just want you to know," he said, "that if I ever did get engaged with the intention of getting married..."

"You don't have to explain," she said, cutting him off as if she didn't want to hear the end of the sentence. "I know how you feel. The next step is to get ourselves unengaged."

"Let's not talk about that until after you get back on your feet," he said. "In the meantime..." He trailed off without finishing his sentence. He knew what he wanted to do in the meantime. She was so close, her lips were only inches away, tempting him, torturing him. She was so warm, so soft, she smelled so sweet, like the fresh air in the garden. There was something in her eyes he'd never seen before. He would have called it seduction if he didn't know better.

Whatever it was, he kissed her once. He could have sworn that lightning struck, despite the fact there wasn't a cloud in the sky. She tightened her arms around his neck and kissed him back. This time it was thunder roaring in his ears.

It could have been gratitude that made her kiss him, but it wasn't that kind of kiss that said thank you. It was the kind that said kiss me again. So he did. Again and again until he staggered to the couch and fell back with her in his lap. She tasted just as good as the last time he'd kissed her, the night before he'd rescued her, but different. Something had changed.

She raked her hands through his hair and he shuddered.

"For a virgin," he said hoarsely, "you're a very sexy woman."

She blushed furiously. But a tiny smile tilted one corner of her mouth. A knowing smile that said she was aware of herself as a woman, a sexy woman at that. He hoped he'd had something to do with the change in her. Because she had changed. Whether she knew it or not, she was not the same woman he'd taken home from the wedding.

When he finally, reluctantly disentangled himself from her and propped up her ankle, he went to the kitchen to heat something for dinner, another thing he had scarcely ever done before in his life. There had been no need. There was always a restaurant, a food service, a hotel or a servant. But tonight he wanted to prove once again that he was not what she thought he was. Not what he once was.

He was amply repaid for his efforts by the wide-eyed look of surprise on her face when he appeared in the living room with two plates of food. Surprise and delight. He wanted to surprise and delight her every night. So he did, every night that week. With different dishes he ordered and had delivered, or prepared from what she had in her freezer.

When he insisted on returning day after day, Anne only managed a weak protest. When Rafik decided to do something, it was difficult to stop him. She should be grateful he was helping her so much. She *was* grateful. But she was worried, too. Worried that when it was over, and it would be over before long, she was going to suffer. Suffer more than she'd ever suffered before.

Because she'd fallen in love with him. Fallen in love with a sheik. It was so absurd it was ridiculous. She, an elementary schoolteacher who'd never had a ball gown, or attended a gala or mixed in high society, who'd never even had a serious boyfriend, much less a fiancé, was in love with a handsome, wealthy sheik. A man who had no intention of getting married to her or anyone.

She hadn't fallen in love with him because he was rich and handsome, she'd fallen in love with him because he was kind and thoughtful, intelligent, humorous and good company. As if it made any difference. It was hopeless. She knew it. He knew it, too. Though he didn't know how she felt, unless he was a mind reader.

She didn't know how much longer she could keep it a secret. If he stayed around planting in her garden much longer, she was going to have to be more careful. No kisses, no touching, no lingering looks. The best thing was to break off the engagement as soon as possible. He'd said he didn't want to talk about it until she was back on her feet. She prayed her recovery wouldn't take that long. But from the looks of her ankle today, she was worried.

As he worked with her day after day that week, she grew increasingly anxious. The more she saw of him, the more they worked together on the garden project, the closer she felt to him. She knew it was going to be hard to let him go, but she knew it was inevitable. By the end of the week both the garden and her ankle looked much better.

They were sitting at her kitchen table eating a dinner he'd put together as if they were an ordinary couple. His shirt was covered with grass stains. He looked nothing like the groomsman she'd spotted staring at her in the church the day of Carolyn's wedding. He looked like an ordinary man. But he was far from ordinary. Though she was able to walk now, he insisted on making her dinner and waiting on her. But that wasn't why she was so terribly, impossibly, madly in love with him. It was who he was and it was who she was when she was with him. She was having so much trouble keeping her love from showing, it made her heart hurt, if that was possible.

"We need to talk," she said, knowing she had to face the music. Knowing it wasn't going to get any easier.

"I thought we were talking," he said, pouring her a cup of coffee.

"I mean about our engagement. About, you know, how to dissolve it."

"Is that what you want to do?" he asked carefully.

"It doesn't matter what I want to do. It's what has to be done. We've been living a lie. It's not important to the people at my school, but your parents have got to know the truth."

He studied her face for a long moment. "All right, I'll tell them."

"What will you tell them?"

"That it didn't work out. What do they call it? Irreconcilable differences. A mutual agreement to disagree. Of course they won't be happy about it."

"They'll be angry with you."

"Probably. But I can handle them. We can still see each other, can't we?" he asked.

"What for?" She had to make a clean break. No more Rafik. If she sounded brusque, so be it. If she continued to see him, it would break her heart.

He looked taken aback. "I'll miss you," he said. "I can't imagine not seeing you. I guess you don't feel the same."

"Of course I'll miss you," she said, "but I can't depend on you forever. You've spoiled me terribly and I have to get back on my feet, both literally and figuratively. You've missed a week's worth of work. Don't you think it's time to get back to your life?"

"My life before you came into it? I can't remember what it was like."

"All the more reason for you to do whatever it is you do. Now that I can walk, I have to get caught up. The summer's half over and I haven't accomplished half of what I'd planned."

She was proud of herself for sounding so matter-of-fact. Proud of herself for not giving in to the tears that were building behind her eyes. That threatened to overwhelm her. She was afraid if he didn't go soon she'd fall apart. She'd beg him to stay. She'd implore him to stay engaged to her. She'd collapse under the weight of her secret love.

He got to his feet and leaned against the counter. "I guess I wasn't ready for this," he said. "I didn't realize how much I was holding you back."

"I didn't mean that," she said. "You've been a wonderful help to me and I'll never forget it. I'll never forget you."

He stared at her. His face paled under his bronzed skin. "That sounds like goodbye," he said.

She swallowed hard. She tried to say something, but the words wouldn't come. She didn't move. She couldn't, not when she felt like she was made of stone. If he kissed her she'd lose her composure altogether. She willed him to leave. Now. Without another word. Leave her to suffer alone. Leave him with a positive picture of her, cured of a sprained ankle and cured of her attachment to him. Free of pain. Back to normal. But she didn't know what normal was anymore.

He got the message. "Well, goodbye then, Anne. I wish you the best."

She forced a smile. "Thank you." She got up and walked him to the door.

This time she barely got the door shut before the tears came, rolling down her cheeks, hot and heavy. She'd got what she wanted. She'd gotten rid of Rafik. Forever. Yes, it hurt. But better now than later. She'd get over it. It was all a fantasy, anyway. A dream that couldn't come true. Falling in love with a sheik was doomed for failure, disappointment and let-down.

It would have been easier if she'd been teaching. If there had been a class of eager little children waiting for her each morning so that she'd have to get up and pull herself together. But it was summer vacation. She hosted the bird-watchers' group, heard them exclaim about what she'd done to the garden, heard them make suggestions about further plantings, but after they left, she felt let-down.

According to their suggestions, she made a list and ordered more plants from the nursery, so many they covered every available space, stacked high in her shed and on every plot of dirt. She might have overdone it, but that way the garden wouldn't feel empty without Rafik. So she thought. And it would provide her with a reason to get up in the morning.

Still she had to force herself to go to the garden every

morning. Once there, she'd sit and sip tea and stare at the chaos she'd created, overwhelmed by the amount of work she had to do, feeling more alone than she ever had in her life. It was his fault. His fault for making himself a part of her life. Her fault for letting him do it.

She turned off her phone just in case he tried to call her. If she heard his voice she might crumble. She might blurt out a confession that would embarrass them both. When there was a knock on her gate one morning, she jumped out of her bench. Her heart pounded like a jackhammer. But it wasn't Rafik.

It was Rafik's brother, Rahman. She felt all the air leave her lungs. She was crushed, but she was relieved as well.

"I tried to call you but I got a busy signal," he said.

"Come in," she said, opening the gate. "How are you?"

"I'm fine but the family is falling apart. Ever since Rafik told the parents he wasn't going to marry you."

"Oh, no. I hope he put at least half the blame on me. You know it wasn't all his idea to call it off."

"It wasn't? He said it was. He said he wanted to be a playboy again. You can imagine how that went over."

"Do you believe him?" she asked.

Rahman shook his head. "He's changed. I can't believe how he's changed. He's working night and day. And he's in a foul temper. You'd think Father would be pleased about his new work ethic, but he's not. He's furious with Rafik. He wants a daughter-in-law. He wants you." Rahman pointed his finger at Anne.

"But as you know, Rafik doesn't want a wife. He may not be a playboy anymore, but he still doesn't want to get married. He doesn't want me. Maybe if I went to see your father and explained that I can't marry Rafik. Not because he's a playboy but...but... No, I'll say I can't marry him because I don't love him."

"Don't you?"

She bit her lip. She couldn't lie anymore. Not to Rafik's brother. Not to anyone. What did it matter? It was over. All over.

"You don't need to answer," Rahman said. "I can see the answer in your eyes. Just as I thought."

"It doesn't matter how I feel," Anne said. "What's important is that I share the blame for this breakup. I knew it was going to happen from the beginning. I was a willing participant. Now I have to accept my responsibility. I'll go see your father and tell him...tell him something."

"It's worth a try," Rahman said.

The next day Anne dressed carefully in her one good suit and went to call on the old sheik. She didn't make an appointment, and she hoped to avoid running into Rafik. She was lucky. She didn't see Rafik, and she was ushered into the corner office where Rafik's father was in charge.

Massoud Harun stood up and greeted her warmly, asking her to sit down and offering to send for some tea. Anne shivered inside her suit jacket knowing that as soon as she'd spoken her piece, he wouldn't be feeling nearly so cordial toward her. Then he sat down and flexed his gnarled fingers thoughtfully for a long moment.

"To what do I owe the honor of this visit?" he asked finally in his usual formal manner.

"I feel it's my duty to tell you what happened between your son and me," she said. "I'm afraid you've been misinformed. It was I who called off the engagement."

"Oh?" he said.

She took a deep breath. "You see I have never been in love with Rafik."

Instead of being shocked, Sheik Massoud just nodded as if she'd said it looked like rain. "I understand that," his father said. "In my country love is not a prerequisite for marriage. Most often, as in my case, marriage is arranged by the family, based on mutual respect and understanding. Very often, love follows marriage. But this is America. You're an American. If it wasn't love, then tell me why you agreed to this engagement in the first place."

Anne's mind raced. She could have said she never had agreed to it, that she'd been pressured into it by the very man who was sitting opposite her. But she wasn't there to make things worse, she was there to heal a family quarrel. She should have had a backup plan, but she never dreamed not being in love wasn't a good excuse for calling off an engagement.

"For money," she said impulsively. "I wanted his money."

The old sheik regarded her solemnly. "Money, is it? How much?"

"Enough to buy acres of marshland for a bird sanctuary. It would cost millions."

"Money is not a problem. Is money all you really want?" His gaze was shrewd and intense.

Anne nodded and turned away, unable to look into his eyes. He saw too much. Murmuring some excuse, she stood and left the room. Blinded by tears she rushed down the hall, out of the office and down the elevator. The only good thing about the meeting was that she hadn't run into Rafik. But what else had she accomplished by lying to an old man? Nothing. She hadn't even made sense. She'd told him she didn't love Rafik and that she only wanted his money.

His father was probably scratching his head right now trying to understand why she'd broken the engagement. It wasn't as if Rafik had gone bankrupt. He was still rich. As his father said, money was not a problem. So what was the problem? The problem was that she'd fallen in love with a man who had no intention of getting married, and she had no intention of having an affair with him, even though he was the most attractive, the kindest and the sexiest man she'd ever met. But those were words she could never say to the man's father.

If Rafik thought hard work would impress his father he was wrong. He'd been working night and day since the day Anne told him not only did she want to dissolve their engagement, she didn't even want to see him anymore. He'd walked around in shock for a few days, then he'd decided to put his energies to work and try to forget about her. But he didn't forget about her, her face appeared before him when he least expected it. In the middle of a meeting, in the middle of the night when he tossed and turned in his bed trying to figure out what he'd done wrong. Trying to think of how he could persuade her to see him again. And his father continued to glower at him.

Until one day he called him into his office.

"I owe you an apology," his father said. "Your ex-fiancée was here to see me. She said it was her idea to terminate your engagement. You led me to think otherwise."

Anne, here? Anne came to see his father but not him? It shouldn't hurt so much to hear that, but it did. Why didn't she just thrust a knife in his chest and be done with it? "Does it matter?" Rafik asked wearily.

"I think it does," his father said. "The woman told me the reason was she didn't love you."

"That's true," Rafik said. "Our engagement was based on mutual need. Not love." If she loved him she wouldn't have been so eager to call it off. She wouldn't have shoved him out of her life. She wouldn't have let him go so abruptly. She would have called him by now, told him how much she'd missed him, as he'd missed her. Or come to see him to tell him she couldn't live without him. Told him how she couldn't sleep at night just as he couldn't. She would have an ache in the middle of her chest as he did, a hollow feeling inside his ribs. She would not be able to eat, would have trouble concentrating. She wouldn't see the point in going on without him. That's how people felt when they were in love. He knew because he...he...*he* was in love. Absurdly, impossibly, unequivocally in love with Anne Sheridan. The realization hit him with the force of a thunderbolt.

Massoud got out of his chair. "Are you all right?" he asked anxiously. "You're pale. Let me get you a glass of water."

"Thank you," Rafik said, staring at the wall, but seeing nothing. Gratefully, he took the glass from his father and downed it.

"If I may continue," his father said. "She told me she wasn't in love with you, but I don't believe she was telling the truth."

"I'm afraid she was, Father," he said grimly.

"As you know, I'm somewhat of a student of human nature. Her words said one thing, but her face and her eyes said quite another. I believe she has fallen in love with you although she did not wish to admit it to me. Instead she invented a story about being after your money so she could have a bird refuge."

"Very creative, but neither is true. She made it quite clear that she doesn't love me and though she does want a bird refuge, she wasn't after me for my money. I'm quite sure of that."

"What do you intend to do about it?" his father asked.

"Buy her the bird refuge," Rafik said. "Though it must be our secret. If I have a chance to convince her to fall in

love with me, it must be for myself and not out of gratitude.''

"Of course," his father said. "But how...?"

Rafik shook his head. "I don't know how...I just know
I must try. Because life without Anne is miserable. The last
time I broke an engagement, or rather my fiancée broke it,
I felt only relief. So much relief I decided never to try
again. I would play the field and that way avoid another
situation like that. But this is different. Very different. I've
never felt the way I feel about Anne. I feel that I'm not
worthy. So before I go any further in my pursuit of her, I
intend to make a success of this business. I have to prove
to you, and myself and Anne that I'm not the playboy I
once was.''

His father was unable to conceal his broad smile. He
patted his son on the back. "That's my boy," he said.

After Anne's conversation with Massoud Harun she was
at a loss to know what to do next. She turned her phone
back on because she thought she'd hear from someone in
his family. She thought she'd hear from Rahman at least,
telling her her attempt had failed. That his father still
blamed Rafik for their breakup. She thought she might hear
from Rafik, but why would he call her? He'd walked out
of her house and out of her life. Instead she got a call from
Sally, her bird-watching friend who'd helped her get ready
for the gala.

"Did you hear the news?" Sally asked breathlessly. She
didn't wait for an answer, she was too excited. "We got
the bird sanctuary. All twenty-five acres of marshland."

"I don't believe it," Anne said, sinking into a chair at
her kitchen table. "How...? Who...?"

"An anonymous donor," Sally said. "Isn't it wonderful?
All that land for the birds for nesting and feeding. All the

bake sales and car washes we had, raising nickels and dimes. Then someone comes along and buys the whole thing.''

''I thought we'd asked every foundation, every philanthropist around for the money. How did this happen out of the blue?''

''I don't know. I heard from Liz who heard from Andy who heard…I don't know,'' she repeated. ''And I don't think we ever will know. Some bird lover, obviously, who wants to remain anonymous.''

After she hung up, Anne went outside and paced up and down in her garden.

Money is not a problem, she heard the old man say. *Is money all you really want?*

Could it be? No, of course not. Why would he buy the marshland when his son wasn't going to marry her? Maybe as a consolation prize? *Though you tried to convince me otherwise, it was plain to see that you've fallen in love with my son. It was written all over your face. I'm sorry that he has no intention of marrying you, but you can have your marshland. Please don't think all sheiks are alike. Have a nice day.* No, that was ridiculous. Even rich people didn't throw their money around like that.

Anne decided to put such useless speculation out of her mind. Instead she hired two high school boys to help her with her garden. She intended to have it finished by the time school started in two weeks and she did. Throwing herself into the work, she told herself it had all been a dream—everything that had happened so far that summer. The dream was over. This was reality. The boys arrived every morning at eight and worked like demons. She made lunch for them and they all worked all afternoon. She knew people said that the young generation, Generation Y, was lazy, but whoever said that didn't know these boys. She tipped them handsomely at the end of the summer, and they went back to school with their wallets bulging as well as their muscles.

The garden looked wonderful. They'd paved a flagstone walkway, planted native plants that attracted birds and more fruit trees. The trellis was covered with vines.

I have a garden that I'm working on that would be perfect for a wedding.

Why had she ever first voiced that thought to Rafik's mother? Now she couldn't get it out of her mind. Couldn't stop imagining the chairs set up, the punch bowl, the minister in his black robe....

Anne went back to school with much relief, some eagerness and a little apprehension. On the first day, when the teachers got together in the lounge before class, she was able to deflect questions about her engagement. When asked about a wedding date, she was vague. She never said she wasn't engaged anymore, but it was obvious she didn't have a ring. And most people were too polite to pry.

Her students were a joy and the best she'd ever had. Of course she said that every year, but this year it was true. It was so good to look forward to school each day and to have lessons to prepare and papers to correct every evening. It left her less time to think about Rafik. To wonder if her talk with his father had done any good. She feared not. The old man had seemed to see right into her mind and know exactly what she was up to. She'd tried. But maybe she could have tried harder. She thought about the bird refuge, too, and wondered if she'd ever know who'd donated it.

A few weeks after school started, open house was held at Pinehurst School. It was a chance for parents to see what their child's teacher and her classroom looked like. Anne bought a new dress for the occasion. A simple sheath in a raspberry color with a matching cashmere cardigan. She wore it with a three-strand pearl choker and just for a moment as she stood in front of the mirror in her bedroom, giving herself a last critical look, she wished she were dressing for someone other than parents.

She remembered the anticipation she'd felt, the churning in her stomach, the weakness in her knees the last time she wore a new dress. The black dress she'd worn to the gala was tucked away in the back of her closet. She'd probably never have an opportunity to wear it again. Still, she wasn't sorry she'd bought it. The look in Rafik's eyes when he came to pick her up had been worth every penny she'd paid for it.

The campus looked beautiful that evening, lit by the occasional gas lamp. Her room was bright and cheerful and the parents all told her how happy their children were to be in her class.

She had just said goodbye to the last parent when she looked up to see Rafik standing in the doorway. She reached for something, anything to hold on to and desperately gripped the back of a chair with one shaking hand.

''Hello, Anne,'' he said. ''You said I could come to the open house, remember?''

Remember? She remembered everything. Remembered him in her classroom after they'd told the whole staff they were engaged. Remembered how confused she'd felt. Afraid to care about him. Sure that he didn't care about her.

''Yes, of course,'' she said briskly. ''I'm sorry, it's just about over. I was just getting ready to lock up.''

''I wanted to talk to you for a moment, if you have time.''

''Here?'' Her voice almost cracked. Her heart was pounding, her face must be the color of her dress. She'd thought she'd never see him again, now he was here, in her classroom.

He nodded.

She made her way to her desk and sat down behind it. He leaned against the wall with his arms crossed.

"You're looking very lovely," he said solemnly. "That color becomes you."

"Thank you," she said. "You are, too. I mean, you look fine." Actually he looked almost pale, if someone who had a year-round tan could look pale, and as if he'd lost a few pounds. Her mind was spinning. Rafik here, in her school. Why, why, why?

"I'll get right to the point," he said. "I came to tell you that though I always said I would never get married, I've changed my mind."

Her heart fell. Rafik was getting married. Her lips felt so stiff she could barely speak. "Really?" she said. "Congratulations. I'm sure you'll be very happy."

"Are you? Are you sure, Anne? I wish I could be sure. The woman I'm in love with hasn't agreed to marry me yet."

She licked her lips. This was torture. Pure torture. Why was he doing this to her?

"In fact," he continued. "She almost threw me out of her house the last time I saw her."

"That's terrible," she murmured.

"That's not all. She told me to get back to my life. That I'd held her back from accomplishing what she had to do."

"I don't know why...what you want me to do about it."

"Do? I want you to tell me what to do. You're a woman. What do women want?"

"Did you tell her," Anne said. "Did you tell her how you felt?"

"You mean that's all there is to it? I just tell her that

I'm in love with her? That I fell in love with her the first time I saw her in her pink bridesmaid dress, but I didn't know it at the time? It took me days, weeks before I knew what had happened. It might have been the day she threw my money all over the floor, or the day I saw her in her garden with dirt on her toes, or the night I danced with her...."

Anne's eyes were full of tears. She couldn't move. She couldn't speak. She was overcome. She heard his words, but she couldn't believe them. She put her head down on her desk and sobbed.

He was across the room in a half a second. He sat on her desk and lifted her head so he could look into her face.

"Anne, stop. Stop crying. I'm sorry. I shouldn't have said it like that. I didn't know what to say, how to say it. I didn't mean to upset you. I just wanted to tell you how much I love you, to ask you, to beg you to marry me. If you don't, I don't know what I'll do. I'm not the same man you met at the wedding. I've changed. If you don't love me now, I understand. My father says love comes after marriage so there's always hope. Give me a chance. I beg you not to say no."

He stared at her, waiting, waiting for her answer. She blinked away her tears and managed a watery smile.

"Of course I'll marry you," she said softly. "I love you, too. I'm sorry I almost threw you out of my house, but I couldn't go on seeing you and knowing that you'd never marry me. It was too painful. You recall you were very determined...."

"Don't remind me," he groaned. "I was a fool. I had no idea what I was talking about. I'd never been in love. Never thought it would happen to me. Not until you came along. Not until we spent so much time together. Then suddenly you were gone out of my life. It was terrible. It was as if the sun stopped shining. I haven't been very good company, as my family will attest.''

''Tell me one thing, did *you* buy that marshland?'' she asked.

''Would you love me more if I did?'' he asked.

She shook her head. ''I couldn't love you more,'' she said shyly. It would take a while before she could say things like that without blushing.

''I bought it, but I didn't want to buy your love,'' he explained. ''I just wanted you to have it.'' He got off the desk and pulled her up into his arms.

She wound her arms around his neck and kissed him. He kissed her back, deeply, possessively. She grabbed fistfuls of his shirt and got lost in the rapture of his kiss. He loved her. It would take a while to get used to it. But she had time. She had a whole lifetime.

Epilogue

It was a small affair. Only the immediate families and a group of close friends attended the garden wedding of Sheik Rafik Harun and Anne Sheridan. The bride wore the groom's mother's wedding dress and walked slowly up a flagstone path to the strains of a string quartet playing the "Wedding March." The groom, who wore the traditional headdress as befitting his status, stood at the trellis which served as an altar. His eyes gleamed as his beautiful red-haired bride appeared from behind the foliage. His brother, who served as his best man, handed him the ring, which had been in the family for generations, to place on his bride's finger.

There were many tears that day. Tears of joy, tears of happiness and sentimental tears. But mostly there were smiles, toasts and congratulations as the caterers brought out trays of smoked salmon, crab cakes and brochettes of lamb. Everyone wanted to take credit for bringing the two together. Carolyn said it all started at her wedding. Rafik's father told his mother he knew about it before anyone else.

Jean declared Rafik to be the luckiest man alive. Rahman insisted that Rafik was luckier.

Only the newlyweds knew for sure who was the luckiest. As they winged their way to their honeymoon in Paris, they decided they were the luckiest couple in the world. And the happiest.

*   *   *   *   *